# The Man Next Door

# BRITT
# HOLMSTRÖM

# The Man Next Door

A Novel

CORMORANT
BOOKS

The publisher gratefully acknowledges the support of the
Canada Council for the Arts and the Ontario Arts Council for
its publishing program. The publisher also acknowledges the
financial support of the Government of Canada through the
Book Publishing Industry Development Program for its
publishing activities.

Cover design by Angel Guerra.

Printed and bound in Canada.

Cormorant Books Inc.
RR 1
Dunvegan, Ontario
K0C 1J0

Canadian Cataloguing in Publication Data
Holmström, Britt, 1946-
The man next door : a novel
ISBN 1-896951-10-4

I. Title.

PS8565.O639165M36 1998   C813'.54   C98-900963-7
PR9199.3.H65M36 1998

*To the memory of my father,*
*Bror F. Holmström*

# SVEN

A seven-year-old boy sat on a couch, dangling his legs. Nothing unusual in that; he often sat there swinging his legs from side to side, or sometimes back and forth, kicking the front of the couch with his clogs. This evening was to be different, however. Later on, way past his bedtime, he would for the first time be overpowered by an uncontrollable urge to kill. He wouldn't succeed, of course. He was too small and skinny, and he had no weapon apart from his wooden clogs. But he would try. After his humiliating failure it would be almost forty years before he was again overcome by that blind, unyielding need to rid the world of somebody who, in his eyes, had no right to be in it. That time he would succeed.

But that evening, when he was seven and lonely and bored, was when it started.

It was late on a hot Saturday night in June 1941. Only a few hours before the sweltering Sunday when Hitler sent his army to annihilate the Russians. It was four days before the Engelbrecht Division crossed through neutral Sweden on its way from Norway to Finland, leaving the prints of Fascist boots on Swedish soil. In Germany, a mere hop and a skip away, the systematic slaughter was going full tilt, but the little boy, whose name was Sven, didn't know that. He wouldn't have wanted to know. Nobody wanted to know. And over in Copenhagen — so close you could see it on a clear day — the Germans had dropped in for a visit on April 9 the previous year, on one of those first perfect days of spring when the sun dazzled from a sky of cornflower blue. They had come to "protect" the Danish people, Pa said. "They're too fucking dumb to look after themselves, those Danes. Listen carefully and you'll hear the gunfire when they shoot a Communist!" Pa must have relished the idea, because it broke him up every time. Sometimes Sven would open the window and politely listen. If he really concentrated, he imagined he could hear the thunderclaps of German guns as they killed people. He didn't like it at all, but he didn't dare tell Pa.

The lengthening shadow of that large black boot was falling everywhere, trampling everything in its way. That was what they said on the radio, and their voices were sombre. You knew it was no joke. It was a dark time for mankind, they said. Sven didn't like the dark so he worried.

But according to Pa there was nothing to worry about. The Germans knew exactly what they were doing, he proclaimed. They were going to save the world from the Russians, and the world ought to show a bit of gratitude. They weren't fighting the Danes, they were helping them, which was different. People had to realize that. The dumb fucks ought to be grateful. Pa had also declared that the only annoying thing about the war was this business about rations and ration cards, which he considered a personal affront. First it was coffee — coffee, for God's sake — then it was sugar, and about half a year later it was bread and flour. The following month it was pork. New Year's Eve, for a special treat, they had clamped down on butter and margarine. Even worse was when they cut the four litres of *akvavit* a month down to three. However, said Pa, that was no problem because he, Rune Andersson, had contacts in useful places; he was a man of resources. Pa would never lack food or drink.

Sven found it reassuring to have a father who knew everything. And if the Germans had to save Denmark from the Russian barbarians, it was mighty decent of them to go to all that trouble, considering how busy they were. That was what Pa said. Only he said the Danes had to be saved from the English. The English were barbarians too. You could tell because they drank tea, just like the Russians. They put milk in to disguise it, but that didn't fool Pa.

In the meantime their life plodded on as usual. There was lots of *akvavit* to be had, what with Pa's personal ration being approximately fifteen litres a month. Herring and bread, butter and cheese were bountiful, as were the sausages made of sawdust and dead Communists that Sven refused to eat.

Ma and Pa were sitting at the table by the window having their Saturday booze-up with Asta and Kjell. Because that was what they always did. That was the way it was. Kjell walked with a limp due to an injury from his days as a sailor, when he had got beaten up in Shanghai by a six-foot-four transvestite from Melbourne, so he had not been able to sign up for army duty. Instead he'd joined the Home Guard. Stiff as a rod, he tried desperately to stretch his meagre frame another ten inches to fill his uniform. He strutted in front of Ma like a brilliantined rooster.

"You sorta have to take two steps before your pants move," noted Ma.

Pa refused to admire the bold warrior. He snickered resentfully as the little shit paraded around like a fucking general. Pa was not easily outdone, so to emphasize his disapproval he snorted loudly and smeared a contemptuous gaze at the preening hero. Then he smiled a scornful smile, one of his very best, the kind that made a deep crease in his round left cheek. When he did that, you knew he was about to launch into a tirade. And sure enough, there poured forth a rationalization as to how he himself had no time to spare for such infantile crap, blah, blah, blah, although he would have signed up first thing that April 10 had it not been for his bad heart, blah, blah, blah. Shit, had he been able, he'd have gone to Finland, he'd have walked all the way, fought barefoot in the snow, and killed with his bare hands.

"Really, Kjell." Pa smiled, pausing just long enough to stick a cigar in his face. "Really. I mean, don't think I'm not a patriot. I am. I know what you're thinking. You think you know me, my gimpy little buddy, but you don't. So wipe that dumb fucking grin off your face, you self-righteous little prick, because you're looking at a *real* patriot here! One who cares, Kjell — one who cares for more than himself!" Pa stabbed himself in the chest with his left thumb, a gesture that here was a valiant hero whose heart beat passionately for his country. A man who'd look grand in black boots polished to reflect an admiring world. "If Sweden is invaded, I'll be the first to lay down my life for my homeland, just like that, no questions asked. I'll fight the Russians till I drop."

"It's the Germans we have to worry about, you ass-kissing Nazi pig," interrupted Kjell, sadly shaking his curly head. He emptied another glass to fortify himself against Pa's perverse logic.

"Bullshit, my man. They're the ones who are going to save Europe, and I'm all for it. I'm for what's right, and I'll gladly die for it. That's the kind of man I am." Pa's eyes misted over as he listened to himself. "And furthermore," he added, with a wave of his cigar, "Hitler's got get up and go, if you know what I mean. Takes no shit from nobody. Doesn't piss around. It's what the world needs. A leader who can stand up and tell it like it is. Take charge. I admire a guy like that."

In fact Pa, who felt a strong bond with "real men", had tried to cultivate a Hitler-style moustache, but Ma immediately vetoed it, telling him he looked more like the fat guy in Laurel and Hardy. He had shaved it off at once, but he had sulked so hard that his cheeks drooped. He started to look like Churchill instead.

Ma, if she noticed, didn't give a damn. She knew better. Besides, she was preoccupied with her own ambitions. In June 1941 she was dreaming of becoming a nurse, the Florence Nightingale of Sweden, if by any chance it turned out that Pa was wrong and the Germans did invade. She didn't share his views about Hitler, and she was perceptive enough to notice that very few people did. She didn't know where Pa got these weird ideas. It was embarrassing sometimes. Hitler was evil, everybody said so, and he was ugly too. Ma had the hots for Clark Gable. Clark Gable was a real man. He could invade her any time.

Ma was a feeble-minded romantic who at the time had a vision of herself as a glorious angel of mercy. Shrouded in virginal white, she floated, breathtaking and celestial, among stacks of bloodsoaked soldiers dying painful deaths in a field hospital somewhere in southern Sweden. Their tortured cries echoed down the foul-smelling hallways of hell. But when these brave heroes saw the golden mirage that was Edith Andersson from Malmö, the light that was fading fast in their eyes flickered one last time, in a glimmer of eternal gratitude for her unselfish presence. They died with smiles of bliss cracking their dry lips as their bloodstained hands reached out for her. This preview of heaven made their sacrifice more than worthwhile.

Edith loved her vision. It was spellbinding being the centre of the universe. She rolled the scene and over and over again in her head, while heartbreaking violins sobbed between her ears. It damn near made her weep, it was so spectacular. Much better than *Gone with the Wind*.

One thing Ma knew for sure: Clark Gable would never have left *her*.

But once again Clark had not been able to make it to their little do. Ma's only admirers were the same old ones, Pa and Kjell. And then there was the old bag that was Asta Jönsson, her decaying body slumped on the chair closest to the window. Asta's poor mind, if she had one, appeared lost in a dim Never-Never Land. She was sublimely indifferent to Hitler, the war, and Clark Gable. She would declare, unasked, that she really didn't give a rat's ass. If people wanted to kill each other, let them. They were all foreigners anyway.

This she'd bray joylessly to nobody in particular. She was a marionette; her body and its appendages lay piled in a heap on the chair, coming to life only when unseen hands saw fit to pull her strings. The hands would let go just as suddenly, and she'd fall back into a bundle of stick-like parts, silent and immobile. It was uncanny.

The fifth person in the room — the only one who ever paid attention to anything Asta said — was Sven, the bleary-eyed little boy over on the couch. The grown-ups didn't regard him as company. He was just a kid, and kids didn't count. Still, he was there, an invisible consciousness, waiting and watching as always. Watching the grown-ups at the window, which was open to the night and let in sounds from the outside world. Unnoticed and unthought of, like a fish below the water's surface, he hung suspended.

The weather was listless that night. There was a wind hovering over the rooftops and streets, but it was too hot and lazy to move fast. The curtains fluttered limply once in a while as veils of cigarette smoke dragged towards the night. Out in the summer night, up in the vast heavens, there would be stars. Bright yellow stars, Sven hoped, even if he didn't get to see them. He liked stars.

Music and shouts and drunken roars wafted into the room, as always on weekends, from the amusement park two blocks away. The sounds floated into their midst on bits of wind torn loose. Odd bits of tra-la-la from the dance bands, a drawn-out note from an accordion. Ma hummed along with the fragmented tunes of a smoochy tango, rolling her shoulders as if she had an itch in a strange place, blowing smoke through her nostrils to the rhythm of the music.

It looked stupid.

Pa had got out the deck of cards and was shuffling with an expert hand, a sharp look of concentration on his shiny face. He was a gambling man and he played to win. There wasn't much to win, but he was determined to win it.

"Is it legal for you to play cards in that get-up?" he smirked.

Kjell smiled benignly back at him. Being more or less a soldier, he felt handsome and invincible. Significant. He could afford to laugh at Pa, to stare, indulgent and unabashed, at Ma's great tits as if being in uniform gave him the supreme right to do so. According to Pa, Kjell was just a dumb fuck whose only ambition in life was to grab Ma by the tits and never let go. Like a tattooed little leech. So Ma would treat him to the odd wiggle and shake to keep his ambitions alive. She liked doing that, and Pa thought it was hilarious. It made him feel proud. Once when Pa was really pissed he had unbuttoned Ma's dress and tried to pull a tit out in full view, saying to Kjell, "Bet you'd like a feel of this, eh?" Kjell had drooled over his poker hand and looked pained. That time Sven had quickly left the room and gone to bed. It had made him feel strange. He didn't understand grown men. They always made him uncomfortable. He didn't want to grow up.

Asta had sat there on the same old chair, a scrawny figure slumped in a world of her own. Just as she did now. The invisible hands controlling her strings were resting. Her mouth hung open and her sometimes oddly flickering gaze was for the moment glued to some non-specific point out in the street. Maybe she was blind and nobody had noticed. Blind eyes glued to some long-lost memory. If she had memories. Nobody knew and nobody cared.

Nobody thought of Asta as someone with a past. Nobody thought of her at all, except Sven. He thought of her a lot.

Because nothing in the whole wide world was more loathsome and scary than Asta, and that was the truth. Sven had come to this conclusion at a very early age, and since then it had become an obsession. She was a slimy detestable creature from somebody's horrible nightmare. Not his nightmare, he didn't want it, *ever*. But he lived in fear that one day she would touch him, grab him by the arm, perhaps, so that he would never be able to use that arm again. It would rot like the arm of a leper. It would putrefy and fall off.

This was no joke.

Asta was a snake. Or more like an octopus, actually. It was as if she had no bones in her body except in her wildly waving arms. She sat there with a cigarette butt hanging out of the wide wet hole in the middle of her face, where other people had mouths. She was hideous. Pa said that Kjell only lived with Asta because she supported him with her salary from the stocking factory so he didn't have to work, because Kjell didn't like work very much. It didn't agree with him. It made him tired, or some such thing. And these days, Kjell said, he was just no good at clipping those piddly little coupons for rationed food. Albeit a necessity for survival, it was woman's work. Women had smaller hands so they were better with those tiny scissors. And a man had to eat.

That was why Sven sat on the couch and stared at Asta across the room. He was bored yet fascinated. Alert. He had to be vigilant because one day she was going to slide off her chair and come slithering across the floor towards him, no longer in human disguise, but as her true reptilian self. Then she would try to gobble him up. He knew this for a fact. Slurp, burp, and he'd be gone. That was why he always kept his clogs on when she came over, so he'd be able to kick her in the face just before she sank her yellow dripping fangs into him. The kick would only delay her, so he'd quickly jump up on the coffee table and hurl himself to the ceiling lamp, where she couldn't reach him. From there he would swing himself to safety somewhere. Straight out the window, maybe, whoosh, grab onto a lamppost outside, his reflexes absolutely perfect, sharpened by his acute survival instinct. He'd slide down the lamppost in a flash and disappear into the dark night, never to be seen again. Maybe go to sea.

Yes. Yes, he would. He'd go and fight the Germans. Just to spite Pa.

Sven was bored. He was tired too, and his back hurt. There was never anything to do except sit and silently force time to move forward. Push it with his mind, butt it with his forehead. That and stare at the grown-ups, who did what they always did. Drank and played cards. Shouted and laughed. It never failed, on and on they went. It was late now, he should have been in bed long ago. Nobody noticed him anyway. But he sat there, silent and stubborn. The room was his world. It didn't matter how shabby or fragile this world was, not that he would know, he had nothing to compare it with. He needed to belong, to have a mum and dad. He felt he had a right to them, somehow, and he was aware of his rights. Always would be. There had to be order and justice in life.

An amazing event had taken place earlier in the evening. Kjell had, for some inexplicable reason, brought Sven some delicious chocolate toffees. Unprecedented behaviour on Kjell's part. Perhaps it was in celebration of his fancy Home Guard uniform; no explanation was given, just "Here kid, catch!" Now Sven was chewing the very last one, which meant that it was eleven o'clock and he had sat here for five hours, because he had made a rule that he was only allowed to eat one every hour on the hour. There had been six sticky, chewy toffees wrapped in striped red and gold paper, and he had unwrapped the first at one minute to six and popped it into his mouth at six on the dot. He was a firm believer in rules.

He looked over at Kjell, prepared to smile at him and show how grateful he was, but he had long ago faded from Kjell's consciousness. The grown-ups were playing cards seriously now, loud and preoccupied. Playing cards was a battle, not a game. Pa had that tight intense look that made his fat cheeks wobble. He couldn't stand even the thought of losing, so he cheated as often as he could, and that took concentration and careful planning. If he didn't win tonight there'd be hell to pay, Sven could tell from the look on his father's face. Pa wasn't going to lose to a limping loser in a uniform four sizes too big.

Sven picked toffee from between his teeth. That was definitely the end of the candy. For something to do, he cocked his ears to the festive noises from the park. They sure knew how to have fun over there. He heard an orchestra strike up a waltz. Drunks were whooping and screaming somewhere down the street, having a great old time. They must have just left the park. A bit later he heard a tango, hot and smouldering, one of Ma's favourites. She shut her eyes and heaved an amorous sigh as Clark Gable swept her across a vast ballroom under a sea of crystal chandeliers.

It looked *really* dumb.

Time crawls sluggishly down the road to eternity when you're only seven and you're too tired to think straight. When you're sitting on a couch, kicking the air with your clogs, while the rest of mankind is doing the tango in the park. Your body grows stiff, as if aspiring to reach rigor mortis and have done with it. Apart from the never-changing scenery of the grown-ups performing their usual histrionics, there was nothing to look at except the two pictures on the opposite wall. Sven liked them a lot. While their landscapes were bleak, they were not without hope. His gaze would home in on them once in a while for support, for a bit of rest. Even when he was alone, he would sometimes go and hide in those scenes so empty of people and noise. Their desolate lack of colour blended with his, and he became one with them. It was oddly reassuring.

A lifetime dragged by until finally they started playing the last waltz down in the park. "They're playing the last waltz," announced Ma, as Clark swept her back onto the dance floor. Then the music stopped dead. It was followed by the usual choir of whooping and singing as the drunks spilled out of the park and scattered into the night. Sven wondered what people were doing out there, why they didn't go home to bed.

The grown-ups were still playing cards. They were really pissed now, and had reached the querulous stage that meant they'd keep it up most of the night, unless Pa won the Big One. They always finished with the Big One.

"Full house!" squealed Kjell, and triumphantly banged three kings and two aces on the table.

"You fucking cheat!" hollered Pa, and damn near exploded. He had been dead sure that time: a straight, ace high, sweet as you please. No cheating, either, that was what hurt. It was an honest hand. Always the same thing. Honesty fucking well did not pay.

"You tattooed asshole!" he bleated. It was a really sweet hand he had there, a fine hand. An honest one. He deserved to win, he really did. This time of all times.

"You fucking tin soldier!" He whined on and on, like a broken record. "You frigging clown! You cheated, you bow-legged little bastard, admit it! You fucking cheated!"

"Listen to the Nazi." Kjell smiled, sweet as a choirboy. "Poor ickle Nazi-poo!" And he giggled that funny drunk giggle of his. It came through his nose in little bursts while he smiled from ear to ear with his mouth closed. His face looked like a rubber mask.

"Nazi asshole," he said when he opened his mouth again. "You think I don't know what you're up to with those guys? That fucking whatshisface.... You think I haven't seen your DNSWP propaganda stuff? They're such losers, for God's sake. Why the fuck would Swedish workers want anything to do with the Danish National Socialist Workers' Party? You're fucking warped, Rune, you know that?"

"Oh, what the hell," interrupted Ma, thinking out loud, philosophical like, as she lit another cigarette. "Are we playing cards or what?"

The querulous stage evolved to the tired stage. It took a thousand years. Sven sat over in his territory, semi-catatonic, only a small part of him still on alert. Smoke stung his eyes and his eyelids kept drooping, yet he had no intention of giving up. He never did. If he fell asleep on the couch, they would forget him there and he would wake up freezing at dawn with the window wide open and no blanket to crawl under. It was an awful way to wake up.

The night crawled on. His eyelids grew heavier.

Just as his eyes were about to close, a terrifying scream cut through the night. A single razor-sharp manifestation of pain. It sliced through Sven like a cleaver, emptied his head and filled it with ice. Was it the end of the world? It was a woman screaming as if all the world's suffering had found a sudden outlet in that piercing scream. And then it was gone. The world's silence covered it up. There was no aftermath. The night went on as before. Had the Germans arrived? Was it war? Sven could hear no guns, no goose-stepping boots.

"Reckon someone knocked up a virgin!" declared Pa. He couldn't resist an indulgent grin, though he wasn't by any means finished sulking.

Kjell giggled wholeheartedly, he couldn't help it. When Rune was in the mood, he was a real riot. But that was that. They continued to stare dull-eyed at their cards, seeking those elusive four aces.

"Heaven help a knocked-up virgin," croaked a long-forgotten voice.

It was Asta and she was talking. She was coherent. They all stared at her, slightly sobered by the spectacle. Usually she lost the ability to speak after the third glass.

"What the hell do you know about that?" enquired Edith with supreme disdain. Clark Gable still had a manly arm around her.

"I got knocked up once. Got pregnant just like that," explained Asta, straightening her back with all the brittle dignity of a drunk. "I had a kid. A long time ago, long before you did. I had a kid. So there.... And don't think I didn't, because I did. So fuck you.... I know. I know. Was a virgin, too...."

The invisible hands pulled spasmodically at her strings. Her arms jerked and she dropped her cigarette.

"Is that a fact? You never told me," interrupted Kjell. He was a bit put out because he liked to be in on things, being a regular gossip. But apart from that, he was basically indifferent. It wasn't all that interesting. Asta was like a faithful old dog, shabby and neglected, with mangy fur. A bit foul-smelling at times, but tolerated out of habit, even when she pissed on the rug.

That was when the little fish became alert.

Sven pricked up his ears, his mind reeling. Asta had a child? A real child, like him? That couldn't be! He wouldn't let her, it wasn't right, it was abnormal! She was a reptile, she couldn't have human babies. He felt frightened and angry. His head went all hot inside.

"No shit. So where's the kid?" Edith wanted to know.

"The kid,..." echoed Asta and blinked. She'd already forgotten what she'd been talking about. "The kid?... Well, I gave it away, is what I did. Gave it away. Was a boy...little baby boy...what the hell was I going to do with a kid? Chrissakes. Was only a kid myself...dammit all...what was I supposed to do?"

"When was that?" Edith was curious in spite of herself; she wasn't quite sure what to think about this. Asta was too stupid to lie.

"Can't remember...was sick. I remember that. I was sick.... Was the same year Branting died. I think. Yes, it was...in February. I remember. Sad, wasn't it? Hjalmar Branting dying...fine prime minister...fine man.... Yes...was my birthday that week. When Branting died."

"Hell of a present you got then, eh?"

"Yeah...sure was." Asta's lights were about to go out.

"Who was the father?"

"Can't remember his name. Tall guy...always wore brown shoes."

"Are you sure you had a kid?" double-checked Edith, while Clark Gable nibbled her left ear. She wanted to be absolutely certain.

"Sure? Fucking right. Why wouldn't I be? I know what I know."

"In that case the kid would be about sixteen now," observed Rune, who had a head for numbers.

"Could be," mused Asta. "Was many years ago now."

"Sure was!" shouted Kjell with a benign grin, and he banged a fist on the table. "Especially when you're having fun! Eh?"

"Wasn't much fun," mumbled Asta.

"If it was the year Branting died, you would have been around nineteen," calculated Edith, happy to have caught Asta lying. "That ain't exactly a kid, is it? Huh?"

"Was to me. Still had my dolls," maintained Asta. "Was a virgin too. I was. Not like you."

"What's that supposed to mean?"

"Never mind. Wasn't a slut, is all I'm saying."

"Yeah, and I am, is that what you're getting at?"

"Ladies, ladies! We're having fun!" Kjell waved the cards in his left hand and the glass in his right to remind them of the ongoing festivities. "Let's sing!"

And so on.


Sven had been born on October 9, 1933. In the same week and the same city where Gustaf Rydberg, "The Grand Old Man of Swedish Art", died. Edith had read that in the paper and thought what a coincidence it was. She decided at once to name the newborn child Gustaf. Not having realized that she lived in the same place as such an important personage, she now wanted to make up for it. If she named her son Gustaf, he might grow up to be a great artist. He certainly wasn't much to look at, this kid of theirs, so it would be just as well if he had something else going for him. And Gustaf wasn't a bad name. The King of Sweden was named Gustaf, and if it was good enough for the king it was good enough for her. Pa had already vetoed Clark.

Gustaf wasn't good enough for Pa, however. No son of his was going to be called Gustaf, no way. It was the name of some old fart. Besides which, she knew piss all about art. Aside from the pictures her drunk cousin Sigge had painted, that was. If those were even art, which he personally doubted very much.

It was the same year that Hindenburg made Hitler *Reichskanzler*. Rune thought, hey, there was a suitable name for the kid. Something to live up to.

"Hindenburg Andersson? Are you out of your mind?"

"No, you dumb tit. Adolf. Adolf Andersson. It's manly. It's got muscle."

Fat chance. No goddamn way were they going to name the kid after some slimeball German with a stupid hairdo. Edith was adamant. There was a limit, and Adolf was fucking well it. So Sven it was. You couldn't get more bland than that. It suited the kid perfectly.

15

They were not in a very good mood that year, neither Rune nor Edith, which may have accounted for their conduct. There was a heat wave that summer, and Edith, big and heavy in her seventh month, sweated and suffered and sulked. Felt ugly and clumsy. Looked ugly and clumsy. Sullen and unadored, she was irritable and whiny. Rune was in a frenzy. His soccer team, Malmö FF, his boys in blue, didn't win the national games as he had predicted and bet on extensively. They didn't even come in second. They hobbled into ninth place, like a bunch of one-legged cripples, and Rune was inconsolable. He felt personally insulted and humiliated. Ashamed to face the world.

Then he had some cockeyed excuse for a son.

That same October there was a municipal election in Skanör-Falsterbo, just south of Malmö. Although only 52 per cent of the eligible voters could be bothered to go out and vote, 12 per cent of the vote went to the Swedish Nazi Party. The right took 57 per cent, but the Nazis got two of the twenty seats on the city council. Ten per cent. It was the same year that the extreme right called for "Sweden's freedom from Bolshevism and prohibition against associations that aim to overthrow with violent means the old Swedish society, a society of justice."

Into this society of justice popped Sven. He didn't cry a lot and that was a relief. But he wasn't what Ma had expected. She had decided on a lovely little girl whom people would look at and exclaim, "My God, she's beautiful, she looks just like you!"

"Christ, he's ugly," said Pa. "Look at him. No hair. No muscle." He had wanted a little girl too. Or a real little man who looked just like him.

"He's not all that ugly," protested Ma weakly.

"Sure he's ugly," maintained Pa, "and I bet you he's stupid too, the little bastard. Just look at him. No get up and go. That kind of thing shows right away."

Still, they kept him. They didn't have to, of course, but they did. Actually Pa did make enquiries about adoption, which he didn't tell Ma about, but changed his mind when he found out that they wouldn't get any money. He was never one to give anything away.

So they kept their cockeyed offspring, and now Sven, seven going on eight and no longer cockeyed, was sitting on a couch staring at a prematurely aged woman named Asta. The gargoyle, as he perceived her. The secret mother. The troll.

He felt inconsolable. Sick.

"So who did you give the kid to?" Edith kept nagging for information.

"Didn't say...he was adopted or something...the hell was I gonna do with a kid?"

One minute later she sank like a stone straight to the bottom of her murky consciousness. Thud. There she sat, like a prehistoric deep-sea creature with staring eyes and motionless fins. No longer present but part of the shadowy landscape of her mind, way down in the mud where her thoughts hid. The others soon lost interest in her pathetic little scandal. It was hardly an original story.

That was when the little fish surfaced. As Asta sank, Sven rose to the surface, dizzy and free — as if he saw daylight for the first time, and was blinded by it but unable to resist it. He shot from the couch, flew through the room, fuelled by his suddenly combusted hate, and attacked Asta with such force that she fell off her chair.

Suddenly Sven existed. The skinny kid from the couch existed. The world raised an eyebrow as he attacked. He felt exhilarated and powerful. He was like a mindless buzzing mosquito, not dangerous but irritating and persistent. Easy to squash but fearless. Flames of unformed thoughts leapt through his head as he kicked Asta furiously where she lay on the floor beside the overturned chair. There was an expression of vague surprise in her slack, empty face. Sven kicked and kicked and kicked with his little clogged feet. He wanted to kick her to death, that was what he wanted to do. He wasn't sure of the meaning of death, but he knew that dead people no longer existed. They never came back, and he very much wanted Asta never to come back. He wanted her gone. It was a strong, pure feeling that burned bright and hot in his head. He kicked some more, tried to kick her pasty face to make her features disappear. But she managed to avoid that, hiding her face behind her arm as if they were playing peek-a-boo. He kept kicking, glad he had his clogs on, oblivious of the other people in the room as they sat and stared, so surprised and drunk that it didn't occur to them to stop him. Or perhaps they were too intrigued. Or maybe they just didn't give a damn.

"You goddamn whore shitbag! I'm gonna kill you. Whore!"

It was his own wild voice spewing his father's familiar vocabulary into the silence of the room. Hearing it, he stopped his unexpected performance as fast as he had started. Hearing his own voice, he ran out of power and his head went cold again. Less than two minutes had passed. Asta lay by his feet, holding her head, curled up like an embryo. She didn't move, didn't make a sound. He stared at her with sudden indifference, not caring if she was dead or not. Overcome by exhaustion, he ran to the bedroom and slammed the door.

He threw himself on his bed and hot wet tears of hate washed his face. He had never dared to hate before, and then all at once he had found out how. And it was so easy! It was such a great feeling, but it made you really tired. He kept on hating as he cried, soaking his pillow — hating Asta, hating all of them, Ma and Pa and Kjell too. He wanted all of them not to exist.

But at the same time he felt ashamed. Not of what he'd done, oh no. He felt ashamed of *them*. All of them. He didn't know why. He just had a sudden suspicion that they weren't very nice.

He stopped crying, confused. For a brief moment he was amazed at his thoughts. He had imagined those unseeing eyes popping out of Asta's head and rolling across the floor like a pair of old marbles. But he felt he was in the right, he had done nothing wrong. He'd paid her back for having a baby and throwing it away.

She wasn't nice. You didn't throw babies away.

He felt dizzy. Everything was so strange, so nasty and ugly, and there was no way out. And then there was that eerie feeling that he didn't understand, that feeling caused by suddenly having his existence confirmed. It was not good news.

He wondered what Asta's baby had looked like. How many arms it had had.

The door flew open, and Pa came marching into the bedroom like a field marshal laden with medals, fat and bombastic. He halted his troops by the bed and gave Sven one very hard, stinging slap across the face. Sven's glasses fell off. Pa hit him again, mainly for the hell of it, to show who was boss. He didn't say a word to the child. Not a single reprimand was uttered. It wasn't all that important. Having won the battle, he marched triumphantly out to rejoin in the revelry of his faithfuls.

Asta lay curled up asleep where she had fallen, a discarded doll. The others continued to play cards. Sven lay in the dark bedroom and cried and cried and cried. In the end he cried because nobody cared that he cried.

That was the first time he lost his temper and wanted to kill somebody. That was the first time he expressed his ill-formed opinion for the world to hear. It wasn't much of an opinion and it was feebly expressed, but Sven didn't have the gift of the gab. He didn't have the slightest idea how to express the unidentified frustrations that burned in his head, so he kicked and screamed to extinguish the flames, to make everything nasty go away. And the world listened to his shrill voice and really didn't care.

But for a while it felt better. It cooled his brain, it cleared his thoughts.

Afterwards, the humiliation made him shut up for almost forty years — long silent years that he cautiously plodded through. Until he lost his temper just once more. One more time a conflagration would erupt inside his poor brain, already fevered and aching from too many thoughts about too many things. One more time he would have to put out the blaze, next time by killing a man. And it would feel right.

But he knew nothing about the future that night when he was seven and heart-broken. Had he known at the time — on June 21, 1941 — it wouldn't have made any difference. At least, that was the conclusion he came to in his old age, as he looked back over the empty landscape that had been his life.

What had been had been.

He would never know that the young man he killed was Asta's

19

grandchild. Knowing that would have made a difference. And that was only one of the ironies of Sven's life.

The years went by and dragged the little boy with them, and he had no choice but to grow up. He turned into a well-behaved and tidy man, a man who wore a dark blue tie when he dressed up and a discreet striped brown tie for work. His eyes were pale blue behind his glasses. He had a nice straight nose, a rather elegant nose, in fact, below which cowered thin lips tightly pressed together. He had limp, soft brown hair that he kept cut short. He used dandruff shampoo and he showered every day. An average man.

This was what he had become, and it didn't surprise him a bit. It was what he wanted. A seclusive individual, he didn't let anybody into his private world. It was a well-insulated place, built with care, bit by bit, thought by thought, over the years. He'd had lots of time to erect his sturdy fort. It was constructed to last for as long as he did. He himself was much less sturdy.

Everything was well planned in Sven's adult world, because if you plan your days and years like a scientific project — with materials and methods, the hypothesis clearly defined, following certain basic rules — it is possible to survive without major trauma. But only if you're very, very careful, and practise stringent self-discipline.

Sven was very, very careful. He was a dull and humourless man who kept himself on a short leash. But he had principles and he knew his rights. If he was small-minded and petty, it was because he wanted to be; it was needed in order to fulfil the plan. It was part of his mental survival kit.

But who was he?

There was nothing in his apartment that would help identify or betray him. It was furnished with good-quality, uninteresting furniture: a sofa-bed in anonymous beige, a matching armchair that was comfortable and sturdy. In the corner by the window facing the courtyard stood a TV on a wooden stand. He'd gone all out and bought an expensive German brand.

There was some reading material lying around, but nothing revealing. Stacks of thick, well-thumbed history books would have told something about the person living there. Dog-eared magazines of child pornography would have revealed something else. But there was neither. There was a newspaper basket, but it was empty apart from yesterday's paper. A bookcase with detective novels and a row of volumes from a book club: twenty-four of them, one dutifully purchased every month for two years. That was all. The rest of the shelves had been given over to, among other things, a black telephone, a china figure of a boy in a round green hat playing the violin, and a glass bowl with assorted candy in pretty wrappers. Did he have a sweet tooth, perhaps?

In the corner by the window that looked out on the street stood a round teak dining table and four chairs. The dining set didn't really fit in; already out of fashion, it looked unused, as if bought in a weak moment when dreams of what could be had temporarily clouded reality. It was his fancy table, his Sunday best. Was that revealing? He had a small table in the kitchen with two chairs, all painted an old-fashioned blue. A peasanty sort of shade. You would have thought that was enough, for why would one person need two tables and six chairs? Especially a person who never had company? But that was the way it was. He had seen the dining set in a newspaper ad. It had looked tasteful and elegant. The way a table should look for a fancy dinner party with linen napkins folded into clever shapes, and crystal glasses and polished silverware, even if you only invited yourself. You always ate at your best table for special occasions, it was the civilized thing to do. He liked to think of himself as a civilized man.

Sven ate his Christmas dinner at the teak dining table, sitting on the chair opposite the window, with the dark winter sky as his only companion. There were Christmases when it snowed, and that always made him happy; there was something peaceful and reassuring about the slowly falling white stars. This was the time of year when he'd take the red four-armed candleholder from its box in the hall closet. He'd lift it out carefully, dust it with a kitchen towel, and put four white candles in it. These he would light just before he sat down to eat. It was his Christmas ritual, his bit of solemn ceremony. He would read a detective novel while he ate, one of four new ones that he bought himself as a Christmas gift. If it was snowing he'd sometimes just watch the snow. He didn't mind being alone. What made him feel edgy and anxious was the thought of people knowing he was alone. That was as embarrassing as having some kind of disease, something contagious. It was something to stay well away from. Watch out, there's a lonely man, don't go too close.

It worried him sometimes. Not while he was eating his Christmas dinner, but now and then the thought would stir up from its thorny nest in the back of his mind. The thing was this: a lonely life, or a life so perceived, you could always lie about. You could hide it with words. But a lonely death would be humiliating. And eventually he was going to die. That thought was perplexing. You can't hide for very long when you're dead. You start to reek after a while, at which point the neighbours will grow suspicious and call the police who will then come and break down your door, expensive security locks and all, and carry away your rotting remains in a plastic bag. And people will say "Oh, isn't that pathetic! The wretched old man! What did you say his name was?" He'd read about cases like that. Unwashed old men in stained underwear in rooms piled high with decade-old newspapers.

He grew cold with fear at the mere thought of this happening to him, his life and putrefying body being revealed in so vile a fashion. If there was one thing he was almost fanatical about, it was keeping scrupulously clean — as if a lack of human odour helped him remain anonymous. After thinking about this in depth for a considerable length of time, he decided what he'd do if he ever felt he was about to drop dead: he would call the city morgue or hospital or whomever you called, tell them to come and pick up a dead body, give his address, and then unlock the door. Then he

22

would crawl into a large plastic garment bag and zip it up from the inside, leaving no mess, no smell, no inconvenience. He had the perfect bag for that very purpose, a mothproof one that he kept his good suit in. He even considered donning his good suit to die in, if there was time — maybe just before he called the morgue. Dress up for the occasion, and exit incognito and clean.

He was pleased with this plan. It had class.

While the two tables and six chairs might have given the impression that there was more than one person living there, a quick look inside the kitchen cupboards told a different story. They were almost empty. There was no more than one of everything: a dining plate, a soup plate, a large spoon, a small spoon, and so on. There were a couple of cans of soup, a jar of coffee, sugar and salt. No herbs, not even pepper; he didn't like pepper. On a bottom shelf to the left of the sink there were usually two bottles of Armagnac. That was his bar. His stash. The refrigerator was home to a loaf of bread, a package of butter, and some salami. No disclosures there, except perhaps the emptiness itself.

Photos would have told a story, but there were no photo albums. There was no past. Nothing pointed to a single bygone event. There was no yellowed photograph of his parents' wedding. No photo of himself as a fat-cheeked baby, or as a young boy with uncombed hair and scraped knees. This total absence of pictorial evidence was rather frustrating. He couldn't prove that he'd had a life. He had not a single photo of relatives at a birthday party, aunts and uncles wearing silly paper hats, cigars sending smoke signals from under bushy moustaches, strings of pearls on stuffed satin bosoms. No holiday pictures of naked children with buckets and spades by the edge of a lake, no groups of flabby grown-ups in ill-fitting bathing suits. Nothing.

Well, there were the two framed paintings on the wall over his dining table. The same two paintings that had hung in his parents' apartment. They had a past, they had a history. The one to the left was in shades of grey, brown, and scattered dark blues and purples. The scene was so empty that it startled the eye. It depicted a landscape that was not only uninhabited when painted, but had always

23

been untouched. There was a river going through the desolation and it looked as if it had recently flooded; the land around it muddy and treacherously wet. Maybe it had rained hard for a long time. There were dark clouds disappearing over the horizon. The few trees in this landscape, far to the right of the overflowing river, had no leaves; they were naked and black, bent in the wind. Whipped into submission by some unseen force. Perhaps it was autumn, perhaps early spring, it was impossible to tell.

It was a barren land yet it always pleased Sven. He had often rested there as a child, and as he grew older he became consciously attached to it, and often sat on the couch studying it. He knew every twirl and splash the water formed along that river, every crooked branch on the trees. He had stood by the edge of the water in imaginary rubber boots and felt the wind splashing tiny droplets of water on his face. It always had a cleansing effect. He felt a sense of belonging.

The other painting was also one of bleakness, if bleakness is the absence of people. The colours were grey, white, greyish blue, and a purplish blue that looked as if it might be carried over from the river in the other painting. A high wall made of large stones dominated the landscape: round, smooth cobblestones embedded in white masonry. Along this wall ran a gravel road that disappeared around a corner in the far distance. The same naked trees could be seen to the right, except that here, on one of the lower branches on the tree closest, hung a small bluish leaf. Here there was no wind, here the trees had always stood still. Conceivably there was something behind that high wall, otherwise there would be no wall. A wall was a border, a divider. Something was being kept in or out. Or both.

Sometimes, as a child, he had closed his eyes and stood on that road. He would not pretend to walk along it, but just stand there surrounded by silence. There was never a sound on that road. Once or twice at the beginning he had felt that perhaps there ought to be birds singing on the other side of the wall, as if in some secret garden. But he knew at once that that was wrong, he knew that that was not the way it was. So he'd stand there, the wall warm against his hand, the stones smooth and round to his touch. It was a friendly touch. He never wondered where the road might lead, only what might be found on the other side of the wall. He felt at home there, that was all that mattered.

He knew where the paintings came from. Ma had had a cousin who was an artist. An artist and a drunk. His name was Sigge. He went crazy, Ma had said once, that was why he painted. Then he killed himself and that was that. It was what artists did, she said, and she took the two paintings because Sigge owed her money.

When Sven was called up to do his military service he left home for good. He didn't know at the time that it was for good, but he must have had an inkling because he took the two pictures without even asking, and put them in the bottom of his suitcase. He wasn't sure why, but he knew he didn't want to be without them. They belonged together, he and those landscapes. Ma never said anything about it. She probably didn't notice.

These were the only pictures from his past.

Sven had dreams occasionally that involved other human beings. Not often — that would be reckless — but there was the odd weak moment, the rare faultline between the hours, when his hobbled brain broke free for a brief run. At times like that he dreamed a specific dream about what it would be like to have a woman in his life. Smallish and roundish and willing, but not too willing. Sweet and kind and shy and good. At night she'd be there naked in his bed. No, not naked; she was a lady, not a whore, she'd wear a nice nightgown. A lacy sort of affair with long sleeves. But she'd be ready for him all the same, ready and willing in such a way that he would spontaneously assume the role of The Lover and confidently set about his business. He'd know what to do. And his woman would moan shyly but not too loudly, with surprised delight, as if she couldn't get enough of him. During the day she would look after their home while he worked. They would have a nice little villa outside town, with a nice garden and a view of the sea. He had money saved, they would be able to afford it.

He'd return home in the evening and she would serve him good wholesome food. No canned stuff. Fresh fried herring with onion sauce. Roast pork with applesauce. Thick yellow pea soup with big chunks of pink ham and a glass of hot *punsch* on chilly evenings. Good solid stuff that helped build a man. During dinner she would sit and listen to him as he held forth about his day at work, about life, the wrongs of the world, and other deep matters that men ponder. He would be patient and explain and the two of them would be one. She would melt into his world and become part of it in a natural way, so there would be no moments of awkwardness or discomfort, no clumsy mating ritual as they got to know one another. Like a pretty little spirit, like an elf out of the woods, she would suddenly be there, smiling sweetly, and it would be as if she'd always been there. Without questions, without words at all, they would know and understand each other, the sun would shine, and birds would trill jubilantly in the trees in their garden.

A modest dream, he thought.

The components of the dream were the material of his refuge. In it, he adhered to his rigid goal, which was plain unembroidered survival. His dream might be torrid and dull, might reflect a Spartan soul or one hampered by lack of experience. But it was his life, this dream, and he'd kill to protect it.

Every morning from Monday to Friday at 8:31 sharp, come rain or shine, Sven stepped out into the world, his tie in a perfect knot, two salami sandwiches tucked in his coat pocket. Somewhere between 8:35 and 8:38 he got on the bus and rode down to the train station. It wasn't far. He could have walked and got some exercise, but he didn't. He did walk from the station, two blocks down Skeppsbron, to where he worked, close to the hydrofoil ferry terminal.

By 8:57 he was on the seventh floor of the building where the large import firm he worked for had its offices. He entered the door with his name on it at 8:58 and became Mr. S. Andersson, Accountant. Spot on nine o'clock, he was sitting at his desk. It made him feel good. He'd been working at that same desk for twenty years, never off sick for a day. He'd take his holiday time, but only because he had to — it would look strange otherwise. His job was the glue in the seams of his existence. He didn't acknowledge this fact; he didn't need to, not yet. But he knew.

He was an excellent accountant, meticulous to the point of pedantry. So reliable, in fact, that he was largely ignored, which was fine. If he didn't feel at ease around people, he was right at home among numbers. Be they integers or decimals, small or large, positive or negative, he was in control, and he needed the feeling of being in control.

There are two kinds of ridiculous people. Group A consists of people who deep inside are aware of their predicament, but live with it, in an ill-concealed state of embarrassment. Sven was definitely a member of Group A. He blushed too easily. He was tongue-tied and awkward. Group A members are the kind of people who are only too aware of the source of the snickers they hear behind their backs. They should probably be pitied but seldom are, as they're so easily forgotten.

Group B are the attention-grabbers. These are the people who breeze through life loud and confident, wonderfully assured of their importance. They die of old age still thoroughly oblivious of the fact that throughout their lives they did not exhibit a single endearing trait, totally ignorant of their own grating asininity, no doubt blinded by the limelight they assumed was their birthright.

The overseer of the company, Executive Director Nils Nervander, was a lifetime member of Group B. It's possible that with a name like Nervander he felt it was his mission in life to get on people's nerves. He thought of himself as The Boss. He had power of a sort that nobody envied. Contrary to his firmly held belief, nobody feared him. People hid their contempt behind servile smiles and ignored him. He hated that. Nervander himself was under the thumb of The Big Boss himself, Mr. Uno Hammar — Numero Uno Hammer, as he was known. Hammar was a one-man economic powerhouse, a squat grey-haired wheeler and dealer with a granite chin and eyes the colour of the North Sea during a December storm. Not a guy you'd want to mess with. He buzzed around the globe like a bee in search of pollen. There was nothing ridiculous about Numero Uno. The office seldom saw him, but it made no difference. Having hand-picked his staff, he knew he didn't have to stick around. Sales people sold, buyers bought, payroll payrolled, receptionists received, typists typed, and Sven, the accountant, accounted. Executive Director Nils Nervander, the brother of Hammar's second wife, sat in his spacious office picking his nose as he watched the Copenhagen ferries come and go. Having properly excavated his snout he might, for something to do in the official domain, show off to his secretary by dictating a letter, preferably in a foreign language. While his German was fairly good, he usually got his words mixed up when dictating in English. People were still laughing about the time he had mixed up "excellent" with "excrement". His secretary, fluent in both English and German, never bothered to correct him. He didn't like being corrected, so why bother?

In his glass cage three doors down, Sven too enjoyed a splendid view. Not of Öresund, the strait, with Denmark on the horizon — that was Nervander's special treat. Sven looked out on the inner harbour and the canal along Norra Vallgatan, towards the ivy-clad courthouse and the museum. This was as far as Sven's career was to go; here he had laid his ambitions to rest. He felt he had arrived. This was the corner of the world where he rightfully belonged, and there was nowhere else he wanted to go.

In the cage to his left sat the energetic Mrs. Lundwall, née Miss Nilsson. She was newly married and was very particular to point out that her name was now *Mrs*. She had a man now. When they didn't change the plaque on her door soon enough, she marched straight into the executive director's office and gave him a piece of her mind. "What's right is right" was her guiding philosophy. An old-fashioned girl, Mrs. L. was full of averages. She was of average intelligence, average height, average weight, and used an average amount of makeup to improve her average looks. The only insight

28

into her private life that Sven had been treated to was the fact that she enhanced her own and her husband's existence with half a kilo of shrimps every Saturday evening after payday. A restrained celebration they indulged in with "a little glass of wine". It was her idea of sinful debauchery. "Well, whoopy-fucking-doo," as young Arne in Sales had said upon finding that out. Sven quietly agreed.

Mrs. L. treated Sven with a kindness of sorts, an almost maternal condescension that he did not cherish. The reason for this irksome attention was the fact that Sven suffered a mild case of dandruff. Mrs. L.'s Kent had dandruff, and she reasoned that if her Kent had dandruff, other men ought to be likewise endowed, or it would make her man look bad. Dandruff was honourable. Mrs. L. belonged to Group B of ridiculous people.

The cage to his right was stuffed like an eiderdown pillow with Fat Fransson, her elephantine buttocks swelling and hiding what was a very solidly built office chair. She always wore dresses with flowered patterns that made her look like walking Botanical Gardens. The massive arms that protruded from these flowerbeds ended in surprisingly dainty little hands. Her manicured nails were polished with a pearly pink. She was not without vanity and her manners were girlish and soft. She had several chins that all trembled in unison as her fingers typed invoices with inhuman speed.

But what intrigued Sven the most was the fact that, despite her gargantuan proportions, she had a couple of years earlier been impregnated by an equally mountainous husband, and had given birth to a tiny, very beautiful girl child. Sven's mind had boggled, like everybody else's. The whole office had boggled for weeks. It had been impossible to get any work done. Some people nastily claimed that the child had to be adopted because Fat Fransson had never grown any bigger, but others said it was because she'd already reached critical mass. Sven imagined that she had a secret cavern deep inside for the child to grow in. A dark red cavern with a Mickey Mouse nightlight spreading a golden glow over the growing fetus curled under a soft blanket, its head resting on a red satin pillow with lace trim. That stuff must still be lying in there somewhere, deep inside the mountain range of her body. Nor had she decreased in size after her baby's exit from that cave. And now she was the proud mother of a tiny angel with golden curls and the astonishing blue eyes of a doll. Since the day her little Pia had been born, Fat Fransson, madly in love, had never stopped talking about her. Hourly reports were broadcast with regard to what little Pia had just accomplished that was just too enchanting to be withheld from the rest of mankind. Every unused surface in Fat Fransson's office swarmed with framed photographs of little Pia. Yet Fat Fransson was not at all ridiculous. She should have been, with her vast bulk, incessantly babbling about her sweet angel, but she wasn't. Human warmth gushed out of her like lava from a volcano. She was a happy woman, and it's difficult to sneer at happiness. Happiness is strength, and it is not easily come by. It has its own dignity.

Just across the corridor sat Bertil and Arne, two louts in their early twenties, immature but aggressive. They were in Sales and Marketing and belonged to a different generation, a different world. They lived in a far-away land where Sven had never set foot. He didn't know their language, didn't understand their jokes, and failed to recognize their priorities. They mostly ignored him.

Everybody needs somebody to hate, and the office was lucky to have a perfect object of loathing apart from Nervander. In the cage to the right of young Bertil perched the notorious Tyra Rankeskar, tall and scrawny, full of self-important confidence, her lipstick just a shade too red and her eyebrows just a shade too black above a nose like the beak of a predatory bird. Tyra was special. She was a gold-card–carrying member of Group B of Ridiculous People. She had forced enough of her self-appointed significance upon others to arouse contempt and hatred in equally massive amounts. The reason for her hugely inflated self-importance was the fact that her brother was the executive director of a large firm. He was rich and lived in a villa out in Bellevue, and if you had a villa in Bellevue you didn't need to worry about status symbols. Most of her many, many unrequested proclamations began with "Director Rankeskar, my brother, said the other day...." There was apparently nothing about which this man did not opine at great length. Next on her list of titillating personalities were her extraordinarily

30

gifted niece and nephew, offspring of said director. Amaretta and Amadeus were eleven-year-old twins whose brains, if Tyra was to be believed, would have made Einstein's intellect compare unfavourably with that of a dew-worm. You better believe it, assured Tyra. "Do you know what they got for Christmas? Electric guitars! And expensive! With huge amplifiers! Of course, my brother, the director, can afford it, money is no problem in that family, but imagine! Those children!" And she'd shaken her stiffly sprayed curls in silent bliss, savouring the knowledge of who was who in the world. (Tyra didn't know that the twins had demanded these instruments, which they couldn't play, after informing their father — Moneybags, as they called him — that otherwise they would tell their mother about the pornographic magazines, most with a *très piquant* homosexual slant, that they had found when they'd broken into Daddy's mahogany desk in search of money.) They had a distinct feeling that Mummy would not appreciate daddy's preference for this quaint and interesting art form. There was one particular picture they decided to keep, one depicting several naked men forming an intriguing daisy chain. This one they mailed to Aunt Tyra who just about dropped dead on the spot, cheeks blazing scarlet, her breathing laboured. She had no idea that men did that kind of thing. And so many of them all at once! She kept the picture. Nobody in the office ever heard about that incident.

Yes, everyone in the office hated Tyra, but they never dared show it; if they did, Nervander would immediately call them into his office to question them about something he had found out. Something they had done wrong or not done at all, which should have been finished last week. Strange how he knew. So in the name of survival they all smiled and listened to Tyra, who would always top their stories with a better one. If somebody was sick, then Tyra was immediately much sicker, only *she* did not take time off work, *she* did not let anybody down, *she* was not one to let a bout of malaria and dengue fever keep her in bed. If somebody died, Tyra hinted that she herself would have been twice as dead, had it not been for her sense of duty.

Good old Tyra. She had viewed Sven with great suspicion when

31

he started work two years after her, an inoffensive young man with slumped shoulders who never looked her in the eye. But there was never a crack in his efficiency and he was never sick, so it was impossible to be morally superior to him. She had long suspected that Sven was trying to outdo her in her zeal to be the most perfect employee, and it was a situation she didn't know how to handle, because the bloody man never said anything. He never complained. After about ten years of distrustful speculation and schemes of revenge, Tyra finally decided that not even germs could be bothered with Sven, he was too self-effacing. Thus, being infinitely more fascinating, she was more perfect after all.

The only person Sven looked forward to seeing was old Sture from the warehouse. He came by once in a while but not very often, as the warehouse was located on the other side of the harbour, and as Sture felt out of place amid all the plush carpeting and fancy what-have-you. When he did show up, he liked to sit himself down and have a little chat in Sven's office. Have a cup of coffee, light his pipe, and philosophize a bit about this and that. Discuss something he'd read in the paper that morning. Impersonal reflections, ponderings about politics, the general decline of the country, how it had been different when he was young, and what the world was coming to. Sven had nothing against this, as he too considered himself something of a philosopher. It sometimes happened that they almost had discussions. Slightly fumbling ones, rather jumbled with regard to direction, but nevertheless there was a distinct attempt to exchange thoughts. Before it went too far, however, Sture would knock the ashes out of his pipe, tuck it away in his jacket, and say that it was about time he left before Nervander started to charge him rent. He would retreat with a friendly nod and disappear back to the warehouse world where he belonged.

Around the corner, farther down the corridor, dwelled a bunch of dangerous creatures: women in their thirties, some of them married, most of them divorced. All of them had children. Even worse, they had hair and lips and eyes and breasts and legs and laughter. They all smelled of perfume. Sven stayed as far away from them as possible, just to be on the safe side. They were all friendly and helpful. Not a single one of them wasted time forming an opinion about Sven, beyond once discussing the fact that he looked a lot older than he was after Berit in Payroll told them his age. They wouldn't have noticed if he had dropped dead at his desk and grown moss. He avoided them all the same, hoping they were not coming to see him when he heard the soft rustle of their skirts in the corridor, the almost imperceptible little taps of their heels.

There wasn't a high turnover of staff, despite Tyra and Nervander. Sven and his colleagues were well looked after. Coffee was free at any time, with two official coffee breaks a day when strong, freshly ground brew was served in stoneware mugs with the firm's logo tastefully incorporated in the design. They all had their own private offices, with tempered glass from a metre above the floor to the ceiling to discourage too much privacy. Good salaries, comfortable chairs, and a nice view. Every Christmas, the last afternoon before the holidays, they gathered in the lunchroom for the traditional hot *glögg*. Here things were not done on the cheap; the *glögg* was laced with three-star Cognac, loaded with almonds and raisins, and served hot but not hot enough to take the buzz out of the booze. The tables were pushed into one long row for this festive occasion, and decorated with real china, red Christmas serviettes, poinsettias from the nearest flower shop. There were plates of gingerbread, almond cakes, and chocolates, and a big Christmas torte specially ordered. Not only that, but The Numero Uno Hammer himself was always present. He knew when to be one of the gang, smiling and beaming good will towards mankind. For one afternoon a year they became a big silly family. And what a family! Rosy-cheeked in the flickering candlelight as their loud shouts of *Hej!* and *Skål!* echoed and brimming mugs of *glögg* were rapidly emptied and refilled. It was the one time of year when Sven got half pissed in public, and chatted (when he had to) in a friendly, mindless manner. They all yelped with helpless laughter when The Hammer condescended to indulge in one of his traditional jokes about loose women with large breasts and members of the clergy. Christmas cheer lifted the roof.

It was also the time of year when Executive Director Nils

Nervander deigned to act like a fellow mortal. He had to because The Hammer from Hell did. He would grin with drunken sincerity and shout, "For God's sake, gang, call me Nils! We're all buddies here, right?" "Well, here's to you, Nils!" they would scream, faces glistening with *glögg* and good cheer, swinging their mugs, never calling him Nils again until the next Christmas.

At four o'clock they all gushed their thank-yous and Merry Christmases, got their coats, and descended on wobbly feet into the darkness of the afternoon. This was the one day when Sven did not wait for the bus. This was the day when he buttoned his coat against the wind and walked leisurely by the train station, over the bridge, and past the Savoy Hotel, across Stortorget and down to Lundgren's Bookstore. That was where he'd made it a tradition to buy his four detective novels. He never rushed this task; the shop was nice and warm, busy and bustling in a comfortable way that he liked being part of, book-buying people being solitary and quiet. At the counter the clerks would ask if the books were to be wrapped as a Christmas gift and he would say, "Yes, please, they're for a friend." They would take their time preparing a prettily wrapped gift, making a fancy bow and curling the ends of the ribbon.

After his annual Christmas shopping he walked home carrying his present, red ribbons fluttering, peering in display windows, looking at all the people, their faces tense with shopping needs, and at the general Christmas rush. He liked being part of this too. Carrying a Christmas gift helped make him part of it. He strolled past St. Petri Church, down Östergatan towards home. He always stopped and bought his Christmas food at Malmborg's supermarket. It was crowded that time of day and year, but he didn't mind as he was still half pissed and full of good cheer. It was the nicest part of Christmas, this routine that suggested some purpose.

His shopping done, he trudged home through the dark streets. He watched a lot of TV. On Christmas Eve, before his dinner, he unwrapped his gift and started reading one of the books. After dinner he cracked nuts and drank Armagnac while staring at the boob tube. It wasn't so bad.

The rest of the year he sat faithfully at his desk. Like a good dog, he loved his master and knew his place. He was content. He'd had his future predicted early in life by his father: "He's gonna work in an office, this one," Pa had said more than once, for God knows what reason. "Sit behind a desk. Bound to, look at him, glasses and all. Good with numbers, the little bastard. He got that from me." Pa was right. Sven was good with numbers. He appreciated the way they worked, the way they didn't let you down. He added and subtracted, multiplied and divided to his heart's content, and when he estimated what the final figure would be he was usually right. It gave him a deep sense of satisfaction.

This was his place in the scheme of things. It was in this place, among these people, that he spent his days. Where he belonged. Where he felt safe. Until they turned on him and his world shattered.

Two people peripheral to Sven's existence were his neighbours on the fourth floor. Two identical dark brown doors stood side by side, like sombre sentinels with matching brass mail slots. His read S. Andersson; the other declared that here lived A. Persson, and that was just about the sum total of what Sven knew about his neighbours, despite the fact that he'd lived beside them for more than sixteen years. Observing some unwritten rule, Mr. and Mrs. Persson both greeted him whenever they met with a friendly and proper nod accompanied by a smile, and sometimes a polite exchange of words. "We've certainly had enough rain this week," they might say. "We sure have, haven't we?" Sven might reply. That would be the extent of their dialogue.

But it meant something.

The Perssons were discreet, considerate people who did their utmost not to bother anybody, and expected the same in return. They still referred to Sven as "our new neighbour, young Andersson",

as they had lived in their apartment for fifty-two years while Sven
had arrived on the scene a mere sixteen years ago. They had lived
there since the day they got married. It was where they had spent
their honeymoon, after a day trip to Copenhagen.

Arvid and Greta Persson's wedding had been an occasion for
rejoicing, the festive start of something grand. A leather-bound
album with yellowing photographs still had its place of honour on
the bookshelf, beside a framed wedding photo. It had been one of
those rare celebrations where everybody was dressed up, smiling,
brimming with hope for the future, because Arvid was marrying
the only woman he would ever love, just as Greta knew there would
never be any man for her except her kind and gentle Arvid. It was
more than romantic, it was a story-book wedding, a happy beginning on Midsummer's Eve. They got married in Greta's uncle's garden, on the lawn by the cherry tree. Greta's veil was held in place
by a garland of flowers. There was dancing around the maypole
and the children got grass stains on their Sunday best, but never
mind — everything was absolutely right with the world. Even when
Uncle Kalle locked Aunt Augusta in the wood-shed and threw away
the key and proclaimed himself divorced and they didn't discover
her until the next day.

It was a solemn occasion as well, because for Arvid and Greta
marriage was a deadly serious business. They were not flippant
people. Matrimony was a lifelong commitment, this they had agreed
on — something you had to care for constantly, like a sensitive
plant. For the two virgins this wedding was the first significant
step.

They moved into the one-bedroom apartment on the fourth
floor. It was quite a treasure back in the late twenties; it had not
only a bathroom but hot water. The street was quiet in those days,
with precious few cars, though the tram stop was around the corner even then. A proud Greta spent her days bustling around their
precious castle, polishing the already shining furniture they had
bought with hard-earned savings and family contributions.

During those first happy years they concentrated on the com-
pletion of step two: having their first child. Their plan and ardent

36

wish was to have two children. These would be the culmination of their happiness, their reason for hard work, the meaning and foundation of their future. Over and over again Arvid and Greta tried to create this first miracle, their first child, be it a boy or a girl, but always in vain. Greta did not become pregnant.

The wait for something to happen grew more despairing as the years went by, their hopes dashed every month when Greta bled crimson blood right on schedule. After seven dragging years of crushed hopes, and increased periods of impotence, it was confirmed that she was unable to bear children. She would never become pregnant and she would never be a mother. This simple truth was delivered in a matter-of-fact clinical voice by a man in a white coat behind a very large oak desk. There were several framed photographs on the shiny surface of that desk. Greta was sure they contained photographs of his smiling wife and many children.

It was a cruel fate for a woman whose life ambition was to be a mother. Greta cried all that summer. Not in front of Arvid; she would never burden him with her weakness. She cried when he was at work, every day until the first day of fall, when the rain and wind brought a swarm of yellowing leaves whirling through the street. One of those leaves, a small golden one shaped like a child's hand, stuck to the living-room window. She looked at it with some surprise as she stood watering her African violets, and said to herself, it must be the hand of my unborn baby waving at me. I know it must. It's my little girl. It's Eva-Lotta. She's saying, "It's all right, Mummy, I don't mind not being born." Greta opened the window and plucked the wet leaf from the glass, carefully dried it, and hid it in their wedding album. It gave her some comfort to know that her unborn child had sent her a message, and she decided not to cry any more. Eva-Lotta didn't want her to. She never told Arvid about Eva-Lotta's hand, he might think she had gone funny in the head. She hadn't, but she knew what she knew.

Arvid too was inconsolable. He would never become a father, he was a family man without a family. So much for setting goals. He didn't cry; he didn't dare do that. Instead he grew more and more humpbacked as the years went by, a beaten man who knew his place and didn't make a fuss, forever quenching the thought of the unfairness of it all.

The core of their existence grew still and quiet as together they began to age. It seemed there was nothing else left to do. Perhaps they thought they might as well get it over with, get it behind them. Their life continued but it never again had any meaning. Events no longer touched them. They didn't feel they belonged any more. They could have adopted children, but never thought of it. It was their own children they'd been waiting for. Their dreams had been modest — they had been willing to work hard for their goal, willing to make sacrifices — and fate had responded by simply ignoring them, as if they weren't important enough. Yet they never complained.

Sven moved into his apartment the same year Greta Persson turned fifty-two. He was never to know their secret lament. It could not be read in the gentle faces passing him on the stairs; such kind faces were surely a sign that these people had no problems, that they were content and happy with their lives. That was Sven's reasoning. He thought he was tragedy's lone victim. He presumed that the Perssons were living whatever kind of life married couples lived, going to the theatre and out to dinner, having excursions in the country.

Year after year they sat there, Sven on his side of the wall, the Perssons on theirs. Sven in front of his TV and the Perssons at their kitchen table, with coffee-cups on one of the many tablecloths Greta had embroidered. It was often the one with bluebells and forget-me-nots tied with yellow ribbons. It was her best one. For sixteen years they co-existed in mutual silence, not wanting to disturb. Arvid and Greta aged quickly but gracefully. The years gathered in soft, ever-deepening lines in their mild faces, as if they never voiced a complaint, never had an evil thought.

Still, they needed each other despite their silence, and acknowledged as much by a gesture once a year. In wordless agreement a tradition had formed. Every year, the week before Christmas, there would be a timid knock on Sven's door. He would open it to find Greta Persson standing there, her cheeks still rosy from the warmth of her oven, handing him a china tray covered with a freshly ironed white linen napkin and saying "I thought maybe young Andersson would enjoy a bit of home baking this Christmas, because I don't suppose he has time to do any baking himself, being such a busy young man. And store-bought cakes just aren't the same, are they?"

After her long speech she blushed deeply. Sven blushed too, making a bow to her curtsy, thanking her and thanking her again, mumbling foolishly.

Fulfilling a need to nurture, Greta Persson had started this little tradition the first Christmas after Sven moved in, and it had continued ever since. It meant as much to her as it did to Sven. During the endless Christmas holiday he would reverently munch every gingerbread, every almond cake, every butter cookie, and whatever else she had filled the dish with. Everything she baked was absolutely splendid, he thought, made to perfection. He always felt a weepy sort of gratitude, but didn't acknowledge it in words.

He didn't know how to show gratitude, never having had a reason to. He was sure there were specific rules as to how this was done and he did what he could. Early on New Year's Eve he strode determinedly down the street to the flower shop on the next block, where, pleased with himself and full of purpose, he picked out the most expensive plant money could buy. It had to be something potted that would last — one of the poinsettias, perhaps, but only if it was large enough, because nothing but the best was good enough for Mrs. Persson. His arms full of blooms, he strode back home and briskly climbed the stairs to ring the Perssons' bell.

The first time he did this, he was scared witless by such blatant, self-inflicted exposure. But it didn't stop him from going through with it, because deep inside he knew that he had nothing to fear from this woman. He could afford the courage, and he needed to make the gesture.

When Greta Persson opened the door and peered up at him, he would hand over the flowers, the carefully washed china dish, and the neatly folded linen napkin, and utter his well-rehearsed speech: "And I would like to thank you very much for your kindness and lovely, lovely baking, and wish you both a very happy new year." Greta Persson would blush with delight at this recognition every year, as young Andersson stood there half hidden behind blazing poinsettias, Arvid nodding kindly from the kitchen doorway. Greta was deeply thankful for the attention and never for a moment suspected that she was the only woman Sven had ever bought flowers for. They would smile a bit awkwardly at each other until Sven started to shuffle his feet, preparing to disappear into his own private sphere until the following Christmas.

The Perssons, like Sven, were people of few words. Most of the time they sat at their kitchen table sipping coffee out of the delicate china cups that had once been "for best". Sometimes they spent a while standing by the living-room window, gazing down into the street where the world went about its never-ending business. It seemed very far away at times. Otherwise, there they would sit, hour after hour sometimes, wordless in their tidy spotless corner of the universe, among their tapestries and finery, their copper pots and well-pruned plants, their china figurines and framed photographs. A transistor radio on the kitchen counter stood silent most of the time. Every so often Greta would get up very suddenly, as if she'd just remembered something, to start what she called "tidying a bit". She would vacuum, do dishes, wash curtains, make the place look "presentable". Maybe do some baking. Something nice to go with their evening coffee while they watched the news on TV. Cinnamon buns were Arvid's favourite.

Like two guardian angels they sometimes stood by the window and watched Sven return home from work in the evening. He always arrived home rather late, they'd noticed that a long time ago. He probably ate his dinner in a restaurant somewhere, maybe over at Konsum's department store. Being a bachelor and all, he likely didn't bother to cook for himself. He walked a bit slumped over, didn't he? Almost like an old man, always crossing the street with those deep folds lining his forehead, as if lost in thought about some important matter. Not a frivolous type.

"He looks lonely, young Andersson, down there," Greta once ventured.

"Yes, maybe he does," agreed Arvid. "You never hear much noise from in there. He's very quiet."

"Yes...do you think perhaps we ought to invite him in for Sunday dinner some time?" It was a daring suggestion. "I don't think he eats properly, the lad. He looks too pale, doesn't he? Tired. Needs a bit of meat on him, I think. Don't you?" She worried about things like that.

"Well," said Arvid, "well now. I don't know about that, Greta. He's a grown man, after all. I mean, what right do we have to go and interfere in his life? Even if you mean well, and I know you do, because that's the way you are. You don't want to put him on the spot. It might embarrass him. Maybe he has a girlfriend who makes him Sunday dinner at her place. I mean, you never know, do you?"

"Well, you may be right, Arvid. You probably are. It would be frightfully embarrassing to impose on him. You're right."

"Yes, I'm sure he's living his life the way he wants to, being a bachelor and all," concluded Arvid, and stirred sugar into his coffee.

"I suppose so. He's a bachelor."

"Right."

"Shall I make some more coffee? There are fresh buns in the bread bin."

End of discussion.

The Perssons continued their quiet existence until the day Arvid was told that he had cancer of the colon, which had spread to his liver and kidneys, and that he had only a very short time to live. He had had terrible gut-wrenching stomach pains for months but had pretended that everything was fine, because he didn't want to upset Greta. She always worried and fussed something awful. But the pain finally became so unbearable that he could no longer hide the large amounts of painkillers he downed with each cup of coffee. Dizzy with fear, Greta ran in ever-narrowing circles, chased by unthinkable thoughts, for several days. Finally she pulled herself together and forced him to go with her out to the hospital, even insisting that they go by taxi, sparing no expense.

It was probably just severe constipation, she told both herself

41

and Arvid, determined not to give those evil thoughts a chance. She knew what he was like. Too many buns and pastries, and he didn't like going for walks if the weather wasn't right, which it never was. It was either too windy or too wet, too hot or too cold. He liked being comfy, did her Arvid.

At the hospital she spent long hours in the glass-walled cafeteria right in the middle of the compound, feeling exposed to the world and very vulnerable. In the meantime poor Arvid was confined to rooms unknown, somewhere in those buildings that she could never tell apart, and subjected to tests with names she couldn't pronounce. What was the problem, she demanded when she saw him again. He wouldn't tell her. Not yet, he said, wait until all the test results are in. What tests? You'll see, he said. She waited.

She sat at the same table in the cafeteria the day Arvid was called back, with a coffee and a cheese sandwich. She never ate the sandwich. A strange young woman sat alone at the next table, with long, unwashed brown hair that hung like curtains around her puffy pale face. The woman sat and stared at people, and every so often she burst into laughter, unrestrained and loud, banging a tight fist on the table, shaking her head.

She would have made Greta uncomfortable had Greta not been worried sick. Then Arvid came into the cafeteria, didn't even bother to get a coffee and a sandwich, sat down opposite her and told her he was going to die. Just like that. "Well, Greta, it seems I'm going to die," he said, looking down at the table, too embarrassed to face her. They weren't even going to operate; it was too late. He had suspected it for some time, he'd almost, but not quite, grown used to the thought. But his Greta had not. She fainted with a moan, right there in the cafeteria, knocking coffee all over herself and the cheese sandwich. Arvid felt ashamed, as if he'd behaved improperly. The strange young woman laughed heartily at the spectacle. She was still chuckling to herself when Greta came to.

"My husband is going to die," said Greta, but without reproach. Saying the words out loud like that, she was facing the naked truth. It was difficult. She repeated herself. "He's going to die."

"Well, aren't we all!" responded the woman cheerfully, and

stomped her feet for emphasis. She was wearing large rubber boots.

Greta and Arvid took a taxi home.

Sven knew nothing of the unfolding tragedy as he sat in his insulated world, deep in his chair, deep in his dreams. Suspected nothing during the next two months, didn't notice that the silence was heavier, more ominous than usual. How silent does silence get? How much does it weigh? Whatever fear Greta and Arvid felt as they waited did not diffuse through the wall to grab Sven by the throat. They kept it to themselves; it would be distasteful to do otherwise. Arvid insisted on staying at home, it was his last wish. There they sat, at their usual places at the kitchen table. Greta had stopped baking. Every so often Arvid's hand would catch hers as it fumbled about on the tablecloth, looking lost — catch it apologetically, angry at his helplessness. He didn't know what to say, feeling that a real man would not go and die and leave a woman to fend for herself.

So he said nothing.

"It's going to be empty," mumbled Greta one day, and immediately felt bad for having said it. She didn't mean to complain. It was just that the feeling was so overwhelming.

"You'll get used to it." He was trying to help her, to be brave. After a pensive bout of silence he continued. "You know, I was thinking that maybe you should move to your sister's house in Tomelilla. You know how Ingalisa's always complaining that the house is too big now that Gustav's gone. It will be nice and peaceful out in the country, Greta. Nice fresh air. And if you take the colour television with you, you can watch it in your room, right there in our bed, and you won't have to disturb anybody. A bit of luxury, eh, Greta?"

"I suppose so," said Greta obediently. "I'm sure it will."

"You must promise me," begged Arvid, eager to ease his guilt. "Then I won't have to worry so much. Will you please promise me that? Will you call Ingalisa?"

"I promise. I'll call her tomorrow. I think she's busy today."

"Call her today, Greta. We have to plan."

"Tomorrow. I'll call her tomorrow morning."

43

"Do you promise?"

"I promise. Tomorrow."

She kept her promise. He made her.

Two weeks later Arvid had to go into the hospital, his pain was too savage. The next day he was dead. Gone. So fast. There was a body in the hospital bed, but Arvid was not there any more. Greta looked at the body and felt a certain relief as she cried. Then she fainted again.

The emptiness at her kitchen table was terrible after that. It wasn't real. It was so very, very wrong that she couldn't face it. She had to close her eyes to Arvid's empty chair; strange how profoundly and stunningly empty a chair could be. She was glad now that she was moving to Tomelilla. She wouldn't have to look at that empty chair any more.

She had spent most of her life in this place and now it was over. Just like that. She had expected something more. Trumpet blasts from the heavens, global upheaval, angels in full regalia descending to let the world know that Arvid Persson was with his God, happy and at peace. But there was nothing like that. There should have been, there really should. Only the same silence as life continued. She looked out the window and the view hadn't changed. It was raining. Cars swished by down in the street. Konsum advertised pork chops on sale. There was an American movie on television.

Death is like that. It doesn't make a fuss.

The air had grown heavier, that was all. It pressed down on her and made her shrink. It flattened her hair against her skull. One mustn't complain, she told herself sternly. While a fanfare from heaven might give death some meaning, one mustn't complain. Arvid is gone. He's not here any more. He's not anywhere any more, that's what's so peculiar. He stopped being, is what he did. He deserves his rest, he's not in pain any more. He isn't at all.

He's dead and gone.

Sven knew nothing of this until two weeks later, when he was climbing the last flight of stairs one evening and was met by a small figure dressed in black. It was Mrs. Persson fluttering towards him. A little black bird unsure how to use her wings. He stopped and stared, his mouth hanging stupidly open. Thinking, it couldn't be....

"Yes, Arvid is dead," confirmed the black bird, shy and apologetic. She did not like to be a harbinger of bad news.

"Christ Almighty!" blurted Sven, as if to protest what she had just said. "Good God...well...my condolences, Mrs. Persson. I...I...don't know what to say. I'm sorry, I don't know what to say." He shook his head and felt inept. What *do* you say?

"Well," mumbled Greta Persson, "it happens to the best of us."

"It does," agreed Sven, grateful, "it does indeed. How true."

"Yes. That's what Arvid used to say."

"Did he?"

"Yes. Yes, he did," nodded the black bird, rustling her wings. "Well, I suppose I'd better say goodbye then. I'm moving to Tomelilla this Friday. To my sister's. I'm going to live there."

A rosy blush spread like a final sunset over her sad face, as if she'd buried her husband in a moment of frivolity. As if she needed an excuse.

"Well, goodbye then," mumbled Sven. He felt shattered.

Greta Persson nodded shyly, patted his shoulder for some reason — it quite surprised him — and disappeared from his life for ever.

Sven was perplexed. He spent the whole evening in a state of confusion, pondering the riddle that was life. Thought about his neighbour, a man he had never known, a man who had never been quite real to him. A man who was now dead. He missed him. Now that Arvid Persson was gone, Sven wanted him back.

He felt sorry for himself. Persson was dead and his wife was moving to Tomelilla. They were not going to be here any more. No more Christmas baking. No one to lavish flowers on at the end of the year. It had been one of the dismally few traditions in his life, and the only one that really involved another human being. No wonder he felt such an intense sense of loss.

No, life would never be the same, he told himself. He had no idea how right he was. Fate was on its way up the stairs to visit him, bringing an end to peace and quiet and unbridled dreaming. Did Fate slither up the stairs like a reptile, cold and vicious? Or did it skippety-hop like a merry troll, unreal but powerful? Did it smile, smirk, or look supremely indifferent? He couldn't hear a thing in the hush of late evening. Fate doesn't huff and puff; it's got stamina. He sensed something, though, something approaching, getting closer. He tried not to think about it. He didn't believe in premonitions.

It was cold and blustery the Monday evening when Sven hurried home from his quick dinner at Konsum's and found a stranger standing on the landing outside the Perssons' door. His new neighbour. It was a moment he'd hoped would never arrive. But there she was, this very small stranger, a mere slip of a thing. Her short dark hair was ruffled by the wind that had blown her up there. Just a kid, really, dressed in baggy black corduroy pants and a long green sweater. She wore cheap black cloth shoes on minute sockless feet and carried a drooling baby on her arm. The baby stared at Sven with supreme indifference and hiccupped loudly. The baby's mother, if that was what she was, was busy hunting for her keys with one impatient hand inside a Tempo bag full of groceries. She turned around for a brief moment when she heard Sven, smiled a quick smile that didn't quite hide her irritation, and turned her back on him. The baby suddenly squealed for no particular reason, looked displeased at Sven, while grabbing a handful of its mother's hair and trying to eat it.

Sven felt awkward as he fumbled with his key. As if he were the intruder. He didn't have a clue what to do for, while he had anticipated this happening, the situation was still too unexpected. He needed time to rehearse. Was he supposed to say something polite like "Welcome"? Welcome to what? How about "Who the hell are you?" Or "Please go away, you don't belong here"? What did you say to an unwanted neighbour, especially one who looked like a runaway? He had expected people his own age or older, not this childlike alien in cloth shoes.

They stood there, the two of them, alone together for a brief moment, rattling their keys in the silence. Sven decided it was safer to shut up and pretend he wasn't there. After all, she had nothing whatsoever to do with him. Except for the fact that he'd lived there for more than sixteen years and had certain rights. He had seniority. It wasn't as if he'd expected it to stand empty from now on, in memory of what had been, but even so.... He didn't give a damn who moved in, he told himself sternly, but he didn't believe it for a second. Of course he cared. What he really wanted to do was give in to a strong urge to stomp his feet and pound his fists and scream and shout until the trespasser disappeared. But he didn't do that, he had no legal right to do anything. He wouldn't have the guts anyway. He vaguely acknowledged this dismal fact as, head down, he made a hasty retreat into the safety of his fortress, locking the security lock, indulging his bunker mentality to the full.

Determined to relax, he decided to make a cup of coffee. He'd spent a long day buried in stacks of monthly reports that had to be finished at once, according to Nervander, or the world as they knew it would come to an immediate end. As a reward for a job well done he'd bought a package of fresh almond cakes. Nothing like a little present when you've been good. He stared at the fresh, crisp cakes in anticipation and to his horror he felt his appetite fade. He could feel it sighing away, like air leaking out of a balloon. It was all because of that intruder out there. He didn't want to be bothered by her but he couldn't help himself. He was weak. The smallest change in routine threw him off balance. And this was a major change. It worried him, it really did; it made his gastric juices boogie hysterically with Konsum's meatballs and pickled cucumber. No use pretending. Things were going to be different, and Sven didn't like that. Life was supposed to go on the way it always had, that was his plan. The road to inertia and boredom was straight as a rod, you never lost sight of the horizon, and Sven appreciated that. Now there was a turn in the road and he couldn't see what lay beyond. He had not taken such factors into account.

It was that baggy ragamuffin next door. She just didn't belong. For one thing, he found her sheer lack of size offensive. Hard to be rude to somebody that short. More important, there were no young people living in this building, and certainly no babies. She had no business moving in. She should realize that a terrible mistake had been made, apologize for her intrusion, and go away. Go and live with her own kind, wherever her kind lived.

Red Alert!

Listen! What was that? Was that the baby crying? How typical. Was this the way it was going to be from now on? Screaming and crying, day and night? No more relaxing in one's own home? Was this a taste of things to come? It wasn't fair.

Agitated, he carried his cup of coffee into the living-room, quenching the weak voice deep inside that said, "Shut up, Sven, don't be such a paranoid twit." He sank into his chair, prepared for torment, for a deluge of evil baby noises for the rest of his life. He still didn't feel tempted to have an almond cake, that was how bad it was. He sat there, ears pricked, holding his breath, though he couldn't hear a thing. Maybe the noise was only audible in the kitchen; it was wall to wall with the Perssons' kitchen. Or maybe the child had stopped crying. Then again, with any luck it was all a hallucination and there was in fact nobody there. Maybe he'd gone crazy. He got up and trudged back to the kitchen. Bent over the sink, he stuck a resentful ear to the wall, thinking how stupid he must look like that.

Aha!

He could hear it again: the baby was crying. No, it was screaming! Good thing the noise didn't carry through to the living-room or he'd be lying awake all night. He snorted to himself and shook his head with alarm.

One would have thought, he reasoned, that if that ragamuffin was the mother she would look after her baby so it wouldn't have so damn much to cry about. Sven knew absolutely nothing about babies, but was of the firm opinion that if they cried it was because their mothers didn't look after them properly. It made sense when you thought about it. That was what mothers were for. Dealing with babies came naturally to them.

He remembered that once in the lunchroom he'd overheard Fat Fransson say that when the little Pia angel was teething she just cried and cried and cried for nights in a row, the poor darling, and that Fat Fransson became so frantic she couldn't take it any more, her heart was breaking into teensy pieces having to listen to the poor thing, so she rushed little Pia off to the emergency clinic in the middle of the night. They were very unpleasant to her, hissing with ill-concealed irritation, "For God's sake, madam, contain yourself. The child is teething!" Fat Fransson's cheeks had shook with indignation at the memory. Recalling that story, Sven could pride himself on some expertise when it came to teething.

Mind you, Fat Fransson was a good mum, she was a mountain of teeming motherhood, and that no doubt made a world of difference. Whereas that promiscuous little so-and-so next door was a kid herself. She didn't look a day over sixteen. Wasn't even married — didn't bring a husband, did she? Were there no rules? No laws? Did the Children's Aid department let children keep their babies if they didn't look after them? What if they didn't know how to feed them, or change their diapers, or do whatever it was you did when they were teething? It was none of his business, he realized, but they were going to be his neighbours, and neighbours were his business. Invisible deaf-mutes would have been his prime choice. Neighbours lived so uncomfortably close, when you thought about it. Just a wall between you and them, a thin slab of concrete, nothing more. Sven had never thought about that until now, he'd never had to. Basically, he figured, you could be standing only a foot from them and not even know it, with just the wall in between. That was a bit too intimate. The thought made him flutter about in his cage like a terrified chicken. He tried not to squawk.

After a while he calmed down and debated having another cup of coffee, and maybe an almond cake after all. You couldn't starve yourself just because you had a new neighbour, could you?

He went back to the kitchen, but as he stepped onto the linoleum there was a furious banging on the Perssons' door. The hammering of fists was followed by a booming voice.

"Open the fucking door! Hey! Lillan! Where the fuck are you?"

Sven's heart stopped dead.

Inside the Perssons' apartment the baby started to cry again. Sven put down his cup with a shaky hand and sneaked out to his front hall, the ultimate snoop, Mr. Private Detective, and glued an eager ear to his door. He heard the Perssons' door open and then the girl's voice excusing herself, more angry than apologetic.

"I was feeding Micke. You could wait ten seconds before you freak out, couldn't you?"

"Easy for you to say, these goddamn boxes weigh a ton. Move over!"

"Where are my plants?"

"Fuck your plants, I'll get them later. Move over, I said!"

The girl was from out of town, she spoke some up-country dialect, but the male out there, whoever he was, was definitely Malmö born and bred. He sounded thoroughly unpleasant.

This was not good.

A door slammed and silence descended. Sven's heart slowly started beating again as he unglued his ear from the door and pattered back to his chair, where he burrowed restlessly while trying to figure out what the hell was going on. Was she married after all, that slip of a thing? Was she living with this guy? Or was he just helping her move? Didn't sound like it, though; it sounded as if he was very much the boss around there. Couldn't be her brother, they spoke different dialects. No, they were both going to live there, he could feel it in his bones. He was going to be stuck with those characters. All alone with them, up here on the top floor. Anything could happen. He was no longer safe.

Listless, he returned to the kitchen and the coffee-pot. There he stood, slowly removing the thermos top from the pot. Pouring a cup, he felt a sudden worry as he thought about the baby in there. Why, he didn't know — maybe because the baby had a name now. Micke. Well, never mind that. He wanted peace and quiet, that was all, and it damn well wasn't too much to ask.

He'd lost his appetite again and didn't bother with the cakes. Wasted money. He hated to waste money. It was all their fault, those delinquents. Was it any wonder he felt resentful? He had some trouble breathing, too; his lungs felt abnormally heavy. He'd planned a nice quiet evening and now it was ruined. Time for a glass of Armagnac. He returned to his chair and put the bottle and a glass on the table. Got up again, irritated, and got his lighter and cigarettes. Sat down again, poured himself a glass a bit too hastily, and spilled Armagnac on the table. Got up again to fetch the dishrag. Wiped the table and went and threw the rag in the sink. Sat down and took a sip, careful not to spill anything, knowing that if he had to get up again he'd go stark raving mad.

He closed his eyes and just sat there, letting the flavour of the Armagnac spread its consoling warmth. It was like being embraced from the inside. Sat there and sat there, and sighed the odd sigh as he waited for another sound. Time stood nonchalantly still. He poured another glass and started to relax, finally. Was lighting another cigarette when an earsplitting blow on his door echoed through the hall and rolled into the room.

Red Alert!

The noise was so startling in the silence of his apartment that he almost swallowed his cigarette. Nobody ever came knocking on Sven's door. It was not something he encouraged. Fear pricked his skin and he started to sweat. It was them, he just knew it. He didn't move and there was another threatening drum solo. My, they were confident. Getting up, he slowly made his way through the hall. He felt himself moving like an old man unsure how to shift his feet. Was he afraid? The hell he was afraid! Not he, said he, and he opened the door with a shaking hand while trying to look both mean and busy.

"Hi there! You got a lightbulb we could borrow? We just moved in next door. I'm Janne Persson. We'll get you another one tomorrow after we go shopping, okay? Can't sit around in the dark, can we?"

Sven stared at the young man. He had hair down to his shoulders and a wide, smiling mouth. The young whipper-snapper stood there, wearing dirty jeans and a jauntily striped T-shirt, demanding a lightbulb as if he owned the place. Mr. Cocky himself, his blue eyes steady with confidence.

"Just a minute. I'll check," mumbled Sven, and forgot to look tough. He didn't know how anyway. Back in the kitchen he remembered that he had left the door open, he'd been too disconcerted to think clearly. What if the guy came sneaking in after him, hit him over the head with a crowbar, and robbed him? Or even...Sven grabbed a box of lightbulbs from the cupboard by the kitchen door and shot back into the hall. The insolent lout was standing there looking bored, whistling quietly to himself.

"Here," muttered Sven, and threw the package at him. "Keep them. I've got lots." He wasn't being generous, he just didn't want this swaggering swine to come knocking again.

"That's great! Thanks a lot, Andersson, you're a real buddy!"

The insufferable punk waved the package at Sven and disappeared. Sven stood silently in the hall for a moment and stared at his feet. Discovered a small hole in his left sock. Buddy indeed! Unwashed good-for-nothing hooligan! Demanding lightbulbs as if Sven were a goddamn convenience store! How very nice for them! He dearly hoped this was not going to become a habit. If it did, he simply wasn't going to open the door. They could knock until their knuckles bled.

He sank into his chair once again, chain-smoking and chain-drinking. There was something about the young lout that made him feel uneasy, but he didn't know what it was. Not wanting to dwell on it, he decided to go to bed; he'd had enough of being awake. First he went to the kitchen and made sandwiches for next day's lunch, seeking reassurance in the nightly routine. There were thuds of distant hammering. Perhaps they were hanging pictures. A bit late for that kind of thing, wasn't it? It was eleven o'clock, a time when responsible people went to bed so they could get up and go to work in the morning.

He put an almond cake in his lunch bag. You shouldn't waste good food. Pulled out the sofa-bed and got in, but had trouble falling asleep as he imagined he heard a baby crying far away. A full moon peeked over the rooftop across the courtyard. The sky was free of clouds and the moon shone white and cold. On the coffee table he saw the silhouette of a glass and a coffee-cup that he'd forgotten to wash and put away. He stared at them with dismay. Not cleaning up was bad indeed. Shaking his head, he got up, carried the things to the kitchen, and washed them, first the glass and then the cup. Dried them carefully and tucked them away in their cupboard.

The night was still without a sound when he returned to bed. The pale face of the moon looked in on him. Its chilly light offered no consolation. His usually comfortable self-pity felt like a lumpy mattress as he tossed and turned, ears alert as a clock struck midnight. No matter how hard he concentrated, not a sound could be heard, but still he couldn't relax. Eventually he fell asleep. At least he thought he did.

By four-thirty he was wide awake again, staring into the darkness. The moon had disappeared. The upheaval of his tranquillity was doing odd things to his mind; it spilled oil on the hinges of some door rusted shut long ago. Lying awake in the very early hours of the morning, listening to some perky starlings on the rooftops, made him restless and uncomfortable, as if he weren't quite alone. He had to look inside that door to see what was there.

Perversely he peeked through the crack in the door, as if afraid of disturbing the musty atmosphere in that forbidden cave. Deep in a corner of the stale darkness lay his memories, in a pile undisturbed for decades. He peered into the shadows and saw himself as a young child, pale and skinny. Christ Almighty, what a scrawny kid he'd been. If that was really him. Was it? Yes, it was. Well, if he was skinny it wasn't his fault; mealtimes were highly irregular, but he'd managed somehow. Children always do. He was wearing glasses, this kid, cheap wire-frame glasses. Pa constantly reminded him how dumb he looked in his glasses, making sure he would never forget. Pointing out that he sure as fuck didn't look like no son of his.

No, he didn't look like his parents. Ma said he had her father's nose, but that was it for genetic lineage. Ma herself was tall and blonde and, in Pa's expert opinion, curved in all the places where a woman ought to be nicely padded. Great big tits and a big round ass. A bright red mouth hid teeth that were a bit crooked, and yellow from years of chain-smoking. She was a woman with more confidence than style. Not an intellectual giant, but she had a cheerful disposition. She wasn't mean and cruel, and she didn't hate her son; she seldom yelled at him and never hit him. She hardly noticed him. Once in a blue moon (and how often is the moon blue?) she'd look up and see him there in the room, and she'd stare at him as if she knew she'd seen him somewhere before but couldn't quite place him. Then it would dawn on her: oh yes, right, I know him, it's my boy! Intrigued by the fact that she was a mother, she'd start dripping maternal love and sometimes even insist he have a sip of her drink. That, in her opinion, was the ultimate sacrifice that once and for all proved her love; Ma was extremely fond of sweet things and didn't like to share with anybody.

She was thoughtless and more than mildly stupid, but she had a large dose of self-assurance and a general joie de vivre. Things like that went a long way. She claimed that she had a good heart and that was why she liked to jiggle her tits and wiggle her ass — it was her way of sharing with the world. It happened sometimes that she got a little too generous, a little too munificent, when there was no particular need for it. But then, who is to judge what is need and what isn't?

She was excessively charitable one night in late January 1933, when she and Rune, happy and newly married, attended a highly convivial shindig out in the eastern part of the city, in an area known for its wild goings on. It was a celebration in honour of Rune's cousin, Harry the Harelip, being released from prison after serving two years for fraud. It was a time to rejoice. Like everybody else attending, she and Rune got violently drunk on Harry's home brew. To say that this generously provided beverage was strong would be an understatement. It had been made in haste for the festivities, but it did the trick, and if it was a bit heavy on the cumin it was nicely chilled. They partied into oblivion that night, or rather, they presumed afterwards that they had. Not too many of those present could remember much, which was a sure sign of success. Two people woke up with black eyes; one tall skinny guy broke a leg, while his friend arrived home with no clothes under his coat. There were puddles of vomit in several places on the stairs and in the yard, and one of those puddles contained a pair of false teeth. Three women got pregnant, one of them Edith.

While everybody said what a great party it must have been, nobody could remember much about it. Among the many nocturnal events that slipped Edith's mind was the time late that night when she staggered downstairs to the outhouses for a desperate pee. Once down the stairs she couldn't make it across the vast yard, but solved the emergency by lifting her skirts, stepping out of her panties, and squatting in the icy moonlight, much too drunk to feel the cold. It was in this alluring position, trying not to pee on her shoes, that she was found by a man from the building opposite, her round rosy rump shining like a beacon in the night. The man, a young Danish visitor to Malmö who was out taking a leak himself, was quite excited by this unexpected treat and almost pissed himself in the face as his eager penis shot up like a periscope scanning the horizon. Land ahoy! he shouted happily. Like a good sailor he steered for that lovely round land straight ahead, wrapping his coat around him to shield his periscope from the chilly night. Considering himself a gentleman, he first politely introduced himself. "Hello there, I'm Mogens from Copenhagen." Edith stood up and said how do you do and let her skirt fall back over her knees, and he asked if she'd like to accompany him on a stroll to the outhouses and help keep him warm. That sounded reasonable to Edith. She was starting to feel the cold, and he was such a nice friendly young man. He had a lovely smile and he really liked her, she could tell, even if he talked funny. So off they went, abandoning her panties in a wrinkled heap on the icy cobblestones. Behind the row of outhouses, protected from the wind, they got to know each other intimately, if briefly, standing up, wrapped cosily in his thick warm coat. The gregarious Dane was full of boisterous little sperm cells, and once in Edith they all hurtled towards their predestined goal. One particularly energetic little guy made it, and Sven was on his way.

While the sperm had their race, Edith and Mogens adjusted their clothing and parted company, waving cheerfully, nice to meet you, you too, and returned to their respective parties. It was an episode that had slipped her mind completely the next day when she tried to get out of bed and fell down, still drunk. No wonder Sven didn't resemble Pa. It was something nobody would ever know. Pa, the real man's man, would never dream that Sven was not his son, never suspect for a split second that a young Danish metal-worker named Mogens Hansen had impregnated his bare-assed wife behind an outhouse on a chilly moonlit night. Not only that, two days earlier this same Dane had also impregnated a young woman named Ilse back in Copenhagen. He was a fertile man, Mogens. Sven never suspected that his background might not be what it seemed. They would all grow old and die and never know — including Sven's half-brother, Hans, who grew up to become a bartender in a bar in Nyhavn. He looked an awful lot like Sven, but the two would never meet, never see a face so like their own and wonder.

Mogens would certainly never know. He joined the Danish underground in 1940 and was killed by the Germans in December 1943, aged thirty-one. His older brother Henning died in a concentration camp, being one of 1,700 or so policemen rounded up by the Germans in September 1944 during a false air-raid alarm. Mogens was killed shortly after Pa became heavily involved with some Danish traitors on the Swedish side.

Sven examined his bargain-basement excuse for nostalgia and turned over restlessly in bed. He saw Pa. Good old Pa. Rune Andersson, trained bricklayer, experienced dreamer, Nazi sympathizer, and massive ego. They had taken him away in 1944 and put him in some camp for treacherous scum. It wasn't the kind of thing you forgot. Pa was a big sturdy man, the Nazi bootlicker; oxlike in body and mind, with small shifty eyes that could exude human warmth when convenient. And he did have an unreliable sort of charm, and a loud jovial personality. Apparently so did Goebbels. Pa was a man who dreamed trivial dreams of success and riches. He did what he could to acquire those riches by performing a string of unimaginative misdemeanours for which he was never caught, as well as stealing ration cards. When they eventually did nab him, it was for something rather more unforgivable. You could blame it on the war, thought Sven, but it would be a feeble excuse.

In Denmark the foreign minister, Scavenius, who was friendly with the Germans, took over from Prime Minister Buhl in November 1942, becoming both prime minister and foreign minister. Maybe because of that, the Germans allowed elections to take place on March 23, 1943, after pumping a lot of money into Frits Clausen's Nazi party. Clausen's party received less than 3 per cent of the vote and that was the end of that fat fool. Danish Nazis instead entered into German service, as *stikkers* — provocateurs, or *värnemager*, as they were called. On Sunday, August 29, 1943, things changed for the worse with the declaration of a state of emergency. Before the day was over, hundreds lay dead in the street in a country supposedly not at war. The Germans took power and from then on the Danish people considered themselves at war. The following October the persecution of the Danish Jews started, and overnight it became serious business. The illegal trips to Sweden started as a full-scale operation at the same time, transporting not only Jews but members of the underground on the Gestapo's list.

In October 1943, the Swedish government sent a message to Berlin that Sweden was willing to receive all Danish Jews. Berlin did not deign to answer. Just as well, or Pa would have been out of a job. While refugees from Denmark were questioned by Swedish authorities to weed out any traitors, a few made it through. One of them became Pa's "boss", and that was how Pa became a Swedish saboteur working for a Danish *stikker*. With the help of people such as these, the Germans were sometimes able to have their patrol boats in the right place at the right time to intercept transports of people, news, or weapons. It was questionable how much harm was done, as *stikkers* were both inefficient and stupid, but harm was done and lives were lost. For example, in December of that year sixty Danes were sent to a concentration camp in Germany. A handful of those sixty — Sven's biological father, Mogens, among them — were sent because information about their activities had reached the Germans via certain infiltrators in Sweden.

That was Pa for you. In the end he didn't have many friends, other than criminals and lowlifes, as he had great trouble tolerating anybody who was not impressed by his banalities. Kjell was one of the exceptions. He had no problem letting Pa expand upon his shallow philosophies to get access to his booze and his food. It seemed an agreeable exchange. Pa sort of approved of Kjell. He approved less of Sven. Sven just wasn't his type of kid.

"Look at the little fucker. He's gonna go far, you can tell, glasses and all, eh, Kjell? Yeah, he's gonna go far, all right. Right over the edge, 'cause he can't see where he's going!"

And they'd laugh themselves silly. They wouldn't be laughing at Sven as much as enjoying their own keen sense of humour and brilliant insight into the human condition.

These comedy routines would often bring forth a drawn out bleat from Asta if she was conscious. Whether her bleat was a sign of appreciation of their priceless wit, or just a detached independent bleat, was hard to say. Her eyes remained glazed, her body spineless and immobile, a small lank creature with yellowing teeth glimmering inside that big wet suction cup that was her mouth.

Sven, the child, was always scared to death of her, long before he tried to kill her, watching her with fascination as she slumped in her chair, babbling incomprehensibly in short spurts in between long silences. Once in a while a word, or a phrase, uttered by somebody next to her would remind her of some long-forgotten tune and she'd suddenly come to life and look as if she was about to have an epileptic fit. She'd start singing and waving her arms. Then, as suddenly as she had started, she'd stop, slump back into her chair and be gone, the puppeteer having a break.

One night, a dark winter night without a trace of moon or stars, she had suddenly acknowledged Sven's existence for the first time. It was an eerie moment. He was only five years old, very shy and utterly perplexed. What brought it on was Ma, who in a fit of bad conscience turned maternal and lovingly ruffled his hair. For no particular reason, the way she sometimes did. Maybe she remembered that she had forgotten to give him anything to eat that day. Unfortunately Asta beheld this scene of Mother and Child and was seized by the drunk's immense sense of gravity.

"Sten!" she sputtered. "Sten! Lissen! What I'm gonna tell you now, you must never forget! Never! Sten! What I'm gonna tell you is this...lissen! You only have one mother in this here life, Sten, only one...are you lissening?"

She reached across the table to get his full attention, and he quickly backed away. He was so terrified he dared not breathe, dared not tell her his name was Sven.

"Now you lissen to me, Sten. You will never ever have another mother...so you must love the one you got...love her, you hear me, is what you gotta do. I know what I'm talking about. You only get one mother...then you're on your own. Goddamn it, then you gotta look after yourself.... And you'll never be able to do that, 'cause you're too little and you don't see too good. So...remember what I said. Can you remember that? Sten?"

Sven nodded hysterically. He was rigid with fear. But Asta wasn't quite finished.

"Well then...Sten. You give your mother a big hug and show her you love her. Go on...now!"

Bubbles of saliva spouted from the corners of her mouth as she stared at him, wild-eyed and fanatical. Perhaps she was having a religious experience. Maybe she mistook Ma for the Virgin Mary. Whatever had seized her, Sven hastily attempted to comply. Awkwardly he tried to put his small arm around his mother's round shoulders, but the gesture was so unfamiliar to him that he didn't know how to go about it. He couldn't quite reach. It was a show of affection he would never have dreamed of trying unless ordered to. Clumsily he patted his mother's neck, doing the best he could. Ma positively glowed at this tribute, swelling with motherly pride. Asta's solemn outburst had just about brought tears to Ma's eyes. Being a sentimental fool, she ruffled her son's hair once more while they all basked in the warmth of their communion. Kjell gave the kid a coin for candy and then they told him to go away. They were going to play cards and had to concentrate.

Here Sven closed the door of the cave where all his dusty memories were thrown. The little boy would stand there for ever, because that part of Sven's mind was in limbo. There was no past or present in there, and the adults would never sober up.

Yet Sven didn't see this child as himself. Was it a different reincarnation or was it somebody else whose life he just happened to know all about? How could a grown man look at a small child and say, hey, that's me? Sven could not, he would not. He said to himself that he knew who he was.

# LILLAN AND JANNE

Lillan's first encounter with Janne, in late September 1978, was a bit of a non-event if anything. It was not a meeting of minds, nor was it love at first sight. The story-line would read more like "Stoned hothead meets sober virgin with whom he has nothing whatsoever in common." Maybe the encounter was inevitable due to some astrological phenomenon, the moon in the seventh house and Jupiter aligned with Mars or Venus, that kind of thing. It would explain a lot. Whatever it was, for Lillan it was unexpected. Then again, she had no expectations that evening. She was standing in a long hallway in a spacious apartment in an old building downtown. There was a party going full tilt, because it was Saturday night and that was when cool people did cool stuff, according to Lena, her new friend from work. Lillan felt stupid and alone, not knowing a soul there except for Lena, who had taken off and left her behind. Lillan took refuge in a dark corner she found by the coatstand, where she hovered like a shy marsupial waiting for the moon to rise. It was there that Janne stumbled into her. He was happily pissed on Villa Franca, the cheapest, most plentiful rotgut ever produced. He had guzzled this while getting stoned on some expensive black Nepalese that an American deserter called Jumbo had dealt him. Very nice stuff indeed. A strong high, but a sweet mellow one. Janne was one happy man as he floated through the open front door, missed a step, and almost crashed into the coatstand. That was when he discovered that one of the shadows in the corner had a face. It only reached to his shoulder, and it had round dark eyes sort of like a squirrel's.

"Hey lookit! It's a little runt!" He greeted her loudly, his wide mouth breaking into a grin as her pale face stared up at him. "How the fuck are you, eh?" Janne wasn't used to anybody looking up to him like that, so serious and attentive. He decided he liked it.

"I'm fine, thank you," answered Lillan, polite and sober. Lillan

63

was always sober. Alcohol made her sick, which was why she was clutching a small bottle of apple juice. She'd brought it along, not knowing what the unwritten rules of partying might be. She'd never been to a party in the city.

"What the hell are you drinking there, runt?" he demanded to know as he stared at her, intrigued, amused, and patronizing. His shoulder-length, not very clean brown hair hung like curtains around his face.

"Apple juice," replied Lillan and obediently showed him the bottle. She felt both flattered and embarrassed by the attention. The guy was friendly in an almost threatening way. She didn't know how to handle that kind of ambiguous attention, not sure if he was pestering her or flirting with her. She took a sip of juice, not knowing what else to say or do.

"Rat piss!" declared her admirer. His face went blank for a second or two, then he remembered where he was and laughed. "You're a cute kid." He patted her on the head and plunged head first into the sea of people in the noisy room. To Lillan it sparkled like the hall of the mountain king in there.

Lillan shyly padded after him, thinking that if people thought she was with this guy they would assume she was one of them. But nobody did. Nobody noticed her at all. Everybody was very busy without doing anything in particular. Just look interesting, Lena had said, but Lillan didn't know how. She thought about leaving, then decided that was too defeatist. Give it another half-hour, she advised herself, and slid invisibly through the crowd to one of the windows. It had a deep windowsill where she immediately parked herself and curled up into a protective ball. She liked curling up in windows and felt at home on windowsills. In windows with lace curtains and begonias in bloom. Like the windows in Grandma's house. Lillan was an old-fashioned girl. In this window, though, there were no curtains and no flowers. There was nothing but some kind of abstract statue that looked like a beheaded pregnant woman with a bicycle-pump sticking out of her navel. Lillan lifted it up and looked at it. It was heavy and had a silver hallmark underneath. Quickly she put it down and turned her nose to the window.

The street below was very quiet. The newly restored façades were lined with rows of dainty wrought-iron balconies much too small for anybody to use. Still, they looked very continental and refined, very nineteenth century. The buildings were probably full of fancy apartments like the one she was in. Expensive ones. She'd like to live on a street like this, she decided. In a sunny apartment in the middle of the city, so she could walk everywhere. The only feature she didn't like was the long dark hallway between the lavish living-room and the kitchen. It made the kitchen too cut off, not part of the home. It wasn't cosy at all, and Lillan was big on cosy. But that was the way it was meant to be, of course, because in the old days when people had servants they didn't want the cook and the maid mixing with finer folk. There was probably a separate kitchen entrance too. Mum would have loved that, she thought. Not Lillan, though; she liked sitting in the kitchen among glass jars of jams and preserves, a cake in the oven and a pot of soup on the stove. Like at Grandma's. She loved to bake and cook, she even liked doing dishes and cleaning house. She was a pottering sort of person with strong domestic urges just waiting to burst forth. Grandma's kitchen had been perfect, warm and friendly, a place where she had belonged. It had had windows where you could sit and watch the pear tree outside. Too homey for words, but that was how she liked it. Someday she was going to live like that again. Someday she was going to belong again.

Lillan was not a very demanding person, but she had faith.

It was getting dark outside. The streetlamps were lit and she could see lights in the windows across the street, golden rectangles behind each and every balcony. There was a wind, and a whirl of autumn leaves chased each other down the sidewalk to the end of the street, where a large church was lit up like an earthly part of heaven. A taxi came around the corner and stopped in front of a doorway opposite. An old lady with a cane immediately hobbled out and starting yelling at the driver. She was wearing a plastic rain-bonnet over her fancy hat though it wasn't raining. It wasn't even supposed to rain. If it did, Lillan would get soaked when she biked back to her rented room over by the park. Lena had made a big deal about her biking, had sighed and shaken her head and told her that, Jesus Christ, nobody bikes to a party! What if you meet some guy? she'd said, what if, what if, what if? That was the problem with Lena: her beliefs led her through a narrow confusing labyrinth of what-ifs and she always got lost. Lillan was too practical to listen. If she wanted cheap, fast transportation to get home in the dark, that was her business.

The vast room was choked with people. Most of them looked drunk or stoned or both. There was a funny smell and every surface was covered with empty beer cans and wine bottles. The music was pounding. The guy who was having the party, Peter or Pontus or whatever his name was, was sending around a strange-looking pipe decorated with ornate silver fittings. He had wide brown eyes with the eyelids half closed, as if they were too heavy to raise. She knew he was the host because somebody had just slapped him on the shoulder and shouted, "Great party, buddy!" But he seemed quite unaware of the fact that he was hosting the festivities. He just sat there on a white leather couch, obviously at peace with the world, puffing the pipe when it came his way. His long legs, clad in tight emerald-green velvet pants, were in the lotus position. If he had any parents, they were not around. Maybe he was independently wealthy and lived here by himself.

Lillan didn't know the host; it was Lena who claimed to know him vaguely, through some mutual acquaintance. But Lena had disappeared almost as soon as she got there, giggling her way down the stairs with an African guy from Senegal who talked in a seductive singsong. Hanging onto his arm, she had shouted up to Lillan, "Stay and have fun, kid, by all means, life is short, don't waste it!" She had lectured Lillan earlier about how she needed to get to know some interesting people, being new in town and all, and how if there were any interesting people their age in Malmö they'd be at this party for sure, because this was where it was at. "Stay on and check out the guys!" Lena had yelled, and then she had been gone. Lillan did as she'd been told, because that was the way she'd been brought up. Just obey, just do as you're told, Mum had always said, and life will be so much simpler. Mum gave orders and everybody obeyed; life was simple and Mum was happy. Until one day when Daddy disobeyed and ran away with another woman. A French woman at that. An avenging Mum had turned to God and life had stopped being simple, because God did not obey Mum either and Dad and his new woman didn't come to the grisly end they deserved. They moved to Paris instead. As soon as Lillan was old enough, she too fled the overpowering voodoo holier-than-thou version of Christianity that her mum clutched like a Zimmerframe. That was how she had ended up in Malmö in the spring of 1978.

Having nothing better to do, she sat there in the window feeling as if she were outside looking in, and passed the time studying her surroundings. It was like going to the theatre and sitting in one of the most expensive seats.

Peter, or was it Pontus, had moved and was facing her way, his elbows resting on the glass coffee table. He didn't notice Lillan perched in the window; he was busy feasting his eyes with undiluted concentration on a girl sitting on the other side of the table. The girl had long black hair that looked dyed and she was wearing an oversized pink and black striped cardigan with huge black buttons. It was like watching two actors in a play without words. All the others were extras, and Lillan was the sole spectator trying to interpret the low-key drama before her. She had to pay close attention in order not to miss anything. She discovered hints of gestures so full of studied finesse she was afraid to miss a single nuance. If she could catch on she might learn something. Peter didn't stare at the girl; his gaze under those droopy lids was light and caressing, but securely anchored on her face. The girl acted as if he was thin air, but if he as much as turned his head to reply to somebody her eyelids would flutter almost imperceptibly and she would reach for her glass of wine with supreme boredom, three of her fingers hanging around the stem of the glass like the wilting petals of some pale flower. It was remarkable that she didn't drop the glass. After a minute or so she'd shake her long hair out of her face and her earrings would tinkle like tiny bells. Lillan wished she knew how to play this fascinating game. The ritual obviously had intricate rules, but perhaps it was a requirement for social interaction with the opposite sex on the more sophisticated level. So different from Lena's "Wanna fuck me now or later?" approach to men. Lillan knew she had a lot to learn, but that didn't bother her a great deal. She thought it might be interesting to be in on what was what. To be one of the cool people.

In fact she had a certain self-confidence that she was largely unaware of. Daddy had said once that she took after his mother, Grandma, because she was just as tiny and kind-hearted and happy. Lillan rested secure in that knowledge, because Grandma had been everything that was right and good in life.

As she sat there reminiscing about Daddy and Grandma, Peter and the girl disappeared into thin air. She searched the room for somebody else to observe. Nobody was doing anything interesting, apart from trying to look interesting, so she decided to study the interior decor instead. The furniture was tasteful and expensive but a bit too modern for her liking. The guy must have rich parents. She wished that she had rich parents who lived together and loved each other and spoiled her rotten. That kind of schmaltzy stuff. She would have liked to have two brothers, an older one with a sportscar and a younger one who was studying to become a concert pianist. Something like that — the details didn't matter. Somebody clever and famous, at any rate. They would be a happy family and have long lazy breakfasts together in a sunny room full of potted plants and read funny bits from the morning paper out loud to each other. Much nicer than a sour-faced mother and sister who most of the time didn't deign to speak to her for fear of catching her imperfections.

As this dream was impossible, she would have to get her own family. She would be the mother. Her oldest son would be named Mikael after Daddy, Micke for short. The in-between child, a daughter, would be called Emma after Grandma, and the youngest boy would be named Frederik because it was such a refined name, it had a regal ring to it. Her husband would be rich, he'd have to be, because she didn't have any money. He'd be the executive director of an international firm, or at least a doctor or something. A doctor would be good, it would be handy if the children got sick in the middle of the night.

She got excited thinking about this future and decided to bike home right away to write down the details.

Then he was there again, the guy with the big mouth, heading straight towards her as if she'd waved him over.

"Move your legs!" he commanded as a form of greeting. "Lemme sit down and rest for a minute."

Lillan complied wordlessly and there they sat side by side with their legs dangling, like children, Lillan and....

"What's your name?" she asked bravely.

They introduced themselves formally and politely, as if it was some kind of game. Maybe it was; Lillan wasn't sure.

"Janne."

"Lillan. Well, my real name is Kerstin."

"Where the hell are you from?" he wanted to know when he heard her dialect.

"Småland," said Lillan.

"No shit! That's why you talk funny!"

"I don't talk funny at all."

"Do too! Are they all that short up in Småland?"

Lillan didn't answer, but he didn't seem to mind. They sat there silently for a while and she went back to dreaming about her perfect future family and their huge gorgeous apartment and their life in continuous sunshine. She couldn't decide the colour of her oldest son's sportscar. A cream-coloured one would be classy but not very practical. Lillan was a practical person, something she'd inherited from her mother's side of the family.

"Hey runt! What are you dreaming about?" Janne's voice was demanding, as if it were her duty to inform him. "Tell me."

"About my family," she said, smiling slightly. It never occurred to her to lie. "I mean, the way I would like my family to be when I have one."

"Family!" sniggered Janne. "Who the fuck needs one?"

"I do," she confessed.

"You're crazy, runt." He shook his drunken head.

69

"Maybe," said the runt.

What a weird little broad! But she had dimples in her cheeks when she smiled.

"So, are you an orphan or what?" he wanted to know. "Seeing as how you want a family, I mean."

"Well, yes — I mean no. I'm not an orphan. But my daddy lives in France. He's married to a French woman, but my mum forbids me to have any contact with him so I don't know where he lives. I was only eleven when he left. Then I wasn't allowed to see my grandma either, because she had contact with my daddy, you see, and Mum was afraid she'd give me his address, which she claimed would be disastrous because Daddy was evil. Then Grandma died when I was thirteen and there was only my mum left. And my sister Gun, but she's like Mum. We don't get along. She's five years older than me and really conceited. I'm not good enough to be her sister. She's just too perfect."

Lillan blushed scarlet and became very quiet, embarrassed to have revealed so much about herself all at once. It had just come out. She didn't even know if he had listened to a word she'd said; he looked too out of it.

"Your mum sounds like a fucking bitch, if you don't mind my saying so. What's her problem?"

"Well, she was always difficult to get along with, then she became super-religious when Daddy left her and it got even worse."

"When you were eleven?"

"Yes, but like I said, she was always impossible. Everything and everybody had to be perfect. Her version of perfect, anyway. And the only thing she ever cared about was having a clean house. 'Creating pleasant surroundings,' she called it. If Daddy came home from his office and was tired and wanted to take a nap he had to lie on the floor because Mum couldn't stand the thought of him wrinkling the bedspread, because then it would look untidy in case somebody came to visit and that would be such a humiliation. She actually said that."

Janne's sullen face broke into laughter. He laughed so long and so loud that several people in the room shut up and turned to

70

stare at him in surprise. Maybe he didn't laugh very often. Or perhaps it was the sheer noise level he was able to produce.

"Fucking hell!" he bellowed. "My old lady says the old hag that adopted my dad was like that. She says we went there for a visit when I was four and I completely grossed the old bat out. Ate all her fucking cakes. They musta been related. Their name was Sandberg. My old lady changed our name back to Persson after that. People like that ought to be fucking shot and pissed on," he concluded firmly. "That's my humble opinion as a practical sort of person."

"I agree," said Lillan, which wasn't quite true, she just wanted to get along with him.

Maybe it was the influence of the stars in the autumn sky, who knows? Maybe it was due to a biochemical reaction. Whatever it was, Lillan and Janne became friends. When Lillan decided to bike back to her room, he asked to come with her so she'd be safe. Lillan didn't protest. It was well after midnight, and she hadn't stayed out that late since she'd come to Malmö. Together they left the window and headed for the hall, where they found Peter with his arms wrapped around a lot of black hair and a pink and black striped cardigan. The two looked as if they were seriously attempting to devour each other. It was an amazing sight. Lillan had never seen anybody kiss with such total concentration. It looked like a full-time job. She blushed and averted her eyes.

"Take it easy there, Patrik!" yelled Janne in the doorway. When he received no answer he gleefully added something so obscene that Lillan had to pretend not to hear.

"I thought his name was Peter" was all she said.

"Could be, who knows?" replied Janne cheerfully. "It's not like I know the guy. He's my buddy Hasse's buddy. Don't know what he sees in that broad."

"What's wrong with her?" Lillan was surprised. She thought the girl was very attractive and sophisticated with her long dangling earrings and green nails. Very worldly. But there was obviously an awful lot she didn't understand.

"Not my type. Her nose is too big" was Janne's judgement.

71

"And she's got too much shit all over her eyes. Makes her look like a fucking Indian."

With such puritan views he must have appreciated Lillan's scrubbed face, her short dark hair and lack of adornments. When they got to her rented room he wanted to come up with her. She thought about it and agreed, tired of being alone, tired of the meaningless state of virginity. Now she'd really have something to tell Lena. Upstairs she let him undress her while she stood quietly outside herself and observed them both with an almost clinical interest. She wondered what it would be like. It turned out to be quite nice, she thought she could grow to like it. Although still stoned and drunk, and eternally irritable, Janne was surprisingly tender with her. Perhaps it was because she was so fragile. Naked, she looked as though she might break in the middle if squeezed too hard. And the fact that she was a virgin really blew his mind. He had to shake his head real hard. Talk about weird shit happening!

The following day was a Sunday and they went to a movie. Janne treated. Then he insisted they go down to Kockska Krogen and have a few beers. That is, Janne had a few beers; Lillan drank juice. He was greatly intrigued. He couldn't get over the fact that here was this little woman who was actually twenty-one years old, who didn't drink anything alcoholic. That was a novel experience as well. All the other chicks he knew drank like fish.

Lillan was impressed too. She'd never been to an expensive place like Kockska Krogen before.

Three months later, Lillan became pregnant. It had never occurred to her to protect herself; it was as if she didn't know the connection between sexual intercourse and pregnancy. She wasn't used to not being a virgin. She told Janne at once. He was, after all, her only friend. He'd know what to do.

"I'm going to have a baby," she said in that straightforward manner of hers, staring up at him with her round earnest eyes.

"No shit!"

"No. I mean yes. I'm pregnant. I thought I'd tell you. I wasn't sure what you'd think."

"No big deal," Janne said, and threw a lavish arm around her shoulders. "No big deal, runt, not to worry. You want to have a baby, have a baby. We're of legal age, we can handle it." He liked Lillan an awful lot. She was too tiny and trusting to be threatening. So inoffensive and useful. She could cook. Real food, too. And God knew she was inexpensive to keep: she didn't drink, didn't smoke, didn't do dope. Nothing. She liked to sit at home and knit and shit like that! Unbelievable or what? You couldn't very well complain about a girl like that. A funny little chick, but she was his and she made him feel good. She made him feel all protective, which he thought was kind of neat, it made him feel all heroic inside.

He had even introduced her to the old lady, which was a big event. It was the first time he had ever introduced a girl to his mother, and the old lady went fucking loopy with delight. Adored her right on the spot, gushed on and on that Lillan was "the right kind of girl". Happier than a pig in shit, the old lady, bless her heart. Could be she was so stunned when he suddenly came visiting with a "fiancée" that she was prepared to like anything female on two legs. But, and there was absolutely no doubt about it, Mum and Lillan became as close as mother and daughter. It was almost as if he were some outsider from off the street. Weird shit. But he didn't mind. Mum had even stopped calling him an idle blockhead and a useless goddamn good-for-nothing, which was good. Janne liked his mum a great deal, but he didn't appreciate criticism, nor did he feel comfortable hanging out with old ladies, so he didn't see her that often. And Lillan never complained when he went out on the town with his buddies for a bit of fun. Life was sweet. So if Lillan wanted to be pregnant and have a kid and play house, that was okay with him. He grandly told her so. Told her that she'd probably be a nice little mummy, being so domestic and cute and all. Everything was going to be just spiffy, he promised.

Yes, Janne had never had it so good.

Lillan thought she had never had it so good either. Happy and pregnant, she waddled about, thinking her fantasy was already becoming reality. She'd never dreamed that it could be so easy for make-believe to come true.

When Lillan was four months pregnant, Janne found an old apartment through his friend Pelle, who had a cousin with contacts. A week later they moved in together and became an official couple, as in "Janne and his girlfriend are having a baby." It wasn't the apartment of Lillan's dreams, just one room and a kitchen. There was no hot water and no central heating, but there was a tiled stove in the room. They had to share the toilet out on the landing with the Yugoslav immigrant worker in the apartment opposite. On the other hand, it was very cheap, as the building was slated for demolition in the near future. It was okay for now, said Lillan, it was a first step. They were hoping to find a proper modern apartment by the time the baby was born. It was all part of her plan, and so far things were going smoothly.

She got exquisite pleasure out of decorating their first nest. She made curtains by hand from bits of synthetic lace she found on sale. Soon potted plants were competing for space on the windowsills — mainly red begonias that she bought at the farmers' market down at Möllevångstorget. She even made a bedspread for the bed that also served as a couch, so intent was she on domestic bliss. Janne would say, "Can I lie on the bedspread or should I lie on the floor?" and they'd laugh themselves silly.

They didn't have much money because Lillan had already quit her job at the tobacco company. Working in a factory wasn't part of her dream, it was only what you did while you waited for it to come true. Now she needed time to be with her unborn baby, to prepare for this miraculous event. Things would work out, she knew that. How could they not?

Janne didn't mind her not working. He was in the process of "getting an engineering degree". He never bothered to clarify the details of this academic endeavour, but he did have a student loan, so Lillan assumed it was okay. Not that he was ever caught studying. Most of the time he was busy with his sideline, his "little firm", as he lovingly called it. The firm sometimes did brisk business. Janne and his pals had developed a smooth operation stealing records and tape cassettes from local music stores and selling the goods at an irresistible price on the street. It was an irregular income, but often quite a generous one, not to mention tax free. There were regular customers with special requests. Most of the profit was converted into drinks and drugs and other tools of pleasure. Janne had a great need for pleasure, and liked to have it without any budgetary inhibitions. Economic restraints always put a damper on his enthusiasm and he ended up in a bad mood.

While Janne went about mixing business with pleasure, Lillan preferred to stay at home and be snug in her playhouse. Her latest project was a baby blanket crocheted in endless rows of pale yellow squares in a simple pattern. It was just adorable and she couldn't wait to finish it. Creating even squares with a small crochet hook was time-consuming and required patient concentration, so it didn't bother her a bit that Janne was never home in the evening. It was peaceful when he was out.

She had a new friend, too. Her name was Amy and she lived in the apartment directly below. Amy would often come up and keep her company in exchange for endless cups of tea and sandwiches. She was skinny, Amy, much too skinny, and with freckles everywhere she looked a bit like a dried-up plant. She had a nervous, almost hysterical energy that made her chatter and chatter for hours on end. While she was both intelligent and well educated, she was entirely unambitious and utterly indifferent to the possibilities of success in what she referred to as "the rat race". She didn't work; it was quite beneath her, she explained. It didn't appeal to her. Not because she was lazy; she just didn't like the idea of servitude, it clashed with her philosophy of life. For that matter, the whole structure of Swedish society clashed with her philosophy. It was fit only for people willing to sell their souls for the privilege of living in a materially perfect society, reasoned Amy. And as she not only refused to part with her soul, but also was too imperfect to dwell in such a perfect society, there was no point in even trying; she would never fit in. She was the first person Lillan had ever met who was receiving social assistance. A bona fide welfare case, she was quite an exotic addition to Lillan's life. Amy had no hobbies and no interests, but was full of opinions about everything from the meaning of life to the effect of the global economy on the environment. Suspended in nothingness and vibrating with unused energy, she often became depressed or manic. She tried to curb her tendency to hysteria by sitting very still while staring at Lillan's increasingly globular stomach, as if she were trying to hypnotize the unborn child.

Lillan suspected that Amy was a bit demented and that this was due to malnutrition, so she always made her a plate of cheese sandwiches, often using up her last piece of cheese, and saying, "Oh, try to eat something, will you, Amy? Please, it will do you good." When Amy was on her own she usually didn't eat, because she couldn't be bothered with the tedium of shopping for food and carrying the damn stuff home just to be stuck in the kitchen cooking and then cleaning up. It wasn't worth the trouble. But at Lillan's she'd suck up sandwiches like a vacuum cleaner. She had nothing against food *per se.*

"What do you want a kid for?" she nagged Lillan whenever she saw her. It had become a form of greeting. "And with a cretin like Janne, for God's sake! I mean, really, are you desperate or stupid, or desperately stupid?"

Lillan's relationship with Janne was a phenomenon that Amy was unable and unwilling even to begin to comprehend. She had a couple of degrees in sociology and psychology, and presumably ought to have had some insight into the intricacies of the human psyche, but she simply failed to understand. She begged Lillan to explain the situation, insisting that she could not grasp this "human tragedy", this "tragicomical relationship", if "relationship" was in fact the correct term, in which Lillan insisted on masochistically immersing herself. If she were at least unhappy, if she felt abused or deprived — but oh no! She sat there, round and rosy-cheeked and content. It was enough to make you puke, seeing her crochet her icky yellow baby blanket as if she were going to win some fucking prize for being cute. Never bothering to be delicate or polite, Amy would slam the teacup on its saucer and once again demand an explanation for this absurdity.

But Lillan had nothing to explain. She had no excuses, and didn't feel the need for any. She was busy counting her double stitches, not wanting the pattern to get out of whack.

"I like babies," she stated when she was finished counting. "They're so adorable. I've always wanted one." She informed Amy that she was going to have three children if everything went according to plan, which so far it had. Two boys and a girl. Mikael, Emma, and Frederik with an e after the d. Amy offered her condolences and mused to herself that if the poor wretch of a kid took after its father, they might as well send it straight to the zoo. There was an orangutan at Copenhagen Zoo that needed an infant to nurse, since its own baby had died. Mind you, why insult an ape by offering it Janne's offspring? She didn't say it out loud, though. Not because of any sense of etiquette, but because she liked Lillan. She didn't understand her worth a shit, but she liked her all the same. Lillan was too naive to be dishonest, and Amy detested dishonesty, at least in other people.

"You're a real cow," she declared fondly. "The size of a hamster, but deep inside you're a real dumb cow."

"Could be," agreed Lillan cheerfully, "could well be. I'll have a lot of milk then, won't I?"

"Christ, Lillan! If you want something small and soft to hug, why don't you go down to Tempo and get yourself a stuffed toy?" Amy seriously thought she was being helpful, trying to avert disaster. "It's so much cheaper and stuffed toys don't scream all night. The world is evil enough as it is, what does it need another Janne for?"

"It's not going to be a Janne," Lillan corrected her primly. "I told you, his name is going to be Mikael, if it's a boy. Mikael after my daddy."

"Is that right?"

"Yes. That's right."

"I see."

"Well then, why don't you just shut up? Have some more tea."

They would argue comfortably until Amy sensed Janne's presence like a dark cloud descending on the neighbourhood and danced off downstairs. Amy and Janne couldn't stand the sight of each other. It was a spontaneous, easily combustible, mutual hatred, a contempt that grew more profound and irrational as the days and weeks went by. Amy let Janne know that he was a severely retarded delinquent with old piss flowing through his veins, failing to supply oxygen to that disgusting slippery gob bouncing around between his ears, and that he was a prime example of evolution taking a huge leap backwards and landing on its ass. She told him all that the first time they met, without pausing for breath, right after he enquired who the redheaded shit-stained skeleton was who was slurping his tea and wolfing down his food.

Janne didn't appreciate her response.

Not wanting to be any less childish, he declared that Amy, that scrawny scarecrow covered with freckles like dried pieces of shit, was in fact not the poor excuse for a female that she seemed to be. No indeed, he claimed, she was an undernourished prancing queer who'd lost his prick in an accident, got it chopped right off, whack. Then it was flattened by a truck, so when they sewed it back on, his crotch looked like a fucking duck-billed platypus, so they had to hack it off again. And now this guy had turned into this simpleton sleazebag slut who had gone nuts because no one wanted to fuck her, or him, or it.

"Oh, how pedestrian," sighed Amy, smiling sweetly, as his monologue ran out of steam. "But I'm a lesbian! Didn't you know? I'd rather fuck your girlfriend than you."

Well, you just didn't talk like that to Janne. He felt himself under no obligation to cater to some fucking lesbian who made herself perfectly at home in his apartment while he was out, drinking his tea and eating his food and never saying as much as a simple please and thank you, oh no, not she, she was just too fucking educated to have to lower herself. And while eating what little food they had in the cupboard she did her best to try and brainwash and disturb his woman who was pregnant and needed peace and quiet.

Amy was bad news. The trouble was, she liked being bad news.

But she wasn't a lesbian. She was having an on-and-off affair with an on-and-off impotent married journalist with a serious drinking problem. What she saw in this wretch was anybody's guess, but she claimed that he appealed to the same instinct that had made her study sociology at university. She maintained that the relationship helped ease her boredom and that his trivial problems and whining self-pity never failed to amuse her. Apart from this part-time lover she also had a patient, long-suffering husband and a three-year-old son back home in the province of Halland, whom she had left half a year previously when motherhood and responsibility had failed to fulfil her and instead had given her a nervous breakdown.

This was a secret she would never dare tell Lillan, who would have been appalled and would have stopped speaking to her at once. In Lillan's world one did not abandon one's children — especially not to pursue absolutely nothing.

Amy was irresponsible and negligent, she was spoiled and selfish, but she was not completely without shame. And she did plan to go home to her kind and understanding husband eventually, one day when she'd pulled herself together. Weekly letters from Arne, about how he and little Mats were doing, kept her guilt alive, but that was all. She did what she felt like because she got away with it.

In the meantime she sat at Lillan's, keeping her company, watching the baby blanket and Lillan's stomach grow. She never went there unless she heard Janne leave first, and she often left before eleven to be well out of the way in case he decided to come home early for a change. Even so, it sometimes happened that he turned up unexpectedly, and there would follow a lengthy exchange of vitriolic comments regarding the opponent's inexcusable physiognomy and lack of mental development. Lillan would turn a deaf ear to the proceedings, not only because it bothered her a great deal, but also because she found it repetitious and silly. She'd retreat into the unheated kitchen, wash the teacups in cold water, and feel her fingers grow numb. If the insults were still hurling about the room she'd go out and sit on the toilet, if it wasn't occupied by the Yugoslav.

The frenzied shouting matches reached flashpoint one night when Lillan was eight months pregnant. She'd grown as round as she was tall. Janne came home much earlier than usual one evening, in a particularly putrid mood. Somebody had sold him some extremely evil shit, claiming it was Lebanese gold — one of his all-time favourites — which it sure as fuck wasn't. Instead of a good strong high he got stuck with innumerable tiny yellow-eyed demons whispering vicious rumours inside his brain. He was in a highly explosive mood and good old Amy was ready with her blowtorch tongue. It wasn't that her insults were any worse than usual, but her timing was inordinately bad.

At the first sight of Amy devouring a sandwich on a plate, he turned white and told her to get the fuck out of his home or he'd throw her out head first. She should have sensed bad weather and left, because after all it was his home, he was right about that. But she didn't. She was in a bratty mood, and she'd got away with being bratty all her life. She languidly poured herself another cup of tea, Janne's tea in Janne's favourite cup, and launched into a lengthy description of the physical and intellectual similarities between Janne and his close and beloved relative, the common earthworm, and how he and his fellow worms shared one of the lowest rungs with him on the evolutionary ladder. She concluded that the only difference between him and his annelid cousin was that the earthworm had a slightly more dignified profile, indicating that its ancestors might have arisen from the more aristocratic ingredients in the primordial pond, whereas Janne's forebears had undoubtedly sprung from the putrid scum floating on the surface of said pond.

Smiling beatifically and feeling pleased with her childish litany, she skippety-hopped out of there singing a catchy tune in excellent French.

She shouldn't have done that.

Even without the bad trip, Janne would not have enjoyed being compared unfavourably to an earthworm. He wasn't fond of worms. Nor did he understand French. Only snobs spoke French. He therefore suspected the worst from her joyful trilling. It took him exactly five seconds to throw himself into his worst fit of rage since Lillan had known him. It was such pure, unleashed fury that Lillan half expected to see lightning. His frenzy broke two of their four teacups, his feet grinding the pieces into the kitchen linoleum while his tightly knuckled fists banged on walls and cupboards. Chairs were hurled about the room, and when it was all over Lillan's flowerpots lay smashed on the floor, mortally wounded begonias going to their final rest in piles of humid earth.

Lillan was horrified. Helpless, she stood and felt the child inside her turn over and over, as if trying to get away from the fury sweeping so close to its universe. She felt the tiny feet kicking at her bladder until she had to go to the toilet, hoping to high heaven that the Yugoslav hadn't locked himself in there again to stink the place up. Sitting locked in the communal toilet seemed to be his favourite pastime. Must be all that weird food he ate. Janne claimed it was because they didn't have toilets in whatever backwater he came from. Whatever the reason, that night he wasn't there; he was probably afraid to come out of his apartment with all the yelling and crashing going on.

She locked herself in the toilet and sat there for a long time in quiet solitude, until eventually the child under her heart grew calm again. She rocked it gently to sleep, swaying slowly on the toilet seat while she sang a lullaby: "Sleep, oh little willow tree, winter still is lingering." When she was a young girl and Grandma used to sing that to her, she would see the small tree sleeping in the snow, waiting for spring to come and wake it bringing roses and hyacinths. The tree would wake and stretch its thin branches and tiny green buds would appear by magic. A few tears ran down her cheeks as she sat humming to herself and her unborn child, her eyes closed to the world.

While she was gone, Janne slowly calmed down. He had come to a decision. As he lit a cigarette he planned a delightfully sweet revenge. The mere thought of it made him laugh out loud. Sometimes he amazed himself! It was a plan distinguished by its utter brilliancy, its unadulterated genius. Humiliation raised to an art form. It was enchanting, that was what it was — fucking enchanting, glowing with the beauty of evil. And it had come to him just like that! The question was, why the hell hadn't he thought of it before? That sleazebag lesbian had drunk her last cup of tea in his living-room. Oh yes!

When Lillan came waddling in again he was grinning a mile a minute, damn near splitting his face in half. He patted her bum lovingly. My little mummy, he cooed, and hugged her tenderly. Kissed her cheeks and noticed how they had filled out.

"So? Have you calmed down now?" asked Lillan, speaking in the slow manner he found so adorable. He laughed contentedly, once again a man at peace.

"Sure I've calmed down, runt. I just needed to get it out of my system, that's all. No problem, everything's cool, believe you me." He said nothing about his supreme scheme of revenge. Lillan was to be protected from everything unpleasant and nasty in life. She was his little woman and she was pregnant with his kid. He was her man and he loved her. Fuck him if he didn't! In his own dubious fashion he loved her, he suddenly realized. The realization made him feel all warm inside, adding the perfect icing to his cake. In an almost fatherly manner he carried Lillan off to bed and tucked her in. "You go to sleep," he whispered. "I'll clean up the mess. Tomorrow I'll get you some new plants, I promise. And I'll buy you a bunch of tulips too, and a vase to put them in. Purple ones." He bent down and kissed her, then did a little dance around the bed. Chuckling to himself, he set about cleaning the place up, quietly so as not to disturb Lillan. She needed her sleep.

Janne said nothing to Lillan about his ingenious plan. His face shone with innocence as he kissed her goodbye, saying he was late for a class at the technical college. It was true that he was late but, having business to attend to, he went straight downtown to look for Uffe, who'd been hanging out around Gustav Adolf Square the past few days, making everybody avoid the place. It wasn't that Janne wanted to be seen in public with Uffe, but Uffe was an integral part of his scheme. In fact, you could say it was Uffe's deplorable physical and mental attributes that made the whole plan so incredible in nastiness alone. Uffe was a creature without a single redeeming feature. At least Hitler was nice to his dog, but Uffe wasn't endowed with even that tiny streak of human likeness. He was a prematurely flabby young man looking far older than his twenty-six years, pale and pasty-faced from spending most of his life in various institutions for maladjusted individuals. He suffered from "severe adjustment difficulties" according to one file — that is, a complete inability to conform, even superficially, to any normal, legal mode of life in any stratum of society, including the very lowest. Uffe didn't care; he considered himself a poet, he said, which explained why he couldn't possibly live among normal people. Look at Bellman, he said. He claimed to have published a highly praised volume of poetry a few years back under a pseudonym he refused to reveal, and said that the impact of his literary genius still reverberated around the globe thanks to his little gem having been translated into English, German, French, Spanish, and Italian. He'd told this to so many people for so long that he now firmly believed it. Nobody else did. Nobody liked him, or cared to be seen on the same side of the street with him.

So it took some internal persuasion for Janne to close his eyes to all this and to kiss Uffe's butt, the mere thought of which almost made him puke. He nearly changed his mind when he got off the bus at the square and spotted Uffe's fat behind over by the kiosk. Uffe was trying to bum a smoke from a bus driver. Making his way to the kiosk, Janne did change his mind. He stopped and decided to pretend he had to make a call. He got as far as pulling open the door to a phone booth before Uffe saw him and came charging like a hippo in heat.

"Hey! Janne!"

Well, maybe it was meant to be. Janne plastered a friendly grin on his face and turned around.

"Uffe! Old buddy! Long time no see! How the fuck are you?"

"Okay, I guess," said Uffe and scratched a sore on his neck. "Got any smokes?"

"Better than that, I got some great Lebanese gold!"

"No kidding?"

"No kidding. Wanna go down to the park and get stoned?"

"You're on!" Uffe would rather kill than turn down free dope, as Janne was well aware.

"You go ahead," said Janne. "I gotta make a couple of phone calls first. Meet you down by the canal by that little bridge. Know the one I mean?"

Uffe was already on his way. Janne went into the phone booth and grabbed the receiver and talked nonsense to himself until Uffe was out of sight, then stood there and debated what to do. Uffe made him sick, he really did. But on the other hand, he hated Amy. He had to do something before he fucking lost it completely. He remembered being compared to an earthworm. That clinched it. He headed for the park, but he didn't hurry.

It wasn't a proud moment of his life, being one of two shifty-looking characters hanging around the bushes by the edge of the canal, where they were least likely to be seen. Uffe was wearing a raincoat and looked like some freaky dough-boy flasher. Janne wondered if, with a gut like that, he'd actually be able to see his own dick if he decided to flash it.

But then they got stoned on that same yellow-eyed demon shit that had made Janne lose his temper the night before. They had to, it was the only dope he had. Thinking about it, he got angry again. Suppressing his increasingly feeble second thoughts, he inhaled deeply and told Uffe about the redheaded lesbian downstairs. About how she needed to be taught a lesson in etiquette. He told Uffe that she lived on the first floor in the building, not revealing that he himself lived upstairs, and that she slept with her windows open. He helpfully informed Uffe that her windows faced the sheltered courtyard and were located right above the bicycle stands, by the old toolshed.

"Like, she has to be taught a lesson, you know, sort of?"

Uffe agreed passionately, wheezing as if he was about to keel over with terminal asthma. It was not a pretty sight. Observing this lardbutt a-heaving and a-hoeing, Janne started to change his mind again, all the while knowing that it was too late. He should have kept his stupid face shut, he decided, as he allowed himself to remember that Uffe was a guy with a well-known weakness for rape. It was a little indulgence of his — his idea of romance. There wasn't a sex club in Malmö that Uffe hadn't been banned from. Even street hookers wanted nothing to do with him — even if he paid triple. Uffe himself now brought up the idea.

"Shit, Uffe, no! Nothing like that, okay? Push her around a bit, threaten her, but no more. I just want her to get scared. Really, I mean. I'll pay you. But, you know...."

"Fuck, buddy, you don't have to pay me!" Uffe beamed magnanimously. He felt truly happy. "At least not a lot. We're pals, right? We got to stick together, right?"

"Right," echoed Janne, hearing how lame he sounded. "Just, you know, take it easy, okay? I don't want anybody hurt. I just want you to scare the living shit out of her, make her want to move right out."

"Not to worry," promised Uffe. "Trust me, everything will be just great. Just terrific. I mean, do chicks fear me or not? Know what I mean?"

"Yeah, I know what you mean. But promise, no rough stuff?"

"Don't worry, good buddy. Don't worry!"

Uffe radiated good will and high expectations while Janne tried to look as if he were somewhere else altogether. Now that everything was taken care of, he just wanted to get the hell away from this freak. Frantically he tried to think up a good excuse. Cleaning out the pipe, he told Uffe that he'd better rush or he'd be late for his exam. Don't want to flunk, do we? Uffe wanted to shake hands but Janne pretended not to see.

They had set the place and time. Tomorrow night. About midnight, to make sure people were in bed.

The courtyard lay deserted and dark when Uffe made his un-announced entry into Amy's life at exactly four minutes to midnight on Thursday night. He heaved his bulk onto the bicycle stands and his face loomed in her window like a sweaty moon. The noise made her look up, startled, but his sudden appearance didn't frighten her so much as infuriate her. The doughy figure that suddenly rolled in between the curtains was to Amy not evil and frightening but offensive and ugly, an insult to her aesthetic sensibilities. She was repulsed to the core of her soul, and immediately told him so, not even bothering to get up. Telling him to get lost, she dipped a cracker in a mug of hot asparagus soup. Not the lonely woman mute with fear that Uffe had dreamed sweet dreams about. Fear was the only emotion that excited him enough to get an erection. Amy's cold acerbic anger did nothing for him. Standing there looking stupid, with a limp dick, cheated out of his midnight fun, he got pissed off. He'd been looking forward to a violent fuck all day, and the realization that he wasn't in any condition to perform was too much. This whore had to be punished and good. Oh, would she ever be! She was gonna get it so bad it just wasn't funny. If he'd only brought his knife! He'd left it in his room in a weak moment, because he'd promised Janne no rough stuff. Stupid idea. The thought of the knife got him excited, though, and he unzipped his pants as he unbuckled his long, stiff belt.

And so Amy was punished. She'd never know how it had come about, or what it was for, but it would teach what was left of her how to hate.

Earlier that same Thursday evening, Janne had been overcome by an intense urge to visit his mother. Lillan had raised her eyebrows, for while Janne was very fond of his mother, he'd never exhibited any need for her company. He never visited her without having been summoned unless he wanted something from her. But on that Thursday evening a trip on a bus and then a streetcar out to the suburb of Lorensborg was something he could not do without.

"I know it's the middle of the week, but you need to get out and about a bit more," he said to Lillan, his face thoughtful and concerned as he gazed into her eyes. "I was thinking about that today, for some reason. You sit at home too much, you know that?"

"Well then," said Lillan, moved by such kindness.

Majken was like a mother to her, which to Lillan was reason enough to visit any time. By seven o'clock they sat on a streetcar, suburb-bound and nicely dressed. Janne felt like an asshole, and hoped nobody would see him wearing a tie. He hadn't worn a tie since he'd been confirmed, but Lillan had made him. He'd given in because tonight of all nights was not the time to argue. They bought a strudel and two kinds of small cakes in the pastry shop on the corner where they got off, as if this was a very special occasion — which in a way it was. A bit expensive but, as Janne said, what the fuck. They had called Majken ahead of time, but she still went into shock when she saw them. Almost as if she didn't believe it was true. She'd just washed her hair and she was standing there in her new blouse and best skirt, wanting to look nice, with a large purple towel wrapped around her head.

"This is too good to be true!" She sighed with pleasure and rushed off to make coffee, a lovely big pot full of strong coffee, they were staying for a while, weren't they, now they'd come all that way? Catering to Lillan as if she were royalty. "You sit down, my girl, and put your feet up, you don't want to walk about too much at this stage, your feet will get all swollen and painful. I know what it feels like, mine swelled up like elephant feet when I was expecting Janne. Probably runs in the family. Sit, I said! Here, put this pillow behind your back. No, no, just do it. Janne, you go get the tray, there's a cake-plate in the cupboard above the stove, you know, the white one with the gold edge that I got from Aunt Lina. Oh, and get a tablecloth, will you, Janne, let's make it really nice, get the blue one with the embroidered flowers. And get the liqueur glasses too! This is a good reason to open the Grand Marnier I bought in Benidorm last year. I've been dying for an excuse to have some. So, let's celebrate! I'm going to be a grandma soon! Janne! Don't forget the spoons! And get the good cups!"

On and on she went, enough to drive you up the fucking wall. Janne was too restless, too easily bored, to get into all the domesticity shit, sit back and have a pleasant chat about trivial crap, especially at his mother's, and this night was no exception. He always felt out of place among all the many knick-knacks that marked Majken's territory, even though he'd grown up here. It wasn't his turf, but that night he sat there and didn't so much as twitch. He was in no hurry, he had no half-baked excuses as to why he had to rush off. As usual he had nothing to contribute to the conversation, he watched TV instead, insisting that there was a movie on that he couldn't miss for the world. Twirling his liqueur glass, wishing he could smoke a pipe of hash, he suffered through a Hungarian film that made no fucking sense whatsoever. Hungarian people doing Hungarian stuff in some crappy run-down apartment building somewhere. Eating sausages and killing each other. Like anybody gave a shit! Meanwhile the old lady and Lillan were deeply immersed in the world of babies, Majken showing some old snaps of a chubby-cheeked Janne in diapers. They didn't even notice he was there, which would have pissed him off had he not reminded himself why they were visiting in the first place. Instead he said, "Mind if I have another glass of liqueur?" as often as he thought he could get away with it, and Majken would absent-mindedly reply, "Sure, help yourself, and pour me just a teensy one while you're at it," before she forgot about him again. Which was fine. He stirred the liqueur with his tongue and coped bravely with his boredom while he stared at the Hungarians yelling at each other in Hungarian as they all boarded a train with a bunch of battered suitcases. Not having paid too much attention, he wondered vaguely where the hell they were going and whether they'd packed enough sausages to last them to the end of the movie.

They were at the old lady's for ever that night, but that was the plan. Didn't get going until it was too late to catch the last streetcar back downtown. They had to take a taxi. Lillan shouldn't have to walk, said Majken, and she insisted on paying for it. Lillan was grateful, she was dead tired. Her back was aching, her spine threatening to collapse, and her feet had doubled in size despite her having kept them up all evening. Back home again, she waddled out of the taxi and dragged her misshapen body across the dark courtyard, Janne's arm protectively around her shoulders. All was peaceful. There were lights on in only a few scattered windows across the yard. The lights were out in Amy's room; she must be sleeping already. Lillan envied her being able to lie comfortably in bed in whatever position she wanted, and not having to get up and pee every five seconds. It had been stupid to sit there and drink cup after cup of strong coffee before going to bed, she should have known better, but it had seemed impolite not to. She didn't want to hurt Majken's feelings when she'd been so ecstatic to see them. They should visit her more often, but Janne never had time. Majken was her mother-in-law, they were family, Majken had said so over and over again. Lillan was her girl now, she had said. Her daughter. That was so good to hear. It was sad that Lillan's own mother didn't even know Lillan was pregnant, but she wasn't about to find out, because Lillan had people who loved her and cared about her now, just the way she was. She didn't need to put up with her mother's daily admonitions and criticisms any more. Now she belonged, without feeling either shame or inadequacy. She made a mental note to tell Amy that next time she saw her, to tell her that she was wrong about Janne, and that while he had a bit of a hot temper — just like Amy, let's face it — he was in fact very kind and thoughtful when it really counted. She'd say something like "I ought to know, I live with him and I'm expecting his child. So you may just have to re-evaluate him a bit, Amy, and be less scornful and critical. At least when you're in his home." That was what she'd say, straight to the point. Kindly but firmly. No more nonsense, enough was enough. She'd tell her about how, when they went to visit his mum, he'd bought the most expensive cakes in the pastry shop. "You know, the ones covered with green marzipan with lots of whipped cream inside?" she'd say. "And why? I'll tell you why. Because they are his mum's very favourite, that's why. He remembered that from when he was little. So don't you come and tell me he doesn't care!" That was what she'd tell her. Then she hoped there'd be no more screaming matches and they could all try to be friends. How difficult could it be? Mind you, she would also point out to Janne that Amy had brought her vitamin pills and calcium pills because she was worried that Lillan wasn't getting enough nutrition for both herself and the baby. And that yesterday Amy had popped up with a package of tea and a teddy bear because, having run into her conscience during the night, she had wanted to apologize. Lillan had been afraid to tell Janne about it, but decided that she would tell him after all, maybe tomorrow. Right now she was too tired.

Before they went to bed, Janne was so considerate that he even went out and banged on the toilet door, yelling at the Yugoslav to "stop jerking off and get the hell out of there because other people need to use the fucking can! Honest Swedish citizens! Not to mention the fact that a pregnant Swedish woman needs to use the Swedish toilet! So a little consideration wouldn't go amiss here, buddy!" She wished he wouldn't yell quite so loudly or use such filthy language, it embarrassed her, but it was the thought that counted, wasn't it? He knew she had to pee really bad and he was trying to help. Janne himself pissed in the kitchen sink, it was more convenient, but Lillan would never dream of doing that. She found it disgusting and was hoping eventually to cure him of the habit. It wasn't hygienic. Janne knew how she felt; that was why he was being so thoughtful.

For somebody who was not a morning person, Janne was doing a very convincing early-bird routine the following dawn. He shot out of bed at seven, giving the impression that he just had to get out and jog ten kilometres before breakfast or he wouldn't feel human. He stretched his arms over his head as if there was nothing he loved more than greeting a grey, windy morning. His explanation for this bizarre behaviour was that he had to prepare for an excruciating exam that was vital to their continued existence.

"Us educated men have to suffer through a lot of shit!" He grinned as he patted the mountain under the comforter. "Gotta get my incredible brain in gear."

Lillan smiled sleepily as she started to roll her globular self off the sofa-bed. Time to piddle again. The baby had started boxing lessons early and was using her bladder for a punching bag. Good thing the Yugoslav left for work early. He'd taped a note to the toilet door, though: "Please for to note goot: Also I have my rites in the toilet, thank you please so much. Griitings. Milo Pasic." Janne was delighted and wanted to frame it.

It was time she was up too, said Lillan, because it was going to be a special day. She was going with Majken to Wessel's department store to stock up on baby stuff. So far all she had was a baby blanket and two pairs of pyjamas. But Wessel's was having a super-sale, Majken had told her, and as she was about to become a grandmother, she was going to pay for everything. She had stubbornly insisted; I've been looking forward to it, don't deprive me of the pleasure, she'd said. To be perfectly honest, she'd said, she could hardly wait, because since Janne had met Lillan her life had taken on a whole new meaning. Lillan had responded that so had hers. Then they had shared a big hug and had made their plans, toasting them with the Grand Marnier from Benidorm — half a glass for Lillan, four for Majken. Life was just a bowl of cherries sometimes.

They had to leave for Wessel's early because Majken had to go to work in the afternoon. She worked in the duty-free shop on the Copenhagen ferry. At a quarter to nine Lillan was ready and waiting under a grey sky at Gustav Adolf Square, badly needing to pee. She was excited. It was to be her first serious layette-hunting trip and she wasn't taking it lightly. As Majken came hurrying around the fountain, the bus pulled up. They ran for it, Majken holding onto the scarf she'd tied around her hair, and were off. At Wessel's, after Lillan had her pee, they were off to the children's department to join a horde of pregnant women all smiling at each other like Mona Lisas, members of a secret society, when their hands met by accident amid the piles of tiny coloured clothes. It was like playing with dolls again, and they had a nice long play until they were both tired out. "Let's go have some lunch," said Majken.

Lillan returned home shortly after one with a pair of large shopping bags spilling over with the most adorable little garments that she had ever laid eyes on. She was almost spilling over herself, too. Majken had of course insisted on treating her to lunch, because Lillan had to eat properly and regularly, that was very important. So there she was waddling like a giant duck with a belly full of beef stew, fried potatoes, pickled beets, and chocolate ice-cream. Feeling wonderfully spoiled, she clutched the bags of loot. They held an amazing heap of stuff. There were the sweetest little pyjamas you ever saw, softer than a summer cloud. Not to mention half a dozen cuddly terrycloth sleeper suits in fire-engine red, sky blue, and canary yellow. With teensy pockets! She wasn't sure what babies needed pockets for, but they sure looked cute! And there were striped T-shirts for when Mikael was a bit older, a whole stack of them that Majken had decided her grandchild could not possibly find happiness without. Here was a bunting-bag so their darling would be warm and snug when the cold weather arrived, and here were the most darling bibs you ever saw, with bunnies and kittens, and teensy-weensy socks! Lillan was still high with sheer delight at these wonders of the world as she carried her load across the courtyard.

She'd never dreamed that life could be so rich and fulfilling. Overwhelmed, she felt a strong need to share; she needed an audience to display her new treasures to, she wanted to hear crowds cheering their approval. She'd have to go and see if Amy was home. Amy wasn't one to squeal with pleasure at bibs and bunnies, but never mind.

Almost bubbling over, Lillan knocked on Amy's door. A rhythmical and friendly knockety-knock sound that said here was a messenger bringing cheerful tidings to the dweller within. Open up, open up, I bring you joy! Two bags full! Cute socks and all!

The answer was a strange animal roar, the howl of a wild creature, so unexpected that Lillan froze and almost peed herself. She stood there for a second or two, or maybe it was for ever; it seemed as if a lifetime rushed by. She stared at her fist resting on the door, stared at her brimming bags for moral support, then squatted down and pressed open the mail slot in the door.

"Amy?" she squeaked into the opening. Her voice was muted with apprehension. She felt as if some beast might charge down the hall and rip the nose off her face. "Amy?" The answer was another scream of rage and madness, and Lillan burst into tears.

"Amy! Amy!" She yelled the name as if it were a magic spell that would put everything right. "Amy! Please!" She turned the handle and the door opened; Uffe had unlocked it the night before. After he'd finished his assignment, he couldn't be bothered leaving the awkward way he had entered. He had quitted the battle field formally, triumphantly, through the door. Amy's punishment took less than an hour, but he was tired out.

Lillan put her bags down and tiptoed nervously through the dark hall. No wild animals attacked. Glancing into the room she saw something that looked like Amy sitting bolt upright on her mattress screaming to high heaven. She was stark naked, her skinny white body covered with black and purple bruises and smears of dried blood. She had a swollen greenish-black mass of flesh where her left eye was supposed to be, and a very fat upper lip that extended up to her smashed purple nose, which had been bleeding profusely. Dried blood coated her chin and cheeks. There was a deep cut from the left corner of her mouth all the way down her chin. This was no longer a face. She was unrecognizable but for her long red hair.

Lillan stared at her and cried helplessly as Amy threw herself at her, clutching her, whimpering, pressing her face against Lillan's bulging front, butting her bruised forehead against her as if trying to force her way inside. The child within kicked angrily; it didn't want company. Lillan gently patted Amy's cold back with both hands.

"There, there, Amy. Sweet, dear Amy," she cooed as her hands became red and sticky. Holding them up, she saw it was blood. Amy shuddered in pain. Her back had been whipped so hard it was striped.

Uffe was a bad loser. He had used his favourite belt, a black leather one with a big vulgar metal buckle. Amy tried to tell Lillan that late last night, after not having eaten all day, she had been having a late mug of canned asparagus soup and some crackers when a stranger's face appeared in her window like a full moon. Uffe had lashed Amy's back so savagely that she had cracked three ribs, although she didn't yet know it, she just knew the pain. Her wounds were deep, and Lillan's tender strokes had started them bleeding again. The sheets were stiff with blood. Amy hadn't moved since the stranger left. She had felt she would never move again. She had felt there was no point any more.

Lillan looked at her smeared red hands, then looked over Amy's shoulder, around the room. Drying asparagus soup had formed an ugly pattern on the floor by the bed. It looked like vomit. The newspaper thrown beside it was splashed with blood. There was a tooth lying by the over turned cup. Not knowing what to do she screamed some more, whimpered and peed herself. Not very help-ful, but it helped ease the terror. She had eagerly skipped into a world that she could hardly have imagined. A world that wasn't supposed to exist. She screamed out of fear, out of anger and be-cause she felt idiotic being there with her offering of teensy socks and bibs with bunnies. Feeling suddenly sick, she ran into the kitchen and chucked up beef stew and pickled beets all over Amy's unwashed dishes. Dizzy but determined, she wiped her face and returned to Amy, carefully hugging her tangled head. Stroking her hair, she thought about how Amy had sat there bleeding, not only all night but all day too, while Lillan was out playing with dolls.

She felt ashamed.

For a while the world ceased to exist. Either the clock refrained from ticking or Lillan didn't hear it. Then Amy's whimpers punc-tured the silence. Poor little Amy. She had been tortured, she had gone mad from the pain and fear, the rage and frustration. Lillan

94

felt like going mad too, but Amy needed help. Yes, that was what she needed — she needed to go to the hospital right away. Lillan would get her there. But then she felt a sharp pain in her stomach, so sudden and intense that she folded over and panted like a dog. It must be nerves. All the horror had frightened the baby.

The pain disappeared and she felt fine again, which was just as well, because Amy had no phone; getting help meant running upstairs to call a taxi, then rushing back down. Or should she call an ambulance? Or the police? Or was it too late for that? What did you do in a situation like this? She looked down at Amy who had stopped screaming and was sitting there cross-legged and staring up at her with one large empty eye. Just as Lillan was going to ask her where Amy kept her clothes she was felled by another stab of pain, a domineering pain that knew how to get attention. She gasped. It seemed selfish but she couldn't help it.

"Holy shit," whispered Amy. "It's time." She talked oddly because her front teeth were missing.

"What's time?" panted Lillan, her face hanging over her stomach as she stared at her friend.

"The baby, Lillan. You're in labour."

"No!" protested Lillan, "I can't be! It's too early! Last time I was at the hospital, they told me I had three more weeks."

"No, you don't."

"I do too! They told me!"

"Never mind what they told you. It's what the baby's telling you."

Amy stood up carefully. Moving gingerly, she tried to pull on a pair of torn jeans lying on the floor. Then gave up. "Go upstairs and call a taxi," she said. "And hurry up! I have to find something to wear."

By the time the taxi arrived ten minutes later Lillan had had two more contractions. The young driver caught the words "in labour", "emergency", and "maternity ward" and considered stopping the car and running like hell, especially as Lillan had another contraction as soon as she had heaved her bulk into the back seat. Christ, he thought, what if she has a frigging baby in my clean car!

Imagine having to deliver a baby halfway down Amiralsgatan, standing on the sidewalk with blood and guts up to your elbows! And not only was she about to pop, she was accompanied by some barefoot pervert in a big raincoat and sunglasses, with a long scarf wrapped around his face. Like *The Invisible Man*. It was eerie.

"Drive and drive fast!" hissed the barefoot freak.

The taxi driver drove as fast as he dared and then some, running two red lights and barely missing a crowded bus. He arrived at the gates of the hospital in five minutes, but within the hospital compound he promptly got lost. Lillan had another contraction and screamed. As he glanced in the back mirror, the weirdo companion hissed, "Breathe slowly and deeply," and the scarf slid down to reveal a grotesque purple face. "Oh my God," thought the driver, "I've got a fucking alien in my car!" After trying to dump them outside the paediatric building and the psychiatric building, in that order, he finally unloaded them at the right place and took off, forgetting to get paid.

As Lillan and Amy hobbled through the door, Lillan's waters broke and splashed all over the floor. She bent double with another contraction as two nurses rushed forward and swept her away, giving the barefoot alien a suspicious glare.

"NO!" screamed Lillan furiously. "Not me! It's not me! I'm okay! I've got three weeks! Not me! It's Amy, she needs help!" She had another contraction. God, it hurt! But all the same. "It's Amy! She's been tortured! Listen to me, you have to help her! Look at her back!"

"It's okay, dear, just calm down now," said a kind voice. "You'll be all right. Just you calm down, dear, we'll look after you. Everything will be fine."

"I know that!" she screamed, frustrated and angry. "Look at her back, for God's sake. Look at her!" She was shrieking by now. It helped ease the pain, but nobody seemed to be listening. She didn't even notice that Amy had left.

"There, there," soothed the voice. "Everything's okay. We have to get ready for your baby."

Lillan was lying down, her eyes stubbornly closed, as people poked between her legs. Somebody said, "She's fully dilated," and soon after that Lillan gave up her effort to help Amy. She let the brightly lit, antiseptic world enfold her. It felt secure. The pain was changing, becoming more bearable.

Less than forty minutes later a baby boy slid into the world. She opened her eyes in time to see him arrive, and she was mute with wonder. A little boy. Her Mikael Gösta. Her real live baby. It was such an incredible sight that she started weeping uncontrollably as they handed him to her. It was a miracle but here he was, her Micke, he was real, he was lying here on her arm wrapped snugly in a blue blanket. He was absolutely perfect. She hugged him very gently, she smelled him and touched him and splashed his beautiful wrinkled little face with her tears. She forgot about Amy, sure that she was being looked after. She was full of the miracle of her child. She felt faint just looking at him. He was the most incredibly exquisite baby in the world.

"Welcome home, Micke," she whispered to the little face with its eyes squeezed so tight. Carefully she touched the downy skull. It had a soft mat of dark hair. Same colour as mine, she thought. Imagine that! She beamed at the doctor, beamed at the nurse who'd come into the recovery room to ask, "What about your family, dear? Do you have a husband or a boyfriend?"

Oops! She'd forgotten! They brought a phone and she called home to find Janne wondering where the hell she was.

"We have a son!" she whispered. She didn't want to wake her baby up. "Mikael. I'm at the hospital."

"No shit! How the hell did that happen? I thought you went shopping."

"I did. Are you coming to see us? I'm going to call your mother."

"Sure I'm coming to see you. I wanna see my son, eh?"

Janne felt proud after all. What the fuck, he said to himself, and called his mother too, feeling a sudden urge to share the accomplishment of fatherhood.

"Dad! I'm a mom!" he shouted. "I mean, I'm a dad!"

"I know, my boy, I know!" Majken had just got off the phone with Lillan and she sounded delirious. "And I'm a grandma! Isn't it just heaven? I have a grandson! I can't believe it!"

"What the hell," admitted Janne, thinking that the old lady was definitely losing it. "I'm a man of many talents. Are you coming out to the hospital to see the kid or what?"

"Try to stop me!" cried his mother. "I've called a taxi already!"

"Okay, Ma. Just take it easy, eh? No need to go nuts."

Amy had disappeared from the face of the earth. The hospital had no record of her. Lillan never saw her again. She thought about her often, and felt the loss, especially during those first few months of motherhood. Nursing her baby late at night, she tried not to remember the sticky blood coating her hands, the raw wounds on Amy's back, the gargoyle deformity where her face had been. Shutting her eyes tightly, she sang to her baby. She was happy, she was determined to be happy, and she didn't want to cry ever again. Amy would be okay by now, her wounds would have healed. Otherwise they would surely have heard.

The day after she came home from the hospital with Mikael, Janne said he'd seen a man carrying some stuff out of Amy's apartment. Lillan remembered with a jolt how she had thrown up all over Amy's dirty dishes. Janne wanted to know why the hell she went all red in the face, but she couldn't tell him, it was too disgusting; she just said that she was worried still. She asked him what the man had looked like.

"Well," said Janne, "I don't know. I don't look at guys, do I?"

"Try to remember," pleaded Lillan. "Was he white or black, short or tall, fat or thin, young or old, handsome or ugly? Did he look nice or nasty?"

"He was probably in his thirties, I guess," said Janne after thinking for a while. "He was tall and had blond hair and a beard. And glasses, I think. One of them intellectual types, you know, the kind with leather elbow-patches on their blazers. Shit like that. Probably smokes a pipe."

"Did you talk to him?"

"No, I didn't talk to him! What the fuck would I have said?"

"You could have asked who he was."

"None of my business who he was, is it?"

He didn't mention that he'd been scared absolutely shitless, expecting the guy to jump him and beat him into raw meatloaf before calling the police. As it turned out, the guy didn't even look at him. But it was as if an ice-cold hand had reached out and grabbed him by the balls and squeezed the life out of them, because the guy was dressed in black, as if he was in mourning. That had *really* freaked him out.

Janne wasn't proud of himself at all. If he'd ever encountered shame before, he might have recognized it. All he knew about what had happened that night was what Lillan had told him: the horror story about Amy's back lashed into bleeding stripes, her ruined face, all the blood. He'd only wanted to curb that spirit. He tried to rationalize that it sure as fuck wasn't his fault, he'd been sitting at his mum's having coffee and cake, for God's sake. He'd been with family. Still, for weeks he waited, jittery and impotent, for something to happen. For the police to come marching up the stairs, for heavenly retribution, for Amy's blood-stained ghost to point a skeletal finger in his direction. Shit, he didn't even know if she was dead or what. He checked the papers but there was nothing there, no scandalous article about a woman beaten to death, no obituary. And how could she be dead if she had walked out of the hospital? Damn it all! Janne had to carry his guilt from day to day, and he was starting to resent it. It was heavy going. He should have been proud to discover that he had a conscience, but he wasn't. It was a handicap he could happily have done without.

Uffe too had conveniently disappeared. Well, that came as no surprise; he wasn't going to step forward to claim a reward, was he? Janne made some discreet enquiries into his whereabouts. One rumour had it that he was back in his old room at the St. Lars insane asylum in Lund. Another story circulating in the streets was that he'd taken the train to Berlin one morning to visit a masochistic whore on the Ku'damm. Somebody else had talked to somebody who had run into him at the train station; apparently Uffe had tried to borrow money for a one-way ticket to Stockholm. A young theatre student who'd just been to Poland for her second abortion said she'd seen him in the bar on the ferry to Gdansk, blind drunk and bellowing a poem in Swedish about a crippled orphan to some equally shit-faced Polacks. No, she hadn't talked to him — she wasn't stupid, was she? That was the last rumour about Uffe that Janne cared to listen to. Like everybody else, he didn't really give a damn what happened to Uffe as long as it was bad. Knowing Uffe, it likely would be.

Though Janne was never suspected of anything — no cops came charging after him, heaven ignored him, and there were no ghosts hovering downstairs in Amy's apartment, wailing or rattling chains — he remained jittery. He got irritable when the baby cried. It sounded like an accusation and he couldn't stand it. Life did return to normal eventually, but very slowly, as if to punish him. The guilt grew less heavy and he learned to ignore it most of the time. Lillan was busy with the baby.

Then came the go-ahead for the building to be demolished. Majken promised money to help them get a new apartment. They'd have to find one with hot water and a bathroom now that they had a child, she said, even if it cost. By February she had found out about a one-bedroom apartment, central location, not far from Drottningtorget, fourth floor. Not very expensive. Signe at work, who knew that Majken's son was looking for a place, said that her Uncle Arvid had died and his wife was selling and moving to Tomelilla. They looked at the apartment and Lillan was delighted. She would no longer have to pass by Amy's door every time she went out. The apartment had remained empty, as the building was about to come down, but that just made it all the more spooky.

Janne was happy too. The tearing down of the building was a sign of forgiveness, the way he saw it, a sign that he could now forget. The whole thing had never happened. How could it have, when the building wasn't there any more? His conscience once again

100

rested, silent and at peace, and he was feeling pretty pleased with himself. Things were once again turning out okay, and he wasn't complaining. Life was good.

They moved into the new apartment on a Monday right after lunch. It was windy and it drizzled a bit as they loaded the van, but cleared by the time they arrived at the new place. They both took that as a good sign. Lillan went up ahead with Micke and wandered around the empty space that was now her very own to do with as she wished. First she checked the kitchen, which faced the courtyard. It was bright and sunny and had an eating area just large enough to hold their table and four chairs. It needed new wallpaper. The living-room was spacious and had a large window over the street. Beside the kitchen was the bedroom. It too faced the courtyard. Lillan looked around and decided it was big enough to hold their new bed, Micke's cot, and probably the dresser too.

Her first real home, with their very own toilet and all! She was standing in the middle of the bedroom, daydreaming and rocking Micke in her arms, when she heard Janne and his friends Hasse and Pelle grunting their way up the flights of stairs, carrying something heavy. Probably the couch.

By four o'clock they were more or less finished. Janne went to get whatever was left at the old place and bring it back in Hasse's dad's old car. Lillan went shopping for food. When she came back she encountered their new neighbour, S. Andersson. He was an odd kind of man who looked so uncomfortable and disconcerted at the sight of her that she thought it best to ignore him. She was also slightly irritated by the fact that somebody could look so scared meeting her. He must be a real recluse. Out of the corner of her eye she could see his hands trembling as he tried to open his door. Maybe he had something to hide. She was disappointed; she had hoped for friendly neighbours, the kind you could borrow a cup of sugar from and gossip on the landing with. People their age. And a small child who could eventually become Micke's friend.

Janne didn't arrive back until late. He'd taken the opportunity to go for a pizza and beer, treating the buddies for helping out. That was fine, except that he'd forgotten to pick up her plants. Not that he seemed overly burdened by guilt. To punish him Lillan made him go and borrow a lightbulb from the strange guy next door. The bedroom light had gone out and Micke wouldn't go to sleep in the dark. She didn't tell Janne that she'd already met the neighbour. Janne came back with a pack of two lightbulbs.

"So, what's our neighbour like?"

"Huh? I don't know. Looks like a loser. Why?"

"Just wondering. What's his apartment like?"

"How the fuck should I know? He didn't give me a guided tour, did he?"

"Just asking. No need to be rude."

"Oh, stop sulking for fuck's sake! I said I'll get your plants in the morning!"

"Do you have to shout? Now you've made him cry again."

"Too damn bad!"

And so on, into another late night, another early morning.

The next evening Lillan stood in her new kitchen, leaning against the stove as she prepared Micke's mashed vegetables. He was having tummy trouble again. The move had disturbed the carefully established routine he seemed to thrive on, if "routine" was the appropriate name for it. The new surroundings seemed to confuse him, poor thing, and the late nights recently made her tired. The fact that he was teething didn't help matters. Then at breakfast, their first breakfast in the new place, Janne informed her that he was planning a big house-warming party on Saturday night.

Brilliant.

"I don't think that's a very good idea," she said right away, deciding to put her foot down. "We just moved in yesterday. Nothing is in its right place yet and the hall is full of boxes to unpack. It'll have to wait, please."

He chose to ignore her reasons because he'd already invited everybody he knew.

"You have to have a house-warming party, for God's sake!" he said. "It's the hospitable thing to do for your buddies and pals. One acquires a home, one shares it with one's friends," he philosophized, looking down at her with an expression that said she had no insight into human interactions, never having had much of a social life. "It'll be great," he promised — the great organizer — as he grinned his "am I lovable or what?" grin.

She did not find it lovable at all.

Micke had slept less than usual lately. He was whiny and hypersensitive, and squealed like a stuck pig whenever Janne lost his temper over his son's constant whimpering and screaming, which was all the time. A never-ending circle of disharmony. Lillan didn't know what to do about it as she watched from the eye of the storm, but she thought it was grossly unfair to yell at poor Micke, who was after all not even a year old. Janne could be insufferably bad-tempered. It was childish, but she didn't know how to curb his outbursts any more than she knew how to defuse nuclear warheads blindfolded. She bit her lip hard and shut up instead. It wasn't easy, but she was learning rapidly. Learning how to read Janne, when to avoid him and when not to. How to cater to his sensibilities. It was hard going sometimes.

Yes, he had his faults, Janne did. He could behave like a spoiled five-year-old and think it was macho. But let's face it, Lillan said consolingly to herself, he has, despite his shortcomings, taken responsibility for me and the baby. That was something. It was more than she had expected, but then again, she hadn't expected anything.

Janne was just a bit immature, according to Majken, but he

was sure to grow up soon. He was only twenty-two, and everybody knew that boys matured later than girls. Fatherhood would help make a man of him. That was apparently what had happened to Janne's dad, and he had become a wonderful dad, albeit for a tragically short time before the accident. So be patient, was Majken's advice, it won't take long. Give the lad a chance and I'm sure he'll do us proud.

Micke had calmed down now and was waving his arms about, demanding his food. She kissed his drooling little face and he smiled at her. She smiled back and kissed him again and he gurgled happily. Janne had gone out and she and Micke were having a quiet breather. Before he left, Janne had nagged Lillan to go out with him. Let's go to a movie, go have a beer somewhere, I've got some money, he had said, not to worry about the finances, everything is cool, runt, and all that.

"Put the crybaby in his cot with a bottle and let's go out and relax for a bit. Have a bottle of our own, eh? Come on, what do you say?"

"You mean leave Micke on his own?"

"Well, why the fuck not?"

Lillan was shocked. She was speechless. Such a horrendous thought would never have occurred to her. It would never have occurred to her that anybody with children would harbour such a thought. There were certain things you just didn't do.

"Not so," said Janne. "I mean, what the hell, why not leave him alone? What the fuck does it matter if he lies here and cries all alone or with us sitting here listening to the godawful noise?" If they went out for a while they would do both themselves and the kid a favour, he explained with irritable patience, as they would then be in the fortunate and unusual position of being able to relax and heal their tattered nerves, thus ending up in a good mood for a change. It made sense — to him, anyway. And if they turned out the light the kid wouldn't know whether they were there or not; in fact, he would probably think they'd gone to sleep, and that might inspire him to go to sleep too. Which would make a real nice change.

"So what do you say?"

"No. Absolutely not." Lillan was vehement. "It's not right. What if something happened? What then?"

"What the hell could possibly happen?" Janne shouted. "He's not gonna get out of the fucking cot and run off, is he? He can't walk, for chrissakes! And it's not as if the whole fucking building is gonna burn to the ground as soon as we hit the street! Is it?"

"It's wrong. Parents do not leave babies on their own. And that's that. It's not even legal."

"Bullshit!"

"It's not bullshit. It's the way it is. And it's the way it should be."

"Bullshit!"

"Oh, stop it!"

She would never ever do that to Micke. She'd rather put up with his screaming for ever. In fact, she'd rather die. The very idea of leaving him on his own made her feel sick. Janne quit nagging her after a while, as she knew he would. He didn't mind going out alone — in truth, he preferred it — but it pissed him off that when he tried to be magnanimous and offer her a little treat, the runt turned him down.

Janne took all this fatherhood stuff with a pinch of salt. It was no big deal. It didn't really have anything to do with him. Babies, he reasoned, were basically for their mums to take care of, that was how nature had set it up. They were the ones who got pregnant, they were the ones with tits full of milk and all that shit. And he had other things to do. He was the breadwinner. Everybody had a role to play in life; that way there was order in the universe.

Lillan pampered the kid way too much, though. She was so deep into this motherhood crap that she didn't know when the fuck to stop. He kept telling her that but she didn't pay the slightest bit of attention to his pearls of wisdom. She went right on gooing and cooing and slobbering. It was embarrassing when he had friends drop by. But it was amazing how pigheaded she could be when it came to that kid. She refused to admit that kids shouldn't be spoiled, she couldn't see how it ruined them. That was something he'd had to learn at an early date. Or so he claimed. He'd done pretty well as he pleased for as long as he could remember, because when Majken came home from her shift at the chocolate factory where she worked when he was younger, she simply didn't have the energy to argue with him.

But that had been a very different situation, it had had nothing to do with being spoiled. He'd been independent. Stood on his own two feet. That was the opposite of spoiled. He took after his dad, and his dad hadn't been spoiled either, according to what Majken had told him. Growing up without being spoiled and pampered and weak was, as far as he was concerned, a family characteristic. A tradition, if you please, and a fine one that ought to be continued. It was genetics, was what it was, in the genes and nature and all that, and you didn't fuck around with nature. He aimed to make sure that Micke was brought up accordingly, to take after his dad and his granddaddy. That way he could never go wrong.

Janne didn't really remember his father, he just imagined that he did. Me and the old man, he'd say if the subject ever came up, we were two of a kind. His father had died at age thirty-two in a train crash up in northern Sweden. Suddenly and unexpectedly he had been gone for ever. Janne had been only four at the time and had not quite understood. Too small to cope with a concept like "for ever", he had refused to listen, pretending nothing had happened. Daddy had got this job up north helping to cut down trees and had gone away on a train and he hadn't come back.

His father's parents, who were called Grandma and Grandpa Sandberg, knew nothing of Janne and his mother at the time of their son's death. Janne, on the other hand, knew vaguely of their existence. They lived "out in Limhamn", which he thought was halfway round the world, maybe in Africa. That would explain why they never came for a visit. They didn't come to the funeral either, Janne knew that too, because he'd heard his mum say afterwards that it was the goddamn limit that those uncaring misers didn't even show up for their only son's funeral, and what the hell kind of people were they anyway?

Grandma Persson, who knew everything, told his mum to go and see them, because she said maybe they didn't even know that Gösta was dead, seeing as he had cut off all contact with them. Maybe they didn't read the paper.

"I told you to send them a letter," said Grandma Persson to his mum. "I told you that last week, didn't I? Give them a chance."

"She told you, didn't she?" echoed the small child.

"I'll send one today," his mum had replied, her lips forming a thin pale line as she went looking for a pen. "I'm going to do it right now," they heard her say to herself. "I'm damn well going to do it."

It was a week later exactly, on a beautiful Saturday afternoon in late summer, that they went visiting. Sunlight slanted golden over the whole city, the way it does sometimes, and a salty breeze swept the air fresh and clean. People still wore summer clothes, looking vaguely surprised that they could. Majken dressed Janne in his Sunday best, polished his new shoes, combed his hair over and over with water until it lay plastered like a cheap wig against his round head. She told him firmly to make a particular effort to behave himself, that one day of all the days in his life. It was very, very important.

"You just have to," she said, "because if you don't behave yourself I'm going to beat the living shit out of you when we get back. Do you understand, Jan?"

She spoke slowly and clearly, as if he were a small foreigner who had trouble comprehending Swedish. Plus she called him Jan, and that was always bad news. He nodded and sighed and wondered why she was behaving like this. Not even Grandma Persson was herself as she kissed him goodbye. Her face had gone all stiff, her eyes were preoccupied, and she didn't smile.

They caught the bus up to Gustav Adolf Square. It looked festive, with water cascading in the fountains and beautiful flowers still on parade in the flowerbeds. A gang of sailors in white suits were eating ice-cream by the kiosk. One of them whistled at his mum when she determinedly dragged him onto the number four streetcar. The streetcar, she informed him, went the whole way out to where they were going.

"I know that," he said. "It goes out to Limhamn. I know that!"

He waved to the sailors. They waved their ice-creams at him, and laughed and shouted things in a strange language.

"I'd rather be a sailor than go visiting," he informed his mother.

"Oh shut up," she said.

She was not herself that day. Not her sunny old self at all. She was wearing her thin lips again. He didn't like them.

"I don't like your lips," he said, just to show her, but she didn't answer.

It was a long way out to Limhamn — they were on the streetcar for hours — but he'd expected that. About a million kilometres, he calculated, but it was pretty exciting. There were new streets everywhere and everything looked so different. It was obvious that they were very far away, because suddenly you could see the sea. It was huge and grey and endless, not like the harbour back in the city, which was full of ferries and drunks going to Copenhagen. Once when they'd been to Copenhagen Zoo a drunk had thrown up on Janne's left shoe on the ferry going home.

Here there was just sea. Water, water, and more water. Way out on the horizon he could see a ship. He'd never realized how huge the world was. He was impressed. As he mused about this, the streetcar turned a corner and they were on a street running along the sea, the water washing into the shore less than a stone's throw away. On the other side of the street, right on the corner, he saw a big old villa. It was white with green shutters and surrounded by a garden café. A whole bunch of nicely dressed people sat around white tables with striped parasols, drinking coffee and eating fancy pastries. They all looked as if they spent every day sitting there eating cake. Janne stared at them, wild-eyed with passion, wondering if the streetcar had perhaps taken them straight to heaven instead of Limhamn. This was something! His greedy eyes absorbed the well-dressed people daintily stuffing themselves, and his heart throbbed with unadulterated envy. The streetcar stopped and he tried to get off but his mum said, no, this isn't it, sit down, for God's sake. He kept staring at those fancy pastries, especially the round ones coated with a thick layer of green marzipan and filled with whipped cream and vanilla custard. There was a big gob of strawberry preserves right in the middle of the cakey part. He'd had one once, when Grandma Persson turned fifty and they had a big party. Oh, he remembered it very well! Now he saw two elderly ladies wearing white gloves and eating those very tortes with delicate little forks, tiny bits at a time. He drooled. He looked at his mum. No use even thinking about it, he decided; she looked too stiff in the face, too out of reach. No pastry for him.

What was the matter with her? This was the strangest she had ever been. She'd been strange ever since Daddy hadn't come back from the train, but today was the worst. He didn't like her dressed in black, either. She dressed in black every day now. But maybe she was extra strange today because they were going to visit Daddy's mum and dad. Grandma and Grandpa Sandberg out in Limhamn. He wasn't sure why they were called that. He didn't think they quite deserved those titles because he didn't know them, he had no idea who they were. Grandmas and grandpas were people you knew, people you went and stayed with when your mum went to work. They gave you presents on your birthday and for Christmas. Those Sandberg people never did. Then again, grown-ups were completely unpredictable, he knew that. You could never figure out what they were up to. The rules changed all the time. All in all, he wasn't overly interested in meeting them. Daddy wasn't going to be there, his mum had said so. For sure. So what was the point?

"Why are we going there?" he asked again.

"Janne, don't bug me, okay?"

They sat silent and after a very long time his mum said, "This is where we get off, I think." So they got off and the streetcar jingled and clanged and rattled around a corner and was gone. They were all alone in an unknown land. It was a strange land, but it was a very nice one. He didn't mind being there. Walking down a side-street, they found themselves in a picture from a book he'd seen once, a lush and verdant paradise where birds sang and fruit hung heavy on the trees. What a day this was! Big gardens, fertile jungles teeming with fruit trees and rose-bushes. He saw bushes laden with gooseberries, too. Late-summer flowers had burst into splashes of colour all over the place. It looked as if the villas were nestling in green secret caverns lit by an amber light from some source within. It was quiet, there too; the only sounds were birds singing and bees buzzing. A sweet scent of ripe fruit, flowers, and damp earth wafted up his quivering nostrils. In this plentiful paradise old twisted apple trees and huge pear trees stretched their branches over the sidewalk to tease him. At one point a large juicy pear dropped right at his mum's feet and lay there waiting to be picked up, big and juicy and round. Janne stopped to claim it — it was obviously for them — but his mum said, typically, that there wasn't time to pick up rotten fruit now, for God's sake, hurry up and don't get yourself dirty.

"But it's for me!" He just had to protest. "It's so beautiful here!"

"Mm," said his mum.

Maybe it wouldn't be so bad to meet that there grandma and grandpa after all, not if they lived in a castle in a magical garden where trees dropped fruit all over the place. But his mum informed him mercilessly that they did not live in a villa, so don't get any ideas, Jan, they live in an apartment building in a brand-new subburp. Whatever a subburp was. There are no villas there, she explained, just apartments. Rows and rows of nice new apartment buildings.

"Well," suggested the child, ever helpful, "we could move here, you and me and Grandma and Grandpa Persson, and live in a big house and have apple trees and pear trees. And plum trees! Plum trees! With those enormous yellow plums on them. Mum!"

"Nah," grunted his mum, "no chance. If you want to live in a villa like that you need money. Lots of money."

"Don't we have lots of money?" The child was surprised.

"Not exactly," she said, and almost laughed. She was pretty when she laughed.

"Why don't we?"

"Janne-boy, just shut up, will you? We're almost there." Her face tightened again, but Janne wasn't finished.

"Go to the bank," he suggested. "They've got loads of money there. I know that because I was there with Grandma yesterday and they gave her money so we could go to the market."

"Janne," said his mum in her Very Firm I-Mean-It Voice, "will you please shut the hell up? Just for a while? I need to concentrate."

But he didn't shut up, of course he didn't. Why should he? It was all too much. He needed to share his thoughts. And besides, he'd decided that he wanted to live in a villa with a big green garden with a huge plum tree smack in the middle of the front lawn. They could live there and every day they could take the streetcar to the café by the sea and eat pastries. He elaborated on this plan until his mum shouted, "Will you for God's sake shut up?" and started walking faster to get away from him.

Then all of a sudden, as if to punish him, there were no more gardens, no more paradise. The street ran out of trees and all that was left was a newly paved road crossing an empty field full of rubble and weeds. Across the field, way over there, were rows and rows of new four-storey apartment buildings that all looked exactly the same, every single one made of yellow brick. They looked very new. His mum's face lit up and she said, "Doesn't that look nice! What if we could get an apartment in a building like that, so clean and modern, on a brand-new street with a brand-new name!"

Grown-ups, thought the child. He didn't understand them. Rows of buildings that were all identical, not a tree in sight, no nothing — no flowers, no bushes, no fruit falling at their feet. And she thought it looked nice! He didn't bother to contradict her, but it was obvious that there was nothing to like, except maybe the field of rubble they were crossing. That looked fairly interesting. There was a whole bunch of wood and stuff lying around. But the apartment buildings on the other side of the field looked so identical that they immediately got lost. The number above the entrance was right, mind you — 4C, it said, right there between the door that said 4B and the one that said 4D — but it turned out that they were on the wrong street. So they had to start all over again, and it took them for ever before they got both the street and the number right.

Majken put a sweaty, determined hand on her dawdling child's arm and pulled him up the first flight of stairs. She was hot, irritable, and nervous, and hoped fervently that Janne would show some manners. He could behave very well when he wanted to. It was just that he never wanted to. "Dearest God in heaven," whispered her brain inside her hot head, "dear God, wherever you are, make sure he doesn't fart or pick his nose or say bad words. Just this once, please?" Majken only prayed when she was desperate, and then mainly for something to do, never thinking to offer anything in return.

Up to the third floor they climbed, along silent staircases, and then they were there, in front of a forbidding brown door with the name "G. Sandberg" on the mail slot. The end of the journey. Majken abruptly terminated her monologue to God as her head filled with ice and her heart exploded in her chest.

"G. Sandberg," she read out loud. "This is it, Jan."

"This is what?"

She pulled her damp fingers through his hair, drying off the sweat more than tidying his hair. Fiddled with herself for a bit, patting her new hairdo, which she could ill afford but which suited her very well. Pulled at her skirt as if she were trying to take it off. Shuffled her feet like a restless horse. Janne silently watched her performance. He was intrigued.

Then she stopped very suddenly and rang the doorbell. A short polite little signal, elegant rather than impolite or pushy. A thin transparent creature with a pointed nose opened the door at once. Janne presumed this to be the grandma, and knew for sure that she had been standing on the other side of the door, her hand ready on the door handle. But she didn't seem the slightest bit ecstatic to see them, which rather bewildered him. When they went to Grandma Persson's she had the door open before they even got up the stairs, and was standing on the landing shouting, "Here comes my boy!"

in a loud voice for all the world to hear.

Not this pointy-nosed one, though. He could feel right away that he would never be her boy. Maybe it was the wrong door? But it wasn't, because the woman asked Majken to please step inside. Her voice was like thin ice, cold and ready to break at the slightest pressure. It had a tone of painful politeness that she seemed to find exhausting. As they followed her into the immaculately clean apartment, Majken noted a hand-tied rya rug on the floor in the hallway. Janne noted a closed door with a noise behind it.

"I hope the child has clean shoes!" quavered the lady. Terror widened her colourless eyes.

The child had spotless shoes, freshly polished and shining proudly on the hand-tied rug, so without further ado they were ushered into the living-room, to the accompaniment of some incoherent mumbling that Janne ignored. The living-room was forbiddingly clean, stuffy, and overdecorated, and he felt completely out of place. The walls were full of framed embroideries. They were mighty ugly, all of old people wearing funny hats in dark gloomy colours. There were china figurines all over the place too. Mostly white-faced ladies in fancy dresses standing on tippy-toe. He didn't like them either. They were the kind that made grown-ups scream if you went near them.

This was not a nice place to be. No toys either, he noticed, but he brightened considerably as he laid eyes on the dining-table by the window. It had been laid with a crisp white tablecloth set with cups and saucers with a pattern of red rosebuds. And best of all, plates full of fancy little pastries, cakes, and cookies galore. Oh yes! None with green marzipan and whipped cream, but what great stuff! This was going to be some party! Maybe this grandma was happy to see them after all. She probably just had a stupid face. He approached the table, his shoulders straight in respect for what his eyes beheld.

The round chocolate-covered ones closest to him were lovely, he knew that because he'd had them before. They had a special creamy filling inside and were all nutty and chewy underneath. He wanted one badly.

"Mum, can I have a chocolate cake?" He delivered his enquiry in a loud voice to make sure he got her attention. "A round one, Mum, like those here," he added, and pointed so there would be no misunderstanding.

Majken blushed, cursed God for never listening, and hushed her son while the pointy-nosed lady excused herself to go and make the coffee. There didn't appear to be any grandpa about, but that didn't really matter when there were tons of cakes around.

Boy, was he going to eat cake! He grabbed a chocolate cake while his mum was looking out the window. By the time she turned around, he had a mouthful of cake and brown sticky spots were forming in the corners of his mouth. She sighed and looked through him as if he'd become invisible. That suited him just fine. He grabbed another morsel, one with slivered almonds and raspberry preserves on top. He turned to his mum but she was still looking right through him. She could obviously hear him, though, because she hissed, "Eat with your goddamn mouth closed," as he shoved another cake in his face.

He didn't remember much of the visit afterwards, apart from the cakes and the strange heavy atmosphere that he refused to be part of. The grown-ups were not having much fun. He recalled his mum's stiff, pale face. It looked like a mask with her eyes peeping through the holes. She didn't even eat anything. All those cakes and she didn't have a single one. That wasn't like her. Halfway through the visit she even stopped telling him to behave. Stopped nagging him about devouring every cake on the table. Oh, those cakes! He would remember them for a long time afterwards.

He would also remember that the pointy-nosed lady, the grandma, made really funny faces. Every so often she looked at him briefly, with an expression of ill-concealed disgust, and every time he dropped crumbs on the rug she frowned in the most hilarious way. Her thin little lips bunched together and hid in the shadow of her nose, and bobbed around for a split second before straightening out to a wobbly line again. He laughed out loud the first time she did it, but that was obviously the wrong way to show appreciation for her fine talent. Instead he regularly dropped large crumbs on the floor and checked her face out of the corner of his eye to see if she'd react. He beamed with delight when she did. It gave him a feeling of power to be able to make her do tricks.

But that was about all he ever remembered.

What he didn't notice, because he wasn't paying attention, was the lady's triumphant expression as she slapped Majken in the face with her frigid stare and said, "Gösta wasn't our real son. He was adopted."

"Adopted?"

"That's right. I wanted him to know that but my husband refused to tell him. I don't know why. After all, it's not the same as having a child of your own, is it? You can never be quite sure of the quality, can you?"

"The what?"

"The *quality*. Gösta turned out to be a great disappointment. Not at all what we expected. We had to put an end to the relationship when he came of age." The pointy-nosed face looked hurt and wronged.

"Is that so?" said Majken in a choked voice. She couldn't decide whether to laugh or cry, but she was overcome by a desire to hit the old woman in the face with a sharp instrument. Knock her teeth down her throat. But she had promised to be polite. "What bad luck for you," she said, trying not to sound sarcastic.

"It was indeed."

"Not good enough quality, eh?" mumbled Majken. She couldn't help herself.

"His problems were of course inherited, there's no doubt about that," declared the older woman in a condescending manner. "There was certainly nothing wrong with the way I brought him up."

"Oh, I'm sure of that."

Deaf to the sarcasm in Majken's voice, the martyr was by now wallowing in memories of how she'd suffered from the inferior infant thrust upon her. She served up a monotonous litany steeped in bitterness, self-righteousness, and self-pity. Svea Sandberg had done her duty, because she was clever and good and knew what was right and proper. She was above the faults and weaknesses that ordinary mortals were riddled with. Nothing was ever her fault. Her self-sacrifice had been impeccable.

It was Gösta, the child they'd been stuck with, who had been no good. Unappreciative. Recidivist. And that wasn't her fault, was it? No, it had nothing to do with her, as she had pointed out to his teachers whenever there was trouble. And there was always trouble. She had done her duty all those long agonizing years, ruining her life and her health for some child of strangers ensconced in her home, expecting to be fed and clothed. But she had never complained because she wasn't that sort of person. She knew her duty.

The D-word again. In later years Majken would sometimes think that it was having heard the D-word one time too many that made her too lenient with Janne.

The simple truth, the Ice Queen went on, was that it was wrong to take on the thankless task of raising other people's offspring. They just didn't appreciate it.

"Then why did you adopt him?" The question was an obvious one. As Majken asked it, she felt a great sense of relief that this frigid bitch was not related to Gösta.

The Ice Queen carefully wet her bloodless lips.

"Well, my husband wanted a son, and I could not carry a child," she explained with curious pride. "It so happens that I am very frail. I always have been delicate and fragile. I had tuberculosis as a child you see; it was a miracle that I survived at all. And that has to be considered, doesn't it? I could not possibly be expected to become pregnant. I'm sure you understand."

"Yeah, for sure." She's probably still a virgin, thought Majken. Too bad she didn't die young; mankind would have benefited from her early demise. Gösta would probably still be alive if his youth had been spared her presence. While she wondered who his real parents had been, she lit a cigarette, just to be a nuisance. She had refrained until then out of politeness, because there were no ashtrays in sight.

"So we got Gösta from the adoption agency." The other woman was still grinding out the replay of her great suffering. "That was in 1925. Thirty-two years ago. In February, just after Prime Minister

Branting died. You wouldn't remember that."

"Right."

"Right. Yes, well," mumbled the older woman. "But all the same. Gösta was an extremely difficult baby. Extremely difficult. Utterly selfish and uncooperative. Whiny and nervous. Always screaming — day and night, day and night, he'd lie there and scream. Week in and week out. Always expecting to be picked up, always so demanding, never thinking about anybody but himself. My headaches almost killed me, I can tell you. I was so very, very tired that you cannot even begin to imagine it. It was difficult to forgive him. Then when he...."

"So you're not interested in your grandchild. Is that what you're trying to tell me?" interrupted Majken. She had been kind, polite, and well-behaved, but there was a limit and she'd just reached it, God forgive her. There was no way she was going to let this insufferable bitch talk like that about Gösta, adopted or not, so she might as well get this over with. "Is that what you're trying to tell me?" she repeated, and lit a new cigarette from the old one before she ground it into the delicate saucer in front of her.

The grey face winced at the sight, then gave Janne a quick, indifferent glance. The woman seemed genuinely astonished that she'd been expected to take an interest in this creature. He was an exceedingly messy, ill-behaved child, and she wasn't even related to him. She made a face as if she'd swallowed poison. Janne had strewn crumbs all over the newly cleaned carpet and now he was standing in the mess, filled to bursting with expensive gooey cakes, contentedly picking his nose. Majken let him. Served the old bitch right. She hoped he'd have a gassy tummy after his cakefest and treat her royal highness to a couple of loud farts. Or some of those silent stinkers he was so good at.

Poor Gösta, she thought. Poor little bugger probably wasn't allowed to fart.

"As I already pointed out, Gösta was adopted, so this child can hardly be considered any responsibility of ours. We are not related, are we?" A sigh escaped her and she cleared her throat. "And if it's money you're after...."

"Money!" hissed Majken. She had a mean hiss. She almost added, "You bitch!" but instead controlled herself and lied gallantly. "You're joking! We won the football stakes a couple of months ago, I'll have you know. A full 25,000 kronor. Didn't you read about it in the paper?" The 25 kronor they'd won looked much better dressed up with three zeroes. "And last year I inherited 50,000 kronor from an aunt in Minnesota, over in America, so we're damn well not after your money!"

The cadaver blushed to an almost human hue, envious and angry, instantly regretting having served coffee and an excess of fancy cakes she could ill afford. Rich relatives in America did not grow on trees.

"Allow me to congratulate you," she managed. It wasn't easy. The only reason she had spent so much on cakes was so this young woman of Gösta's would be too ashamed to ask for money. Assuming that any woman of Gösta's would be capable of shame. And how it turned out that she had had no intention of asking for money! This truly puzzled the old bat and she had to ask, "Why did you come here, then?"

"I thought you were human," explained Majken. Her face was pale and hard as she got up. "I felt sorry for you for being deprived of seeing your only grandchild. But I was wrong, wasn't I? Mind you, Gösta always used to say what a monster you were. That bitch doesn't have a heart in her frigid body, he always said. He was right as usual. Don't worry, we won't bother you again. Mind you, I can't speak for Sigrid."

"Who's Sigrid?" The Ice Queen turned the white of the first snow of winter.

"Oh, Gösta's other woman. The one before me. Didn't you know? She's got eight-year-old triplets. Real evil little brats. Gösta couldn't stand them. But she could use some help. I gave her your address. I hope you don't mind?"

The older woman looked catatonic with fear but didn't utter a word. Hoping she wouldn't drop dead before they were out of there, Majken dragged the stuffed child into the hallway and got their coats.

118

"I want a cake to eat on the streetcar!" hollered the boy, and looked into the living-room, where the old lady was busy brushing crumbs from the tablecloth with trembling hands, the lace trim on the cuffs of her blouse drooping around her wrists. She acted as if they no longer existed.

"I don't like that grandma at all," he informed his mother as she opened the door.

"Me neither," she replied just as loudly, and out she marched, down the stairs, banging her heels on each step.

Janne followed her out to the landing but couldn't help turning around for a last look at the place. The closed door inside the apartment was open now, and in the doorway stood an old man dressed in black, staring at Janne. He held a newspaper in one hand and a pair of glasses in the other. He was very sad, Janne could see that, because his cheeks were wet and his eyes were red.

"There's lots more cake!" Janne called, trying to cheer the old man up. It must have helped because the man smiled. But then he looked sad again and withdrew into his room, quietly closing the door behind him.

"Will you hurry up?" nagged Majken from the floor below.

They walked back through those same heavenly streets with their magic gardens full of secret hiding places, ripe fruit still littering the sidewalks. The shades of green had deepened, the golden glow of the sun had faded, and the shadows fell darker and longer. It was going to be evening soon. They walked fast and didn't talk. As they got to the corner the streetcar clanged past them and disappeared, and they had to wait fifteen minutes for another one. Majken stomped her feet, lit a cigarette, and swore to herself. Janne stomped and swore in sympathy but she didn't pay attention; her thoughts were somewhere else. The street was empty. The wind came in from the sea bringing a salty flavour to the air. It swept through the trees and made them rustle. It was getting chilly. They were all alone.

On the way back to the city centre they once again passed the elegant garden café. All the people had vanished. The white tables and chairs stood empty and the parasols flapped in the wind. A

119

paper napkin was swept along the ground until it got caught around a table leg. On the other side of the street a grey sea lapped the sand with white lace-edged waves.

"They've finished eating," observed Janne. "They've all gone home." Then he remembered what he had meant to tell her. "I saw somebody at that grandma's house."

"Who did you see?"

"There was a grandpa there too. But he slept in. He was very sad. He wasn't happy at all."

"I'm sure he wasn't," commented his mum, and grew two sharp folds between her eyebrows. It made her look old.

"I told him there was some cake left and that cheered him up." He heard his mum mumble something but couldn't catch what it was.

"Don't worry about it, okay?" she said loud enough for him to hear. "It turns out I was wrong about the whole thing. They're not your grandma and grandpa after all. So forget about it, okay?"

"Okay."

It didn't make much sense, but he was used to that. He didn't want that grandma anyway. So he did as he'd been told and forgot all about it, the old woman first and the cakes later. The café by the sea lingered in his mind the longest. The man in black slipped his mind altogether.

He never overheard Grandma Persson and his mum a month later when they talked about old Sandberg's obituary. Nor did he know that in order to "cheer up the goddamn widow", as his mum put it, she sent another letter to Grandma Sandberg, signing it "Sigrid". The letter told "dearest Grandma" all about the triplets desperately wanting to meet her, about the poor tykes all needing special shoes to fit their club-feet. It said that Sigrid was desperately hoping that their beloved new-found grandma would chip in. "On a happier note," she added, "little Laban will be coming home from the Juvenile Detention Centre in another week. Hopefully he will have learned his lesson and will stop lighting fires in other people's homes. Maybe we can come for a visit then and really get to know each other?" Majken put down a girlfriend's address, to which the letter was soon returned labelled "Return to sender — moved", although it had obviously been opened.

After that his mum cheered up considerably.

SVEN

The week that followed the invasion of the delinquents was as un-eventful as ever. There was the odd slam of the door, but by the weekend Sven was less tense and cautiously entertained the daring thought that perhaps life had returned to the unruffled boredom that was his idea of normal.

As if to bless this thought, Saturday dawned radiant, accom-panied by choirs of starlings from a thousand rooftops, as the sun burst forth after a dark and endless winter. Behold springtime, the old pagan gods heralded. And the people, including Sven, heeded their most primitive instincts and beheld. Something started to bubble like champagne in dormant souls. It was one of those crystal-clear spring days that turns the bleakness of winter into a long-forgotten memory. The sun dazzled in the blue sky above; there wasn't a cloud to mar the cerulean perfection. Seagulls swooped manically over the city, shrieking with abandon. Overnight, flower shops and market stalls were bountiful with pussywillows festooned with a profusion of brightly coloured feathers. Fuzzy greens, yel-lows, reds, purples, and blues fluttered in the breeze, announcing that Easter was on its way. It seemed that every single person out and about was carrying a bunch of feather-clad pussywillows. Or a cluster of tulips or daffodils. Bearing these symbols of spring, peo-ple broke into smiles, faces turned towards the sun, cheeks flushed.

Sven succumbed to the spring as well. The same potent pagan instinct made him bounce out of bed and fling open the window. Down in the courtyard a man in rolled-up shirtsleeves was beating a large rug. It was slung over the beam of the carpetholder, hanging in the air like a bright blue flag. He was beating it like a drum, a troll drum echoing between the walls, signalling for everybody to get up and out. Normally Sven would have been upset by the early noise, but today he stood in the window, heeding the signal, feel-ing his lips curve into a smile, glancing heavenward at the white gulls' reckless antics. Such freedom! The mild winds charged unrestrained inland over the southern plain, all the way to the white beaches by the Baltic Sea, waking a dormant nature. By evening bluebells would be shaking their sleepy heads.

Across the yard, the sun was warming the yellow brick façade and a white curtain waved in an open window. Down below, two tots on tricycles circled the man beating the rug, shrieking with excitement, much like the gulls.

"It's spring," said Sven to himself, almost congratulatory. He thought that there would soon be cowslips and anemones in the beech forest. He remembered the beech forest as a giant green cathedral, the sunlight creating great chandeliers in the crowns of the trees. In younger days, back when he still had his bike, he had been out there several times. He had been braver then. He had walked in nature's vast shrine, last year's leaves soft underfoot, listening to the hymns of the birds. It didn't make him religious — he didn't sense the presence of any god — but he did feel closer to some primal source of life. He felt peace there. He was able to gather a few blessed memories.

The last time he had been out there, he had walked in the castle garden at Torup, and afterwards he had had coffee and pastries in the coffee-house in the glade down by the creek. That had been quite a while ago, he realized. It had been crowded that time and he had never gone back. But the air had been fresh, the woods a tender green, the leaves whispering in the wind in a way that softened the hard knot in his chest.

Here in the city the daffodils would soon paint cheerful yellow patterns along the canal. Before long water would cascade in the fountains again, the parks would turn green and there'd be throngs of tulips in the flowerbeds, there'd be sidewalk cafés with striped awnings. The ice-cream stands would open up. Then it would be summer and there'd be people lazing about all over the place.

But for now it was spring, a spring so inebriating that even Sven's inert soul could sense it. It felt like a seed about to germinate. A restlessness gripped him, his toes trembled and twitched.

He was human after all. Leaving the window open, he decided to give in to the sudden urge to join the world, to be part of mankind and walk in the sun.

Where to go, what to do, where to start? A walk through the city, definitely, enjoying the air, the sights of spring. While he hastened through his meticulous ritual of getting ready he planned his route. By the time he finished polishing his shoes he had it perfected down to the last detail. First a bus to the theatre, then a long walk through the city centre eastwards to Caroli City shopping centre, where he would have a bite to eat and do some shopping. After that he'd continue down to Drottningtorget, where he'd buy a bottle of Armagnac at the liquor store. Back home he'd make supper, then a big pot of coffee, have a drink with it, and watch some TV. There was a movie on tonight. A funny one, the paper said. That would be an excellent way to spend the first day of spring. He felt so good that he would have hummed had he known how. Tying a perfect knot in his best tie, he was ready to accept the gift of the new season.

Descending the stairs with steps so light that they were almost weightless, Sven joined the world. The bus came breezing along right on schedule, just to please him on this fine day. It was to his dismay chock-full of old ladies in new spring hats. Little biddies in hats made him nervous, why he didn't know. Why did they always dress so neatly? Why were they always wearing those silly hats? Were they talismans against death? The white, carefully combed curls in front of him were adorned with a light blue, upside-down flowerpot arranged in velvety folds, from which a dove-grey feather stuck out proud and straight.

Two stops later the light blue hat was joined by a round beige one with no fewer than three brown feathers waving flirtatiously at him. Why feathers, he wondered. Did these women belong to some secret society that knew something he didn't? The hats appeared to be old friends, and Sven helped himself to bits of their conversation. Having no conversations of his own, he liked to listen in. It seemed that Ebba and Ellen were out visiting the dead and the dying.

"Well, you see, I'm on my way to the hospital to see Hildur. He had another operation last Thursday. They say he won't be able to talk any more, he'll have to get one of those little machines...."

"Oh dear! How miserable for you! Will you be able to manage?"

"I have to, don't I?"

"I suppose so. Isn't your son living in Stockholm these days?"

"Linköping. Yes, it gets a bit lonely. It's all the waiting, too. You never know what's going to happen next."

Sven thought of Greta Persson. Somewhere in Tomelilla, wearing a new spring hat with a feather at a jaunty angle. The thought softened him and he felt kinder. But it didn't stop him from listening in.

"And you're on your way home?"

"Yes. I thought I'd go out to the cemetery and put some daffodils at the fountain in Memorial Grove. For Ivar. Do you know, he would have turned ninety today."

"You don't say! Oh my! Well, time flies. Soon we'll all be gone."

"Just as well, I say. The world isn't what it used to be."

"It isn't, is it?"

"It isn't. No.... One feels a bit out of place these days."

"Yes...I know what you mean. But that's life, isn't it?"

"Mmm...."

They sighed in a soothing unison that Sven envied; then Ebba patted her friend's shoulder and tottered off the bus, feather atremble. A couple of stops before Sven got off, a swarthy dago sat down next to him and started talking loudly and animatedly in a strange tongue to an equally unrestrained friend standing in the aisle. Both exuded wafts of garlic and God knew what, and their laughter and banter deeply offended both Sven and the surrounding biddies, who all looked at each other, acknowledging that this was what was wrong with Swedish society today and they all knew it.

Having had his fill of human closeness, Sven got off the bus. Straightening his tie, like the man of purpose that he was, he crossed Östra Rönneholmsvägen and started his walk at the corner at

Férsens väg. This was where X marked the spot. He was now on his way.

At the corner of Erik Dahlbergsgatan, a flower shop had spilled its extravaganza of feather-clad pussywillow out onto the sidewalk. Bursts of red and yellow, blue and green. Even purple and pink. He had to smile at it all.

He walked on down the street. Crossing Regementsgatan, whom should he see across the road, heading towards the old city library like a battleship going into combat, but Fat Fransson. She was handsomely clad in a dark blue spring coat. No hat, though. Not yet. Securely anchored to her left hand floated precious Pia. Fat Fransson's face shone almost idiotically with sheer delight at having been chosen to guard this heavenly apparition here on earth. Across the width of Férsens väg Sven could see pride glittering in her eyes, roses of joy blossoming across the expanse of her cheeks. Bless Fat Fransson, he thought. It must be all that love that swells her up like a balloon.

He surprised himself by thinking fleetingly of his mother. Or did the thought sneak up on him when he wasn't paying attention? She'd be the same age as the old ladies on the bus. If she was still alive. He hadn't the slightest idea what had happened to her; he hadn't seen her for more than twenty-five years. Not since he'd left to do his military service, lugging the large suitcase with his clothes and the two paintings. He'd never gone back because by the time he was finished his service she had moved. She too might be tottering around in a new coat and a hat with a feather like an antenna. The thought of Ma in an old lady's hat was strange. Absurd and ludicrous and sad. He sincerely hoped she was dead. That way she was sure to stay in the past. Like Pa. Pa was dead, he knew that, Pa had died in the internment camp. Somebody had planted a knife in his fat gut. Ma had said at the time that the guards had not tried to stop the killer, because Pa was a traitor and a Nazi pig and didn't deserve human compassion. Pa was the lowest of the low. That had been back in the forties, in the fall of 1944. A long time ago. But Pa was dead, thank God, safe in the past where he belonged.

Sven hastily banished any further thoughts of his family.

Enough of that, he said to himself; the sun is shining, the birds are singing. Fat Fransson disappeared down the steps to the library garden. Her little Pia skipped beside her, golden curls flying about her head, shiny red shoes adorning her perfect tiny feet, matching her new red coat. Sven thought he heard her singing as she jumped down the steps in her shiny shoes, a bell-like tinkle on the wind.

Crossing the bridge, he stopped and gazed down at the water in the canal. An empty Tuborg beer can was merrily bobbing along, keeping company with what looked like a jellyfish but turned out to be a condom. He blushed. An old man, properly soused despite the early hour, came stumbling by. He too was singing, like a lusty, tone-deaf old troll. Stopping beside Sven, he greeted him like a long-lost brother. He was about to throw a smelly arm around his shoulders when Sven fled. He did not feel *that* pagan.

Turning from Slottsgatan onto Stora Nygatan, he noticed tender green buds on the trees in the old graveyard. Daffodils and crocuses spilled their colour over the graves under the trees. Oh yes, it was spring all right! Even the long dead were celebrating. He would have liked to unbutton his coat, let it flap nonchalant and free in the wind, but he felt too timid. People might think he was about to start undressing in the middle of the road like some pervert.

He crossed the street and disappeared into the shady narrow avenues of the old quarter, down Generalsgatan to the winding Ostindiefararegatan, dipped down Tegelgårdsgatan to Larochegatan and was beginning to feel lost when he found himself in the sun again on the worn cobblestones of Lilla Torg market square. Here the Saturday commerce was in full swing. Outdoor market tables had sprouted in the sun. Burghers intent on parting with their money flowed in and out of the market hall. Outside the entrance some leather-clad faggot held a bag under the nose of a long-nosed friend with a shaved head and squealed, "Doesn't that tea smell just diviiiine!" Christ, thought Sven. As far as he'd heard, real men didn't drink tea.

A gaggle of strange creatures with green, red, and purple hair hovered by the telephone booths. Their tattered attire was held together, more or less, by spikes, nails, and chains. He gave them a wide berth. With their colourful hair they looked a bit like walking pussywillows, but they didn't seem to be a cheerful lot. If you were going to strut around like that, you should at least look as though you were having fun, reflected Sven as he glanced at them. They stood there like a flock of tropical birds on long gangly legs under the mild blue Swedish sky, huddling together in the lapping sea of middle-class values that would eventually claim them.

Sven ventured into the market hall. He didn't go there often, but was always intrigued by the exotic displays of goods. Shark meat and fillet of antelope. Fruit with spikes or reptile scales. Vegetables he would not be able to name if his life depended on it. Hand-dipped champagne truffles. Now, they looked good! He was sorely tempted by the liver pâtés, but dared not step too close in case a salesperson approached him. They looked so authoritarian in their starched, striped aprons, and there were too many pâtés to choose from, with too many French names he couldn't pronounce. Shopping in this paradise of the palate, you had to know your stuff. This was for experts. Most people he saw had shopping lists that....

Ooops!

Who was that standing by the fish counter down the aisle but young Mrs. Lundwall from the office! Expertly pointing a prim finger at a pink mountain of shrimp. What else? Her expression clearly indicated that she was doing the salesperson a stupendous favour by deigning to buy her half-kilo of crustaceans from him. No doubt who was in charge there. And that must be her very own Kent standing by her side like a faithful dog. Tall and skinny and as bland as his missus. He had a splash of freckles across his nose and looked like a friendly sort of guy. Sven made himself scarce at once, before Mrs. L. discovered him. Never knowing what to say to people, he was not one for introductions. Besides, he had no desire to exchange tips on dandruff control.

Fleeing the hall, he scuttled across the square, past the tropical birds, and down Skomakaregatan. He slowed down and turned left onto Södergatan towards Stortorget, past City Hall, where he slunk around the corner like a well-dressed thief. Not until he reached St. Petri Church did he feel safe again. On a whim, and hot from his successful escape, he entered the church and timidly slid into a pew at the very back. The silence and cool air were soothing and he let himself get lost for a while, fairly confident that Mrs. L. wouldn't be taking her shrimp to church.

The church was, as usual, nearly empty. An old woman at the front was praying. No fancy hat, he noticed. Maybe she was praying for one. In a pew in the centre sat a young man in a green sweater, staring at Jesus on the cross. Two older men walked slowly around the periphery, one giving the other a guided tour. When they passed behind Sven he heard them speak German, one of them with a strong Swedish accent. After a while a middle-aged woman burst into the church, a large bag slung over her shoulder. Striding purposefully up the centre aisle, her heels thudding on the stone floor, she stopped, lit a candle, and stared at it for several seconds, lost in thought. As unexpectedly as she'd entered, she turned and strode out again. She seemed to know exactly what she was doing and why, to know exactly where she was going next. Sven envied her that certainty and confidence. He decided to leave too, inspired by her resolute stride. Before he left, he looked up at the highest point of the ceiling, as if to check if there was a God looking down. There wasn't.

Sven left for more mundane matters.

Now there were only a few steps left on his program: having a bite to eat, and shopping for bread, salami, and coffee at Malmborg's supermarket. The mall was crowded, even more than usual on Saturday afternoons, which were usually bad enough. A mass of humanity was pushing and jostling, surging forward. He knew right away that he wouldn't be able to handle it, and decided just to shop and go home. Grab some pork chops or something else that was easy to fry up, a can of potatoes to heat. He had run out of steam, and once again felt a strong need for the solitude of his home. Concentrating on patience, hanging onto it tooth and nail, trying to breathe slowly, he was eventually released from the imprisonment of the nearly immobile queue at the cash register. He left with a trembling sigh of relief, still more or less sane. Carrying his bag past the liquor store at Drottningtorget, he looked in at the line-ups and fled onwards past Schougen's Bridge, almost home again. Turning the corner onto his own street, he slowed down and relaxed. He'd done it. He'd had his long walk through the spring day, he'd looked at this, he'd observed that. He had sat in a church, he had seen Fat Fransson and Pia, escaped Mrs. L., and done a big shopping. Now it was time for his reward. Fresh coffee and a bun. He had splurged and bought cinnamon buns because he was so pleased with himself.

Back up on the fourth floor, he heard voices coming from the Perssons' hallway. He kept thinking of it as the Perssons' apartment because it still said "Persson" on the mail slot. Those stupid people probably couldn't read. Putting his bag down, he hurried to get out his key. He had not the slightest desire to encounter the intruders. Not that he had laid eyes on them all week, but the day before, when he had come home from work, their door had been wide open. Anybody could have walked right in. Now, as he unlocked his door, he heard the young swine shout, "Where the fuck is my green T-shirt?" The language that came out of that mouth — it was deplorable. And raucous and loutish, but that was to be expected. Sven slammed his door, making sure it banged loudly, showing who was who around here.

Once again he was burdened by the feeling that things were not the same since these people had moved in. Deep inside he felt his privacy eroding; he felt the challenge of their indifference, their lack of need for such privacy. He didn't understand their alien ways. He wanted respect, he deserved it. Not only had he been there first, but he was older. And he'd given them two lightbulbs. They owed him. Not that he would let it ruin his evening, absolutely not. But it was on his mind as he put the kettle on and unpacked his groceries. There was something in the air that the burst of spring could not hide.

Later that evening, just as he lowered his tired butt into his comfy chair, there was an ear-splitting explosion outside his door. Somebody was shooting! Paler than death, he fell backwards into the chair, immobilized by the sheer terror of what would follow. He dared not breathe. Or think. It was as if the explosion had momentarily obliterated him, leaving a cardboard effigy in the old chair to fool whatever enemy was approaching. For ever he sat there, and eventually sounds started to seep into his cardboard ears. Gradually he returned to life. The sounds turned out to be screams followed by a sulphurous litany out on the landing. Were they killing each other?

"Fucking asshole! He dropped my bottle of vino! It fucking exploded! You stupid prick!" It was an unknown young voice, shrill with indignation and vivid in its suffering.

"Cheap piss anyway," declared a more cheerful individual. "Even the bottle is substandard quality!" Other voices laughed and whinnied. They echoed down the stairwell.

"Substandard quality! You fucking cheap shithead snob! I didn't see you bring any wine!"

"I drank it before I got here to make sure I wouldn't drop it."

They all neighed and snorted like a herd of raunchy horses; then the loud voice of the punk next door announced that Lillan would clean up the mess and that nobody was to freak out because "My dear old buddies, it's party time!" A large group of what could only be Indian braves greeted this announcement with war whoops and a stomping war dance.

Sven imagined war-paint and tomahawks as he quietly retreated into shock, which his survival instinct deemed the safest place to huddle. But thumping music and loud voices caught up with him even in that state, and he felt as if he were sitting exposed and naked, with no walls surrounding his fort, as war-painted punks did a ceremonial dance before they scalped him and stole his cinnamon buns.

This was the end.

As darkness fell, he acknowledged that he was cowering alone, that the walls of the fort were still standing and it was probably safe to go into the kitchen and get the Armagnac. He got up very slowly, defeatism weighing heavy, his breathing laboured. The noise was louder in the kitchen. The baby was crying and somebody was laughing like a hyena. Another horde came charging up the stairs and leaned on the Perssons' doorbell. More tribal shrieks greeted the newcomers. Somebody burst into song. A door slammed.

Sven returned to his chair and poured himself a generous glass of Armagnac. Sat looking out at the darkening evening sky and wondered what had happened to the beautiful spring day. A day so benign, so full of promises. He stared at the walls and felt locked in a box. His fort was standing but he was trapped. He looked for refuge where he usually found it — in his two paintings — wanting desperately to run down that road and disappear, or to put on rubber boots and a raincoat and go splashing at the edge of the river, the cleansing wind in his face. To be embraced by silence.

Those young criminals were having a party in the Perssons' apartment, where Arvid Persson had sat quietly waiting for death. They were in there blaspheming, shouting, laughing, and drinking. Taking drugs, more than likely. Showing no respect. Sven had never been to a party, apart from the ones Ma and Pa used to have when he was little. At least Ma and Pa had never played noisy music, though they would often sing or yell all night and keep him awake. Well, history was repeating itself. He heard the baby screaming. It sounded upset and frightened. Then he heard another tribe of yahoos thumping up the stairwell. How many people were they going to crowd into that place?

He tiptoed out into his front hall fuelled by masochistic energy and heard an older, deeper, male voice, then a female voice squealing like a stuck pig. Somebody banged violently on the Perssons' door. The door opened and a tidal wave of noise spilled out. Sven took a step backwards.

"Is this the bacchanal where plentiful wine and reverent and willing women are ready to rejoice and celebrate the prodigal arrival of the great god Pan?" It was the deep male voice holding forth.

"What the fuck's he talking about?"

"Come on in, Pan! Get pissed! Get fucked! Get fucking pissed!"

"That's no god, that's Vicke! Hey, Vicke, my man!"

"Greetings, my pimply pagan pal!"

Sven's eyes popped. Were they having one of those orgies in there? Having sex in front of the baby? Should he call the police? What would he tell them — my neighbours are having an orgy, I think? Were orgies legal? What exactly did you do at an orgy? What should he do about it? Damned if he knew. He dragged himself back to his chair, knowing full well that he'd do nothing, the din from next door mocking him. He sat down, his heart beating somewhere up in his throat. If he wasn't careful he might spit it out. He thought about the saintly Greta Persson and what she would think if she knew what was going on in her tidy home.

Oh, the injustice of it all! He was frightened and he was angry. No, more than that, he was absolutely furious. Such exhausting emotions when you lacked the courage to act. After a while he gathered enough wits to get up and switch on the TV, turning the sound up and staring at some program as incredibly and stupefyingly boring as only Swedish TV can be. In the free world, at any rate; he'd read somewhere that they actually had worse programs in Albania, but that was no consolation. Emptying his glass, he refilled it to the brim and took a gulp, determined to relax, to get a little drunk. But it was hard work, he wasn't sure he was up to it. There was supposed to be that funny movie on later, maybe that would cheer him up. He'd watch it and have another large drink.

Every so often there were voices booming and echoing outside his door. Drunk, boisterous, and uninhibited voices. At one point he heard a girl's clear voice singing what sounded like a hymn, all the way up the stairs. What strange people! And the music was louder than ever. He could feel the floor vibrating and hear the windows rattling. Absolutely insane! It shouldn't be allowed! Sven became so overwhelmed with dismay and frustration that he nearly burst into tears. He took another tour through the hall, too agitated to sit still. There was no sound coming from the baby any more, just thumping music, laughter, and shrieks. Ma used to shriek like that when she was pissed. A shrill sound that could cut glass. He hated it.

He trotted back to his chair. Poured some more Armagnac, started to watch the movie while wondering listlessly what it was all about. The stupid bastards weren't speaking Swedish, were they, and he had trouble reading the subtitles. The noise from next door surrounded him like a sticky mist. It was starting to seep into his head and cloud his vision. And surely it was getting louder? He had trouble breathing, his chest hurt. The room seemed foggy. Trying to take a deep breath, he wished for a brief moment that there were somebody he could call, somebody he could complain to. Somebody who would come over and do something. Or console him and tell him what to do. Somebody who would be happy to hear from him, who would say, "Why don't you come on over and spend the night here instead, we'd love to have you!" Then maybe he wouldn't feel so trapped.

Eventually he surrendered, hoisted the white flag, and unfolded the sofa-bed. Climbed in and lay there on a raft in a noisy sea, ever alert. At two-thirty in the morning, as the merry-making got more and more unrestrained, he was convinced that he would never again be allowed to sleep. They would party through all eternity. Maybe he had died and gone to hell, punished for God knows what. No doubt for being the offspring of a Nazi; things like that caught up with you. He was just getting out of bed to go for a pee when he heard that girl's voice again, singing another hymn in a clear soprano. Two-thirty in the morning! Two-thirty! He went off to listen at the door once more, as there was nothing else to do. He was prepared for anything now that the boundaries of the civilized world had been torn down and all rules abandoned, now that anarchy reigned. The song was quickly interrupted by a suggestive male voice.

"Ah, Mam'selle Hansson, lovely shepherdess! You trill like an angel!"

"I thank you, kind Victor."

"What other talents does the lovely shepherdess possess?"

"Ooooh! My talents are many, kind sir! Mostly I hide them."

"Oh, where, fairest maiden?"

"Ooooh! Have a peek under my skirt!"

"No undies! Oh, such hidden delights! What say, oh fairest one, we skip downstairs and fornicate in the sandbox, under the glittering stars of heaven?"

"What the hell, Vicke, what the hell?"

"That a girl!"

Eager feet galloped down the stairs. Rigid with shock, Sven managed to rush to the living-room window that overlooked the courtyard. Surely they weren't going to...? But sure enough, they appeared below, ghostlike in the moonlight. It looked as if she was leading him by the....oh my God! She was! She really was! Sven had to open the window furtively to get a better view; this was beyond belief! Murmurs and giggles from the sandbox floated weightless on the night breeze as the man stepped out of his pants and fell upon the fair maiden, his white butt a reflection of the moon.

They were doing it in the sandbox! They were actually doing it! Sven's heart went into overdrive. He had a painful erection, and his eyes were glued to the spectacle below. Then, from the Persson's window, a voice burst into the night like fireworks.

"Look at that! Vicke's fucking Lena in the sandbox!" A second later a choir of voices spilled an encouraging chant into the court-yard. Sven hid discreetly behind a curtain.

"Keep on fucking! Keep on fucking! Keep on fucking!" The cheering spectators exploded into helpless laughter as the lovers in the sandbox waved happily without interrupting the more imme-diate task at hand.

"That bitch will fuck anybody," declared a female voice, and at that precise moment four policemen burst into the courtyard and broke up the free show. It was unclear if the lovers had finished or not. The guy named Vicke got up, turned his back to the police, and wiggled his scrawny butt suggestively as he pulled up his pants. One of the policemen kicked him and he stumbled over his pants and fell headlong into the sandbox. Meanwhile the young hussy calmly climbed out of the sandbox, brushed sand from her behind, and let the hem of her crimson skirt fall languidly to her ankles. She smiled beatifically at the men in uniform and remarked on what a lovely night it was.

Next door somebody became frantic, "Hide the shit! Don't flush it, pleeeeease! Oh noooo!" This was followed by the sound of many feet stampeding out the door. Somewhere in the building a clock chimed three times. A few minutes later calm descended and there was once again silence in the world — that is, apart from a small child crying. Sven was still too upset, too shocked and too excited, too tumultuously bewildered to care. He lay in bed hopelessly awake, the image of the two going at it in the sand glued to his incredulous eyeballs. For the moment, at least, the vision blocked out the fact that tonight was the end of life as he had known it.

It was twenty past eleven on Sunday morning when he woke up, astonished to realize that he had actually slept. He must have slept, he reasoned; otherwise what could he have woken up from? Remnants of the previous night hung like stale smoke in his head. Fear and anxiety had left an acrid taste in his mouth. The sky hung heavy over the city in a shade of dirty dishwater. As if yesterday's spring extravaganza had been just a tease, a badly timed April Fool's joke designed to lull him into a false sense of security. To make him feel stupid. Or maybe he never had gone for a walk, because the sun never had shone; maybe he had dreamed it all while he slept.

He got up and peeked down into the courtyard. It lay deserted now with not a trace of what had taken place. No imprint of a bare butt in the sand, no used condom carelessly hurled aside for some little kid to find. Nothing. It was thoroughly disappointing. How can you trust your memory if there is no proof of what you remember? The desolate Sunday silence reigned supreme, taunting him. The whole human race could have perished overnight, for all he knew. Well, it was Sunday, and Sunday was dismal no matter what.

Dragging his traumatized husk to the kitchen, he found comfort in the ritual of making coffee. Very strong, very black coffee with lots of sugar. It was nearly lunch time so he made some sandwiches too. With salami, as if everything were normal. "A man has to eat," he said out loud, making himself jump. He'd never talked out loud in his life.

Not a peep from next door, though.

Sven sat there like a stick figure, slurping his coffee, mechanically chewing his sandwiches, his shoulders drooping in his blue striped bathrobe. He was tired and emotionally drained, but somewhere in his head a hitherto unknown part of his brain was buzzing. He ignored it and turned on the transistor radio that usually sat unused on the kitchen table, feeling a need to hear a human voice, but even that was no consolation. His brain had gained at least twenty kilos overnight and weighed his head down something awful. Inside his distended skull he saw a replay of the scene in the sandbox. The two of them humping away with total abandon, waving to their audience. But the image had ceased to excite him; now he felt insulted. And somehow exposed, which made no sense. He hadn't been the one with his bare ass bobbing up and down in the sand. All the same, he did feel exposed. Or maybe "vulnerable" was a better word. He was still safe behind his locked door, the walls were still standing around him, but they seemed thinner. He had a vision of them growing transparent. Soon the delinquents next door would be able to see him sitting there, and they would jeer and throw things at him. Broken wine bottles and used condoms, the filthy detritus of their miserable lives.

There was no turning the clock back.

He missed the Perssons so much it hurt, even though he had never known them. They had been such good people. He missed their gentleness and kindness. He had been safe with them. That was what he mourned, his safety. When you were safe you didn't

140

have to stand eye to eye with your cowardice and your humiliating inability to act.

And of the quarter-million people in the city — of all the crooks and criminals, nutcases and lunatics, drug addicts, rapists, and murderers, foreigners and other rabble — of all the teeming mess of humanity, why had he, Sven, respectable citizen, been singled out to have this riff-raff living next door? Shouldn't such rabble live among their own? There must be some slums left somewhere. Or maybe they'd all been torn down, and all the outcasts had received fat government hand-outs to go and live among hardworking, tax-paying, respectable people. Some perverse kind of integration process. Go and live among the people who pay the taxes that provide for you, go and live there and ruin their lives.

Sven shook his gloomy head, wobbling his heavy brain, trembling with anger at the injustice of it all. Anger was good, though; anger helped loose the knot of cringing fear that tightened even more if he gave it a glimmer of recognition. It could easily cripple him. He poured another cup of coffee; it was a normal thing to do, and he desperately wanted to be normal. While he did so the sun came out. The world lit up briefly, but a minute later the light was gone and it looked like rain. Only to be expected. Why would it be a nice day? Hell, that would be expecting too much. After all, it was Sunday.

He lit a cigarette that tasted like an ancient sock stuffed with dung, and filled his empty head with smoke. It never did rain. Afterwards he wished it had.

When he was pouring his third cup of coffee, his subconscious, uninvited as always, decided to send him an old memory to reflect on. It took him a while to recognize as his the recollection of a Christmas Eve a lifetime ago. He couldn't have been more than five. Such a small child. Yes, the memory was his, but as he scrutinized it from several different angles he felt strongly that he didn't know the child as himself. This child had loved Christmas so much, a long, long time ago. And now, out of nowhere, crystal-clear pictures from across the decades started to flash on the screen of his mind. He could smell the smells too if he tried.

There were heaps of brown cabbage and ham for dinner. Little tasty meatballs, almost crunchy on the outside (now, how could he remember that?), those little sausages he was so crazy about, and several kinds of pickled herring. There was black bread, two kinds of white bread, and three kinds of crispbread. And rice porridge, of course. Pa must have made a lot of money as a bricklayer in those days. It was before the war, before he got involved with the Nazis. Though who knew what other scams Pa had been into?

Wherever it came from, whoever paid for it, there was lots of lovely food to eat. Except for *lutfisk* — that was a no-no. "We're having none of that soapy slime on my table," Pa said every Christmas. Ma's complaint was equally ritual: she liked *lutfisk*, it was the right thing to have, it belonged on the Christmas table, with lovely thick sauce made with grainy mustard. It was tradition and therefore Christmas wasn't quite the same without it, said Ma, but like a good wife she gave in, for it was messy to prepare and you got your hands all smelly. Sven didn't care, he didn't like it either.

Around the table, celebrating Christmas with them, sat Asta and Kjell. Always Asta and Kjell. There were some other people as well that year, but he couldn't remember who. Two blonde women and a man in a black suit. He didn't remember the details of the early part of the evening very well, except that he ate until he got stomach cramps and then kept eating anyway, making the most of the opportunity. After dinner they doled out presents. He got a box with twelve crayons and a big drawing pad, some chocolate, and a new shirt. The crayons were the best. He'd wanted some for a long time.

They must have had a Christmas tree, Ma was too sentimental and traditional to do without one. She might sacrifice the *lutfisk* but there would have been a tree for sure. No Santa Claus, how-

ever. While Pa was the right shape for that role, he had no intention of strutting around in a dumb hat with a bunch of cotton
stuck on his face. Besides, the kid was too old to fall for that crap.
He looked like such a clever little fucker in his glasses, he was probably too smart, so why bother?

"Am I right, kid, or what? You don't believe in that shit, do
you?"

"No."

"Too smart, eh?"

"Yes."

"See! What'd I tell you? He doesn't believe in it!"

While Sven remembered that long-ago evening, his subconscious shoved forth another bit of dubious memorabilia: here, what
about this then? And he remembered that that was the year Ma got
a fancy dressing-gown with ruffled lace trim. It was a gift from Pa.
She tried it on and it aroused much admiration, all tied up with a
string of obscene comments. Pa and Kjell yelped and howled like
wolves in heat. At the time Sven didn't understand why, but it was
something grown men did in certain situations. All the raunchy
revelry over this dressing-gown reminded Kjell of his good old days
as a sailor, and he launched into stories that were greeted with
yowls of jubilation, especially from Pa. Stories that Sven didn't comprehend, but that were obviously gut-splittingly hilarious. Even
Asta had a coughing fit and went all googly-eyed and red in the
face, as if she was about to croak.

It must have been around that time that Sven went to bed,
taking his crayons and his drawing pad. What he remembered clearly
was waking up in the middle of the night to find the light still on
in the bedroom. His parents' pull-out bed was untouched so they
must still have been up, although none of the usual noise could be
heard from the other room. It was undoubtedly very late. They
had probably passed out. Sven had woken up because he had stomach cramps and badly needed to fart but couldn't. He grunted a
bit, then decided to draw a picture with his beautiful new crayons.
Something Christmassy and pretty. The apartment smelled like
Christmas, whiffs of brown cabbage and ham, candles and Christ-

mas tree, so he started to draw a Christmas tree. That was right, that was it! He could still see it quite distinctly in his mind's eye. It was a nice green Christmas tree with pointed branches. How puzzling that he could remember something like that so many years later! A Christmas tree with an angel on top. The angel was almost as big as the tree, with lots of yellow angel hair, all curly, and big eyes, like a cow almost, and a halo around her head. The halo was the same colour as her hair because there was only one shade of yellow crayon, and a halo had to be yellow and so did angel hair, according to the rules of the child he was then.

Treading cautiously along the path of this memory, he could almost feel how pleased he had been with his work of art. Proud. No point showing it to anybody, though, so he carefully put the pad away under his pillow.

How odd that he should remember that old drawing. Such a trivial detail. A tree dotted with red and blue balls, and a candle on the tip of each branch. Yes, he could recollect the candles; they too had little golden haloes.

He'd tucked the pad away under the pillow, and was ready to crawl under the blanket, only to discover that he badly had to go to the toilet. The unheated toilet was out on the landing so he put on his socks and a cardigan. The bedroom was closest to the front door so he didn't have to pass the living-room. They would all be completely drunk that late and wouldn't notice him anyway. But whatever they were doing, conscious or not, they wouldn't be a pretty sight.

After sitting on the icy toilet seat until his butt turned blue, farting with relish, he felt much better. He decided that he now had room for some leftover meatballs and sausages. He tippy-toed back through the cold hallway and stopped by the living-room door, where the tile stove spread an irresistible warmth. Too nosy not to peek inside, he saw Pa snoring his face off on the couch, his face as reddish purple as the beet salad they'd eaten earlier, food stains on his shirt and unbuttoned fly. A true gentleman. Somebody had thrown Asta, the marionette, on the table by the window. One arm hung lifelessly over the edge, the other was curled beside her in an overflowing ashtray. He noticed a bowl of nuts beside the ashtray and wondered where it had come from. It hadn't been there earlier. That made him a bit upset because he was very fond of nuts.

Ma, the pin-up girl, was awake. She was dancing, undulating silently as if under water in her flounced and frilly dressing-gown. It was of shiny baby-blue material, almost see-through, he noticed with surprise. Well, it was a gift from Pa, and Pa knew how to dress a lady, he'd said so when she'd opened the gift. Then he noticed Kjell sitting in the armchair opposite the sofa, staring hollow-eyed at Ma's solo performance, ogling her with the single-minded stubbornness of a half-wit.

"Eh, Edith," he babbled, almost incoherent. "Eh, come on, eh!? Show 'em to me, eh! Just once? Come on! Is Christmas, for fuck's sake!"

And Edith smiled foggily and with supreme confidence, lost in a dream. Sven stood there silently, knowing full well that he shouldn't be there, that he ought to be in bed, asleep, out of the way. Yet he remained riveted to the spot, fascinated by a world where he didn't belong, staring as Edith pushed a blonde curl from a round cheek and smiled with a mouth whose red lipstick had smeared down to her chin. She looked hollow-eyed and unreal, almost as transparent as her new gown.

"Pretty snazzy with this lace and all," she teased, in a dull sort of voice. She was a baby-blue nylon goddess twirling carefully on unsteady legs, letting her breasts sway under the lace, turning herself on. Sven thought she seemed even more a stranger than usual.

"Jeeesus Christ, Edith, give me a break! Show me your tits!" Kjell's glassy stare had been tenaciously glued to Edith's lacy front.

Curiously Sven watched Edith's dreamy smile spread across her face like an oilspill, as if she'd suddenly noticed that it was Clark Gable sitting there and not boring old Kjell. She slowly undid the pearly buttons amid the lace and bent over Kjell. Like a royal princess offering a jewel-encrusted hand to be humbly kissed. Edith, naked under her nylon splendour, offered her large breasts — all she had that was of any value.

Kjell, the faithful dog, tried to sit pretty, but he got carried away and started to moon and whimper and go on in the strangest way. Her royal highness indulged in a smile, benevolent and supreme, observing the antics of her eager lapdog, disregarding the contempt she felt, glorying in what she perceived to be her carnal power.

It was all beyond the comprehension of the child in the shadow of the doorway. This was a one-act play that he neither enjoyed nor understood. He was unsure about what was taking place, but it made him thoroughly ill at ease, the way he felt when he watched Pa pick his nose in public. If he was to draw a picture of that scene with his new crayons, he decided, he would have to mix all the pretty colours into a smelly shade of ugly. Except for Ma's swelling breasts — those he would colour a glaring piggy pink. Like two lumps of sugar candy. Huge lumps that dominated the picture, but ugly and fat. He would draw Kjell as a small dog with a pointed nose. He'd have straggly whiskers that trembled as he made funny little animal noises. Or perhaps a mouse with wavy hair, although he wasn't sure how a mouse would look with wavy hair. Not even Kjell looked all that great with greasy waves all over his head. He'd look good with whiskers, though. And in the background there would be a bunch of arms and legs in a pile, like people who had fallen apart.

But Sven the artist was never to be. He sneaked silently back to bed and fumbled under the pillow for his drawing pad, his stomach hurting again. He never did bother with the meatballs.

How astounding that he should remember all that now, recalling the picture he never drew even more vividly than the scene he witnessed — how he would have mixed the colours, and the shade of grey, like ashes.

What he could not for the life of him remember was what had happened to that drawing pad. He couldn't bring to mind any picture he had drawn — not a single one — apart from the grand green Christmas tree with the angel and the burning candles and their haloes of golden light.

By late afternoon the solitary confinement had Sven in a strangle-hold and he was ready to climb the walls. He'd finished his fifth cup of lukewarm coffee, having moved to the living-room, where he sat staring morosely at his two paintings. Both landscapes were letting him down, shutting him out, refusing to give relief. He was on his own with nowhere to hide.

Maybe that was what did it, or perhaps it was some inexplica-ble impulse, an unripe caprice sprouting in the cracks where the light was reaching now that he was coming unglued. Whatever it was, he got up as if in charge and, ignoring his customary meticu-lous ablutions, dressed without washing or shaving, put on his coat, and said to himself, "I have to get out!" Decisively, just like that. Didn't even brush his teeth. To hell with it, he thought. Didn't put on a tie either, just grabbed the wrinkled shirt and pants that he hadn't hung up before going to bed. There had been no point, had there? When world order crumbles into anarchy and madness and you're standing in the rubble you feel pretty foolish hanging up your pants so they won't get creased. Sven had rebelled before go-ing to bed, and he was still rebelling, striding out and slamming the door behind him. He was angry, but still cowardly enough that he dashed down the stairs to avoid encountering the delinquents, in case they thought he was the one who had called the police. That filth had ruined his life and, as well as his rising anger, he felt utter dejection. He reached the street and started down the wind-swept sidewalk. There wasn't another human being in sight. He took that personally.

He thought about how he had always lived a life that was pre-dictable and uneventful, carefully avoiding the word "dull". A grey existence, but a tasteful grey, he'd always thought. The discreet grey of a good suit. His had been a garrisoned and uninvolved exist-ence. Now that way of life was gone and he wanted it back. It was a good thing he had not known how quickly it could be wiped out, or he would have lived in fear. As he did now that the walls of his fort had turned to brittle glass. He shuffled along the deserted street, a mean wind slapping his face. He took that personally too.

When he arrived at Drottningtorget he stopped, momentarily stunned as he glanced at his feet. There he was, plodding around downtown in his old checked felt slippers. Normally he would have dropped dead on the spot, but at this moment the lapse just seemed to confirm the breakdown of the rules and standards that had been the bricks and mortar of civilized society. It was like being beaten to a pulp, he guessed — towards the end you didn't really feel it any more.

Across the square, over the old market hall, the clouds hung ragged and dirty. Still it didn't rain. The market hall was a museum now. Even Drottningtorget was not what it had once been. He could remember when there had been markets there. He remembered horses drinking from long wooden troughs outside the hall, or standing with bags of oats tied to their muzzles. The smell of horse manure, exotic in the concrete jungle. Nothing was what it had been, nothing was what it ought to be. He'd been betrayed. What had happened last night, he knew deep inside, was not an isolated incident, it was the future. It was his fate, it had finally found him. The game had been cancelled, the cards reshuffled, and he'd been dealt a useless hand. No wonder Pa hated losing a card game.

Sven realized all of a sudden that he was starving, and in his slippers he resolutely shuffled across the street to the hot dog stand, where he bought a large fried sausage, mashed potatoes with onions, ketchup, and double pickles. The ravenous hunger of a condemned man. Food in hand, he strode to the nearest bench and without even thinking about it plopped himself down beside two older gentlemen presiding there. Another first for Sven, parking himself on a bench with strangers and devouring a hot dog, all at the same time. Sitting unabashed beside strangers who were, as a quick glance now confirmed, not quite respectable and not quite sober. Maybe Sven didn't notice; maybe he failed to see clearly the two ageing drunks, both wearing suits, one wearing a striped tie. The suits were neither new nor clean, and both had buttons missing. Closer inspection would have revealed little holes and rips here and there. The striped tie adorning one of the men had been used as a napkin for some time. Yet Sven, a stickler for detail under normal circumstances, didn't notice. A sensitive nose would have picked up a not very pleasant smell, but Sven's nose was out of order. The man closest to him, the one without the tie, had a hole in his left shoe where the sole had come loose. His big toe, obscenely naked, stuck out at a jaunty angle. Its black-rimmed nail badly needed trimming. But being shod in slippers, Sven was not about to scrutinize footwear. Besides, he was in a frame of mind where such things had temporarily lost their significance. His set of moral values, a long and tedious list, was folded and stuck in his back pocket.

So there he sat, amazed at the ease with which he did so, perversely enjoying himself. The two drunks must have sensed it. They both glanced sideways at him and greeted him with imperceptibly raised eyebrows, as if he were a distant acquaintance they thought they ought to recognize. The man next to him gazed curiously at Sven's slippers and gaily wiggled his unmanicured toe. Nobody said anything, not at first. Sven chewed his food in a companionship that he would have abhorred only yesterday. After a while the two boozers decided that he was harmless and recommenced their gruff conversation, like old dogs barking at each other. It sounded as if they were having an argument, but it soon became obvious that this was their normal mode of communication.

"Damn right you are," muttered the one at the far end of the bench as he ground his cigarette butt to dust under a dirty shoe. "Damn right."

"Oh yeah!" growled his friend. "And at our age it's worse! It ain't fair. Not a goddamn place to go on a Sunday."

"Or any other time."

"You said it. If you don't want to play frigging bingo with a buncha old bats."

"Bats in hats."

"Damn right you are."

"Damn right."

"You said it."

A short but meaningful silence descended after this outburst. Sven scraped up the last bit of pickle and cold mashed potato with his plastic fork and greedily gulped it as the old lads started up again.

"I really miss the beerhall that used to be over there," sighed one.

"Me too." The other belched in profound agreement.

"Yeah."

"Yeah."

"Yeah. Say, remember that beerhall down on Östra Förstadsgatan, halfway to Värnhemstorget?"

"Yeah! I remember!"

"They had a restaurant in front. I used to go there all the time. But, you know, in the back mostly."

"Yeah. Me too. Have a beer. Sit and talk for a while."

"Yeah! No harm in that."

"Yeah. It was real nice."

"Yeah."

"They had good food too."

"Damn right they did."

"Yeah."

"I sometimes ate dinner there," declared Sven without warning. His voice was loud and clear and he blushed when he heard himself, but he didn't regret having opened his mouth.

The two old regulars stared at him. Not in an unfriendly way, just a bit surprised. The naked toe was wiggling again. Sven blazed forward.

"They knew how to cook a pork chop at that place," he explained, as if to excuse his interrupting. He wasn't familiar with the etiquette of the bench.

"Yeah! Ain't that the truth!" The boozehound next to him looked dreamy. "And they gave you those pickled cucumbers."

"And potatoes and carrots!" sighed his pal.

150

Sven felt oddly comforted by this. He almost felt a sense of belonging. Here were people with whom he shared a past, united by pork chops and pickled cucumbers.

"They gave you lots of applesauce too," he contributed, showing that he spoke their language.

The old boys beamed at him.

"You got that right! And when Anna-Greta was working, you know, the tall one, she always gave you extra gravy and potatoes."

"Yeah! Anna-Greta. She was always nice to us."

"Real nice."

"Yeah."

"But it's gone now."

"Yeah, it's gone. There's a store there now. But that place is gone."

"Lots of places are gone. Too many."

"It's a shame. You hardly recognize where you are any more."

"Damn right. Makes you feel lost."

"Yeah."

They all nodded in unison.

"Yeah, it's all different these days," proclaimed the geezer in the middle. "Now they got them damn Chinaman restaurants. There's one right down on Östra Förstadsgatan. Know the one? Makes people go all slanty-eyed, that food. It's crazy. Real nuts. Why do you think Chinamen look the way they do?"

"Ah...I don't know," confessed Sven, assuming the question had been directed at him. It was something he'd never pondered.

"Well, you see," explained the old guy who seemed up on these matters, "it's on account of all that weird crap they eat. It ain't normal."

"Is that right?" Sven was dismally unfamiliar with this theory. It didn't sound very logical, but he wasn't about to contest the facts. He was relishing this moment of togetherness.

"Yeah, darn right," nodded the other guy. "I seen it on TV. Birds' feet and monkey brains and all kindsa shit. Goddamn disgusting if you ask me. You'd never catch me eating that shit."

"Me neither. Octopus and snakes." The other drunk went wild-

151

eyed just thinking about it. "And dogs! They eat their goddamn dogs!"

"Oh dear!" said Sven.

"That's right. Dogs. Fido with applesauce, I kid you not. Jeez! Only you don't get no applesauce, only bamboo and lumps of stuff coming from God knows where."

The other old-timer laughed grimly and they all shook their heads in unison again, fully determined never to sully their insides with Chinese cuisine. Sat united in brotherly self-absorption, three squinting figures in a row at dusk, in a desolate square in the chilly urban landscape.

Sven, whose very foundation had fractured, felt a strong need for compassion. Not pity— not at all, no — but some gesture of consolation and understanding. Before he really knew what he was doing, it all came gushing out. He talked as he never had before. A detached part of him listened to his voice telling his bedraggled companions about being held hostage in the twilight zone. His monologue was awkward and groping, unpolished and without nuance, but it betrayed the intensity of his need. And the old boys understood, they really did; he sensed that and lapped it up. They were on his side. Sven needed to expose the unfairness of it all, the violation, the arrogance, and they needed just as badly to condemn it. They were familiar with wrongdoing, they'd endured it too, he could tell by the way they nodded and shook their grizzled heads in all the right places.

"It was after two in the morning. And they were getting louder and louder. Then finally somebody called the police. And when they got there this couple I mentioned was down in the sand-box...they were...you know...doing it...?"

The old boys overflowed with sympathy for Sven and vicious hatred for all young people. They uttered murderous sounds on Sven's behalf, smearing soothing ointment on his wounds. Together the three indulged their loathing of anybody amoral, promiscuous, deviant, corrupt, and perverse. That is, young people.

"The bastards should be put in an institution," concluded the old guy in the middle, and wiggled his toe violently.

152

"The whole frigging lot of them," agreed the other one. "Learn to behave in a civilized manner. Too much babying and pampering going on."

"You said it, Hilding. Pampering."

"Damn right."

"Yeah. Shave their heads, I say. Put them in uniform."

"Teach them discipline."

"Yeah. Discipline."

"Yeah."

"It was different when we was young. Back then you did as you were told or got a beating. A good one."

"Damn right."

"You got beat till you bled."

"Yeah. I remember that."

"Yeah."

The old boys grunted in unison, shoving their hands deeper in their pockets. The wind was growing colder. It was getting dark. Fog came crawling in from the strait. By now all the comfort and support had helped Sven recover a feeling similar to that of normalcy. He was starting to feel nervous and ill at ease. The streetlights came on, illuminating him and his bench companions, slippers, toe, and all. He noticed the bottle in the brown paper bag between the two geezers. It looked empty. He sat up straight, back on alert, blushing as he realized that he was fraternizing with two of society's outcasts. The lowest of the low. And in his slippers! He was sitting on a bench in a public place wearing slippers and wrinkled clothes, unshaven and unwashed, just like his companions. He felt himself blush an even deeper red.

"I guess I better get going...," he mumbled oafishly as he hastily got up. "Ah...see you...."

"Yeah. Sure. See you," replied the grumpy twosome, sensing the change of atmosphere. They were used to other people's discomfort. It had been Sven's lack of it that had surprised them. All in all, they didn't really care.

"Did you see what he was wearing there, Malte?"

"Slippers!"

153

"Yeah! Real nutcase, eh?"

"You said it."

"We shoulda hit him for some cigarettes."

"Yeah. Too late now."

"Yeah. That's life, eh, Hilding?"

"You said it, Malte."

Sven bolted down the street, across the bridge. Safely out of sight, he stopped at the kiosk to buy an evening paper and cigarettes, then continued home at a brisk pace, hoping not to meet anybody and have to hide his feet. Where did you hide your feet when you were out walking?

It was cold and the wind was pinching. An empty bus rolled by. It was getting foggier. Nobody saw him, nobody was out.

Tomorrow was Monday again.

He forgot to sneak up the stairs when he got back, too preoccupied with his shameful adventure. He was embarrassed, but a little pleased as well, that he'd enjoyed himself. As he shoved his key in the lock, the neighbours' door flew open and he went cold with fear. The young punk came tearing out, wild-eyed and pale, his hair uncombed.

"Was that you calling the fucking cops, you prick?" Janne hissed the words and stared furiously at Sven with bloodshot eyes as he scratched his right armpit with his left hand.

Sven got his door open in a hurry, so nervous that he dropped his evening paper. He didn't dare take the time to bend and pick it up. The ape looked as if he was going to hit him.

"N...no, that certainly wasn't me," he muttered, scared and sullen, and slammed the door shut, immediately putting the safety chain in place. For a long time he stood immobile, waiting to see what would happen next. He heard the guy shout, "You fucking drunk!"; then their door slammed and everything was quiet. Still, he didn't dare open his door to grab his paper. Let it lie there, he figured. I'll get it in the morning on my way to work. How he hated himself for giving up so easily. He ignored the voice inside him that asked in disgust, "Is that how deep your cowardice is, Sven? You don't dare pick up your own evening paper from your

154

own doormat?"

The programs on TV were more stunningly boring than usual. Typical Sunday fare. There was nothing to do but shoot yourself or go to bed early. He decided to go to bed. Stupidly, he hung up his wrinkled clothes and put them away. Then he crawled into bed, both marvelling and fuming at the nerve of that young pig. Calling him a drunk! It was all too much.

At least there was no noise. Outside, over the rooftops across the courtyard, he briefly glimpsed the moon between two clouds. Maybe it was clearing up and spring would be here after all.

"You could have said something," the contemptuous voice pointed out. "You could have told him what you thought of their behaviour last night. But oh no!"

Sven pretended not to hear.

The night was as soundless as in the good old days but, having caught mistrust like a terminal disease, he still couldn't sleep. He tossed left and right in vigorous exercise, trying to find some new way of hurling himself into the arms of Morpheus. No such luck. Finally he got annoyed with himself. His nitpicking brain kept dissecting every detail of the weekend's events. It did so with its usual pedantic determination and it took its own sweet time. He'd have preferred not think about the weekend at all, but he had no conscious control over his thoughts. And being so unused to any events taking place in his life, he found it difficult to grasp what had happened all at once. His only conclusion from his analysis was that he should never have talked to those two outcasts, he should never have so much as contemplated sitting on the same bench. Because one didn't do that, did one? And why not, he asked himself, although he knew the answer. One didn't do it for the same reason one didn't take a piss standing in line at the bus stop, that was why. It made you a social misfit and you had to give up your membership in civilized society. There was a handful of those outcasts at every square, around every fountain and statue — wretches who didn't belong, didn't fit in, were not let in. Most of them were middle-aged or older, like some endangered species. The majority were men. They were never sober and never clean. They were pariahs that you looked right through, as if they weren't there.

Everybody knew that.

Sven knew it too, yet in his moment of defencelessness he had broken the rules. Yes, he had done the wrong thing. But it wasn't his fault; he'd been a helpless victim at the time. It was the fault of the people next door. Of course, if he'd had a modest amount of courage and faith in his fellow man he would have had a talk with his neighbours, a friendly if firm chat that would have had pleasant and positive results, after which they might have coexisted in a more harmonious fashion. He knew that too, but rejected the knowledge. He was not ready to admit that he was a passive bystander of his own fate.

Eventually he fell asleep, exhausted and discouraged by the disturbing results of his late-night analysis. It was after two o'clock, once again. A foghorn bellowed in the night. Rain started drumming on his windows, splashing in the courtyard below, cleansing the sandbox. It was a safe and familiar lullaby. Bad guys didn't come out when it rained.

He was sleeping deeply when the alarm clock had a nervous breakdown. Its bleating cut into his head and dragged him back from oblivion by his nerve ends. It was raining still, wet sheets of grey lashing the windows. Half an hour later he was standing by the kitchen window with a cup of coffee, glaring miserably at the wet concrete below, at the sandbox where he had watched his one and only live sex show. Once in a while he heard the baby next door squeal. It suddenly occurred to him that he was late and he rushed to get ready. Ran down all four flights of stairs. Dashed out into the rain without his umbrella, rushed to the bus stop, and sprinted onto the bus just as the doors were closing. It was the first

156

time in his life that he had been late for the bus, the first time he had ever had to run to catch it.

Hot from his run, he stood catching his breath and dripping rain in the mute morning crowd. He was looking forward to a quiet day in his temperature-controlled office, the place in the world where he had a function, where he was needed, where he was part of a team. Where there was a routine to follow that didn't alter no matter what. The thought of normalcy and tedium cheered him no end.

He arrived at work four minutes early, as usual, and passed good old Tyra in the hallway, where she was holding forth to a small gathering. He mumbled a damp good-morning but nobody answered. As he threw a glance in their direction he noticed that Tyra had gone quiet. Her sharp eyes were lit by some strange fire as she gave him a disdainful nod. She took a breath and went on in a loud voice about how she *never* would dream of cleansing her face with soap and water, *absolutely* not, a cream cleanser followed by a toner, blah, blah, blah.

Sven hung up his wet coat and noticed that the group in the hall were staring at him while pretending they weren't. It was painfully obvious. Tyra's freckled hand played nervously with her fake pearl necklace. Mrs. L. was giggling for no apparent reason. Fat Fransson looked so sad that her cheeks were drooping. Not knowing what to do, he smiled shyly and sat down at his desk. As he had every morning for years.

Monday morning was the best time of the week. There was a full and busy work week ahead. The in-box was full of invoices and reports, enough to keep him going at a quick clip all day. That was how he liked it. Later in the afternoon, Sture from the warehouse was supposed to stop by. Outside, the rain fell steadily, obscuring his view. The ivy-clad courthouse looked as if it were melting. Somewhere a foghorn bellowed. In the street below, umbrellas on legs were heading for the ferry.

Three times before coffee break that morning, he looked up to find himself eye to eye with Tyra, who was watching him like a hawk from across the hall. Her eyes still shone with that lunatic light. She seemed restless. Maybe the crazy bitch had finally gone around the bend. The first time he looked up and found her gaze on him, she almost blushed, at the same time dripping condescension. Clever trick. The second time he turned sideways to reach for a pen and there she was again, transfixed, her painted chocolate-coloured eyebrows raised halfway up her lined forehead, giving her an expression of simpleton surprise. Weird woman. Sven gave her the beginning of a timid smile and turned away. What else to do? It was only a question of time before Tyra lost it completely, everybody knew that. The woman was batty. Still, it made him edgy, her taking it out on him just because he had the misfortune of being right in her line of vision. Maybe it was, what did you call it, that thing women got? Menopause? She was past fifty, good old Tyra, ripe for the inevitable change of life. He'd read somewhere that they went kind of loopy when that happened. And let's face it, Tyra was pretty damn loopy to start with.

Sven looked at her out of the corner of his eye. Now she was pretending to work, but it was blatantly fake. All she was doing was shuffling the same bunch of papers around. Then all of a sudden she bolted out of her room and into Fat Fransson's. She looked as though she had just sat down on a sharp tack; too bad she hadn't. Arriving in Fat Fransson's office, she closed the door and started ranting about something. Fat Fransson looked intrigued for a change. It must be good, whatever it was. Next thing he knew, Tyra had flitted in to pour her heart out to Mrs. L., and soon they were both staring at him. Sven was starting to feel alarmed. It was as if the world was conspiring to drive home the fact that life had changed. As if his working days had to be ruined too, in the name of consistency. Or was he going through a change of life so complete that it affected everybody around him? Or had they always behaved like this and he had never noticed, until the shock of re-cent events shoved him into another dimension and he attained some kind of heightened perception? No. That sounded a bit far-fetched, didn't it?

He stood up abruptly and beat a hasty retreat to the bath-room, needing to sit where nobody would stare at him. Perched on a toilet seat in peace and quiet, he looked up now and then, fully expecting to see Tyra's powdered beak hanging over the cubicle wall, sniffing him out. After a while his paranoia subsided and he almost fell asleep.

It wasn't until later, when he was sitting in the lunchroom chewing on a salami sandwich, that it became clear that there re-ally was something odd going on. It had been years since Tyra had deigned to eat with her fellow employees. She always had lunch at home, as she lived nearby and her old mother still cooked for her every day, breakfast, lunch, and dinner. But here she was, deli-cately nibbling on a sandwich, explaining (although nobody had asked) that "Mother made it this morning. It's a lovely shrimp salad with just a tad of curry for that extra tang."

Then she launched into a tirade about the weather. The glori-ous, glorious sunshine of Saturday. The "azure of the sky." She actually said that, and it raised a few eyebrows. Fat Fransson was describing how she and little Pia had gone shopping for shoes for Pia, and how expensive they were, but how it was worth it because they were absolutely perfect for Pia's dainty feet.

Sven wanted to say, "Yes, I saw you by the library," but Tyra was still looking at him and he couldn't speak. He kept chewing his sandwich, but the bread seemed dry and he had trouble swal-lowing. Tyra, who had actually kept silent during Fransson's lengthy tale, had finished nibbling and sat smoking a cigarette, the filtertip sticky with red lipstick. It looked as if it had been dipped in coagu-lated blood. Sven tried not to meet her eyes.

Berit from accounting was saying that they had taken a drive out to the beech forest by Torup's Castle yesterday, whoever *they* were, to have a walk and a cup of coffee, but that it had been too windy and unpleasant. Mrs. L. added her two cents' worth about how she and her Kent had walked to her in-laws for Sunday dinner, as they did every Sunday, and had a roast with mushroom gravy, and although she didn't care for mushrooms it had really been quite good, but oh my, it had been so cold walking over there that her knees had gone almost blue because she was wearing a short skirt, silly old her, but really, that was how cold she got, they should have taken the bus as Kent had suggested in the first place....

As everybody's eyes glazed over, Tyra lit another cigarette and interrupted expertly.

"Yes, it sure was nippy," she declared, in a tone that implied that they needed her to confirm the weather conditions. "It was certainly no weather to sit outside."

"That's for sure," seconded one of the secretaries.

"It must have been unpleasant for the drunks I saw hanging out up on Drottningtorget," mused Tyra, as her eyes threw daggers Sven's way. "We drove by there yesterday afternoon on our way back from a lovely Chinese restaurant. There were three of them sitting there, all red around the nose, though that was probably the booze. That kind of person probably doesn't feel the cold. And would you believe it, one of them was wearing slippers! I mean, for God's sake! Can you imagine?" She glowed as she slammed down her last card. Five aces! Tyra had won the Big One!

Saturday night he had watched a live sex show. Now he was watching a woman have orgasms and he didn't even know it. He was too preoccupied shrinking through the floor. They all knew. They must have known since early morning. He wanted to die, still he vaguely wondered if she ate monkey brain or fried dog at the Chinese restaurant.

The silence was painful. Sven's gut turned to ice, his face burned with shame. The people around him looked embarrassed and uncomfortable but their excitement shone through. Tyra stared at him, her triumph complete. She had finally got him. She had revealed his secret. Her cheeks were as red as a vampire's after feeding.

So that was it. The end.

When Sven had shrunk to a two-inch shadow of his former

self, when his inner demolition was complete, he looked wearily at his uneasy colleagues. Nobody met his pale eyes. But that's the way it was with outcasts. His gaze travelled on to Tyra. She stared back, but the bleakness that met her eyes made even her look elsewhere. She chose to be fascinated by the wallpaper. Sven sat there feeling stark naked, thinking, "I will cease to exist right now. I'll go up in smoke. I'll fade away." But he had a pain in his chest, a feeling of hot and cold, that he remembered from long ago. From back in 1944. When they came and took Pa away and he never came back. When a higher power came strutting into the yard and squished Sven like an insect, as men in uniform led Pa out the door.

Here it was again, that higher power, getting him with the other foot. And again time stood still, again the camera stopped rolling, and he sat pondering death.

Distantly he became aware of the shuffle of feet and the scraping of chairs as people got up one by one to leave the scene of the slaughter, hoping they hadn't been splashed by the blood. Forced conversations sprouted as they walked out the door. Tyra was the first to leave. Close by, he heard shreds of an unnecessarily loud exchange about a movie somebody had been to see that was absolutely terrific.

Soon the lunchroom was deserted. It was one o'clock. Still Sven sat there, discarded and useless. There was no need to rush, was there? There was no work to go back to. He felt oddly light-headed and relaxed, almost entranced. So this was what dying is like — a slow, weightless drift into nothingness. It was quite pleasant.

Smiling crookedly to himself, he thought how easy it should have been to stand up to Tyra, stare her down and tell her what he thought of her. To explain to his colleagues, not that it was anybody's business, why he was sitting on that bench in the cold wind, wearing his slippers. But it was too long a monologue to attempt in a room full of people. They weren't used to hearing him hold forth, it would have been unnatural. He couldn't have done it anyway; he would have blushed and stuttered and made a fool of himself. As Tyra well knew.

It didn't matter now. The damage had been done, and Tyra would fight sharp tooth and long red nail to maintain her story. And the fact was, she wasn't lying. He couldn't accuse her of falsifying the truth. He had been sitting there, unshaven and sloppily attired, in genial brotherhood with two pariahs. He had enjoyed it, too, maybe she could see that in his face as she drove by. He had been painfully sober at the time but he couldn't prove that, so what was the point of trying?

The star witness had performed. The jury had reached a verdict. The judge had passed sentence: I condemn you to hang. An appeal would be humiliating. Besides, what would he say? "Excuse me, but delinquent punks tore down the wall of my fort and I had nowhere to go. They were going to scalp me. Please forgive me my transgression"? Not likely.

So now he had a reputation. What a joke! Here he was, a most forgettable man — damn near invisible — yet a man disgraced. Suddenly he was a degenerate, somebody it was debasing to be seen with. Somebody with a bad smell. Funny, wasn't it?

Sitting immobile in the empty lunchroom, his heart still barely beating, he remembered a drunk he had once seen down by Värnhemstorget, an unwashed fragment of a man who'd fallen unconscious at the entrance to a shoe shop. Like a pile of dirty laundry he lay there, lifeless and alone, while people walked in wide circles around him. Customers leaving the shop stopped and walked backwards a few steps, like a movie in reverse. There was a vacuum around the wreck lying there, until the police arrived to drag him into a paddy-wagon. Crossing the street in disgust, Sven had thought how outrageous it was that these drunk and useless people should be allowed to walk free and upset respectable citizens. How there ought to be a law. How the policemen had not been nearly as rough as they should have been.

He smiled at the memory. At least, he thought he was smiling, though he couldn't feel his lips move. Sipping some cold coffee, he looked at his second sandwich and reflected that now he never had to eat again. He no longer needed fuel. Well, he said to himself, that's something.

With his head filled with helium he got up and floated out of the lunchroom, totally at ease and eerily free. Nothing could hurt him now. Maybe he *was* dead, maybe he was a spirit. That must be why he didn't weigh anything. Floating to his office, he passed Tyra's cage and gazed benignly in at her in a bless-you-my-child manner that made her visibly uncomfortable. His face showed no shame; he looked rather as though he had had a religious experience, and had passed on to whatever lay beyond. There was something untouchable about him, as she would explain to the others when he'd left. Something that dampened her cheap triumph, but she wouldn't mention that part.

Sven got his coat in the same dreamlike state. They all observed him, some more openly than others, but nobody said anything as he floated out the door.

Then he was gone.

That was quick, he observed with surprise as he stood in the elevator for the last time. Just like when Pa had walked across the yard that day. Across the yard and out the door. So that was how easy it was. You got up, walked through the door, and you were gone. Before you even knew what you were doing, you'd done it.

A minute later he was standing, forlorn, on the sidewalk. He took a deep breath and strolled into the city. What else was there to do? The rain had stopped and the sky lay draped in colourless folds over the Savoy's roof as he crossed the bridge. The air smelled fresh after the rain. He found himself walking by the canal along Norra Vallgatan, going not east towards home but in the opposite direction, towards the museum. "Early retirement," he proclaimed to himself. It was not an attempt to be amusing. "Passing the time of day. Getting some fresh air."

Following the canal all the way around, he reached home eventually via Södra Promenaden and Exercisgatan. It didn't take as long as it should have. He knew that his false sense of freedom would end as soon as he set foot in his apartment. The spell would be broken and there would be nothing left.

And sure enough, it broke as easily as a soap bubble. *Ping!* and it was gone.

He sat down in his chair and stared into space. Space was all there was at the end of the road. Distraught, he thought about what he would do for the rest of his life. Going back to work was out of the question. He could have explained, but he had chosen not to. That was his own fault. But it would have been pointless anyway, he repeated to himself, pointless, pointless. The story had already taken root and was growing as he sat there. Fertilized by imagination, it would blossom into a flower that would last for quite a while. Tyra would prune it and water it and keep it in a sunny spot. And people would talk. "He was always a bit odd," they'd say. "Yes, he was, wasn't he? So quiet." "Funny we never noticed that he was drunk." "Oh, that kind knows how to hide it!" If he went back they would avoid him, while he sat in full view in his cage with his shame and embarrassment. And he would feel ashamed. He had been brought up to feel that way. It would be unbearable.

No. He would send a letter with his resignation. A few formal sentences. His life was over, but how could he explain that without sounding pompous and ridiculous?

He smiled. My life is over, but I'm fit as a fiddle. Looking around his tidy room for some answer to the riddle of his life, some reflection of himself, some proof that he was there, he found nothing. He gazed long and hard at his two paintings — maybe he was hiding in there, standing by the water's edge in his boots. Or walking along the road, his hand trailing the wall. But no, both scenes looked flat and uninviting. There was nobody there. Without really deciding to do so, he got up, walked around the coffee table, and sat down on the folded-up sofa-bed. After a minute or so he lay down and curled up like an overgrown embryo wearing a tie. He had tried to be a good boy all his life — almost fifty years, for crying out loud. But it hadn't worked out, had it? He had messed up. Was it the criminal in him? The bad blood from Pa flowing in his veins? If so, he couldn't help it, could he? You didn't choose your parents. Or had he been born to be punished? What for? What had he done?

Curling up tighter, he closed his eyes and went to the place in

164

his head where the memories hid. He didn't go there often, but he knew the way by heart. It was not a nice place, but he could hide there, and nobody would find him.

It was in the summer of 1944 that they came and took Pa away. Shortly after the Allied forces invaded France, though Pa had nothing to do with *that*. He hadn't been around much lately, though. He had joked that he had now joined the real army, as he called it. Pa's employers had started to get a lot busier after August 29 the previous year, and things really started rolling after October, thanks to the good old Gestapo and SS General Pancke. After the Germans deported 481 Jews from occupied Denmark to Theresienstadt concentration camp, the first large wave of Danish refugees reached Sweden, and before long the illegal transport of both Jews and resistance fighters was a full-time operation. At the same time, weapons and medicine were being smuggled from Sweden to Denmark.

Ships, fishing-boats, cutters, barges — whatever was available was used. Even if a Danish ship's secret cargo was destined for a Swedish harbour, it generally met a Swedish contact vessel in the strait and transferred its hidden passengers. This was to mislead anybody spying for the Germans on either side of the water. Sven had read about all this later, choking on the shame of having been associated with the wrong side. People arrived in Sweden hidden in empty water tanks, oil barrels, camouflaged lockers, in boxes labelled "Handle with care. Machinery. Made in Germany". Another trick was to unseal and reseal German railcars meant to transport goods through Sweden. These were carefully unsealed, filled with refugees, and resealed. On arrival in Sweden the seals were broken to check the contents and the refugees were released. Imagination and sheer nerve knew no bounds.

After August 29, 1943, about 6,000 Danes were sent to concentration camps. Around 20,000 made it to Sweden, half of them in late 1943. By November of that year a Danish general named Knudtzon had organized the first Danish army camp in Sweden, with about 550 men. By spring 1944, five battalions, with 3,500 officers, were ready and eager to fight the Nazis.

There was another, much smaller and shadier group hard at work as well — the Nazi lackeys, the traitors, the *stikkers*. This small band of Danish traitors, their noses firmly up the Nazi ass, had people in Sweden as well. It turned out that Pa was one of these. This was his "army". There was his old pal Henning Jensen, who had lived in Sweden since the mid-thirties and was married to a Swedish woman. He spoke good Swedish and often posed as a Swede. He had been joined by Hans Madsen, who came over with false papers in 1941, while the ferries were still running. Then there was Ole Pedersen, who had come via Helsingør on October 5, 1943. On the run from the Resistance after murdering one of their men, he slipped through when the rush of refugees was the greatest. The weather was on his side; a savage storm lashed the coast that night, and there was pandemonium in Hälsingborg harbour. Customs officers and military personnel didn't know what had hit them. Huddling in the cold and the rain were more than a hundred young Jewish women, most of them clutching infants in a futile attempt to keep them dry. Equipped with a new beard and papers identifying him as a freedom fighter, Pedersen pushed his way through this chaos and headed for Malmö. He claimed he had worked for the Bröndum gang, which impressed Pa no end, as they were probably the worst of the groups terrorizing Denmark with the approval of their German masters. He also claimed to be a personal friend of SS General Werner Best, but that at least was a lie. Madsen, who deserted Clausen, the vain Danish *Führer*, after the election, was apparently in contact with Kröyer, the Nazi lawyer, but probably not with the Germans directly. As for Henning Jensen, he had been a contact man for the Danish Nazis since the start of the occupation. Pa had got involved with him way back, helping push Nazi propaganda and similar filth. Jensen was a man

Pa admired, a real man. Pa had been happy to be of help; he firmly believed in the Master Race, of which he considered himself an indisputable member. He was honoured to be in with the big boys.

Their job, which was largely voluntary, was to infiltrate the transport operations, intercept "Radio Betty", the Resistance's illegal transmissions, find out what seagoing vessel carried whom and what and when, and where it might meet another ship to transfer cargo. Pa was to infiltrate Dansk-Svensk Flygtningetjenste, an organization that transported refugees across the strait on a daily basis, on more than a dozen different vessels.

Sven would never know the exact extent of the damage done before they all got caught, but he had been told that people had been killed because of what Pa and the bad guys had done. Two Jewish families and three resistance fighters had lost their lives just in the week before the gang was finally stopped: brave people who had done nothing wrong. It was Pa and the bad guys who had done all the wrong. His Pa was an evil man. Ma had told him that.

They weren't clever, these traitors. Most of them were small-time criminals who saw the German invasion as their chance to advance themselves. In their eagerness to please, they often fell for the disinformation regularly sent to mislead them. But they stumbled through their botches and persisted in their treachery. In their dreams they wore shiny black boots and carried a big hard gun.

The resistance in Denmark grew daily, and in early 1944, after the shameful murder of the priest-poet named Kaj Munk, it became unstoppable. In response, the German Schalburg Korps took to roaming city streets and blowing up buildings left, right, and centre, seemingly just for amusement. The people of Denmark considered themselves at war. Around that time, the resistance group Holger Danske smuggled two men, wanted badly by the Gestapo, over to Sweden via Bornholm. Once in Malmö, the pair got busy infiltrating the small group of traitors to which Pa had attached himself. It wasn't difficult. The *stikkers* were as stupid as they were devious, and pitifully credulous when it came to flattery. Posing as close friends of the mass murderer Henning Bröndum, the men from Holger Danske impressed Pedersen's group with their credentials, and the group was soon caught and transported to two different camps. None of the traitors lived very long. Pa and another Swede were killed "by accident" in camp. The Danish traitors were transferred back to Denmark after the war and swiftly dealt with. Pedersen was sentenced to death.

Sven would always remember that day in 1944. It was a Thursday afternoon. He was sitting in the yard, on the rotting old bench by the bicycle shed, munching on a splendid sandwich. It was a masterpiece: a thick slice of homemade bread, twice the size of his hand, spread with a generous layer of real butter, topped by an exquisitely fried egg, its surface golden, its edges crisp. Having watched him sitting there since late morning, old Mrs. Göransson across the yard had taken pity on him and insisted he eat it.

"Have those darn people locked you out again?" she asked as she stuck her disapproving face out her kitchen window. When she thought of the Anderssons over in 4B, disapproval came naturally.

"They're doing business," Sven replied in an uninspired attempt to defend his parents. He had no idea what they were up to. Ma had been busy cooking lunch for Pa and his new friend Pedersen, a tall skinny man who never said anything except "yes, yes" in Danish that Sven could understand, and Jensen, who always looked angry. They were having fried fish and potatoes and beer. That was all he knew. Sven would have liked some lunch too, but he wasn't invited.

"Oh, they're doing *business,* are they?" Mrs. Göransson snorted, her eyes flooding with contempt. "Are they indeed!"

He could tell by her snort that she knew better. She knew that Rune Andersson was the only man around who had never been called up. Not even in April 1940. He had "medical problems" and could not be expected to fight for his country, should it come to that. She had her own opinions of his "medical problems".

"Are they indeed!" she repeated, and looked at the skinny boy on the bench, thinking what a shame it was that the wretched lad always had to sit in the yard by himself. Shaking her head, while staring absentmindedly at the well-fed begonia on her windowsill, she said, "Well, boy, you'll have to have yourself a sandwich at least, you can't sit without food all day. You'll faint and fall off the bench and hurt your head."

"I'm not hungry," he replied, if not very convincingly. The truth was, he was extremely partial to food, and never got enough of the stuff — especially during the last few weeks, when things had been worse than usual. There wasn't much food in the house so Ma never cooked unless Pa was having a meeting like today. She went dancing a lot, though.

"You must eat, child, or you'll grow up stunted like a dwarf. I've seen it happen. Now, you just wait there while I fry up an egg." Offering food was the only way Mrs. Göransson knew to help. Having plenty of family on various farms on the southern plain, she didn't often lack flour, butter, and eggs. "And if you're still hungry after that one, let me know and I'll make you another. You're a growing boy, remember that."

And so he was munching his delectable treat when four policemen and three grim-faced men in suits and overcoats came trooping into the yard. Marching by Sven as if he weren't there, they disappeared into 16B. That was where Sven lived. Something must be happening! Nothing ever happened in the yard, but now the police were coming to catch a bad guy! Right here in their building! And he'd get to see it! He debated whether to hide behind the garbage cans in case there was a lot of shooting. You never knew, did you? Maybe there were spies hiding in the vast attic, evil Russians or something. They probably had machine-guns! Even Pa would have to listen when he told this story. Pa would be impressed.

He still hadn't decided whether to hide when the men came trooping back out, leading Pa, Pedersen, and Jensen, all in handcuffs. Sven stared at them, his open mouth full of food. His heart stopped beating, and dropped like a stone into the icy cold of his gut. Pieces of half-chewed egg sandwich fell out of his mouth onto his lap.

The whole world stopped for a very long time. Nothing moved: all the clocks quit ticking, the soldiers on the battlefields stopped shooting, the wind stopped blowing. Then, as the earth slowly started spinning again, the procession marched across the yard and out the door into the street. Doors slammed and he heard cars revving their engines. Somebody shouted something. The cars drove away and a hush fell over the world.

Pa was just like that.

It all happened so fast.

Sven was alone again, numb with incomprehension, his eyes as blank as his head. After a while, his only thought was that Pa had not looked at him. His Pa had not looked at him. Sven had sat there and stared at Pa, willing him to meet his eyes, to exchange some form of communication, some secret message only the two of them would understand. But Pa had not done so. He must have known Sven was sitting there, but he hadn't acknowledged him. He hadn't noticed him any more than he had noticed the handful of sparrows hopping on the ground. Sven told himself that it was because Pa was ashamed that he didn't dare look at him, but he didn't believe it. He knew it was because his presence was not important enough to register on Pa's eyeballs.

That was the last time he ever saw his father.

He sat on the bench by the bicycle shed. Mrs. Göransson came out to get her bike, patted his shoulder without saying anything, and left for her afternoon cleaning job. It seemed he sat there for days. Way up in the sky he heard seagulls shriek and laugh. Later in the afternoon a girl his own age came out from 16C. Her name was Ingalill. She had short brown hair framing a serious little face, and that day she was wearing an ugly, ill-fitting brown skirt and a knitted vest. They didn't talk to each other, didn't play, they were both alone in their separate worlds. But he always remembered that girl, and the way she stood across the yard with her skinny back to him, throwing the two balls against the wall. A yellow one and a green one, thudding rhythmically against the brick wall. Once in a while she lost her rhythm, dropped a ball, and had to chase after it. Then she patiently started again. At one point she dropped the yellow ball and it rolled all the way to where he sat and stopped dead by his feet. She ran over and quickly bent to pick it up. When she stood up again she stared right at him for a brief moment, her eyes full of terror, and whispered anxiously, "There's a war." She

170

turned and ran back to the wall and started throwing her balls again.

He didn't reply. Empty of words and empty of thoughts, he sat rigid until she disappeared. Not until then did he get up and make his way upstairs, bent and heavy like an old man. Step by step he climbed to what had been his home, wondering if it was still there.

Ma was standing in the kitchen, chain-smoking and swearing a blue streak. He'd never heard her use such foul language, and he'd heard quite a lot in his short life. To say that she was furious would be an understatement. Yeah, sure, she'd known Rune was not a totally honest man, but shit, who was? So she'd known he stole ration cards and stuff like that, but hey, they had to eat, right? That was how a man looked after his own, she'd always figured. That was okay, that was what separated the men from the boys. But when the cops came and said he was a war criminal, and found the box Rune had hidden in the closet, well, Christ, that was when she lost it. The box contained 7,000 kronor in cash and a brand-new passport made out to Sigurd Bergström but with Rune's photo in it. And to top it off, get this, a couple of photos of some naked whore with tits bigger than hers. In one of the photos the whore was sitting on Rune's lap and he had one hand on her left tit and the other between her legs.

So that was it, as far as she was concerned. She'd had it! What a prick that man was! No need to stand by him after this. From now on she'd say they'd never been married, and change her name back to Edith Berggren. Pretend that Rune fucking well didn't exist. She was a single woman again and life was full of possibilities. But that didn't mean she was too outraged to think clearly. They said he was a war criminal, for Christ's sake. How could he have done the things he had? People had been killed. She was married to a fucking murderer! One thing for sure, though, it had nothing to do with her. She'd had no idea. Good thing, too; you got four years for not reporting stuff like that. Luckily they believed her. They'd had their eyes on them for quite a while, they knew what was going on. She'd been under surveillance, would you believe it? They'd checked her out. But she was okay. Plus she had a kid to look after,

171

didn't she? Pa would get at least ten years, that was the minimum, probably more. They could shoot the scumbag for all she cared.

When Sven came walking into the kitchen, his face white and his eyes wild, she stared at him briefly, raised her voice an octave, and went on with her fire and brimstone litany about what she'd do to that fat fucking prick if she ever laid eyes on him again. Whether it was the detailed description of what she would do to Pa's private parts, or just the aftermath of the shock, Sven suddenly threw up fried egg sandwich in a smelly puddle on the kitchen floor. Ma stared at it in disbelief, shook her head, and threw her cigarette stub in the barf.

"Oh Christ! That's all I fucking need! Thank you so very much! Well, you just get down on your knees there, kid, and clean it up. I'm going out, I gotta get out of here. But I'll tell you one thing, when I come back I want to see a clean floor. You got that?"

"Yes." Sven nodded weakly, feeling dizzy. Then he threw up again in the same spot. He stood staring at the mess until he heard the front door slam. As soon as Ma was gone, he left the kitchen and went to lie on the couch. It felt good. He fell asleep right away and didn't wake until late in the evening. It was dark and the streetlights were on, casting strange shadows into the room, but they didn't scare him. Not tonight. The apartment was silent. Ma must still be out. That was good in a way, because he would have time to clean up and make the floor nice.

The congealing mess on the kitchen floor almost made him sick again. He wasn't sure how to clean it up, but he did what he could by wiping it up with the dishrag and flushing the mess down the sink with running water. It was disgusting; there were big lumps that wouldn't go down the drain, and he had to pick them out by hand and throw them in the garbage. Then he got down on his knees and scrubbed the floor, using a hard brush he found under the sink and some of the soft green soap Ma used for washing dishes. Pleased with the result, he felt he deserved a late-night snack, and peered into the pantry to see what he could find. While there wasn't much there, he was soon sitting at the table having a midnight feast of some crispbread, an end of sausage, and three pieces of herring in onion sauce that were past their prime. He washed it all down with cold water from the tap. It was so cold he almost threw up again.

By the time he was finished it was after midnight and rather chilly as he sneaked barefoot out to the toilet on the landing for a late pee. Back in bed he curled up under the blanket and squeezed his eyes shut. A soft rain drizzled against the window and he listened to it for a while. It sounded like voices whispering far away. He pretended they were angels come to watch over him, and before long he was sleeping deeply. He slept on as the rain stopped and a crescent moon appeared from behind a cloud.

He didn't dream.

It was past eleven o'clock the next day when he heard Ma's heels tap their way up the winding staircase. He knew it was her right away, those high heels echoed against the stone stairs like a tired machine-gun. Sven was sitting at the kitchen table in his underwear, having a late breakfast. Or early lunch, depending on how you looked at it. Three pieces of crispbread and the last two pieces of ancient herring. He'd been up since eight, sitting in the window, looking down the street to see from which direction Ma would pop up, turning it into a game. I'll count to ten and she'll come around the corner from the left. I'll count to twenty and she'll come from the right. At eleven o'clock he had given up. He was sitting there planning how he'd live his life if she never came home, when he heard her steps. A minute later she hauled her weary carcass into the kitchen and stared at him bleary-eyed. Her hair was a mess and she had bags under her bloodshot eyes. Just looking at her, Sven could tell that she hadn't slept at all. He never found out what she'd been up to, or where she'd been up to it, but he knew it was none of his business. Her tired eyes shifted from the boy to the floor and she observed, without spending any undue energy on enthusiasm, that the kitchen floor looked pretty damn good. Dragging her gaze back to her son, she told him what a good boy he'd been. But, she added, now he had to go outside, or promise to be very quiet, because she had to hit the hay real quick. She was dead beat and she needed sleep, lots of sleep. She was sure he understood, he was such a good boy, he knew how to look after himself, didn't he?

"Yes."

"I'll cook us a nice dinner tonight," she promised, so unexpectedly that she took herself by surprise.

Sven blushed at all the attention. It paid to be a good boy. He didn't really believe her hasty promise — experience had taught him better — but it was nice of her to offer. And you never knew, perhaps it would be different with Pa gone. Maybe it would be worthwhile to be very, very good all the time. Considering this possibility, he sat quietly at the kitchen table, leafing through some of Ma's ladies' magazines (not rustling the pages too loudly) and listening to her snoring away in the living-room. Somewhere in his chest a hopeful little bird fluttered foolhardily as he waited for Ma to metamorphose on the couch and wake up a doting mother. She might even look different. It could happen. Icky larvae turned into butterflies, he'd seen it in a book at school. It could happen.

Time dragged on, almost forgetting to move forward. The sunbeam from the window crawled across the floor towards him, warmed his face briefly, and crawled on. Still Ma slept. He didn't dare go out in case she woke up. If she'd changed, he wanted to know right away. Besides, he was used to just sitting, he'd done it all his life. It wasn't difficult once you got the hang of it. You could do a lot of thinking while your body was inert. Or you could not think at all, and then it was as if you didn't exist. That was useful sometimes. But right now there was an awful lot to figure out. Nothing was going to be the same ever again, Ma had said so last night. The police had taken Pa. He wasn't coming back. Sven had heard all that, but the finality of it was inconceivable.

It was hard to know what to think when you were eleven and

nobody ever told you anything. You were standing there, totally ignorant of what was going on, and suddenly fate shoved a new script into your skinny little paw and said, "Here, kid, the play has changed. These are your new lines. Hope you know the language."

Luckily Sven had an absolute and stubborn will to live and was going to do so come what may. Having lived amid the inane vagaries and hypocrisies of adults his entire life, he had learned not to ask questions, but to seek answers by other means. He wasn't helpless.

Consequently, as the sunbeam inched its way across the floor, he was inching himself into his new existence. He was reshaping his brain like a lump of clay, kneading it with the hope and strength that a child's practical single-mindedness is capable of, putting the remodelled lump in place in his head, satisfied that he would survive if he tried very hard, if he was stubborn enough, if he avoided looking too closely at what went on around him. Sitting on his chair throughout that afternoon, he slowly turned into the person whose self he would always inflexibly cling to. He may even have grown slightly taller, visibly older, as he sat there.

By the time Ma woke up around four, Sven had undergone a self-imposed metamorphosis, while she seemed her good old hung-over self as she got off the couch and fumbled for her cigarettes. She did try to pull herself together, she really did, stumbling out to the kitchen sink for a quick wash in cold water, then into the bedroom for a change of clothes. Wearing her everyday dress, with her hair more or less combed, she reappeared in the doorway.

"Come on then!" she said to Sven. "Let's go down and get some food for dinner."

Sven got up, dazzled with the wonder of it all. Going shopping with Ma! That was a first. He followed her silent back down the spiral of stairs, across the street and up towards Möllevångstorget, then down Bergsgatan a few blocks. There was a store much nearer but Ma went right by, pretending not to see it. Standing in the other, unfamiliar store he looked around at the customers to see if they noted the picture that he was part of, the splendid mother-and-son motif. Nobody seemed at all impressed. Meanwhile Ma spent almost five kronor on potatoes, crispbread, and herring. Afterwards they went to the tobacconist and she bought cigarettes and a newspaper. The shopping finished, they walked home again, side by side. Sven got to carry the newspaper. No words were exchanged apart from "Here, you take the paper."

That night they had mashed potatoes and fried herring. Sven ate in silence, not knowing what to talk about, but it didn't matter; they were eating together. Besides, Ma was reading the newspaper she'd bought and never even looked at him, except when he was finished and stood up.

"Are you full?" she asked and glanced up at him.

"Yes, thank you," he replied, standing straight and formal. "It was very good."

"What? Yeah, sure." She waved her cigarette in the air. "Do the dishes, will you?"

Sven was happy to help out. He felt sated and content, which was just as well. It would be another couple of weeks before Ma indulged her culinary skills again.

He washed the dishes and glasses, carefully dried them, and put them away on their shelf while Ma smoked, drank ersatz coffee, and read her magazine. Half an hour went by before she uttered another word.

"Well," she said finally, "there's nothing in the paper about it. Just as well." She threw the paper on the floor and got up. "I think I'll go back to bed now. I gotta get up early tomorrow and go talk to the police. Commissioner Hansen or something."

"You do?"

"Yeah. Gonna help them nail that prick real hard. I better go and check if I got something to wear."

She went and dove into the walk-in closet in the hall. Sven followed her like a shadow. She had pulled the cord of the closet light and was standing there holding up Pa's good suit. It looked for a moment as if she'd skinned Pa and this was the pelt.

"Look at this!" She smirked and looked pleased with herself. "Pa's good suit. Well, he won't be needing that where he's going, will he?"

"No."

"We'll sell it. Get some money out of the bastard, eh?"

"Yes."

"Here, kid, take it." She threw the suit at him. Despite its size he was unable to catch it, and it landed over his head and hung there. "Check there's nothing in the pockets."

Sven pulled the brown pin-stripe off his head and dragged it into the living-room. He put it on the couch and slipped his hands into the pant pockets. He felt like a pickpocket. If Pa had walked in the door right then and seen him do it, he would have belted him hard. But the pockets were empty. Sven smoothed the wide lapels on the jacket and stuck his hand into the inside pocket, caressing the cool silky lining. There was a rustling noise. His eyes popped out of his head when he pulled his hand out and saw his fingers clasping several folded hundred-kronor bills. More money than he'd seen in his life.

"Ma!" he squealed. "Ma! Ma!"

"What the hell is it now?" She stuck her scowling face out of the closet.

"Look, Ma!" He was hyperventilating with excitement. "Money!" he added helpfully.

"Jesus fucking Christ!" She stared reverently at the bills. "How many are there?"

She glided over the floor, hypnotized by the money. There was a sweep of predatory claws as she snatched it up.

"Five hundred kronor," she whispered. "Come to mama, my sweet babies." She kissed the bills passionately. "And just think, clothing rations end this month! Now I can buy a new dress! And a hat! And stockings!"

"Can I have something too?" dared Sven. "A real chocolate bar?"

"Sure you can, kiddo!" laughed Ma. At that moment her benevolence knew no bounds. "Sure you can! I'll put a ten-kronor bill on the table before I leave in the morning. How's that? You can buy whatever you want."

"Ten kronor?" That was more than he'd ever owned. "I can

buy anything I want?"

"You bet!" She smiled and ruffled his hair. "And get yourself some food too, 'cause I don't know when I'll be back. I have to run some errands later on. Okay?"

"Okay."

"Good boy."

Ma plunged back into the closet, rummaging and throwing clothes around, singing to herself. She was hunting for more loot, like a pig rooting for truffles, and it obviously paid off because she emerged from the mess with a scrunched-up ten-kronor bill she had dug out of the pocket of one of Pa's shirts. Inside the bill was a gold ring with three green stones. She whooped with glee. She knew the ring was stolen, she wasn't born yesterday, but that didn't mean she couldn't keep it. Finders, keepers, you better believe it. It was probably worth quite a bit of dough. Well, good. That prick owed her. She whistled and hummed as she tidied up the closet, turned out the closet light, and strode triumphantly out into the hall.

"We'll be just fine, kid," she declared, and patted his shoulder. "Now I'm gonna have me a little drink and celebrate our luck. Then I gotta hit the hay. You can amuse yourself, can't you?"

"Sure," said Sven.

"If you need anything, you just let me know, okay?"

"Okay."

"Just don't bug me tonight, because I'm real tired. Okay?"

"Okay."

"Good-night, kid."

As soon as Ma went to bed, Sven followed suit. He lay in bed listening to the lullaby of her light snores. They sounded calm and reassuring. Not long after, he fell asleep too. It was that night he first had the strange dream that would haunt him off and on through the years. That night the dream was so vivid that when he woke up he was convinced it had really happened. Except that in the dream he had been a grown man and had lived somewhere else. He'd worn a suit. A black suit, not a brown pin-stripe. It was as if his subconscious had already stopped treating him like a kid.

A stranger with an official voice that meant business had called him on the phone and said that his ma had died and he had to go and sort out the estate. In the dream he knew that this meant cleaning all the old stuff out of the apartment. The voice said to take whatever he wanted, because it was all his now, and to get rid of the rest. There were new people waiting to move in. He had to hurry.

Next thing he knew, he was back in the apartment, only it looked completely different. For some reason it was the middle of the night yet the whole place was simmering in a bright yellow light that didn't come from any lamps. It was dead silent. Sven, an adult wearing a suit, stood in the hall looking around. There was a brand-new rug on the hall floor. She must have just bought it, he thought; she certainly didn't know how to weave. The colours were bright shades of blue that brought to mind summer skies, corn-flowers, and bluebells. The walls were covered with white and blue striped wallpaper and hung with beautifully framed paintings of ships. Why ships he wondered. The bedroom door was firmly closed and he knew, the way you do in dreams, that opening it was against the rules.

The living-room had grown much larger and was unrecogniz-able. "Parlour" would be a better word to describe it. Heavy white lace curtains draped the windows and there was new wallpaper here too, in a pale yellow pattern. All the woodwork was gleaming white. The sofa and chairs were upholstered in pale green satin, and grouped around a table on a deep carpet of forest green. On the table stood a huge bouquet of yellow roses. Everything was spotless.

Behind the folds of lace in the windows he sensed, rather than saw, a profusion of tropical plants. He could smell their cloying scent. The apartment had become a place where dignity and peace ruled. A place to take tea and read gentle poetry. A place to hold your cup with your pinkie sticking out.

I'll take all this with me, he thought. It's mine! I like this furniture, I want to live in a room like this. Nothing bad can happen in such a room. And it's mine! Incredible!

He turned around and went to the kitchen. This was where he'd spent most of his time as a child. It had changed too. It was twice as big, but for some reason it had the same shabby table and chairs standing on the same cracked lino. The porcelain sink was still chipped and had only a cold-water tap. But the walls! The walls were studded with brand-new cupboards. It seemed there were hundreds, but how could that be? However many there were, now it was his job to go through every one of them and empty them. He had to do it quickly, the people moving in were waiting down in the street with their bundles. They were Jewish refugees from Denmark.

He noticed that he was conveniently carrying a very large, old-fashioned suitcase with leather straps and a big lock. He opened it up and parked it in the middle of the floor so he could throw in whatever he found worth keeping. If he recalled correctly, there wouldn't be much. The first door he opened surprised him by revealing a wide assortment of vases. Big ones, small ones, of crystal and china and cut glass. Hand-painted ones and silver ones. Yet Ma had never had a flower in the house. How bizarre! He picked out a tall vase made of bone china in a blue and white pattern, and put it carefully into his suitcase. He liked the shape of it. Next he grabbed a crystal vase so narrow it would hold only a single rose. Very sophisticated. He couldn't resist a third one, a square silver container with handles, a manly kind of design. Might come in handy, he thought. Anyway, they're all mine.

He went on to the next cupboard, full of expectations. And the next, and the next, flinging open doors, staring in amazement at the cornucopia, the vulgar hoarding. There were dishes galore, whole sets serving twelve, white with gold edges, others with patterns of rosebuds and primroses, dainty coffee-cups on delicate saucers. There were cake plates in all sizes, though Ma had never baked a cake in her life. There were Orrefors crystal glasses. Wine-glasses with fragile stems, schnapps glasses, punch glasses, five kinds of cut-glass tumblers and goblets. He found artfully blown decanters from Venice with matching liqueur glasses. One set was of smoky pink glass with a gold pattern, the other dark green with a silver motif. Piles of silverware spilled out of drawers. It needed polishing, it hadn't been used for a long time. He picked up a spoon and rubbed it against his shirt-sleeve until it gleamed. I'll keep the silver, he decided, and threw a pile into the suitcase without breaking anything. He was amazingly confident and coordinated all of a sudden, and knowledgeable about the quality of all he saw.

The hue of the golden light never changed as he went from cupboard to cupboard, but the air seemed slightly heavier as the night wore on. He found stacks of linen tablecloths, lace tablecloths, embroidered ones, big and small, linen and cotton towels with the initials EB embroidered in silk, folded tapestries, yet another set of dishes in Royal Danish china. Four cupboards were given over to ornaments and figurines. Shepherdesses and ladies of the court, horses, dogs and playful kittens, ivory elephants, men with accordions, girls holding baskets and flowers, ballerinas and angels. What purpose could they possibly serve? Sven grabbed a couple at random, an angel and a horse, for the hell of it, and hurled them into the suitcase that never filled up. The more he threw in, the emptier it seemed. Its mouth stretched like the beak of a giant baby bird.

Finally there was only the pantry left. It was three times larger than he remembered. The top shelf was groaning under the weight of thousands of chocolate bars. There was dark chocolate, milk chocolate, chocolate with nuts, raisins, liqueur, cherries, strawberry cream, truffle, nougat, and praline, all mixed up in a mountain of excess. Suddenly he was a child again, a greedy child in an adult's suit. He grabbed chocolate bars with both hands and hurled them into the gaping suitcase. It swallowed everything so voraciously he kept expecting it to burp. The other shelves were laden with everything he'd ever dreamed of: juicy, chewy licorice boats and raspberry boats, sourballs, sweet candy, hard candy, chewy candy, soft candy, gumdrops, fudge, toffee, butterscotch, salty licorice. There was candy he didn't know existed, and candy that probably didn't exist. Sweets in all the colours of the rainbow. Oh my, he sighed. Did Ma have a sweet tooth, or what? Even candy stores didn't have this much stuff, or half this much, or a third this much. How could she afford it? Where did she get it? And how come I never noticed? Did Pa buy it for her? Or steal it? Never mind, it's all mine now! In a frenzy of greed he fed his starving suitcase everything in sight, shovelling it in until the shelves were bare. Still the amazing suitcase wasn't full.

Before he was through he found a second pantry, a much smaller one, and confiscated twenty jars of homemade strawberry jam, forty jars of pickled herring in dill, and a loaf of homemade rye bread still warm from the oven. He followed that with a dozen large smoked sausages. The rest he left. A guy could only eat so much. The refugees waiting in the street could have the rest; they were probably hungry.

The suitcase was finally starting to fill up. Beside the stove was a small stone urn filled with fresh butter. This he placed on top, as a finishing touch. Freshly baked bread wasn't the same without butter. What a haul! Talk about a jackpot! And all his! The suitcase was now so heavy that a normal human would not have been able to budge it, but Sven had no trouble pushing it across the floor, past all the open cupboards still exposing their opulence. Wouldn't the refugees be happy moving into all that!

He had to stop in the kitchen doorway. It was impossible to get the loaded case over the threshold, which had grown almost a foot high. Climbing over it, he decided that this might be a good time to take a break and plan his strategy. Have a treat and replenish his superhuman strength. He stuck his hand into the suitcase and pulled out a large chocolate bar. Oh yes, milk chocolate! That was the stuff. It was studded with fat hazelnuts, he could feel their hard globes under the wrapper. He quickly tore it off, the sooner to get his teeth into that tempting brown surface, to crunch all those plump nuts, his very favourite. He was drooling all over his suit.

But just as the chocolate reached his lips, it was as if a mean finger pressed a button. Everything changed. All the reckless joy of his discovery poured out of him in a cold stream. He heard his own stern voice, a grown-up voice, announce that all this chocolate, this whole mountain of goodies, was his only because his ma was dead. She hadn't offered him a single piece of chocolate in her whole life. Not a gumdrop, not a toffee, had been bought with him in mind. She had never baked. Not once had she made him a sandwich with strawberry jam. She had never made jam. She'd never bought jam either, for that matter — not that he knew of. He was never meant to have any of this. She had had no intention of sharing it with him. Pa had given it to her with all the money he made. Sven wasn't to have any. He wasn't invited. He got to see this secret kitchen, these stuffed cupboards only because Ma was dead.

He shivered in the yellow, buttery light and cursed loudly, breaking the heavy silence. He abandoned the bottomless bag in the doorway and left, determined never to return. Knowing the truth, he was too proud to take anything, even to want anything. Passing the bedroom door he noticed that it was open. In the doorway, wearing her blue nylon robe, stood his dead ma, looking at him curiously.

"I thought you liked chocolate, my boy." She smiled an insinuating, sickly-sweet smile. Her red lipstick had smeared over her white cheeks. She had no teeth.

"You're dead, bitch!" he screamed, and ran all the way down the stairs, across the yard, and into the street, where he could finally stop and breathe. The refugees who were supposed to move in had disappeared. A big black car drove by. Pa sat in the back but didn't see him. He was wearing his good suit and smoking a cigar.

Sven woke up sweaty and disheartened, wishing he'd kept some of the chocolate after all. It was too late now. He got up and plodded into the kitchen. It was the same old kitchen as always, so there went that hope. And there was Ma, not the slightest bit dead, slurping coffee and smoking a cigarette. As soon as she saw him, she ordered him to get dressed and go for a newspaper.

"Can we get some strawberry jam?" he asked. It was worth a try.

"I don't think they have any," said Ma.

"Mrs. Göransson does," Sven informed her. "Maybe we could buy some from her."

"Never mind that old bitch." Ma blew a rapid stream of smoke through her nose. They weren't bosom buddies, Ma and Mrs. Göransson. "How do you know that, just out of curiosity? That she has jam, I mean."

"She said so. She's got family in the country. She gets eggs and butter and jam. She told me."

"She did, eh?" Ma was all ears. "How about that? Well, well. Tell you what, why don't you go down and sweet-talk the old bag? Tell her you're hungry 'cause there's no food at home. Which ain't no lie. Tell her you'll pay. Show her this." Ma pulled a wrinkled ten-kronor bill out of her pocket. "She doesn't want you to go hungry, does she?"

"No. That's what she says."

"She does, eh?"

"Yes. You have to eat, she says. Or you faint."

"Oh yeah. Well, I guess she's right about that. Go on then, go and ask. Look hungry."

Mrs. Göransson had a list a mile long of stuff to say about his parents, none of it the least bit nice, so it took a while. But in the end she let him have a jar of jam, four eggs, and a bit of butter for a decent price, just because it was him and he was a special boy. That was what she said. She would happily have given the boy the food, she told some of the neighbours later, but it wasn't hard to figure out who'd sent him down to beg, was it? Because that boy would never go begging on his own, she said, I know him, he's not like that, he'd rather go hungry. The neighbours, Mrs. Hermansson next door, Mrs. Lundberg from 16A, and Mrs. Kvist from 16C, all agreed. Fair enough to make that shameless slut pay for what she got, was the verdict. "She's depraved, that one," added Mrs. Kvist, and nobody contradicted her. "Too drunk to cook for that kid. If she's ever at home at all, that is." Mrs. Hermansson shared the fact

184

that, the day before, Edith Andersson hadn't rolled home until lunchtime. Looked a total wreck, too. They all nodded and knew what they knew. And then there was this thing with Andersson being taken by the police. Well, it was no great surprise, you could see that one coming. Strange there was nothing in the paper. Must be really bad.

Tongues wagged in the summer breeze, rumours blossomed on the grapevine, but Sven didn't hear any of it.

"Good work, kid," praised Ma when he came back with bread and a newspaper from the store and the goodies from Mrs. Göransson, walking proud and feeling indispensable. But Ma was standing in the hall getting ready to go out. She reminded him that his very own ten-kronor bill was under the sugar-bowl on the counter and said she didn't know when she'd be back. "Either tonight or tomorrow" was her rough estimate as she disappeared with a cheerful wave.

Sven was going to ask if she wanted some jam before she left — it was raspberry jam — but the door had slammed and she was gone. He stared at the closed door and the hopeful bird inside his chest stopped fluttering and pecked at his heart with its angry little beak. He ignored it and decided to go and have a sandwich. With lots and lots of jam. It was he who had got the jam, so he deserved it. And after that he thought he might check out the kitchen cupboards, seeing as he was alone and had lots of time to kill. Just in case. He didn't really expect any surprises, though, so he wasn't too disappointed to find nothing. Besides, it meant that Ma wasn't hiding anything. Washing jam off his face, he put the ten-kronor bill in his pocket and decided to go for a walk to look for something to buy, now that he was rich.

Life changed after Pa disappeared. It would have helped had time

185

stopped for a day or so while Sven adjusted. As it was, it was too sudden. There should at least have been a dress rehearsal. He managed as best he could, patiently making himself at home in his new role as a fatherless child. And as the child of a war criminal in a country not at war. It was much harder than he had expected, even though he lived in the same place, wore the same clothes, stared out the same windows. Time slowed down considerably, and he found that, the more lethargic the movement of time, the more muted the sounds of the world. That was how his hearing became less acute.

The loneliness was an old habit, an established way of life — all he knew, really — but now it felt different. This might have to do with the lack of sound, for it certainly was quiet. That was the strangest part. Before they had come and taken Pa, there had always been people around. Not only bad guys like Jensen and the rest, but other people too, coming and going, whether to drink and party or to argue and fight. He'd been alone in their midst, but at least they'd been there.

Asta and Kjell still came by for a while after Pa was gone, to drink and play cards as in the good old days. But it wasn't the same. Asta looked worse than usual, Ma said there was a cancer in her, and Kjell didn't laugh or flirt with Ma any more. Soon that tradition was gone too, and there were no people to sit close to, no raucous voices telling dirty jokes, no shouting, arguing, laughing, or singing, nobody to listen to, nothing new to learn, no interesting swear words to memorize. He missed those voices. Life became one long deafening silence while he waited for Ma to turn up and take notice of him. Cook him dinner if he was lucky. There was of course much less food now that Pa wasn't there to provide stolen ration cards. Still, it was cosy when the smell of cooking wafted from the kitchen, the sound of fish sizzling in the pan, Ma singing to herself. He lived for those moments. But she was so terribly busy these days that it didn't happen very often. She was gone all day because she had got a job at the stocking factory. Usually she was gone in the evening too, and sometimes she didn't come home all night. Especially Saturday nights. You gotta have a bit of fun while you're still young, she maintained, and she was still young and attractive and sought after. Often she had a boyfriend stay overnight in the apartment. When that happened, Sven stayed in the bedroom until the coast was clear.

Ma had rearranged the furniture so that she had the fold-out bed in the living-room. It's a much better arrangement, she had explained to Sven as he helped her push it across the hall, because that way we each have our own room and we won't get in each other's way. That sounded reasonable to Sven, who obediently made himself scarce. Not that Ma ever demanded that he stay out of sight; he was more or less invisible to start with. It was Sven's own decision, after he ran into Ma's first overnight guest. He padded sleepily into the kitchen early one Sunday morning to find a stark naked man pissing in the sink. A pale and rather hairy stranger, just standing there pissing a steady stream playfully shaking the last few drop from his half erect penis while farting contentedly. Sven looked on in dismay and quickly slunk back to his room. He didn't want to have to say good-morning to a butt-naked stranger who had just pissed a waterfall into his sink. Sven had spent Saturday night cleaning the kitchen, not because he had to but for something to do. He'd zealously scrubbed the sink with a piece of steel wool. When he was finished the sink had been sparkling clean, cleaner than it had ever been. Until that disgusting pervert dirtied it. Sven strongly disapproved, but he didn't say anything to Ma because she looked happy these days. He liked her to be happy. And if that meant strange men pissing in the sink, so be it. He just wouldn't clean it again.

Too much silence does funny things to your head. First your ears go all peculiar, probably from lack of use, and a strange empty echo blocks out the world. Then silence seeps into your head very slowly and, next thing you know, all the world consists of what's inside your skull. Your thoughts become loud and you forget how to talk. Making sound becomes unnatural. But eventually Sven got used to that too. When he did speak, he spoke softly so as not to alarm himself.

In the fall when school started things got a bit better. He had

187

somewhere to go during the day. He didn't make any friends, it was best not to. Besides, he wasn't sure how to go about it. Ma had actually surprised him with a new schoolbag, a blue knapsack. Every afternoon he trudged home with his knapsack on his back, never in a great hurry. Sometimes he saw that girl, Ingalill. She went to a different school and walked back from the opposite direction. They never talked, but once in a while she smiled at him. Sometimes he thought about loving her, but didn't know how.

In the evenings he did homework at the kitchen table. If he finished too fast he did it over again. Math was the best; he liked writing numbers, the processes of adding and subtracting, multiplication and division. They kept you busy and in the end you were rewarded with a straight answer. They kept the silence at bay as well, because you could count out loud. He was best in math in his class. Not a mathematical genius, that would have been too much to hope for, but he was good at it. Of course, that made him a bookworm and he got teased by some of the other boys at first. That didn't last very long, though, because he was so indifferent to their taunts that it took the fun out of it. He bored them out of his life in no time at all.

What did trouble him was the fear of somebody finding out that his pa had been put away in a camp for traitors because he had helped kill people. But if anybody ever found out, nothing was said. Before Christmas that first year Pa had his "accident" at the camp and died. Now he no longer had a father who was a traitor and an informer. He was just fatherless. That made everything so much easier.

Saturdays and Sundays he trudged about town. Sunshine, rain, or snow, out he went. First he walked up to Möllevångstorget. It was fun strolling around when the market was on and the weather was good. After the war, when life returned to normal, there were heaps of fruits and vegetables, bunches of flowers everywhere, housewives with their net bags, kids running around, drunks hanging about the statue with their bottles. He could get lost in the crowd. If he had money he'd buy an apple or a plum. Sometimes he bought cherries, white cherries when they were available, and walked along eating them. He didn't spit the pits onto the sidewalk but discreetly into his hand; then he put them back in the bag. He never made a mess anywhere.

Sundays he strolled down towards Gustav Adolf Square. The Salvation Army often came there to entertain in the afternoon. A small group of men and women in uniforms played guitars and sang hymns, always looking so blissfully happy that they annoyed people. Some guys would make loud jokes about them, but they didn't seem to care. Their eyes shone with a light that said that, not only did they have a one-way ticket to heaven, but they were going first class. Sven wished he could somehow invite them home to play and sing in his living-room and take away the silence.

More often than not he'd wander down to the harbour, where the Copenhagen ferries had come and gone until the Germans stopped them. They started running again when the war was over in 1945. He'd go down around Kockums shipbuilding yards. He liked the sea. He sometimes wished he were one of the seagulls travelling on the railings of the ships. Often he'd just stand in the outer harbour somewhere and gaze out over the strait to the line where the vast expanse of cold deep water met the sky. That's where Denmark was. And the Nazis. In the fall of 1944 there was a lot of killing and blowing up of buildings over there. It was done by guys called Hipo-men. Sven imagined them sort of hip-hopping around and shooting people for the sheer fun of it. A week after Pa disappeared they even blew up Tivoli. Sometimes he would squint and stare with great concentration, imagining that he saw columns of smoke rise into the sky.

One evening in September 1944, that first fall without Pa, Sven stood with thousands of other people and watched the grand opening of the magnificent new theatre. It had glass walls at the front so you were able to admire the opulence of the foyer. It was to be called Malmö Stadsteater. Being a child, he had managed to squeeze into a prime position at the front. He had arrived at six; the official ceremony didn't start until seven, but already there were thousands of people patiently waiting. Sven couldn't take his eyes off the huge crystal chandeliers glimmering inside, every piece hand-made of the finest Orrefors crystal. Then all of a sudden there was a lot of commotion. The royal party had arrived. Awed, Sven watched as old King Gustaf V walked by, tall and thin and bent with age. He was eighty-six that year. The King of Sweden! How kind he looked as he smiled and waved to the people! The theatre was opening with *A Midsummer Night's Dream*, and Sven was sure it was all a dream. When the crown prince looked in his direction Sven waved madly and the prince waved back! He really did, and he smiled, too! Sven kept waving even after the prince moved on.

It started pouring with rain but Sven remained glued to the spot, entranced, staring in at the beautifully dressed people, trying to make out the royal family and the nice prince among them. They all looked resplendent under those fairy-tale chandeliers. It was a wonderful dream. When all the beautiful people went to take their seats for the performance there was nothing more to see, and he walked home in the dark, elated and soaking wet. The next day he got a cold and a fever. He lay in bed shivering but he didn't mind, for every time he closed his eyes the crown prince waved at him and smiled.

If only life were always that exciting. Usually he had a vast amount of time to endure and precious little to fill it. A lot of it was spent walking. He walked west towards the museum, or in the opposite direction towards Värnhemstorget, passing only a block from the street where he would live as a grown man. He ambled along the canal, a sandwich and an apple in his knapsack. Sometimes he stopped and threw stones in the water. There were times when he took off down streets unknown and got lost. It was more exciting than scary because he knew that if he kept going for long enough he'd get to a familiar spot. It also killed a lot of time.

One Sunday around supper time he saw Ma all dolled up in a new red dress. She was about to enter a dance place called The Hippodrome, arm in arm with a man in a blue suit. He was a tall man wearing one of those dumb-looking hats with a wide brim that were so popular. Sven wanted to smile but felt thoroughly embarrassed, as if caught somewhere he shouldn't be. Ma didn't see him, though, she was laughing too hard at something the man had said. She laughed so hard that she almost fell out of her shoes, and the man had to grab her and hold her up. It was just as well she didn't see Sven, she was having such a good time. That's what she had told him, that she deserved to have a bit of fun before it was too late. The jitterbug was sweeping the country that fall, and Ma couldn't get enough of it. She thought it was the wildest thing ever and went dancing as often as she could. That was why Sven didn't want to disturb her; he didn't want to take her fun away.

Ma forgot his birthday that year, but she always did, so he wasn't too disappointed. Christmas, on the other hand, was wonderful. Christmas Eve she was at home cooking a lot of food, every Christmas from 1944 until Sven was called up to do military service. People would come for Christmas dinner, different people every year, and there would be laughter and loud voices. Asta and Kjell were there in 1944, the first Christmas without Pa. There was no ham that year. After that they disappeared for good. The man with the blue suit was there too. He brought a teddy bear for Sven.

"Holy shit!" he exploded when he saw Sven, who was eleven and tall for his age. "I didn't know your boy was that big! Didn't you say he was only three?"

"The hell I did!" laughed Ma, rosy-cheeked from the stove. She had in fact told him just that.

"Jeez, doll, you must have been a kid when you had him!"

"Yeah, I was," said Ma. She was thirty-five that Christmas, but officially she knocked off at least a decade.

Whatever else kept her busy, Ma stuck to her Christmas traditions. Two days before Christmas Eve she and whatever boyfriend she had at the time would come home carrying a big Christmas tree. They would spend the evening decorating it, fortifying themselves with *glögg*. Sven got lemonade and became hot and flushed hanging up the old decorations that Ma kept in a big box in the closet. When the tree was finished, tinsel and all, they'd light the candles on the tree, have something more to drink, and crack nuts. Sven got to sit with them for a while before he was shipped off to bed.

Christmas Eve, while the grown-ups partied, he'd stuff himself with everything from ham and meatballs to candy and cakes — especially after the war, when food became readily available. There were always presents for him, he never had to worry about that. Not very many, but he never went without at least one. Often he got two, sometimes three or four; it depended on who was there. Ma's boyfriends usually brought something for her boy. Even a teddy bear counted as a present.

The Christmas table was laden with ham and meatballs (except in 1944), both red and brown cabbage, and lots of potatoes. He liked brown cabbage and meatballs the best. Since Pa was no longer in the picture there was also *lutfisk* with mustard sauce, which he didn't eat. Not to mention sausages, several kinds of herring, and *Janssons Frestelse* with lots of anchovies. Usually it was a potluck party and everybody brought piles of stuff, and as there were always lots of people, ten or twelve or so, crowded around the table in the kitchen, there were tons of food. It looked wonderfully festive in the old kitchen, with candles fluttering amid plates heaped with food and red napkins. Ma hung decorations from the lamp in the ceiling and Christmas tapestries made of paper on the walls; they always featured Santas on sleighs in a winter landscape. Sven got to sit with the grown-ups — he was always the only child present — and eat as much as he wanted. For dessert there would be rice porridge with a hidden almond, but he never got the almond. For some reason, Ma's boyfriends always did.

Christmas Eve in 1944, Kjell and Asta gave him a sweater. The man in the blue suit, Ivar was his name, brought the teddy bear. Ivar's brother, Göte, came with a woman in a green dress. They gave him some chocolate. Ma gave him two books. That made five presents. Sven was happy. They all drank a lot, but both Ivar and Göte were the quiet type so things never got out of hand. There were no fights. It was a great Christmas even without the ham. He didn't miss Pa at all.

The New Year's Eves were worse. He had to celebrate alone, something he wasn't much good at. Ma had to go out dancing on a night like that — it's tradition, she said, you know what I mean, especially now I'm a bachelor girl. If she remembered beforehand she'd buy Sven a bottle of pop and a cake, which would be gone right away as he was always hungry. He'd go to bed early but he always woke up when the church bells started ringing at midnight. He would crawl out of bed and climb onto the windowsill to see the fireworks over the rooftops. People would start singing and shouting out in the street. It got very rowdy. When it calmed down he'd go back to bed. The next day Ma would come home in the afternoon and cry, "Happy New Year, kid!"

In that predictable manner the seasons came and went, each October adding another year, another few centimetres, to his growing frame. The solitude he'd always known grew with him.

The older he got, the less he saw of Ma. There were times when he wasn't even sure if she still lived there, or had moved to some boyfriend's place, or had been run over by a bus. He'd go and check the closet to see if her clothes were still hanging there. Whenever he did lay eyes on her she had a new boyfriend. He didn't know if she kept changing boyfriends or if they kept changing her. First there was Ivar with the blue suit, but he was gone before spring and instead there was a man with a beard and a checked shirt who smoked a pipe and said, "Mmmm...," in a thoughtful voice, but he didn't last very long either. He was replaced by a tall blond guy named Rolf who always wore a black jacket. Rolf looked much younger than Ma. After a month or so he was gone too. After Rolf came a much older man, tall and thin with a long nose. His name was Hjalmar and his teeth were long and yellow. Then he disappeared. Maybe he died, he'd looked kind of sick. After that there was another old guy, named Rasmus, who had curly hair and a tooth missing. After Rasmus there was a really old guy with grey hair named Svante. He had a gimpy leg and walked with a cane. Sven wondered if he could dance with a leg like that. It seemed she picked older and older boyfriends. Or maybe they picked her. Whichever way, she was a busy lady.

After a while it didn't really matter whether she was there or not, her absence had become a way of life. When Sven finished school at sixteen he got a job in a carpentry shop. The pay wasn't great, but the old guys there were nice to him. If he brought no lunch they'd share their sandwiches with him. But usually he had enough money for both food and clothes, and the odd treat as well. It sometimes happened that he came home and found money under the sugar-bowl on the counter, which was where Ma always put money after Pa was gone. She put it there irregularly, for Sven to have some food in the house, as she said. He wished she'd write a note with the money once in a while, telling him how she was, where she was, what she was doing. Sometimes he thought of writing a note himself, telling her that he was almost grown up now and had a job, because he wasn't sure she knew.

In 1951, the year after the death of King Gustaf V, Sven was called up to do his military service. That meant he was now a man. The crown prince who had once waved at Sven was the new king, Gustaf VI Adolf. There was a transit strike in Malmö and the streets were empty of buses and streetcars. Lots of people were out walking. A goofy-looking guy called Snoddas became popular with the most inane song ever to hit the airwaves; Sven couldn't fathom why it was such a hit. Black rust destroyed the wheat harvest in southern Sweden, and foot-and-mouth disease spread across the country, as young Sven Andersson was ordered to travel north to some place he'd never heard of to don an ill-fitting uniform. It was something he'd been dreading, an unnecessary and pointless imposition, but he had no choice. He sat alone on train after train and watched the length of the country go by. It engrossed him; he'd never been anywhere before. There was a lot of country to see, he realized, and the scenery kept changing. He had no idea what province he was in half the time.

Military service turned out to be a fairly pleasant experience. He gravitated to a couple of quiet guys in the barracks, Roland from somewhere in Värmland and Evert from Södertälje. They seemed to be the only other young men who didn't drink like fish and hang onto their adolescence tooth and nail.

All in all he quite enjoyed himself until a couple of weeks before he was due to leave, when he got a postcard from Ma. He would have gotten it sooner had she put the right address on it. The postcard had a picture of the Castle Mill windmill in Malmö on the front. On the back she had written, "My boy! I have mooved to Sune's and gotted ridd of the apartment. Your stoff is in a box in the attick. Sune says you can stay with us untill you find a plaice. We live on Västergatan. Your Ma."

Who was Sune? And what was his last name? And where on Västergatan, for crying out loud? The stupid cow. She hadn't changed. Oh well, he told himself calmly, he should know better than to be surprised. But he had no intention of moving into a strange man's home. He'd leave that to Ma. Come to think of it, she was a stranger herself. He didn't know the woman at all. He stared at the card and shook his head. Kept turning it over to look at the windmill, imagining her living in it with a strange man named Sune.

"Bad news from home?" asked Evert.

"Nah." Sven sounded indifferent. "It's from Ma. She's moved. I'll have to rent a room for myself."

"Better to have some privacy, isn't it? Somewhere to take your girlfriend?"

"I guess so. I was going to do that anyway."

"She'll still make you a welcome-home dinner, I bet. My mum is making a huge roast."

"I don't think so. She forgot to give me the address."

"She forgot?"

"That's my ma for you."

"How will you get ahold of her, then?"

"I won't. But that's okay."

"You don't care?"

"I'm used to it."

"Really?"

"Really."

"Well, maybe she'll remember and write again."

"Maybe."

"I bet she will. Want a cigarette?"

"Sure."

And that was that. Two weeks later he shook hands with Evert, who was off to university, and Roland, who was bounding back to Värmland to marry the homely blonde girl in the photo in his wallet. Sven knew he'd miss them. He boarded the first train heading south, and once again watched Sweden pass by. Somewhere south of Stockholm he fell asleep. Hours later he woke up and saw the familiar buildings of Norra Vallgatan across the canal. He was back in Malmö again. It felt strange. At the train station he looked out towards the Savoy Hotel and thought, "Well here I am, back home again." Remembering that he didn't have a home, he bought a newspaper and sat down decisively on a bench to look through the "Rooms to Rent" column. Calling up the first possible number from a phone booth, he had such an anxiety attack that he started to stutter and had to hang up. After a while he tried again, and quickly agreed to come and see the room, before he could make a fool of himself. It was in the west, out on Mariedahlsvägen, on the fifth floor. The rent wasn't all that cheap and the landlady wasn't a fountain of human warmth, but she seemed willing to accept him. Why she needed the money he didn't understand; her apartment seemed huge and was full of what looked like expensive Gustavian furniture. The room for rent was large and bright, close to the front door, and there was a bathroom across the hall. He was pleasantly surprised.

Across the street two parks, Slottsparken and Kungsparken, spread out as far as he could see. The museum was over to the left, behind the Castle Mill windmill, the one featured on Ma's postcard. He took that as a sign that he was in the right place.

The room had a hotplate and a big green armchair with a floor lamp behind it. The bed looked comfortable. There was a small table with two chairs by the window, and a bookshelf by the bed. He liked it. It was a definite step up. Away from the old quarters around Möllevången, westward towards where "better people" lived.

Indoor toilet, hot running water, a beautiful view. Could he be so lucky?

"What will Andersson be doing?" Mrs. Hultén demanded to know.

"I will be working while I study to be an accountant. It's a correspondence course," he heard himself explain. He was impressed by what he heard.

So was Mrs. Hultén. One or two frown-lines disappeared from her forehead. Accounting was a most honourable profession. Her late husband had been head of accounting for a large firm. And young Andersson appeared to be quiet and self-effacing. She liked that in a man. Well and good, she decided, he may have the room.

He moved in that evening, hung up his two paintings, and became an extremely dependable young tenant who paid his rent on the dot every week. It was a pleasure to have him. Every Friday at six o'clock he put the money on the table in the hall; that was the way Mrs. Hultén wanted it. He didn't run into her very often once she'd confirmed his reliability. She was either out or somewhere deep within the overstuffed apartment. There weren't many visitors except on Sunday afternoons at two o'clock, when the doorbell rang and she came scurrying to open it to a gaggle of little old lady friends. When they'd been swallowed up by the apartment and Sven dared leave his room to go for a walk, he'd see their coats hanging in a dapper row beside his. He found the order and neatness of this life very soothing.

A few years later he finished his course and, a week later, landed the office job that was one of his two goals in life. Mrs. Hultén congratulated him by putting a vase of red and white carnations in his room. He didn't know how to thank her, so he didn't. Now he started saving money so that one day he could fulfil his second goal and get his own apartment. A room and a kitchen and a bathroom with hot and cold water would be fine. But there was no rush. He liked his big sunny room. He loved the beauty of his view, felt peace of mind sitting in his window looking out over the trees, green and lush in summer, rust and gold in the fall. He found equal comfort in their barrenness in winter. The proximity of the parks made it convenient to go for a walk, a visit to the museum. He bought a bike with his first pay-cheque, a second-hand blue Monark, feeling young and brave. Every weekend he biked out to Limhamn, around Pildammsparken, and later out into the country, to Torups Castle or all the way to Lund and back.

He ventured over to Copenhagen on the ferry and discovered the scars left by the Germans, walked respectfully along the streets where so much blood had been shed. He was amazed how cheerful the people seemed. It was a lovely city to roam aimlessly in. The second time he went he walked from the ferry all the way to the zoo and spent the whole day there. Once he dared to go into Det Lille Apotek on St. Kannikestraede for a plate of expensive Danish specialities and a cold beer. It was the bravest he ever got. The herring was especially good and he ended up having two beers and an *akvavit*, getting half tiddly. Afterwards he went for a long walk. He liked the old quarters around the restaurant the best. He sometimes wondered what the people around him would think if they knew what his Pa had done. Once in Nyhavn he walked by the bar where his biological half-brother worked as a bartender. At the moment Sven walked by, his brother was busy mixing a fourth Tom Collins for a very thirsty businessman from Aalborg. The businessman saw Sven and thought how much he resembled the bartender, who a second later handed him his drink. "Your twin brother just walked by," said the businessman from Aalborg. "Is that right?" said the bartender. "Was he riding a pink elephant?" They both laughed.

Sven lived at Mrs. Hultén's for ten years, surprised at how fast time passed. He wasn't planning to move even then, but she had a heart attack and died. It came as quite a shock. The day after, from out of nowhere, her children appeared: a son from Stockholm with a snooty wife, and a cheerful daughter from Kristianstad with a fat, chain-smoking husband. Sven hadn't known she had children. They'd never been to visit. While they squabbled over family heirlooms and the Gustavian furniture, Sven hunted for a suitable place of his own. When he saw the fourth-floor apartment beside the Perssons' — just off Östra Förstadsgatan, a couple of blocks from the canal — he knew he'd found his home.

He attended Mrs. Hultén's funeral, a lone male among her four remaining lady friends on the visitors' side of the funeral chapel. After the funeral he went back and packed his few belongings, and moved east, turning down the offer of Mrs. Hultén's son to sell him the furniture in his room for twice what it was worth. He had already ordered new furniture. He wanted everything to be new, to have been owned by himself and nobody else.

When the new furniture arrived, he arranged and rearranged it until everything was placed in a way that felt absolutely right. Finally he had a home. Standing in the middle of his very own living-room, he felt a deep sense of accomplishment. He had the good job he'd always wanted, an office with his name on the door, a home with furniture that was all his. His two paintings hung on the wall by the dining table. Everything had gone according to plan. He was his own man. He went to his very own kitchen and put on his very own kettle, and made himself a cup of coffee.

Back in the present, in the same domain where he had once so proudly surveyed his new furniture, Sven sat blinking as the fog in his mind started to lift. Glancing out the window, at first not sure if it was night or day, he noticed what looked like a clear blue summer sky. The sun was shining. Birds were trilling with unconditional cheer. His window was open. Who had opened it? What had he missed? Where had he been? One by one the hazy curtains drifted aside while he blinked and blinked, newly born, wondering what had been going on. For a brief moment he was convinced that it was the day after he'd left Mrs. Hultén's. His first day in his new apartment. He had to shake his head at the folly of that notion. He wondered vaguely if he'd been sitting in his chair for weeks on end, dead to the world, slowly gathering dust. Had he not eaten?

Had he not been to the bathroom? A quick look at his shirt told him that he didn't look grubby, which was a good sign. Nor did he smell. On the other hand, he had no clear memory of any recent events, apart from a particularly painful one lurking in the shadows. Whatever it was, he didn't want to face it right now.

He tried hard to quit that stupid blinking. Closed his eyes to the bright sunlight and wished he could fall asleep again. It was healing. The King had smiled at him. Such a kind smile it was. Then the crown prince had waved and smiled at him too. And here he sat, a middle-aged man in a clean shirt, no longer a child, not knowing what day it was. Still, he couldn't have slept for that long if he was wearing a clean shirt.

Getting out of his chair, he tentatively made his way to the kitchen and brewed some strong coffee to help clear his head. He was pleased to remember how to make the coffee, measuring just the right amount into the filter. Cup in hand, he sat at the table and waited. Here I am, he thought, waiting for myself to arrive. I hope I get here. After a while his brain rewarded his patience by producing some recent memories. Oddly enough, they all featured food. Fried plaice with rémoulade sauce, fillet of beef and pommes frites, pork chops with applesauce — he must have gone out to eat. Either that or he'd gone around the bend. That was possible. No, he told himself, I must have been to Konsum's. No recollection surfaced of putting his coat on and walking down there, ordering food and eating it, but he must have done so because he wasn't the slightest bit hungry. A second or two later his brain threw him a memory, teasing in its clarity, of a walk in a Kungsparken resplendent with spring flowers and budding green. That must have been what brought on the nostalgic recollection of the years at Mrs. Hultén's. How he used to sit at the table by the window and look out at the parks below. Admiring the way they changed with the seasons, and the light airy green of spring, so new and clean. Watching the afterglow of a summer's day when he came home from work. Being able to see the Castle Mill so black against the landscape in winter when the trees were skeletons. He remembered that view more clearly than anything else.

Contemplating all this, he realized that he had been an old man even when he was young. His lack of surprise at this discovery brought a mournful smile to his face. He put his hand to his lips, as if to erase it, and noticed that he'd recently shaved.

A moment later he marvelled at the sensation of ice-cream chilling his tongue. That's right, he nodded to himself as it all came back, I bought one of those ice-cream boats, the kind with jam in the centre and chocolate on top. I bought it at the kiosk on Slottsgatan, outside the entrance to the restaurant in the park. On a sunny afternoon with hardly any wind. He had stood by the gate and the ice-cream had started to melt and drip into his hand, and he had wiped it with his handkerchief. He had walked back home after that.

What had happened to his memory? Where had it gone?

Confident now that he could handle it, his mind brought to the surface another walk, a slow stroll out to the East Cemetery. It was always very tranquil out there, he remembered. It was as if the hustle and bustle of the city didn't reach its green refuge. He had seen a little old lady tottering about, carrying a potted plant with yellow flowers in full blossom. She looked lost and doddery, poor thing, and he wondered if she was looking for her own grave to curl up in. It wasn't a morbid thought by any means. She looked as though she was ready for that lasting peace, and this shady expanse of green stillness was a perfect place to rest your weary bones. The tranquillity was broken only by bird-song. The people who came to visit always carried flowers and spoke in hushed voices, and kept discreetly inside their auras of loss. It was a place where pastoral serenity took the edge off your sorrow.

He had sat dreaming on a bench by a newly raked path under a rustling beech. He could still see the lines the rake had made in the gravel. He sat there for a very long time, joining the dead voluntarily. They made good neighbours. Carpets of purple crocus, yellow daffodils, and white wood-anemones had time to blossom around him while he dreamed. In a tree branch above, three chaffinch eggs hatched in a nest before he finally got up and left.

Only half awake, he had walked back home, all the way down

201

Sallerupsvägen, past Ellstorp, an area that had been a new suburb around the time he went off to do his service. He'd read about it in the paper. One-bedroom and two-bedroom apartments with hot and cold water and central heating. He'd thought at the time that he might want to move there. But by the time he left Mrs. Hultén's, having moved up in the world, he wouldn't have dreamed of it. Just as he came around the corner to his street he saw the neighbours leaving. That young missie and her hooligan hero. He hovered in a doorway while they crossed the street and sauntered in the opposite direction, in no particular hurry, apparently off to nowhere special. Only when they were out of sight did he dare climb the stairs, but he could afford to do so at a leisurely pace, not having to worry about running into them. He was only on the third floor when he heard the baby screaming. It screamed loudly and shrilly — as always, poor thing — as if in great pain. Sven wondered why on earth the babysitter didn't do something to console the little guy. Whatever it was you did with babies. Rush him to the hospital? Bounce him up and down and coo at him?

Sven was parked in his chair before it hit him that perhaps the baby had been abandoned and lay screaming all alone with nobody to comfort him. He jumped out of his chair, his thoughts ahead of his body, charged down the hall, and flung open the door. Rang their doorbell without a moment's hesitation, so positive was he that nobody was there. Besides, if somebody did open the door, he'd ask for the hooligan, knowing full well that he wasn't there. Is young Persson home, he'd ask. I need to talk to him.

Nobody came to the door. Inside the apartment the little guy cried his heart out, frightened and upset. Unprotected and vulnerable. It was terrible. Sven felt it was safe to open the flap of the mail slot and peek inside, but the hallway was dark and he couldn't see more than a metre of floor anyway. Another useless endeavour. Meanwhile the child kept crying. Not long ago Sven would have found it merely irritating. Now, as anxiety drove him back to his chair, he unexpectedly burst into tears. It felt good and he didn't try to stop; he couldn't have stopped anyway. Hiccuping and sniffling, he let go with total abandon. The release of all those emotions, whatever they were, became overwhelming, and he went on blubbering for over an hour, wondering where it all came from, until he was completely drained. At last, feeling hollow and chilled, he made for the kitchen, where he put the kettle on while honking into several paper towels.

All this he remembered now, as he sat in his clean shirt, freshly shaven. He also remembered that it had all happened only yesterday. He remembered how he had listened by the kitchen sink and heard nothing but silence. The child had cried himself to sleep. Or maybe Sven had cried the child to sleep. Or maybe the child was dead.

Strange how time had started to bend and twist and turn upon itself. It had always been so linear. But yes, that had been only yesterday, he was positive. He had sat by the table in the kitchen with his cup of cooling black coffee, just as he was doing now, listening intensely, keeping guard. Hoping the child in there would sense that there was another human being close by, watching over him. A guardian angel. Yes, he had sat there with his cold coffee until well after midnight — it was thirteen minutes to one, in fact, but it didn't matter how late it was because he didn't have to get up and go to work in the morning, did he? Work. Work was something he didn't want to dwell on. He'd rather dwell on the fact that it was close to one o'clock when those scum saw fit to return to their abandoned child. They weren't very noisy; if he'd been asleep he wouldn't have heard a thing. As it was he heard plenty, thank you very much, standing motionless by the front door like a snoopy ghost. Out on the landing the little floozie's voice had whispered something, sounding shrill and anxious. The loudmouth punk had answered with a typical hooligan hiss, "Oh for fuck's sake, stop fussing and open the goddamn door!"

Sven had not charged out like an avenging angel to heap moral wrath upon their useless heads. No, he had padded back into the kitchen and dumped his cold coffee in the sink. He hated himself for doing so. Sat down and felt stupid, angry, and helpless. And cowardly. Cowardly most of all. His sense of helplessness had always fit him like a second skin, but for the first time in his tedious life he acknowledged that he felt helpless only because he was such a goddamn coward. "Coward!" he said out loud. The word itself was ugly. Spineless and afraid, it curled in on itself and hid its head. He'd fallen apart, and in the shards of his former self stood all that was left: a coward. Not a middle-aged accountant with a nice office and a view, just a coward. Was that the reason for the unpleasant event that had ended everything? Ask it straight out, Sven: was that why you gave up your job?

Was it cowardice that lay behind it all, a chronic disease that had made him destroy his life with such blind determination? As if there were no choice? Was the reason, the answer to it all, really that simple and banal? He refused to answer the question, didn't want even to contemplate it; it would just confuse everything; he didn't have the energy; it was bad enough as it was. Leave it be. Never mind.

No — let's face it, he'd always been very comfortable in his cowardice, he'd felt right at home. But now he was tired of it. Tired of feeling stupid.

Now, back in the land of the living, he sat very still and thought about what had happened. Thought about the child next door. The reason he was doing so was out of focus, but somehow it was important. It was obvious that he would have to keep an eye and ear on those people from now on. Record their comings and goings. Make sure he was there at all times. Keep notes if need be. It was his mission, his new job. He was a vigilante now.

Around seven-thirty he heard them leave. The sound of their door slamming propelled him out of his chair and into the hall with such force that he almost crashed into the front door. And yes indeed, suspicion triumphantly confirmed, they were both leaving. The delinquent was as loud as ever. "Cheer the fuck up!" he bellowed at the little slut, who as usual mumbled something incoherent. Maybe she was retarded? Their footsteps descended, his quick thuds followed by her slow clip-clop, and then they were gone. Sven went to the kitchen and waited ten minutes, his ear against the wall like a barnacle, but he heard nothing. The little guy must be sleeping. Or had they taken the baby with them? He hadn't thought of that, had he? What to do now? Ring the doorbell and risk waking him just to make sure he was there? Dumb idea. How about a light knock on the door in case they had a babysitter. That would be okay. It had to be okay. It was his duty.

Next thing he knew, he was standing outside the Perssons' door, knocking softly with the palm of his hand, almost stroking the wood. Nobody came to open it, but he'd known that all along, hadn't he? For a moment he wished desperately that old Mrs. Persson would come to the door, smiling her gentle smile, saying, "Don't worry, young Andersson, I'll look after the little one." What a relief that would have been.

Damn that woman! Why did she have to move?

He returned to his lair. An hour later the baby woke up and cried off and on for a while. Sven rejoiced briefly in having been proved right. Supersleuth Andersson was onto them now!

And so it continued for five nights in a row, while the sleuth restlessly paced his apartment, which seemed to have shrunk to an alarming degree. The fifth night the child cried inconsolably for more than an hour, while Sven sat fretting in his contracted kitchen, chain-smoking and drinking black coffee, determined to keep vigil. He could have used a razor; he hadn't shaved for five days. Some soap and water wouldn't have gone amiss either. But he didn't have time to think about trivialities like that.

# LILLAN AND JANNE

Lillan stood by one of the bus stops down at the Värnhemstorget terminal, discreetly wallowing in shame. Not because she wanted to feel that way, not because she had planned to feel that way, and she certainly didn't intend to continue. But at that moment she was helpless to escape her penitence. Suffering the famous "guilty conscience" she'd heard so much about. It was there, stuck in her mind like a special sort of headache. As if she didn't have one of those too. The guilt headache was worse, though; it was heavy with jagged edges and was cumbersome to drag around. It was difficult to cope with the baby's stroller, a heavy shopping bag, and the weight of remorse all at the same time. She was no longer sure she could cope, and her predicament was starting to scare her.

She had tried to persuade herself that she had absolutely no reason to burden herself with so much guilt, that she had done nothing wrong and had hurt nobody. And that, furthermore, nothing was going to happen. In fact, she told herself eagerly, in fact life was improving, it was better than usual. Micke slept while they were out, and both she and Janne could relax a bit. And that wasn't so bad, was it?

But it was bad, and she knew it. All she wanted was to be able to relax at home in the evening. To have peace and quiet — that was it, that was all, not only for herself but for Micke. When life was peaceful Micke was such a happy little guy. A bit clingy lately, but not edgy and nervous, as he often was when Janne was at home and in a bad mood.

Janne's moods were hard to figure out. Anything could trigger them. Like the other night when, restless as usual, he just had to go and see this particular movie that, as it turned out when they got there, was no longer playing. Well, could he accept that? Oh no, not his lordship! He started kicking the wall outside the movie theatre, swearing and yelling, huffing and puffing like the Big Bad

Wolf. People stared at him and fled into traffic to get away from him. Then they had to go drinking so he could calm down after this traumatic setback. That is, Janne had to go drinking; Lillan stuck to juice. But service at the busy pub was too slow for his lordship, who lost his temper again and insulted the waitress. He then failed to see what the fuss was about when the owner of the pub, a big burly guy, steamrolled through the crowd and insisted that calling his waitress "a dogfaced cunt" was not only grossly insulting but also indicated a particularly nasty gutter mentality. And as such a gutter mentality was not welcome in his establishment at any time, it would be most gracious of Janne to get the hell out and stay out. Otherwise the police would be called to assist in his removal. It would also be a real treat, said the owner, if Janne never again showed his ugly mug in that particular watering hole.

Well, that did it. After Janne knocked the table over, several people helped the owner expel him from the pub in a manner that was so painful it left bruises. Out on the sidewalk, Lillan stood with her face to the wall and cried with shame. True, it was an unusually gruesome night, the worst one to date. But it was frustrating and humiliating and she couldn't live like this. The shame was starting to wear her out. Still, if Janne had to lose his temper, and he obviously did, better he do it out somewhere than at home. Better that Micke could sleep and not have to listen to Janne screaming and swearing and breaking furniture to the sound of loud rock music.

Lillan studied her excuses as they sashayed down the runway in her tired head but, try as she might, she couldn't fall for their cheap rhinestone glitter. That kind of thinking just wasn't her style. Nor could she turn her back on his rage and ignore it. Maybe it was true what Janne said, that she was too highly strung due to the hormonal changes in her body. It was something that happened to women, he said. They didn't have men's natural ability to relax and enjoy life, according to him. And if she was so highly strung — which, according to recent medical research, was not a healthy state to be in — it was to everybody's advantage if she got out and tried to enjoy life while she was still young. And hey, summer was coming, the sun was shining! "We're young!" said Janne. "Let's go out, have a beer, stay cool, meet people." Never mind that she didn't like beer. He meant well. He said he did.

But how could you not worry about a baby, so small and helpless? Whatever Janne claimed, deep in her heart Lillan knew that you did *not* leave your baby alone even if he was sleeping soundly. It was just plain wrong.

"What if there's a fire?" she had desperately pleaded the first night he dragged her out.

"The kid's too young to smoke in bed." Janne cracked up at his own joke.

"What if there's an earthquake?"

"Oh, for fuck's sake! An earthquake?"

"Okay, maybe not an earthquake, but what if somebody breaks in and finds Micke and thinks he's just so cute and decides to kidnap him and sell him to some rich people in America who can't have children? Or to some pervert? That happens. I've read about it. What then?"

"What about getting the hell out of here before it's too late, eh?" Janne literally pulled her out the door. She didn't even have time to get her jacket on.

She then had to spend the evening sitting in some pub by Lilla Torg with some people she didn't know, whom Janne didn't know very well either, all of whom found her boring because she didn't say much and didn't laugh at their jokes. She was too busy worrying about Micke. Janne, on the other hand, was in fine form, and charmed several people from Hamburg into buying him beer.

After a long nervous blur of noise, people, beer, and smoke, they finally got back home. It was close to one o'clock. She rushed to Micke's crib and there he was, unkidnapped and sleeping. A picture of innocence and sweetness, thumb in mouth and rosy cheeks. It just about broke her heart. If he'd been crying earlier, she'd never know.

"See!" Janne smirked. "See! What did I tell you? No problemo! My kid can look after himself!"

She was forced to admit that maybe, just maybe, she did fuss too much. The thing was, she liked fussing. It came naturally. Babies needed to feel secure, to be cuddled and cooed at. Micke loved it when she fussed over him. She loved it too. Fussing was fun.

Besides, it wasn't all that long ago that Janne had happily disappeared every evening without a thought of asking Lillan along. She'd been content to stay home and play house, to make curtains and bake cookies. But no more, oh no. Starting a week ago, she suddenly *had* to come along, to be by his side like a faithful little shadow. He never explained why; at least, he had no plausible explanation for this need for them to play Siamese twins. Not even Lillan was gullible enough to accept "Well, hey, you're my wife, more or less." She wondered if perhaps Janne was jealous of Micke, but decided that he wasn't that insecure.

Only Janne knew the reason for his change of heart, and he wasn't talking. He would have sounded whiny and immature if he'd been forced to explain that the very structure of his life had crumbled, that his social life had fallen apart. His three best buddies, Hasse, Bengt, and Pelle, had all let him down real bad. They'd let go of the safety net of their brotherhood and he had crashed to the ground. That was how Janne saw it, anyway. They'd let him down in different ways, but they had all betrayed him by leaving him behind and not giving a shit. Janne felt the pain.

Take Hasse, for example. Prime example. His very best buddy from way back in high school, for fuck's sake. They'd been through thick and thin. Blood brothers. Screwed the same chicks at one point. Well, suddenly Hasse went and got himself engaged to some bitch named Eva from Trelleborg. And from then on Janne was expected to go for a beer or a movie only as a couple, or Eva wasn't pleased. Janne was no longer good enough on his own. Brilliant, eh? And if *that* wasn't bad enough, then Hasse and this bitch moved in together, or rather, Hasse moved into Eva's apartment in Segevång, way the hell out east, right next door to the nuthouse. Good place for her. And no sooner were they all settled and snug than they bought a bigger colour TV, subscribed to every fucking magazine available, and read articles about the royal family, how to maintain a happy relationship, how to prune your houseplants, and forty ways to use leftover meatloaf. Real middle-class shit. Talk about enrichment! And then they went to Greece for two weeks and came back with two bottles of ouzo and suntans and souvenirs and a shitload of expert opinions on Greece and the Greeks that they cheerfully forced on people they invited over for a "Greek evening". Well, fuck me gently, Janne thought, appalled at the very idea. But he went, he didn't want to be left out. Lillan thought it was just wonderful because she got to bring Micke along.

Well, it was awful, he felt like shit. There were eight people in all, or rather, four couples, because in those circles you didn't count unless you were a couple. Two of the couples Janne didn't know, they were friends of the bitch from the sticks. Everybody but Janne had a great old time drinking retsina and ouzo and eating grilled lamb and some crap in yoghurt that Janne wasn't dumb enough to touch, all to the accompaniment of fucking godawful Greek noise they called bazooka music or some such thing. It was torture the way it grated on his eardrums. He sulked really hard to make the point, but nobody was the slightest bit interested, which pissed him off because sulking can be very tiring. Lillan was happier than a pig in shit, showing off her baby and laughing and talking and going on. That kind of bullshit was obviously her idea of a good time. All flushed and bright-eyed, she babbled about babies with two other new parents. They too had brought their brat along. It was lying in a big woven basket with handles. The kind you go mushroom-picking with, for chrissake. The kid even looked like a big fucking mushroom, come to think of it, all bald and bland and featureless. Let's face it, you didn't drag babies to a party. Not that it was much of a party. He damn near flipped at one point when the other new mother suddenly hauled out a huge tit and commenced nursing the mushroom. Right in front of everybody, while they were eating. And then this guy Leif, the father of the fungus, started talking fatherhood with Janne.

"I feel such joy and fulfilment when I watch Agneta nurse our son," sighed the fool. His long idiot face flashed gooey love at his wife and child like a goddamn lighthouse.

"No shit," said Janne. He stared at the guy with hardcore contempt, to no avail.

Janne and Lillan left early, and Janne had a suspicion nobody missed them. Not even Hasse, the fucking hypocrite. He'd told Janne when they got there that he was thinking of buying a car. Hasse had definitely joined the enemy.

But Hasse wasn't the only one. There was also Bengt, a friend Lillan had never heard of and never would. He was a goner too. Bengt of all people — Benke the buddy, Bengt with the rich parents, Bengt the thief and pusher, Benke the party boy, the lover boy. Who was always a pleasure to be around. This same Bengt was one day inexplicably overwhelmed by an intense longing to do good. Of all fucking things! The asshole decided to become a priest! Oh yes, old Benke was determined to strut around in a dog collar with his head stuck in a Bible. He was going to be not just a priest but a missionary, if you could fucking believe it. This was what he said, his exact words: he wanted to ease the pain of the world's suffering. Or some such shit. Spread the word of peace to all those tormented souls suffering in silence, all those starving stick-like people whose pain was visible only in their eyes. That was what he said. Somebody ought to ease his fucking pain.

Janne had been with Bengt when he'd revealed his saintly plans to his jewel-bedecked mother. The poor woman spilled gin and tonic on her Saint-Laurent silk blouse, all her bracelets made a racket as she wiped her blouse and hyperventilated.

"Oh dear God, help us!" she moaned. Did she mean with Bengt or with the blouse?

"He already did." Bengt smiled benignly, which would have been funny if it hadn't been so sad.

Bengt had always been ashamed of his rich parents, not just because it was cool to denounce your bourgeois roots, but for real. This was something Janne could never fathom, envious as he was of all that wealth and what it could buy. But as Bengt explained, infinitely patient, they were wealthy because they never shared; they just hoarded their pitiful money and material belongings, looking down their surgically altered schnozzes at anybody with less status and shit than them. And yet they weren't happy. This, according to Bengt, was an utterly pointless and ludicrous existence for which he would now do penance, and do so joyfully. Janne said he'd rather have their pointless existence, dressing in silk shirts and lunching at the Savoy. Bengt smiled ruefully and shook his saintly head. He also liberated a large amount of his mother's jewellery before he left home, sold it, and sent the proceeds to Save the Children. He got quite a bundle for her diamond earrings alone. His father's chequing account suffered a similar fate, much to the advantage of the world's suffering. Bengt's parents underwent a less noble form of suffering, and had to renew their Valium prescriptions twice in a month.

Janne and Hasse made a few desperate attempts to save Bengt from himself, trying to talk sense with the poor bastard, sharing some quality black Nepalese with him. Talking various girls into fucking him senseless. Bengt declined. Offering to take him to the psychiatric ward for emergency treatment. But Bengt just smiled that fucking smile so full of self-righteousness and otherworldliness, so mild and humble. It was enough to drive you crazy. The last time Janne saw him, he'd cut off his hair, all those long wavy tresses, and was dressed in clothes of such striking conservative cut and colour that they would have gladdened his poor sedated mother's heart. To top it all off he'd started wearing a pair of cheap round wire-rim glasses. Christ, Hasse said, he thinks he's fucking Gandhi already!

Bengt departed from their lives, sprinkling blessings like holy water as he left. He was now generally assumed to be lolling in the safe and good hands of the Lord, those same heavenly hands gently ushering him onto the worthy path of self-sacrifice and self-denial. The mere thought of such nonsense caused Janne considerable grief and bitterness.

The third friend — make that *former* friend — was Pelle. Good old Pelle the pal. It turned out the two-faced bastard was a faggot! Janne was shocked to the core, being an old-fashioned lad in many ways. Always proud of being a man, he was not about to be seen hanging out with some pansy, thank you very much. What if word got around that he was gay too? What if people got the idea that he and Pelle were going steady, for fuck's sake? Then what? Let's keep things in perspective here, let's think about more than ourselves and our perverse little pleasures, eh? That was what he told Pelle when he found out — straight to his face, no holds barred, man to queer. Pelle got very upset and disappointed, which served him right. He even cried, for God's sake. It was disgusting to watch.

Apparently Pelle had been aware of his sexual orientation for a long time, but had kept it a well-guarded secret. But then he fell madly in love with this sleazy smarmy dago, a fucking Arab called Ahab or Abdul or some stupid thing. Whatever he was, apart from a queer, he made Pelle want to come bursting out of the closet. Janne could not, would not, believe it. Pelle was already living with this Arab and was busy learning to cook weird food. Turned out Pelle loved to cook. Of all things! He should have stayed in the fucking closet, locked the door, and shoved the key up his ass.

One Saturday Hasse and Eva met Pelle and his faggot friend down in the old Market Hall. Pelle, the blushing bride, introduced Ahab the Arab and explained that they were hunting for exotic vegetables with strange names, and goats' cheese, or was it goats' eyes, shit like that. Hasse said that Eva said she thought the Arab seemed quite nice, considering. Yeah, right!

A few weeks later Pelle's bedroom looked like a scene from *A Thousand and One Nights*, at least according to Hasse, who went there to pick up the records Pelle had borrowed. This was while Janne and Hasse still hung out a bit and exchanged information. A few weeks later Pelle and the Arab invited all the old pals to one of their dinners, wanting to treat them to Middle Eastern food, but Janne declined with condescension, mainly to hurt Pelle, and told him that he didn't approve of the company, and had no intention of eating that weird faggot food. Lillan had wanted to go because they said she could bring the baby, and because she liked to beg recipes. Not a chance, ruled Janne, and so it was. Pelle stopped pestering him after that.

After the scandal with Pelle, it was useful to be seen hand in hand with Lillan, in case people got any funny ideas. He didn't tell Lillan that, though. He didn't want her to get vain or anything just because he needed her around.

And so it was that Janne's happy old life was no more, and he found Lillan to be the only constant in a cruel world. He had no choice but to make her his pal. It wasn't the same — she didn't understand the rules, didn't know how to enjoy life — but what could you do? Until something better came along, she was it.

Lillan found being a pal very tiring. She never got a day off, was always on call. Was never allowed her own thoughts or opinions because they were inferior. If she could have had her way, she would have stayed home every evening, had a cup of tea while she knitted and watched TV, then gone to bed early so she could get up with Micke, who got whiny if she didn't. He started to squall and then the noise woke Janne and he flipped, of course, and started yelling about how he needed his sleep. Not a morning person, Janne. His lordship seemed to expect a baby to lie silent until he felt like rolling out of bed sometime around lunch. It was all so unfair.

That was why she was standing by the bus stop in the late afternoon, yawning and trying to keep her eyes open. Micke, typically, was full of beans, squirming in his stroller, struggling to get out and go walkies in front of a bus. Lillan was barely staying upright, Tempo shopping bag at her side, stroller in front, bravely trying to be grown-up but feeling utterly cranky. Finally she yapped at Micke to sit still, poked around in the shopping bag for the packet of biscuits, tore it open, and shoved some biscuits at him.

Two old ladies nearby displayed their disapproval through meaningful frowns that didn't hide their glee at finding another young person to condemn. Lillan turned her back to the sour-faced harpies. There was an old bat like that living next to Majken's. Always had time for a word of malice like "Your son doesn't visit very often, does he?" One day, thought Lillan and shuddered, my mother will be like that.

She wanted to go home to bed. No, first she wanted a nice hot bath, a bubble bath, then she wanted to sink into a welcoming bed, one without Janne in it, pull up the cover, and float away. Most of all she wanted to be a child again, to be back at Grandma's and have Grandma come and tuck her in, sing her a lullaby, and pull the curtain in the window to the garden. The window with the pear tree outside. In the fall you could smell the fruit when the window was open. The thought of it made her want to cry. Dream on, Lillan, she said to herself. Dream on.

She'd gone to bed after two the previous night. At five Micke had woken up and wanted juice, after which he'd refused to go back to sleep because he wanted to be with his mummy and play. So good old Mummy had to stay up and try to keep him quiet in the kitchen while his lordship snored on. She drank coffee until she felt sick; at least it kept her awake. It was the fifth night in a row she'd been deprived of sleep and she couldn't take much more. Her hair was greasy. She had bags under her eyes and her complexion was pale and gloomy. She looked like a zombie on a bad-hair day, and she knew it. Her back hurt from carrying Micke around half the time. She had to; he clung to her like a baby monkey to its mother, grasping her fur and hanging on for dear life.

However, this was what she had decided: tonight she was going to bed early in order to sleep and sleep and sleep, and that was that. Janne could yell himself blue in the face, she didn't care, she wasn't going anywhere but to bed. With luck he'd go out by himself and stay out. She was going to sleep. And so was Micke. She'd bought a bottle of cold medicine for children that caused drowsiness and she was going to give some of this blessed brew to Micke at exactly seven o'clock. After that they were both heading for Dreamland. Tomorrow night she was invited to Eva's for a girls' night that sounded like a lot of fun. Janne had actually promised to babysit, after she made a fuss and said she'd refuse to go unless he did her this one small favour. It wasn't asking too much.

But first, a good night's sleep. And if that didn't suit Mr. Janne Lennart Persson, well, too damn bad. He could go to hell and stay there. She couldn't care less, she realized, and it pleased her no end.

What a miracle healer sleep is! Lillan got ten straight hours of it, no interruptions, just sleep, sleep, and more sleep. It was going to be the best sleep she'd ever had, she had told herself as she got ready for bed that night. By eight-thirty she'd been curled up between clean lavender-scented sheets, still warm from her bath, feeling as if she'd died and gone to heaven. She stayed awake for a while listening to Micke, worried that he would refuse to go to sleep, but the medicine worked and he was soon snoozing as soundly as she had hoped he would, his thumb in his mouth like a little cork.

Before she went to bed, she riveted a pair of serious eyes on Janne. It was showdown time at the O.K. Corral. She tried to stand tall, ready to draw.

"And you!" She shot straight, looking as resolute as she could. She was so determined this time it wasn't at all difficult. "You, my good man, either shut up for the rest of the night or go out. Go wherever you want, do whatever you want, for as long as you want. Because I am going to bed, and I am doing so in order to get some much-needed *sleep*. Which I intend to do *all* night *without* interruption. And I do not want any noise *whatsoever*. No music, no TV, no nothing. Not a peep. Do you understand?" By now she was starting to enjoy herself.

"Go ahead, runt, sleep yourself silly." Janne grinned up at her from the couch, overflowing with love and understanding.

She felt a tiny nip of disappointment. Now that she had worked herself into a state, ready for a shoot-out, he could at least put up a bit of a fight. She stared dubiously at the sympathetic smile plastered on his face.

"I won't disturb you, my darling," he promised. "I'll go out and leave you alone, and furthermore, I will sneak back in very quietly. I won't be late, either, I promise, because I'm pretty beat myself."

Lillan thought how funny he looked when he attempted to come across as sincere, but she knew better than to say anything. Janne removed his feet from the coffee table, got off the couch, patted her freshly bathed cheek, and disappeared into the bathroom to smoke a joint. Lillan stared at the closed bathroom door and shook her head, but decided it wasn't worth the energy to care what he was up to. She went and stood by the bed for a few seconds, savouring the thought of sleep. The wonderful state that was soon to be hers. Unable to resist for long, she jumped in. Oh, the ecstasy, the joy! She sighed so deeply that her whole body almost deflated. Then she was off.

When she woke up it was after seven in the morning and the world was a vastly different place. The sky was bluer than ever in the narrow opening between the curtains. Starlings were singing jubilantly; she could hear them clearly even with the window closed. And, most miraculous of all, Micke was still sleeping! As was Janne beside her, his arms and legs flung in all directions, his breath noisily exhaling puffs of stale beer, his hair reeking of cigarette smoke.

Lillan slid noiselessly out of bed, putting her feet right where the warm strip of light from the window fell on the floor. It lit up her toes and she wiggled them. After checking on Micke she sneaked into the kitchen, happy once again with her existence. She relished the silence of the sunny morning, rejoiced in the solitude at the table, alone with her coffee and morning paper. She sat at exactly the same spot where Mrs. Persson had sat for so many years.

This was what life should be like all the time, thought Lillan as the sun warmed her face. She had four slices of toast drenched with butter and marmalade, wishing she could enjoy breakfast like this every morning, her hard-working husband doing important stuff in his office, Micke still sleeping. She smiled to herself, so easy to please, and thought things were just fine the way they were.

Janne and Micke woke up almost simultaneously. She heard them thrash about and, with a song on her lips, rushed in to pull the curtains, throw open the window, and kiss them both, Janne despite severe sewer-breath. For a moment all was domestic bliss. Micke gurgled happily as she changed his diaper. She served his lordship coffee in bed, which pleased him no end.

"This ought to be a daily habit," he proclaimed. "A new family tradition."

"That's what you think, buddy!" said Lillan, and they rolled around on the bed and laughed like new lovers. Micke squealed with delight at such a happy spectacle, greedily soaking up all this dollhouse harmony. Later his daddy even shared little pieces of toast and marmalade with him.

"Tonight it's my turn to go out and have some fun," reminded Lillan, and downed a fifth slice of toast while she was at it.

"Oh yeah? And where the hell are you going, may I ask?" enquired Janne. He looked suspicious but harmless, with a gob of marmalade sliding down his chin.

"You've got marmalade on your chin. And to refresh your memory, I'm going to Eva's. Your friend Hasse's fiancée, Eva. Don't tell me you forgot?"

"I forgot. So what? Hey, that rhymed!"

"Are you listening?"

"Besides, Hasse ain't my buddy no more."

"That's beside the point."

"Is not."

"Is too."

"Is not. Let's make some more toast."

Eva had called a few days ago to invite Lillan to this special event that only girls were invited to. She wouldn't say exactly what it was; it was supposed to be a surprise. Lillan refreshed Janne's selective memory and he laughed heartily and scornfully. Heartily at Lillan and scornfully at Eva, for no other reason than that he couldn't tolerate the bitch who had stolen his buddy.

"Janne! Do you remember or are you just being a jerk?"

"Oh, riiiight! How could I forget! Oh, I am a jerk! I am! The event of the year! Are you taking your knitting to the festivities?" he mocked, pawing under her bathrobe in a distracted manner.

"As a matter of fact, yes, I am going to take my knitting," she said angrily, and hit his groping hand. She saw nothing funny in it. "I happen to find it relaxing."

"Gee, how I wish I could come," he sighed, and batted his eyelids. "I could bring my knitting too. We could have an orgy and poke knitting needles up Eva's butt."

"Don't be so stupid. Just remember I have to leave at six. You got that?"

"Yeah, so?"

"You won't forget?"

"Why would I? Do I look senile, or what?"

"It's just that Eva insisted we be there by six-thirty sharp, I don't know why. So please, *please*, remember that you promised to stay home with Micke. Just tonight, one night of your life. You do remember promising, don't you?"

"Yeah, yeah, I know!"

"It won't be a problem, because he'll go to sleep around eight. It'll give you a chance to spend a little time with him."

"Yeah, yeah, no problemo."

"There's a movie on TV. I read about it in the paper. An American one with lots of gangsters and guns and stuff you like."

"Yeah, sure." Janne got up and scratched his crotch. "I'm having a bath."

"You promise you'll stay home and look after Micke?" she pleaded with his naked back.

"For fuck's sake, Lillan! I promised, didn't I? What's the big deal? Do you think I'm fucking retarded?" He slammed the bathroom door.

"Thanks, honey, I love you!" she called sweetly, wanting to smooth things over. He probably didn't hear her, he'd already turned the water on. Well, never mind. She picked up Micke, whose face was covered in marmalade, and cleaned him off while cooing to him.

"Today Mama and her precious Micke-boy are going to go visit Grandma Majken. Then we'll all go for a long walkie in the park. Micke-baby like that? We'll have ice-cream!"

Micke drooled and looked adoringly at his mother's face. He grabbed her hair with both hands and leaned his face towards hers.

"Mummymummy," he babbled.

She kissed him on the nose several times and hugged him. He smiled from ear to ear.

"Mummy," he said again, more clearly this time.

She looked into his face and made up her mind not to go to

Eva's, not wanting to leave him ever again, but she decided to say nothing to Janne in case she changed her mind. It was just as well, because later that afternoon she did, after a long chat with Majken. She didn't reveal that they had gone out and left Micke alone, she was far too ashamed to tell Majken that. Besides, she wasn't planning to do it again, no matter what Janne said. That kind of thing was over with, as far as she was concerned. She did confide, however, that she was a bit worried about Janne babysitting.

"Heavens above!" said Majken. "Why shouldn't he look after his own child for a few hours? Do you really think that's asking too much?"

"Well, no, not really."

"Absolutely not. Has he ever babysat before?"

"Well, no."

"There you go then! I take it you want to go to this girl, what's her name, Eva's?"

"Yes, I do," said Lillan, after thinking about it. "It would be nice to go someplace with just girls." She'd been looking forward to spending a relaxed evening at Eva's, secure in the knowledge that Micke was not all by himself. And Janne had said, "I promise," while looking deep into her eyes, and if you did that you either kept your promise or you went to hell. She decided to trust him.

"I guess I will go after all."

"Good girl!" Majken approved wholeheartedly. "You deserve to get out a bit. I'd offer to babysit, you know that, but I'm on the evening shift all month. But trust me, it will do Janne good to take care of his own flesh and blood. Teach him a bit of responsibility. God knows he could use some. It's all my fault. I was far too lenient with that boy. You can blame it on me."

"You've been wonderful, Majken. You're the best, you really are. And he's okay, really." With Majken for a mum how could he not be?

"I hope so. I want you to have a good life."

"We do have a good life. And we have you," said Lillan and gave her a big hug. Then Micke wanted a hug too, so they all had a big hug. Then they went for ice-cream.

It was late in the afternoon when they got home. Lillan gave Micke a bath to remove several layers of chocolate ice-cream, and dressed him in a pair of clean striped pyjamas so Janne wouldn't have to bother. Before she hopped in the shower she made some beef and onions for Janne to heat up when he got home. She showered quickly and gave Micke his supper. When she got out her one and only dress, it was twenty to six and Janne still wasn't home. First she started to fret, then she got angry. At four minutes to six he sauntered through the door, apparently without a care in the world, and couldn't understand what she was getting so worked up about. He shook his head and stared at her as if she'd just messed her pants.

"I'm here, for fuck's sake! What do you want? A marching band?"

"Never mind, Janne, never mind. It's okay, really. But you will stay home and look after Micke, won't you?"

"I promised, didn't I?"

"Yes, you did."

"Well then? He's my son too, you know."

"Thank you, honey. I'll be leaving then. There's dinner for you on the stove and I already fed Micke." She kissed him and put her jacket on.

"Have fun. Don't give my love to that bitch!"

"I forgot to tell you, you'll have to change his diaper before he goes to sleep."

"No problemo."

"Thanks." Still she didn't move.

"Well, are you going or what?"

"Just making sure. Oh, and he likes some juice before he goes to bed. There's apple juice in the fridge. Take it out now so it won't be too cold. Otherwise it might give him a tummy-ache and then he won't be able to sleep."

"Goodbye, Lillan."

"Bye. Oh, and he likes his teddy bear when...."

"Goodbye, Lillan!"

"Bye." She smiled and blushed as he shoved her out the door and slammed it behind her. She remembered one last thing but didn't dare ring the bell, so she squatted down and opened the mail slot. "And don't forget to leave his night-light on!" she shouted into the hall, released the mail slot, and ran down the stairs before she changed her mind again.

*****

A while later that evening, Lillan is taking it easy on Eva's couch. It's a big cushiony job covered in a fabric splattered with huge blue flowers. It's like sitting in a flowerbed. And so comfortable — you sink into it and you never want to get up. The whole room is decorated in shades of blue, with the odd splash of white and yellow. Lillan likes it a lot. On the wall behind her hangs a painting of daffodils, large and bold and bright. The shaggy carpet under her feet is pure white. It's a cheerful room. Lillan, equally cheerful, is sipping tea, feeling grown up and independent. The five other young women are drinking wine. There is Eva, the hostess, of course, and her sister, Lisbeth, who is seven months pregnant and whose condition has already brought forth delicious horror stories about four-day labour pains, life-threatening complications hitherto unknown to the medical profession, and red-eyed she-devil nurses.

Beside Lillan on the couch sits a chubby blonde girl named Åsa whom she has never met before, and next to Åsa another blonde girl, a tall skinny one named Isabella whom she met when Eva and Hasse had their Greek evening. On the floor by Lillan's feet, with her elbows on the glass coffee table and her chin in her hand, sits a young woman who looks familiar. After a while Lillan recognizes her; she's the girl with the long dark hair whom Lillan saw the night she met Janne. The one who was standing in the hall devouring Pontus or Peter or whatever his name was. He had his arms wrapped around her like vines around a slender sapling. Tonight

225

the girl is dressed in a long red skirt and a large black shirt, but Lillan recognizes that face and all that hair. Yes, that's her, all right. Lillan is good with faces. It's almost like meeting an old acquaintance, thinks Lillan, who doesn't know many people. She pokes the girl's shoulder politely to try to get her attention. The girl turns around and smiles.

"I remember you," says Lillan. "I saw you at a party almost two years ago."

"You did?" The girl looks a bit perplexed. She lights a cigarette and studies Lillan's face with grey eyes that seem to sparkle under the surface. "Where was that? Must have been some do if you remember me! Did I make an ass of myself again? I'm afraid I don't remember you, and I've got a brilliant memory."

"Well, I'm not that memorable. It was over by St. Petri church. At some guy's apartment. Named Pontus or Peter or something like that. You were kissing him in the hall." Lillan blushes violently when she says that, realizing that it might be rude to point out such an intimate detail. But the girl in the red skirt smiles a crooked smile and taps her cigarette against the edge of the ashtray.

"Oh yes!" She nods slowly. "His name is Peter. I remember that night very well. God, it was a long time ago! Feels like a lifetime."

"Almost," agrees Lillan, grateful that she's not been condemned for being terminally rude. "A lot has happened since then."

"You're not kidding!"

"So you're not together any more?" That's probably too nosy, but it's already out.

"Who? Peter and I?"

"Well, yes. I'm sorry, I didn't mean to be nosy."

"Never mind. And heavens, no." The girl laughs briefly and grows serious again. "No," she says. "It would never have worked, not in the long run. We were too different. Unfortunately. I never met such a spectacular kisser."

"Why wouldn't it have worked out?" Lillan is painfully aware that she's prying but she really wants to know. It's a learning experience. And she likes this girl. "You two seemed crazy about each

226

other, the way you were kissing."

"Christ, you remember that too?" The girl laughs and shakes her head.

"I'm sorry!" says Lillan, and blushes.

"Don't be. Horny as hell was more like it, if I remember correctly."

Lillan's blush turns a deeper shade of crimson and she feels really stupid. She apologizes again.

"Stop being so damn sorry," says her new acquaintance. "It's all right. That just happens to be how it is. And you can't live on that for ever, can you?"

"I suppose not," says Lillan. "I don't know, I haven't been around much. My name is Lillan, by the way," she adds and stretches out her hand.

"I'm Katarina. It's nice to meet you." They shake hands. Katarina is wearing a dangling silver bracelet that tinkles like little bells, and Lillan remembers that at the party her earrings had tinkled like little bells too.

"I hope I haven't made a fool of myself?"

"Christ, no!" Katarina pats Lillan's left knee. "Not at all. The thing is, Peter comes from a fairly rich family, and I'm just a working-class kid. My dad worked in a factory, my mother cleans offices. That's the way it is, and there's no goddamn way I'm going to apologize for it. But needless to say, his parents didn't quite approve of me. The socioeconomic gap was a bit too wide, shall we say. So you may as well be realistic. Saves you from getting disappointed, doesn't it?"

"I suppose so," agrees Lillan, who comes from a fairly rich home but has never stopped to think about it because she's never had any money herself.

"Trust me," says Katarina and lights another cigarette. She sure smokes a lot.

Conversation bounces light and easy among the women. They're all in a good mood, drinking vino and eating pâté, shrimp, and toast. Lisbeth is telling a joke about a horny nun when the doorbell interrupts the punchline. Eva rushes to answer the door.

She comes tripping back into the living-room radiant and smiling, chirping and clapping her hands like some frisky scout leader introducing a new game. The others are laughing raunchily at Lisbeth's joke and don't pay attention to her.

"Girls! Girls!" Eva is shouting, eager and a bit impatient. "Look! Anja could make it after all! Aren't we the lucky ones!"

They stop laughing and turn five blank faces towards Eva, wondering about her flustered flapping. None of them has ever heard of Anja.

"Anja!" exclaims Eva, as if she's announcing some royal highness, and indeed the obese creature in her floor-length embroidered purple gown has a majestic demeanour. Her pudgy face is surrounded by mousy brown hair in a badly cut, not very royal frizz. It looks like the result of a botched home perm. She doesn't enter the room, but remains like a portent in the doorway.

"Don't tell me you never heard of Anja?" Eva is astonished by their ignorance, and glares at the indifferent faces of her friends. Lisbeth confirms that they have indeed not heard of this person.

"Well, I'm going to give you a real treat. Anja is a fortune-teller! She reads cards! You have no idea how fantastic she is. I can't believe you never heard of her."

"We have now," mumbles Isabella, and Åsa giggles.

Anja is regal and grandiose in her embroidered tent. A sibyl and a mystic, she is conscious of her superiority. By now two of the faces have started to express interest. Lillan remains neutral; she doesn't see the point of such nonsense. Katarina looks scornful; she turns her back on the sibyl and makes a funny face at Lillan, who almost surrenders to laughter. Isabella's face expresses only condescension as she lets her eyes take in the dimensions of this supposed oracle. Isabella has some respect for fortune-tellers, just in case, because you never know, do you? But fat broads with bad hairdos are not worthy of her consideration, so she is not sure what position to take. Isabella is spoiled, always has been, and is conveniently narrow-minded when she wants to be. She doesn't approve of people who fail to please her discriminating eye. And this lardo lady is ugly. She has the kind of face that invites contempt. Isabella turns to her friends and rolls her baby blues heavenward. It's heartless, but does she care?

If Anja cares about this show of scorn and disrespect, she doesn't let on. She's built up a fairly sturdy armour of self-confidence over the years. And if that isn't enough to protect her ego, she's got her special powers. The discovery of something nasty in the cards, for example. It's always a pleasure to see a snooty face crumble into whimpering little bits. Anja glides into their midst and parks her bulk in a large chair and smiles coldly at Isabella, who smiles icily back.

"Do you want tea or a glass of wine or something?" fusses Eva. "Something to eat? I've got some fresh...."

"Just a cup of tea, please," deigns Anja. "Herbal tea if you have any."

"Oh, no, I'm afraid I don't." Eva wilts on the spot, having to admit such neglect.

"Never mind," forgives the sibyl. "Ordinary tea will have to do. With a slice of lemon, if you have some."

Eva perks up again, for she has lemons in the fridge; her honour is saved. She scurries off to put the kettle on. Meanwhile Anja is trying to look amiable as she studies her public. They're not much younger than she is. Lisbeth with her big stomach, the two blonde girls whispering together on the couch. The girl with the long black hair sitting on the floor chain-smoking, an inscrutable face behind the veils of smoke. The tiny girl with the short dark hair who sits knitting up a storm in the corner of the couch. A variety of personalities, some of them easier to read than others.

"So...who are you all?"

"Lisbeth."

"Åsa."

"Isabella."

"Katarina."

"Lillan."

"I see. Well...pleased to meet you," says Anja. There's an awkward silence. A moment later Eva comes flapping in with Anja's tea and tries to get the conversation going. Still, the mood remains subdued. Anja has intruded like a grown-up at a children's party. She's not one of them.

They try not to resent her, at least at first. But she sits there like a bloated Buddha, the Indian cotton of her dress straining around her. Her two chins appear to tremble, not in unison, but out of step. It looks highly intriguing, and Katarina tries not to stare. It's difficult to determine if the fortune-teller is unfriendly, conceited, or just preoccupied with the significance of her position. Maybe she's in touch with the dark forces through some incantation echoing in her head as she sits there. Maybe she'll turn them all into toads. She talks sparingly, using words and gestures that give little whiffs of the mystical realm she's ordained to serve. A channeller of information from what can't be explained. Bit by bit, hint by hint, she lets them become aware that she has *knowledge*.

Does she realize that they resent her? Do they realize it themselves? Before she arrived, they were lounging around without a care, like a bunch of monkeys picking fleas off each other. They talked about anything they felt like. Giving birth, politics, work, the latest fashion, you name it. Before Lisbeth's dirty joke, Åsa was talking about how she always grows zits on her forehead when she has her period, which was something everybody could relate to. Katarina said her hair goes all greasy and dull. Isabella said she gets bad breath and has to chew gum all day. All of them get bloated. Lisbeth gets the runs and Eva always grows a big zit on her nose. Things like that bond you. Then the bloated bodies and the zit on the nose reminded Lisbeth of the joke about the nun she'd heard earlier that day.

And then Anja came and interrupted. She is not one of them. Fortune-teller or not, she is excluded. No doubt she has periods too, but they don't want to know about them. Anja compensates by being superior. Still, they do try to be polite and they ask ingratiating questions about her special gift. Anja answers in a manner that implies that she is doing them a favour. This is not how to win friends and influence people, but Anja — special gifts and dark forces aside — is more resentful than bright.

230

"And what you don't have, you pretend to have," whispers Katarina to Lillan as she lights another cigarette.

Lillan smiles, nods and knits. It's growing dark outside and it looks as if it might rain. Eva fusses and fawns, trying clumsily to rebuild the ambiance, but it's tough going. Things are not turning out the way she'd hoped.

"She's as phony as she is fat, I bet," whispers Åsa to Isabella, who nods and grins.

"Let's wait and see what she predicts," mumbles Lisbeth, who is willing to give the sibyl a chance. She feels bad for her sister.

"Now girls!" chirps Eva, all fluffed up mama bird. "It's time for Anja to read the cards. Get ready! Here comes the future!"

She gets a tray and clears the table while Anja graciously looks on. Her chins have started to vibrate again. Maybe she is absorbing cosmic powers, or receiving messages from the other side. They're obviously powers to be reckoned with, judging by the vibrations. Eva finishes clearing the table. Nobody offers to help.

"I am not having any cards read," declares Katarina, and crushes her cigarette stub in the ashtray.

Eva stares at her in disbelief. "You don't want your cards read?"

"That's what I said."

"But why? I don't understand, Katarina. I really don't...."

"I do *not* want my fortune told, okay? I do *not* wish my future revealed, true or imagined. I do not have the slightest desire to hear some stranger's interpretation of what will happen in my life. That is my right, isn't it?" Katarina is really pissed off, for some reason.

"Sure it's your right. I just wanted to surprise you guys." Eva's getting flustered, but then she's easily flustered.

"Don't worry about it, okay?" Katarina tries to smooth things over. "It's just me."

"Okay, I guess. If you're sure...."

"Trust me, I'm sure."

The fortune-teller sits silent. This heated exchange has nothing to do with her; it doesn't reach her elevated realm. The others seem curious enough. It's hard not to want to know, isn't it? Even if you don't really believe it, it's kind of exciting, right?

While they dither in internal debate, Anja takes over and starts giving orders. They all form a semicircle on the floor while she parks herself in the middle of the couch. Moving slowly and with precise gestures, she lifts a hand-carved wooden box out of her large velvet bag. With silent ceremony she carefully sets it on the table in front of her, using both hands, as if it's very fragile. Plunging a hand into the front of her robe, she fishes out a small key that hangs on a chain around her neck. She lifts it over her head and takes her own sweet time with the ritual of turning the key in the lock. Is that a horned figure carved on the lid? It's hard to see; she flips the lid open too fast. Inside the box, on a bed of black velvet, rests her precious deck of cards, powerful cards designed especially for her. Ordered from America, she explains in a hushed voice. From California, she adds, hinting at arcane rituals and blood sacrifice. The backs of the cards glimmer with figures in gold on a red background, in a pattern of strong oriental flavour.

They're all quiet. It has begun. For the moment at least, Anja has their attention.

"I will start with you," she declares loudly. A pudgy finger ending in a purple-polished talon points to Isabella.

Isabella leaves the semicircle and glides up to face Anja across the coffee table. She sits down languidly arranging her slender legs in a semi-lotus position. It sometimes happens that Anja sees events in the cards — both events that have happened and ones that will take place — but only when the currents are very strong. Usually she makes things up as she goes along. As far as this blonde babe is concerned, she doesn't hesitate to spread it on thick. She doesn't like the bitch. She doesn't appreciate the way she rolled her eyes earlier, not giving a damn if Anja saw or not. But Anja saw, she is more observant than she lets on. Now Isabella has to be taught a lesson.

First Anja flatters her. It's so easy. She greases her vanity until she can slide down it. Then down she goes, as low as she can. She hits hard but in a matter-of-fact voice, digging in her talons where it will hurt the most. The bland expression on her face reveals no malice or glee. She's good at this.

"According to the cards, the man you're living with is homosexual. I see a young man by his side. A very young man. They are very intimate." She looks directly at Isabella, her eyes still expressionless.

Isabella glares back and laughs shrilly. "What a load of shit! Can't you do better than that? You obviously don't know Fredrik!"

"Of course I don't. I've never met the man. I'm only reading the cards. I'm just the messenger." She looks modest.

Isabella's pissed off and doesn't want to hear any more. She gets up and rejoins the semicircle. Nor are the others overly impressed by this turn of events. They've all met Fredrik, who is famous for being a tit-man through and through. This reading is an outright lie. Katarina smiles her introverted little smile, leans forward, and pats Isabella's hand.

"Don't believe that crap for a minute," she consoles her, and turns to stare in disgust at the purple mountain. "Was that really necessary?"

Anja ignores her and calmly studies her cards. Katarina and Isabella exchange a glance of unity.

"My turn!" shouts Eva moronically, and she bounces up to take Isabella's place. She kneels in front of Anja as if to be blessed.

Anja shuffles her cards, silent and mysterious. She lets Eva cut the deck, and lays out the star, straight tidy spokes of cards. Anal retentive, thinks Katarina, observing the meticulous preparations. Eva looks excited with her star shining on the glass heaven of the coffee table. She is to be rewarded, and she knows it. Anja beams indulgently at her. Eva shines along with her star.

"Yes," she gushes, "there are indeed babies in the future. Not this Christmas, but it looks very much as though Christmas next year will bring a special little bundle."

"Will it be a boy or a girl?"

"That far ahead I can't tell. But there will be a baby, I can tell you that much. And it will be a beautiful, healthy baby. What more can you wish?"

"Mum will be happy," says Lisbeth. "Then she'll have two

grandchildren. And my baby will have a little cousin."

"Oh, I'm so happy!" Eva is bubbling and bouncing up and down, her bum hitting her heels like a witless yo-yo.

"Whose turn now?" asks Lisbeth.

"It doesn't matter. Whoever feels like it."

Lisbeth is obviously hot to trot so she goes next. She too is rewarded with a star full of good tidings, and a new car too. Nothing to complain about there. To top it all off, Anja relays the message that Lisbeth's first-born will be a girl. Lisbeth and Eva shriek and hug upon hearing such joyful tidings.

Katarina still refuses to participate. Åsa isn't overly enthusiastic, not wishing to find out that her boyfriend has contracted syphilis from buggering three-legged aliens. She declares that she has to go to the bathroom and excuses herself. Lillan has brought her knitting into the semicircle and is absorbed in working on a sleeve for Micke's sweater. She's not paying attention. Her purl stitches have a tendency to be too loose.

"You there." Anja points at Lillan, wiggling a purple claw. "Lillan. Is that what they call you?"

"What?" Lillan looks up. "Me?"

"Yes, you. Do you want me to read your star?"

Lillan hesitates. She doesn't really, but she feels a bit sorry for the poor fortune-teller. They haven't been very nice to her. After all, she has taken the trouble to come all the way to Eva's, bringing her box of special cards from America and all. Considering that, it seems impolite to refuse. She puts her knitting down.

"Sure," she says. "That would be interesting. I'm kind of nervous, though."

"Don't be." Anja studies Lillan's face, which is too earnest to ruffle her mystical feathers. She gets the cards ready, lets Lillan cut the deck, and lays out another star. Lillan looks on curiously.

Anja sits quietly for a while, absorbed in the cards. Her cheeks are flushed.

"So, do you see anything interesting?"

Raising her eyes from the cards, Anja focuses on Lillan.

"According to the cards, you recently became a widow," she

says, somewhat uncertainly, for Lillan doesn't look or act like a widow. She's too young, for one thing.

Lillan laughs. "I don't think you got that right. I don't plan to become a widow for a long time. Actually, come to think of it, I'm not even married!"

They all laugh at this, but Anja doesn't budge. She shakes her head and studies Lillan seriously, trying to discover something that only she knows how to look for.

"You're a widow," she repeats stubbornly, her mouth a tight line between the globes of her cheeks. She's sweating. This is one of those enigmatic stars she has no control over, one of the ones where she doesn't have to fake it. But she can't tell them that. So what is wrong? The cards clearly state that this young woman is a widow. And that's only the start, but she's afraid to reveal more. It's not as if she *wants* her to be a widow.

"No ma'am!" chuckles Lillan. "I most certainly am not. And I ought to know!"

True enough. Anja shakes her head and looks genuinely distraught.

"What else do the cards say?" Lillan wants to know.

"I don't know," mumbles Anja. "Do you have a child?"

"Yes." Lillan looks alert. "Why?"

"There's a problem, but I don't know what it is. It will take a while, whatever it is. Your child will suffer, but it looks like your dad might help you. It's not very clear."

"My dad!" Lillan bursts out laughing again when she hears that. "I haven't seen my dad for more than ten years. Try again!"

"I'm only telling you what's in the cards," maintains Anja, trying not to show her discomfiture. "And it's all in here. You cut the deck. I can't help it." She's starting to sound whiny. "And the cards say you're a widow," she insists for the third time.

"Jesus Christ! Do you have to go on about it?" Katarina is getting pissed off again. They ignore her.

"I'm not a widow."

"Yes, you are."

"Oh, for God's sake!" interrupts Katarina again. She looks furious. "Don't you think she knows if she's a fucking widow or not?"

"I'm only stating..."

"...what's in the cards," mimics Katarina. "And your precious cards know more about Lillan than she does herself? Do you really believe that?" She leans towards Anja. It's a threatening move. "Well, do you?" she repeats, emphasizing each word.

"Yes, I do." Anja's answer sounds mechanical. "Not always. But in this case I do. This is a real one."

"Then you're fucking stupid," contributes Isabella.

"Right on," says Katarina.

Åsa is nodding her agreement. Eva and Lisbeth look perturbed.

"It's not worth arguing about, is it?" Lillan smiles at them, ever cheerful, because it's too absurd to take seriously. She's not the slightest bit worried. "We'll set the record straight. I'll simply go and call Janne and ask him if he's dropped dead lately. How's that?" She gets up from the floor.

"Good idea," says Katarina. "Do it."

"Yes, go and call him right now," seconds Åsa.

"That's right. Let's show her who's right around here."

Lillan giggles and goes out into the hall to use the phone. She is in no hurry. They listen as she dials, and soon hear her in a conversation. They can't make out the words, but she's talking. And you don't talk to dead people.

"You see? She's talking to him. What do you have to say for yourself now?" Isabella is scornful and triumphant.

Anja says nothing, but feels downhearted. She is supposed to be right, yet for once she doesn't want to be right. Being right has lost its appeal. In silence they listen as Lillan puts the phone down, and watch her come back, slowly, as if she is having a dizzy spell and is afraid of falling. She is pale and has a strange look on her face.

"What's the matter?" asks Eva, overcome by a nasty feeling that something is not as it should be.

Lillan's eyes are huge and dark and frightened; she looks like a lemur. Katarina gets up and walks to her, feeling she might have to hold her up.

"A policeman answered the phone," mumbles Lillan with a frown, not yet understanding, but desperately trying to.

"A policeman? What are you talking about? What happened?" They're all shouting at once.

"Something terrible. I have to leave right away. I must go home right now. I should have stayed home tonight, I should have stayed home, I shouldn't have come." She bursts into tears. "I really am a widow," she sobs.

They all stare at her with pained expressions. They're all in shock, Anja included. But Katarina pulls herself together and grabs her bag.

"I'll drive you," she says very gently. "I live next door and my car's downstairs. I'm not quite sober, but who cares? Come on, Lillan."

She puts her arm around Lillan, maternal and protective, and Lillan huddles against her as if she's cold. Katarina has to lead her out. They're followed to the door by a pale and shaken hostess chewing helplessly on her lip, not knowing what to say or do, feeling it's partly her fault for having invited them. In the living-room Isabella is glaring hatefully at the fortune-teller, who sits forlorn and alone, her importance discarded like an old toy.

"Are you happy now, you fat cunt?" yells Isabella, and she sweeps the precious cards off the table. "Are you pleased with yourself? How the hell could you?"

"Yes, how could you?" echoes Åsa, slamming a fist on the table. "You bitch!"

Anja has by now succumbed to the horror of it all, she feels like a spider in the centre of a terrible web. Gone is the queen and her regal mannerisms. The demoralized sibyl is reduced to the sum of her insecurities.

"It wasn't my fault!" she whispers. "Don't you understand? Something happened and I saw it in the cards. It wasn't my fault!" Two large tears escape her pleading eyes and make their way across the hills of her cheeks.

No, they don't understand. They are not prepared to understand. They do not wish to be compassionate in the face of her vulnerability; they find it distasteful. Anja does not have the kind of face that evokes sympathy; distress makes her look pathetic and ludicrous. This misfortune brings out the primitive in people. The women didn't like her when they first met her, and now they despise her. Even their hostess has given up trying to be friendly.

"If I had known, I wouldn't have done a reading, I swear. I had no idea, no premonition. I don't foresee these things. If I did, I could prevent them. It wasn't my fault!" Anja is whimpering again. It's not a pleasant sound. Two more tears appear in her eyes, and follow the first two downhill. She gives up and starts gathering the cards together, throwing them into her wooden box. Nobody offers to help, though her ungainly bulk makes it difficult for her to reach around the floor. Then Isabella picks up a card at random, tears it in half, and throws the pieces at her. Åsa follows suit.

"Guess you'll have to get a new deck now. All the way from California," taunts Isabella. "Seeing as you've done enough damage with this one."

Anja is crying uncontrollably. She throws the wooden box in her bag, abandoning her torn cards still scattered on the floor. Heaving herself up, she wades through the hostility to the door, wishing only to be out of there fast.

Eva is standing in the doorway, biting her nails, looking perplexed, wishing Hasse would come home and save her. She's feeling guilty too; after all, it was her idea. She hadn't even consulted the others, that's how confident she had been. And here is poor Anja staring helplessly at her. Eva stares back and lets her by, following her into the hall, trying to curb the reproach she feels, to be a good hostess, to find a kind word. But she can't think of anything to say.

"It wasn't my fault. Do you understand that?" pleads Anja one last time, hoping for a word of forgiveness before she steps over the threshold. It doesn't come. Eva steps aside to let her out, watching Anja's round shoulders drooping sadly towards the elevator. Then she shuts the door behind her and joins her friends. Isabella and Åsa are still savagely ripping already torn cards into shreds. There is nothing else to do. Lisbeth is holding her hands over her stom-

238

ach. The baby is kicking feistily and Lisbeth is praying that it hasn't been influenced by the dark forces around it. Hoping that it won't be born with horns, like in that movie she shouldn't have gone to see. She looks at her sister.

"What do we do now?" she wonders.

"I don't know," replies Eva. "I feel so stupid."

"I just feel furious." That's Isabella.

"Me too." The echo of Åsa.

Meanwhile their thoughts are with Lillan, wondering what's happened. Eva has entirely forgotten that she was supposed to pay Anja, whose services don't come cheap. She had planned to take up a collection among her friends, convinced that, in their admiration, the girls would give generously.

Janne had really and truly meant to keep his promise when he first made it. But since then several days had passed, and somewhere along the line he had changed his mind. He had not done so consciously, it's just that he more or less forgot about it, to the point where he no longer has any intention of staying home, it's ceased to be a priority. He has now made other plans that make babysitting inconvenient. This change of heart doesn't bother him because, as everybody knows, it's the thought that counts. And as he actually thought he was going to stay home, he's morally in the clear. There's no way he could have hacked staying home anyway, for no sooner is Lillan out the door than the kid starts yowling and howling like a rabid wolf cub. It's pathetic. Janne dangles toys in front of the little fucker, and when that doesn't help he sings "Brown Sugar", including a really great guitar solo, but the little shit doesn't appreciate it at all. He keeps crying for his mama. And a man can only take so much. Janne loses his patience after fifteen minutes. If the kid isn't going to appreciate his efforts, he has only himself to blame.

"Shut up, kid!" he hollers when he's had enough.

Well, fat lot of good that does. He gives up and dumps the kid in his cot. Grabs some apple juice from the fridge and pours Micke's bottle full, goes back and shoves the bottle into the squealing mouth. "Suck on that," he orders as he leaves the room. He firmly closes the door, waving at the kid as he sucks his juice and stares forlornly after him.

Off to better things! Janne zips back to the fridge and gets a can of cold beer, stuffs some good hash into his pipe, then retrieves a porn magazine he's hidden in a jacket in the hall closet. Let the party begin, he chuckles. He's a happy man. He gets comfortable on the couch with his cold beer, his fragrant pipe of mellow mood, and his magazine. With his pants around his ankles he's soon oblivious of his son's plaintive whimpers.

Having sown his wild oats in a paper towel, he feels much better. So good, in fact, that he has to pull up his pants and get another beer. He lights a cigarette and entertains indulgent thoughts about the evening ahead. Estimating that Lillan won't be late — she won't have the guts, she'll probably come charging back no later than ten or thereabouts — he'll only have time to pop out for a quick brew or two. Better than nothing. He ran into some guys last night who were cool enough to qualify for buddyhood. He knew two of them vaguely from a few years back, and established contact again by attaching himself to them and offering them a pipe of his best green stuff. They all had a good time after that. He knows where they're hanging out tonight and he plans to attend, maybe get his social life back in gear. The future looks bright for an enterprising young man.

To add to the general sweetness of life, the evenings are warm now and the cafés and pubs have moved tables outside. Janne intends to join his new pals at a sidewalk pub, have a glass of beer, and check out the babes, who are shedding more and more clothes as the weather warms up. Is there anything as perky as a pair of tits bouncing under thin cotton? Or a pair of nice round buns wiggling in a pair of tight shorts? Is there any more delectable sign of summer?

Lasse, one of the guys from last night, told him about when he went to this disco down on Engelbrektsgatan the week before. There, among a resplendent parade of babes, he saw this luscious suntanned young thing, just back from Mallorca as it turned out, swinging a mane of golden hair down to her butt as she swayed to the music. It made Lasse go all woozy with lust. He asked her to dance when they played this slow bluesy number, and when she agreed he immediately plastered his body against hers. Drunk and horny and happy, he let his fingers do the walking, seeing what he could get away with. She was wearing one of those skirts made of Indian cotton so thin it's only coloured air. That's how he found out that the little tease was wearing nothing underneath. Lasse's fingers kept walking, running, poking, really digging for gold. He figured he basically got away with a complete gynecological examination. And the whole fucking time this broad was pretending nothing was happening. When the music stopped she smiled sweetly, cool as a cucumber, shook the blonde tresses out of her eyes, and disappeared. Meanwhile there was Lasse, so hard he couldn't fucking walk. Humiliating, yes, Lasse had said with a smirk, but worth it. Except that when he asked her to dance again she turned him down.

Janne laughed so hard he squirted beer out his nose, and said yes, he had experienced more than one cock-tease in his time, and wasn't it just sooo fucking typical? This was an outright lie, for Janne has always been satisfied with the one-man-band routine. Make that a one-man-hand routine. He's never been very attractive to the weaker sex.

He's not heavily endowed with social graces at the best of times, and around females he has all the finesse of a caveman. Getting pissed and lumbering up to some alluring beauty, it just isn't enough to grunt and burp and drag her off by the hair while scratching your crotch. It would be easier if it was, but as Mick Jagger so helpfully points out, "you cain't always git what you want." How true that is, thinks Janne as he sits there sipping beer, in a reflective mood. Of course, Janne's no Mick Jagger, despite his delusions. Consequently, he was happy in more ways than one when he met Lillan. With her he feels confident, he's in charge. She's not a hot

241

babe but she sure is cute. And he can handle her. He likes her, he truly does, maybe he even loves her — who knows what the fuck love is? One thing's for sure, though: he has every intention of staying with her. They're a team. She's undemanding and content, despite her constant fussing about the kid. Living with her is easy and painless. With Lillan he doesn't feel he has to constantly prove himself. Don't think he doesn't appreciate that.

And will you listen to that? The kid's shut up! All right! Feeling like an expert on infant care, he goes and checks on his son. Sure enough, the little guy's snoozing away. How about that? It makes him go all soft inside. He quietly closes the bedroom door. Now he can get out for a couple of hours and have some fun. There's no risk of Lillan calling home, because she'll be too afraid of waking Micke. Everything's cool, everything's under control. *Alles in Ordnung*, as the Germans say — though what do the Germans know about having fun?

Five minutes later Janne struts out the door with what he perceives to be a Mick Jagger wiggle in his hips. He's ready to boogie, and he's not afflicted by guilt. He's put his boy to bed and his boy is sleeping soundly, which is the way it should be. Checking that he has money and his key, he closes the door without making any undue noise. He's decided to buy an evening paper and some candy on the way back, so that if Lillan gets home before him he can say he just popped down to the kiosk when who should he run into but good old...good old who? Never mind, he'll work that out later.

He's just about to strut down the stairs when he sees the weirdo from next door down on the landing where the garbage chute is, one hand on the door of the chute, the other curled into a tight fist by his side. He stares at Janne as if he's seen a ghost, which is a bit insulting. This guy's a fruitcake, decides Janne. Being stoned, he's temporarily endowed with acutely heightened perception — or thinks he is. Ordinarily he would ignore the old fart and run down the stairs right by him, pretending he wasn't there. Today he doesn't, he's not sure why. Maybe because he's too mellow from his pipe. Maybe because the nutcase is regarding him with such a feverish stare. He looks as if he hasn't shaved for a week. It's plain eerie, but it feels as if the guy's created some kind of force field that you can't get by. And then, and how is this for bizarre, Mr. Fruitcake opens his tight little asshole of a mouth and out booms this authoritative voice that is totally at odds with his dumb, bland face. The voice echoes forcefully up the stairs, as if through some damn loudspeaker. It's truly amazing.

"You stay right where you are, you hooligan!" it commands.

Janne stares down in disbelief at the glowing eyes in the grey unshaven face sitting stiffly above the blue shirt collar so tightly buttoned around the man's scrawny neck. The eyes are shooting arrows at him, flaming arrows whooshing right up the staircase. The guy's a fucking lunatic, says a warning voice in Janne's stoned head. He ignores it, though; the situation is just too ridiculous. He knows the guy is a nutcase. But "hooligan", for fuck's sake? Who the hell uses words like that?

"What did you say?" he asks, too surprised to be rude. He's still simmering nicely from the good dope.

"I said, you stay right where you are!" The fruitcake is roaring like a goddamn lion. Then he starts to walk up the stairs towards Janne, not taking his eyes off him for a second. He walks slowly and carefully, as if he has a bad leg or something. Maybe he's shit his pants.

"And who the fuck are you, telling me what to do?" Janne is starting to think he ought to get pissed off. Under normal circumstances he doesn't even acknowledge losers like this, but it's becoming painfully clear that what's going on here isn't a normal how-do-you-do-nice-evening kind of thing between neighbours. What's happening here is unreal. Which means it's time to get moving. Anyway, starting an argument with this demented dipstick is not on Janne's agenda. He's feeling too good, and it's clear this guy is totally unhinged. He needs help, somebody ought to do something, but not Janne, because he's got better things to do. He's out of here. He moves towards the stairs.

"You go back in there right now! He's in there and he's crying, I can hear him! I hear him all the time! You don't go out and leave a small child alone! You don't do that! It's wrong!" The preaching fruitcake is up the stairs now, standing beside Janne, breathing heavily. They're the same height and are literally eye to eye. The guy smells of stale sweat and cigarette smoke. He's got bad breath, too.

"Why don't you fuck off and mind your own business?" Janne's had enough of this moronic exchange. Maybe the guy's drunk or something. Whatever his problem is, Janne is splitting. Unlike this asshole, he's got a life.

But it turns out that his neighbour is not about to let him go. A hand shoots forward and grabs Janne's left arm above the elbow. It's a stubborn grip. You wouldn't think the old asshole had the muscle.

"You're going back right now. He's in there crying all by himself. Do you think I can't hear him? Do you think I'm a fool?" He says this with a slow and deadly calm, but his eyes are so hot they're turning red.

"Yes, I think you're a fool." Fuck it, the guy *is* a fool. And besides, Micke isn't crying, so what's the asshole going on about?

The man's grip on Janne hardens. Janne's starting to feel the discomfort you get when a drunk sits down next to you on the bus and starts broadcasting his opinions of the physical attributes of your fellow passengers. This guy is seriously sick, a bona fide nutcase, and Janne isn't too sure how to behave with people like that. Other than ignore them, which obviously isn't going to do the trick in this case. Should he humour him? What will be the quickest way to get rid of him? Probably to do as he's told and go back inside. Wait until the fruitcake does the same. But what if he doesn't? What if he stays outside the door all night? He's crazy enough to do that. But more important, Janne decides, nobody tells him what to do. Certainly not this dipstick. In the end Janne decides to do what he does best. He starts to bullshit.

"Not that it's any of your goddamn business, Mister Andersson, but it so happens that my wife is at home. I'd show you, but she's having a bath. Besides, if we went in there we might wake up my son. So you just pop back into your hole, buddy, and relax. Everything's A-okay. There's nothing to worry about." Janne even tries to smile at the man, but the smile falls apart from lack of conviction.

"You're lying! I saw her leave!" yells the fruitcake, and for a moment he looks as though he's about to burst into tears.

"What did you say?" Janne feels as if he's being spied on, though he doesn't realize how true that is. He doesn't like the way things are going. It frustrates him not to be in control.

"You're lying!" the wacko shouts right in his face. "I saw her leave! No-good little slut! I saw her! So don't you lie to me, you hooligan. I won't stand for it any more! No I won't! Not any more! I'm not a coward!"

Janne loses what little control he has left. "Listen, you sick fuck, you do *not* call my wife a slut! *Ever!* Is that totally fucking *clear?*" He tries to shake himself loose so he can hit the bastard, but the grip on his arm is like an iron clamp. "Let go my arm, you demented moron!"

"Do as I tell you!" The fruitcake sounds like a whiny kid now, and his lower lip is trembling. What a sick situation! Jesus Christ! What a story to tell the guys! "Do as I ask you!" the fruitcake repeats, almost begging. He's starting to look weak and tired. Good!

"Let go my fucking arm, fruitcake! Right now, or I'll hit you where it hurts."

"Hit me?" The fruitcake's eyes widen in surprise and he seems to be losing control, but his grip on Janne's arm is as firm as ever. "Hit me?" he babbles.

"Yeah, hit you. Hit you hard. Where it hurts. So let go of my fucking arm before I lose my temper!"

"But I'm not the one who's done wrong!" shouts the fruitcake, wild-eyed and desperate. It's as if he's trying to explain complex astrophysics to an indifferent brick wall. "It's you who is bad!"

"Let me go you fuckhead or I'll show you bad!"

"But you're the one who ought to be hit!" The fruitcake shuffles anxiously on slippered feet, conviction blazing in his pale, red-rimmed eyes. His cheeks are flushed with effort. He might explode if he goes on like this. Not a bad idea, come to think of it. "You're the one who should be punished! Don't you understand?"

Janne didn't know whether to laugh, cry, or kick the guy in the balls. He must be deranged. He doesn't smell of booze, nor does he look like a drug addict, though you never know. Whatever his problem might be, he's not normal. Even Janne doesn't like to hit a handicapped person. Insult and humiliate, perhaps, but not hit.

"You need help, buddy." Janne smiles, but his look is more condescending than compassionate; he wants the fruitcake to know who is the superior being around here. The fruitcake doesn't answer. He appears to be thinking hard. Janne lets his muscles go lax, and a second later he jerks his arm free and heads down the stairs. He is splitting this scene.

But before Janne gets anywhere he finds himself grabbed once more, and dragged up on the landing. It looks as if they are overcome with an irresistible urge to do the tango. The lunatic spins him two steps to the right, one to the left, then slams him backwards against the wall by his door. Janne grabs his assailant's shirt as his head hits the wall, and they wrestle again until suddenly the lunatic lets go of Janne and then trips him, quite on purpose. As Janne stumbles, the fruitcake pushes him as hard as he can. Janne flies head over heels down the stairs with an outraged cry, an obscenity that he never has time to finish.

Does he have time to see the grey stairs or the white wall fly by as he falls? Does he catch a glimpse of his neighbour on the landing, staring ashen-faced at the tumbling body? Can he hear the muted sounds of flesh against concrete? Is there time to feel anything at all?

Janne crash-lands against the wall under the garbage chute, his head at an odd angle to his body. Death is instantaneous.

SVEN

Sven stares transfixed at the young hooligan lying there in a messy heap. It looks as if somebody's garbage has ended up on the floor rather than in the chute. His head is at a funny angle to his body, his ignorant mouth hanging open, only now no noise is coming out. About time. A dark red trickle is making its way out of his right nostril, straight down to his right ear. His eyes stare blindly at the ceiling. Lying all crooked and bent like that, he very much reminds Sven of somebody. For a few minutes he stands and ponders, then it comes to him: the hooligan looks just the way Asta used to look when she'd passed out drunk, all sloppy and disgusting with her big slobbering mouth hanging open. How about that! Sven shakes his head in astonishment. What a fate! To look like good old Asta!

But why is this good-for-nothing lying under the garbage chute? What a stupid thing to do! He's probably pissed, he sure looks it. Shameless, his T-shirt rucked up, his stomach showing. Sven can see his belly-button.

Then Sven remembers. The argument, the scuffle, the frustration. And the rage. His brain so red-hot it hurt. And he'd tripped that swaggering punk and pushed him down the stairs. And now he's just lying there.

Wake up and face the facts, Sven tells himself sternly. Get a grip. That guy's neck is broken, any idiot can see that. Nobody would lie around like that who didn't have a broken neck. Sven knows that because he has seen stuff like that in American movies on TV. In America they are always killing each other off, that's why. Usually they shoot each other first, but then they usually fall down great long flights of stairs or out of top-floor windows and end up lying in funny positions like that. He hasn't shot his neighbour, though, that much he knows. Still, dead is dead.

"I've killed a man," he says, slowly and clearly.

He doesn't feel shocked at the realization. It's bewildering, of course, this new role he suddenly finds himself in, but that's only to be expected. It's not every day you commit murder. He also feels a deep sense of relief that makes him comfortably dizzy.

He repeats the awe-inspiring sentence: "I've killed a man." It's overwhelming, overwhelming to the point of incomprehension. But it has power. And what happens now? He stands there waiting but no thunderbolt slams through the roof.

Doesn't anybody care?

He's done the right thing, he's sure about that. The stupid jerk should have done as he was told, and he shouldn't have lied. Because Sven knew what he knew. He met the girl earlier in the evening, when he came home from his dinner at Konsum's. Breaded veal in mushroom sauce. Applecake with warm vanilla sauce. She came skippety-hopping down the stairs, happy as can be, not a care in the world. Looked as if she couldn't wait to get out of there. She had the audacity to smile at him, showing the dimples in her cheeks. "Hi there!" she chirped, sweet as honey. He didn't answer, needless to say. But after that he knew she was out, didn't he? And then, after he threw a bag of trash down the chute, he heard the punk quietly close his front door so he too could sneak out and duck his responsibilities.

Not *this* time you don't, Sven thought, and then that sulphurous cloud came seeping into his brain, growing hotter and hotter until it burst into flame and he found it difficult to see. All he could think was, I won't let him leave, I won't let him leave, I won't let him leave. Not this time. I won't stand for it, I won't. I'm not going to be a coward any more.

And he'd showed him.

Finally something has happened. Sven has walked through the looking-glass. He's stood up straight and taken action. The spell is broken. He stares down at the dead body, trying to feel regret, thinking that he ought to, it's the kindly thing to do. But there's no regret anywhere in his whole body. And that means he's not supposed to feel any.

Just as well, because no matter how he tries, he has a hard time feeling anything apart from lightheadedness, which feels truly joyous. Oh yes, he's done the right thing. There comes a time in your life when you have to stand up to fate and take charge. Push it aside and show whose life it is. Be a man instead of a coward.

"That's what I did," he declares out loud. "I took charge." He stands tall, takes a deep breath and expands his chest, all the while observing the lifeless body below, challenging it to try and get up. I dare you!

Time passes and goes away somewhere, somehow, until the sight of the dead body, a wet stain spreading in front of his jeans, starts to bore him. It's getting dark. The streetlights are on, reflecting in the window on the landing. He hears the swoosh of car tires on wet asphalt. That means it's raining.

"I killed a man and then I noticed it was raining." That sums it up.

Speaking of sounds, that reminds him. He can't hear the baby crying. Must have cried himself to sleep, poor thing. All alone. Again.

Sven returns to the evening, to his duty. He has a job to do. He turns around and checks the Perssons' door, which is locked. It doesn't surprise him to find himself trying the door so boldly. He's in charge now. And this is only the beginning. Without contemplating the matter further, he trots down the stairs to the body. Squatting beside the hooligan, he paws him in a way that would have struck him as obscene an hour ago. He soon locates the keys in the left pocket of the jeans. It's difficult to get them out, the punk is wearing such tight jeans, and the pocket is wet with piss. It's disgusting. Sven has to push the body up a bit, and wriggle his hand into the pocket to extract the keys. He does so with his eyes closed, to avoid looking at the dead face close up.

He gets the keys, stands up and takes a final indifferent look at the man he just killed. He shakes his head, saddened by the silence that surrounds them. It's terrible when you think about it. You can not only commit murder, you can rob the corpse too, smack dab in the middle of the building, and nobody cares. The people on the third floor are just two flights from where he and the punk had their fight. They must have heard something. Then again, the Liljas are old people, they wouldn't dare stick their noses out the door if they heard anything strange. Next door to them is Kovac, a middle-aged Hungarian whom Sven knows nothing about. Maybe he's out. Still, it's obvious that you can pile the building full of dead bodies and nobody will make a fuss. Just step over the corpses, nothing to do with them. Cowards. That was what he had been too, that was the way he would have reacted. But he's changed now, thank God. He's challenged fate and won.

He makes it up the stairs in four great vigorous leaps, almost laughing out loud at his own boldness. Feeling invincible, he unlocks Perssons' door as if he's lived there all his life, and quietly slides inside. It's pretty heady stuff, being an outlaw. Once you leave the world of law and order you're on your own, you write your own rules.

He turns on the hall light, hoping it won't wake the little guy. He is surprised how clean and tidy the apartment is; he expected a filthy mess, a well-established slum with empty wine bottles all over the floor, overflowing ashtrays, used condoms, dirty underwear. Drug paraphernalia, of course, although he has no idea what drug paraphernalia looks like. Hypodermic needles, perhaps, strange-looking pipes and stuff in little plastic bags. Yet when he peeks into the living-room he finds nothing remotely like that. In the window, white curtains frame a row of begonias and African violets — Lillan's re-creation of her grandma's windows, her childhood's happy refuge. It reminds Sven of something, although he can't for the life of him recall what it is. The floor is waxed and shiny, the rugs look freshly vacuumed. The pine coffee table, the couch and chairs in soft shades of rose and green, reveal nothing. It could be anybody's pleasant middle-class living-room. It is, he notes with a tinge of bitterness, a lot nicer than his.

The floor in the hall is covered with a rag rug in shades of bright green interwoven to give a speckled effect. It reminds him of the rug from his dream, only that rug was in shades of blue, of summer skies and cornflowers and bluebells. A dresser of polished spruce stands under a large mirror with a matching frame. Shoes are lined up neatly on a wooden shoe rack. A baby stroller stands in the corner by the kitchen door. A hanging lamp over the dresser is a shade of green complementing the rug. There are two modern posters with splashes of green, yellow, and blue, advertising some art exhibit, one on each side of the mirror.

He's somehow disappointed at being wrong, but it isn't important. He has a job to do. Forward, march, get on with it.

The bedroom door is closed. He opens it carefully, just enough to sneak inside. A small table lamp spreads a dim amber halo in one corner of the room. In the other corner, on the far side of the window where the curtains are drawn, stands the cot where the little guy sleeps. Sven tiptoes up to look. The baby is lying on his stomach, his diapered bum in the air. He's wearing striped terrycloth pyjamas and he's sleeping soundly, thumb in mouth. On each side of the stripy little body a teddy bear sits guard. He has kicked off his quilt and it is lying on top of a pile of toys at the foot of the cot. There's an empty baby bottle on the floor.

Sven stands breathlessly by the cot. It's a solemn moment. He's the child's guardian angel, here to check that the baby is unharmed. Resolutely he lifts the yellow quilt, where bunnies hop in a merry row, and gently covers the sleeping child with it. Folds it for extra warmth. There. Now he'll be nice and snug.

As he stands there he feels a sudden urge. Wonders if he dare do it. He doesn't want to wake the little guy up. For a while he gazes at the rosy globe of the baby's left cheek, the dark down on his round head.

The child doesn't look like his daddy at all.

Then Sven does what he feels like doing. Because he can and because he really wants to. He leans over the cot and gingerly strokes the pink cheek with the back of his index finger. What a velvety soft cheek it is. He slides his hand almost imperceptibly over the downy crown of the baby's head, so silky and sweet. And look at the little guy snooze, eh? Sven smiles and fussily straightens the quilt, moves the teddies so they won't fall over and wake the baby up, picks the bottle up off the floor and puts it on the dresser.

Now the little guy is all cosy and safe. Sven's job is done.

Above the bed is a hanging worked in clumsy cross-stitch: two chubby angels sit on a fluffy white cloud, and under the cloud is a prayer. Sven knows those words. Everybody knows those words.

*God who holds all children dear,*
*Please watch over me down here.*
*Though I may roam to foreign lands,*
*My happiness stays in Your hands.*

He whispers the words, nodding emphatically. Those same words. They had hung on the wall above his bed when he was little. Not worked in cross-stitch, but printed on a small poster, or maybe cut out from a magazine, he can't recall. Funny that he remembers that. He can see the prayer clearly, and above it a picture of a child, rosy-faced with golden curls, kneeling by a bed, gazing heavenward through a window where a lone star shines brightly in the night. God's night light. It makes him wonder what else his brain is hiding.

The memory upsets him. It's so typical, isn't it, letting God take the responsibility, going out and leaving God to worry about it? They didn't even believe in God, Ma and Pa. No, not Ma and Pa, what's he thinking of? The slut and the punk, he means the slut and the punk. God obviously comes in handy as a free baby-sitter.

After a last glance at the sleeping child, Sven slips out of the Perssons' apartment, quietly closing the door.

His old world has changed since he walked through the looking-glass. He slides the key to the Perssons' apartment into his pocket as he surveys his domain. Not only is it getting smaller — that's been going on for a while — colours and shapes look different, as if the objects are no longer familiar. It's disconcerting, but he's a new man now, he has to take that into consideration. Then he happily remembers that he was planning to make some good strong coffee earlier, to go with the cinnamon buns he bought. Good idea, coffee would hit the spot right about now. It will help him return to normalcy. He puts the kettle on, and as he does so, he catches sight of his reflection in the chrome coffee-pot and is amazed to find that he doesn't recognize himself. Is he growing a beard? He refuses to think about the jolt it gives him. It's too baffling to deal with at this point. As he grabs the coffee-pot, it occurs to him that maybe he ought to call the police, to let them know what has happened.

Oh dear! How could he forget to call the police?

Now he's nervous, very nervous. Not about confessing — he can hardly wait to do that, he's a decent, honest man — but about what to say. How do you phrase such a confession? "Good evening, officer, my name is Andersson and I am calling to inform you that I have just murdered my neighbour." No, that sounds too formal. You can't be too formal when you're a killer, it isn't right. It's like dressing up in a tuxedo to go out and kill people. It's not just stupid, it's pompous, and Sven is not a pompous man. He tries to remember the TV cop shows. What do they say? "Good evening, I would like to report a homicide." That's it! That's good! It sounds professional and to the point, as if you know what you are talking about.

He gets out the phone book and soon, much too soon, finds the number for the police. Sitting by the phone, the book in his lap, he closes his eyes and concentrates. The elation of the past half-hour is fast disappearing, his sense of purpose deflating. He feels tired and frightened. He isn't used to calling the police. He isn't used to calling anybody. The phone sits silent on the bookshelf. He stares hard at it, but it doesn't spring to attention. His right hand starts a slow meandering towards the receiver. It takes ages to get there. Meanwhile Sven watches it and waits.

Then, before he realizes what's going on, he's dialling.

It's an interminable process. His hands start to shake and he keeps having to hang up and start over. "I'm not a coward," he reminds himself, and on the sixth try he manages. He almost pisses himself when he hears the voice of a fellow human being in his ear.

The voice is so full of natural authority, so in command, that he forgets what he wants to say.

"Malmö Police," repeats the voice.

"Hello." Sven finally gets the word out. It sounds disconcertingly feeble.

"Can I help you?"

"Yes...good evening...I mean, I...I want to report a neighbour...I mean, a homicide."

"Your neighbour has committed a homicide?"

"No, no...I mean, I've committed my neighbour...I mean, I've killed him. I've killed him. He's dead."

There. He did it.

Once he's confessed to another human being, he feels a peculiar sensation of having parted with his own life. The sensation is strong. He wants to confirm it, to get up and leave and never come back. But for now he listens to the voice in his ear. It takes over with ease, bless it. The wonderful, kind voice knows exactly what to say, what questions to ask, what to do. Everything will be taken care of, Sven is not to worry about anything, he must stay right where he is, somebody will be there as soon as possible. Sven thanks the voice over and over, hugging the receiver with both hands.

"You just stay right where you are, Mr. Andersson, and don't worry about a thing," the voice says. What a nice caring voice it is! Are there really such good people in the world?

Then he waits. He doesn't think about anything at all. His brain has slammed the door on recent events and gone for a rest. He'll just wait here in the heavy silence and breathe very slowly. Sit still and wait for the end.

It isn't long before there are noises on the stairs: the thumping of many feet, a rumble of voices. Somebody rings his doorbell. Sven jumps out of his chair and rushes to the door, almost sobbing with relief. He's been so lonely. But now somebody cares, and he's going to be looked after. He can finally leave all this behind. He throws open the door as if to long-lost friends.

Sven can never quite recall what happened after he opened the door that night. After the strange sensation of seeing the hall filled up with strange men, so much went on at once, that it isn't easy to sort it all out. He's never had visitors before, and suddenly there are three tall men crowding his apartment, full of authority and purpose. Others are poking around on the landing where the dead hooligan lies. They all have serious faces, only one of them is in uniform and it is very bewildering, all these grave-looking men in his quiet refuge.

The oldest of them has grizzled hair and is heavyset. He's the Chief Inspector or something. Sven feels proud to have brought out the big brass. But what really impresses him is how polite and concerned they all are. He was afraid they would break down the door, slam him up against the wall, and frisk him. Slap him around until he confessed. But not these guys. How kind and decent they are! Not a harsh word from any of them. Sven's deeply touched by their kindness, and tries to answer their questions politely and honestly. Does he have a family? No, he doesn't. Is he married? No. Divorced? No. Does he have a next of kin? No. Friends? No. Where does he work? The question upsets Sven, and he stubbornly shakes his head. Don't they want to know why he killed his neighbour? That's why they're here, isn't it?

"All in good time, Sven. We'll do this slowly, one step at a time. We don't want to miss anything."

"That's good," says Sven. "I appreciate that. But you will arrest me, won't you?"

They confess that they will be forced to take him into custody shortly.

"That's good." Sven approves wholeheartedly. "You must do your job. That's what you're here for."

They sit him down in his chair and ask a million more questions, repeating them over and over again. They're very thorough, these men; they expect definite answers, and no half-truths. They repeat their questions to see if they'll catch him lying — he knows that from TV, and he respects the efficient way they go about their work. They're so professional. But it's exhausting. He's had an emotionally overwhelming evening and he wants to get it over with. He wants to leave. This life is finished now, and he wants them to take him to whatever comes next. It doesn't matter what it is, as long as it isn't here. He will be fine as soon as he's handed a new script telling what comes next. He has trouble concentrating, what with the urge to go forward and leave the past behind, all these men and their questions, what with people running in and out. The questions sound irrelevant after a while, and the point comes when he doesn't have the energy to answer any more. That's when he remembers the key. He fishes it out of his pocket and slaps it into the nearest hand of the law. He does this at exactly the same moment Anja points to Lillan with a purple claw and says "You there."

"You better take this, because you have to go in there and take care of the baby." He thinks how very firm and in control he sounds. "But don't wake him if he's asleep."

"What baby?" asks the Chief Inspector, and raises an enquiring eyebrow.

"The baby," repeats Sven kindly. He likes the Chief Inspector a great deal. "The neighbour's baby, that is. In old Persson's apartment. They let him lie there all alone every night. All he does is cry, night after night. It's miserable to have to listen to. The baby, that is, not Persson. He died early this spring. That's why I killed him."

"You killed old Persson too?"

"No, no!" Sven shakes his head violently. He desperately needs them to understand. "Persson died of cancer. Then, you see, his wife moved to Tomelilla. She used to bake me cookies for Christmas. Then *they* moved into the Perssons' apartment. And they're mad, they're crazy. They have sex in the sandbox! And they leave their baby alone all the time. So I killed the hooligan. He's down on the landing by the garbage chute. You must have seen him. He was there, wasn't he?"

"We saw him."

"Well then, there you go. But first you must see to the little guy. The mother is out running around again. She's a real slut, that one. She's never at home."

"And how come you have a key to their apartment?" the law wishes to know. "Were you babysitting?"

"No, no! Of course not! I took it out of his pocket after I killed him." So helpful and eager is he that he seems to have no problem communicating with these strange men. These are such good men, they're going to help him, they're going to take him out of his cage. A burst of exhilaration shoots through him at the thought of it all being over soon. He gazes eagerly at the Chief Inspector, who is nodding in his understanding way.

"Why did you take the key, Sven?"

"To go and check on the little guy, of course." It was self-evident, wasn't it? "To make sure he was asleep. He'd kicked his quilt off, so I tucked him in. He was sleeping soundly when I left. Somebody had to keep an eye on him, don't you see?"

The Chief Inspector nods that he understands, and hands the key to his assistant. "Better go check," he says.

"Don't wake him up!" cries Sven. "He needs his sleep, he cried all evening!"

"Everything will be fine," promises the Chief Inspector, and pats Sven's shoulder reassuringly. "Arvidsson knows what he's doing. He's got two little ones at home."

"Oh, then I'm sure he'll do a splendid job." Sven has all the confidence in the world in Malmö's finest. "Would you like a cup of coffee, by the way? I have some fresh cinnamon buns."

"That's very nice of you, Sven, but we'll have to get going as soon as Lundkvist is off the phone," the Chief Inspector explains, adding that it's getting late, so perhaps if Sven would like to get ready...?

Sven asks if he can change into his good suit and put on a tie, to look decent. Show that he isn't a criminal. The Chief Inspector looks tired but he agrees. Sven is allowed to get ready on his own. They know he isn't going to run away, he isn't a coward. They trust him and he appreciates that.

"You go ahead and dress as nicely as you want," says one of them with a friendly smile. "Nothing wrong with looking respectable, is there?"

"That's exactly what I think." Sven's pleased to have met a like-minded soul. "And I suppose you'll have to take one of those pictures, what do you call them?"

"You mean a mugshot?"

"That's it. I don't want to look like a crook, do I?"

"Absolutely not."

They wait patiently while he gets dressed, empties the ashtray, turns out the lights, and pulls the curtains. He hopes he won't be back. Another thought occurs to him.

"Should I pack a bag?"

"That can wait, Sven. We should get going."

"Not even my toothbrush?"

"Oh, bring it if you want. But you better hurry."

Sven understands that, but he has to have his toothbrush. He never goes to bed without brushing his teeth. He's forgotten that he hasn't shaved or washed for almost a week.

Then they're finally on their way out the door. It's a strange moment. As much as he longs to get away from there, as much as he needs to go forward, it's shocking to have to leave the place. It's been his home and refuge for so long. Until *they* moved in and ruined it. Anger stirs in his head and he doesn't see the young woman with the long dark hair standing outside Perssons' door sombrely observing him as they lead him down past the garbage chute. He had expected to see the punk still sprawled out there, but he's gone. As if it never happened. Maybe it never did? He remembers it, though, he's sure he didn't dream it. Unless he's losing his mind?

"This was where he landed when I pushed him," he explains. "Right there. You found him, didn't you?"

"Yes, we found him. Everything's been taken care of."

"I'm sure it has!" he gushes. "You men are the best!"

They laugh and somebody slaps his back as if they're old pals. Which they are — Sven is sure of that. Real friends when you need them.

Sven gets to share the back seat with the Chief Inspector and Arvidsson, and they drive off down Drottninggatan, along the canal. The dark landscape glistens with rain. The sidewalks are empty apart from a man in a yellow rain jacket walking a large German shepherd. The man is wearing a short black skirt and high heels. Sven stares at him.

"There goes Tage," observes Arvidsson, and waves to the man.

The man raises his left hand in a feminine flutter.

"What's he doing out in the rain? Can't be many customers around in this weather."

"Maybe he's just walking the dog."

"Not really his area, is it?"

Sven has no idea what they're talking about, and is afraid to ask. He's quite sure he doesn't want to know.

The ride to Davidshalls Torg doesn't take long. At the station there are more questions, but that's all right, he's someplace new now. Other people are in control and he doesn't have to worry. When he suddenly gets hungry close to midnight, they send for coffee and a plate of sandwiches with cheese and salami. That night he sleeps soundly in his quiet cell. He's never had it so good. There's nothing to worry about, nothing to keep him awake. He has the whole police force keeping him safe.

Once again Sven has been handed a new script and a new role to rehearse. But this time things are looking up; he's been given a major part. He's the killer. The play ought to be a tragedy. A young man has been killed, a child has become fatherless. Despite that, it soon seems that he is in a farce. He has the right role but the wrong play.

The next morning a stranger comes to visit him. A short, bald-

261

ing man in a greyish-greenish suit. It's no doubt a very expensive suit — it has that smooth silky look to it — but it makes the chubby man look like a mouldy sausage. On top of the sausage sits a chinless face decorated with a snazzy little moustache. Sven takes an instant dislike to the man.

The man says that his name is Ragnar Lindgren and that he is to be Sven's lawyer. Sven says nothing, he doesn't need a lawyer. He is happy where he is. He especially does not want a lawyer who looks like a mouldy sausage sporting a moustache. He giggles softly to himself.

Lindgren looks alarmed but sits down anyway, and takes a folder out of a brown leather briefcase. Putting on a pair of glasses, he opens the folder and reads through some papers. This is mainly for show. He's already been through the report on the accused, if "accused" is the right word in this case. The man is confessing a mile a minute, and nobody has yet got a word in edgewise to actually accuse him.

The report states that the accused called the police in a state of utter confusion to report that he had "killed the hooligan because he didn't deserve to live." When the accused opened the door to the police he was making strange keening noises. He appeared to think the police were old friends of his, and clung briefly to the Chief Inspector. He has confessed zealously ever since, over and over, demanding to be punished, telling the police that they're the best friends a man could have. He kept patting the Chief Inspector's hand while constantly nodding emphatically to himself. Now he wants to put forth a legal demand to be punished, for crying out loud. It's positively pathetic. Talk about right-mindedness.

It's blatantly obvious that the victim fell down the stairs. Perhaps there was some provocation, and an unfortunate accident followed. But this man is legally innocent. But will he listen? Does he embrace the opportunity to go free? No sir, not our Mr. Gung-Ho I-Am-A-Murderer. Lindgren feels nothing but contempt for losers like this, and makes little effort to hide the fact. It is, however, his job to try.

He sighs.

Perhaps he should use a fancier word to help stun this fool back into freedom? Jesus! Looking absent-mindedly important, he shuffles some papers, scratches his neck, and informs Sven, without looking at him, that his file strongly indicates *exculpation*. He puts the file down and looks directly at the self-accused.

Sven has no idea what the unpleasant little sausage is talking about, but feels he has reason to worry. Exculpation? It sounds like a disease. Did the doctor who examined him earlier that morning find something? And if so, does the illness make him not responsible for his deed? "The killer suffered from advanced exculpation and could not be held responsible"? No, that wouldn't be right. He can't accept that.

"There's nothing wrong with my health," he protests. "I'm as fit as a fiddle. I haven't had a cold in years."

Sven stares back at the lawyer and realizes that he has misunderstood. "What do you mean by exculpation then?"

"What I'm saying is that we can easily establish that you are legally innocent. You and Mr. Persson had an argument, a scuffle ensued, and he fell down the stairs. It was bad luck. An unfortunate accident. You were in a state of severe mental stress, having lost your job, worrying about their child, and so naturally you felt it was your fault and...."

"But it *was* my fault! I killed him on purpose! He ruined my life! I hated him! I still do!"

"Sit down, Sven! Calm down! All right? Now,..."

"But I did it! I must be punished! There must be justice in this world!"

"I said, sit down! And stop waving your arms about!"

Sven's moronic attitude does not sit well with the lawyer. If all perps and perp-wannabes were that fucked-up he'd be out of a job. He sighs and begins giving Sven a lecture on how to behave in his role as "the accused". On the etiquette of the defendant. When to confess, what to confess to, and why. When to shut up. How the legal system works and how it doesn't work, how to plan, how to present, what to withhold. In short, how to build a case in his favour, a procedure that will be laughably easy in this case.

But Sven isn't interested. He waves his hands as if the lawyer's elegantly ambiguous phrases are killer bees threatening to sting him, shaking his head while the lawyer glares at him and wishes he could hit him. Hard.

"I'm a murderer," declares Sven, when the lawyer stops talking. "Therefore I must accept punishment as decided by the law. Surely you understand that? You *are* a lawyer, aren't you?"

Lindgren can't be bothered explaining to this deluded moron that the law isn't about crime and punishment, it's not about right and wrong. He studies Sven and can't help sighing deeply again. But it's almost lunch time. He's meeting a couple of colleagues and fellow gluttons at the Savoy to celebrate the fiftieth birthday of one of them, and he doesn't want to be late. His colleagues will appreciate the story of this dim-witted "killer", and will sympathize with his own frustration at trying to communicate with a lunatic. A killer indeed! As if the poor bastard even has what it takes! Most murders are spur-of-the-moment events caused by emotions running out of control — passion, rage, hate, love, what have you. Lindgren doubts very much that this meek character has entertained a strong emotion in his life. Look at the poor sod sitting there with his honest face, earnestly demanding punishment. Trying to help, for God's sake. Who does he think he is? And why the hell does he insist on doing up the top button of his shirt like that? It makes him look as if he's trying to strangle himself. How fucking anal can you get?

The most likely scenario, as already suggested in the initial report, is that Jan Lennart Persson had tried to hit Andersson when he got in his way, but had missed and, being drunk, had fallen downstairs, breaking his neck. Blood tests showed alcohol in Persson's blood, and police had found forty-two grams of hashish in his pocket. Not a very original accident, not even an interesting one. Stupidities like that happen every day, people falling down and breaking things. Sometimes a neck gets broken. That's life, not murder, in Lindgren's contemptuous opinion, and he's a lawyer and ought to know. Andersson is innocent whether he wants to be or not. There is some uncertainty because he provided such a detailed explanation of events over and over again, never changing his story.

As for his insistence on being guilty — and his crazy hang-up about the kid — it is clear that Andersson is mentally ill. He needs psychiatric help, not a lawyer. Well, they did warn him that this might be the case, and now it's confirmed. Andersson is officially demented. Case closed. Lindgren sighs. It's the most he's ever sighed in a single morning. Luckily it's almost time to get going. Lindgren has no business here, he thinks, and he briefly closes his eyes.

"Besides, I have inherited criminal tendencies," chirps Andersson.

Oh no, not that!

"Do you really?" asks Lindgren, trying not to sound too sarcastic. He feels like screaming and banging his head on the table. No, he feels like banging Andersson's head on the table. "Would you care to explain?"

"My father was Rune Andersson. The war criminal. One of Sweden's biggest traitors during the war. He worked for Hitler."

"Did he indeed?"

"And then they killed him. Served him right, too."

"Really?"

Lindgren has never heard of any war criminal named Rune Andersson. He's never heard of any Swedish war criminals. That doesn't mean that such characters didn't exist, of course, but in this case he very much doubts it.

"Check the files," urges Sven, overflowing with good advice. "Then you'll understand whom you're dealing with here."

"I'll do that." Lindgren glances at his watch. If Andersson gets any more helpful, he'll kill him.

"And then perhaps you'll realize that I do *not* need a lawyer. I am guilty, I must be punished. It's that simple. The guilt is in my blood. Lawyers are for people who are innocent and need help to prove it. Who can't speak for themselves. As you've no doubt noticed, I am fully capable of speaking up and telling it like it is. I'm not a coward."

"You don't want a lawyer? Is that what you're telling me?"

"I don't want a lawyer," insists Sven. "I'm guilty as charged."

"You haven't been charged yet."

"Never mind, I'm guilty. And I'm man enough to accept my punishment. I can...."

"Well then," interrupts Lindgren, "I have no business here, do I? If you're sure you don't require my services...."

"I do not!"

Never had idiocy been so convenient.

"I'll be off, then. I do have an important meeting to attend." He hesitated. "You're sure about this?"

"I told you, I'm guilty!"

Lindgren doesn't waste any more time. Soon he's reclining in a taxi, heading for the Savoy and a double whisky he's earned the hard way. No, make that a triple. And a big lunch. He's in the mood for rare meat; he needs to taste blood.

As for Sven, he is genuinely happy to see the back of that mouldy little sausage. Imagine a lawyer who doesn't know right from wrong. What next?

The next person to visit Sven is an unnaturally tall child with a false beard. At least, that's what he looks like at first. The beard turns out to be genuine and the boy a lot older than he looks. He must be, because he claims to be a psychiatrist. With a hearty smile he shakes Sven's hand with firm sincerity, and says how nice it is to meet him and to please call him Olle. He's an intense young man, full of purpose and ambition. He's carrying an immense box full of labels and is constantly in search of appropriate cases to slap them on. If Sven doesn't watch out, he'll end up looking like a well-travelled suitcase.

Sven decides on the spot that he isn't going to like this visitor either. Olle wears a folksy checked shirt and a wide purple tie, which is barely an improvement on Lindgren and his mouldy sausage skin, except the purple tie looks pretentious and doesn't go with the shirt. Ties should be discreet.

"So, Sven," says Olle. He crosses one long leg over the other and hugs his knees with white effeminate hands. He's got knobbly knuckles. "Sven, I thought we might have a talk, you and I."

"Why?" Sven lights a cigarette and notices the immediate frown on Olle's face. He obviously doesn't like cigarette smoke but is too polite to say so. In other words, he's a coward. Sven doesn't like cowards these days, he feels nothing but contempt for them. Cowards are powerless, he knows that only too well. They are pathetic. Killing people, on the other hand, gives you an amazing feeling of power. It isn't a power you've earned, but nobody dares take it away from you. They can insult you and patronize you, and they do, but they can't take this power away. You can be rude to people you don't like, you can blow smoke in their disapproving faces, and they'll let you. It's amazing. Sven likes it a lot.

Olle starts out with the brotherly understanding of a longtime friend. A bit patronizing, but Sven is used to that, and Olle probably imagines that he means well. For the first while he talks about this and that: isn't it nice that summer has arrived, that kind of thing. But then, before Sven catches on to his approach, the questions come flying. First the odd missile, then a full-scale attack. It's too late to run for cover. There are questions relating to how he's feeling, asinine queries about what day of the week it is, what month, what year.

"Do you think I'm stupid?" Sven's too insulted to play games. Not even Lindgren was this derogatory. He lights another cigarette. It's his only line of defence.

Olle keeps at it, diligently scribbling away in the clouds of smoke, pink roses blooming on his bearded cheeks. His tone is kind, his manner coaxing, but Sven keeps his mouth shut. He is not "sharing" his feelings. He doesn't have to if he doesn't want to. After getting nowhere for a while, Olle decides to move on to plan B. Freshly brewed coffee and pastries are brought. Cream? Sugar? It's all very nice and relaxed. Sven eats three pastries and drinks four cups of coffee. The pastries are fresh too.

"Tell me, Sven," says Olle, wiping crumbs from his beard as he jackknifes forward. "Why do you insist on being called a murderer? Can we talk about that?"

"I've already talked." Sven sighs.

Olle scribbles furiously, and Sven watches with disgust the fat lips hiding like juicy red leeches in the man's blond beard. The leeches wriggle as Olle writes. Sven decides he hates him. Olle, like Lindgren, is implying that Sven wouldn't be man enough to stand up for himself, would be too useless to handle a drunken hooligan. As if you needed a university degree to push a punk down the stairs. What Olle is basically saying is that he thinks Sven is stupid as well as cowardly.

It's very disappointing. Before he met Olle, Sven thought that a psychiatrist would at least be able to tell him what was going on in his mind. Tell him why he lost control and why his head went so blindingly hot. He had hoped that a man of his profession would have learned insight into the human psyche and its tangled labyrinths, where it is so easy to get lost. Where you find so many memories that you hoped were lost, emotions you have no use for, stillborn hopes, and hurts that never die. But oh no, not our man Olle. It doesn't matter how many dissertations, degrees, and doctorates you have, if your brain is up your ass. Olle sits there, all pompous in his checked man-of-the-people shirt, licking the red leeches snuggling in his beard. That's his way of appearing immersed in profound analysis. But Sven's senses are painfully acute these days, and he knows that Olle is a charlatan who doesn't care whom he hurts as long as he finds somewhere to slap his colourful labels. He probably gets points for every label he gets rid of. At the end of the year the psychiatrist with the most points gets a free colour TV.

Olle's most irritating habit is to suddenly plunge forward, supporting his elbow on his knee, and emphasize some undefeatable viewpoint by raising his left hand and pressing his fingertips against the soft cushion of his thumb. This makes his hand look like the misshapen flower bud of some colourless, flesh-eating plant. Sven stares distrustfully at the hostile bud whenever it appears. It sways in an imaginary wind and then, just as it seems the bud might open into a hungry flower, Olle destroys it by hitting his hand in the air as if he's burned himself. Sven wonders if he does it on purpose. If it's a form of subtle threat. "Tell me what I want to hear or the bud dies."

In fact the reason for Olle's finger exercises is that this tiresome accused — Sven Andersson, and how's that for an original name? — gets on his nerves. The tedious man appears to have not a clue what Olle is talking about, even though Olle has gone far, far out of his way to use simple sentences. Does this dim-witted man comprehend anything?

No, he does not. The poor bastard is out to lunch. Irredeemably delusional. He claims to be the son of some famous war criminal, and perversely maintains that killing people runs in the family. As though he comes from a long line of werewolves and has no control over his lupine urges. Somebody has managed to locate a record of a Rune Andersson, apprehended in June 1944 for obscure reasons, but there's no evidence that the two are related. Two other Rune Anderssons had been arrested that year, one for petty larceny, the other for pimping.

Sven Andersson is your typical loner. A loser. A sad case. When something caused Jan Lennart Persson to have an unfortunate accident, Andersson saw an opportunity to get attention. This is a man who gave up his job after he was seen with some drunks at Drottningtorget. His co-workers were puzzled, although a Miss Rankeskar confessed that she'd often smelt alcohol on his breath but was too afraid to say anything.

Andersson adamantly refuses to talk about that incident. All he does is shake his head and stare at the floor, his lips pinched together, or stare stone-faced at nothing in particular and mumble, "I didn't know I was wearing slippers, did I?" Figure that one out.

Sven meanwhile deduces that Olle's full of crap, so he's no longer listening. There's no reason he should waste his time when all he gets in return is more insults, more slaps in the face. He isn't a nobody any more, and he damn well refuses to be treated like one.

"I don't want to listen to any more of your nonsense," he says, and sighs deeply for emphasis. Having observed Lindgren's long-suffering sighs every five minutes, he's picked on the trick to exhale very slowly. He lights another cigarette and, in a burst of inspiration, lets it hang in the corner of his mouth the way Humphrey Bogart did in *The Maltese Falcon*, or was it *Casablanca*? But the damn thing falls out and lands on the floor.

"You don't want to listen, eh?" Olle enthusiastically catches up this new twist in the yarn and scribbles wildly, missing Sven's Bogart impression. Here's something he can get his analytical teeth into. Defiance is a challenge he can handle. All he has to do is find a soft spot where his teeth can get a solid scientific grip and draw blood.

"You don't want to talk and you don't want to listen. What do you want, then? If you don't mind my asking."

"I do mind you asking."

"Why do you mind?"

"Because I feel like it."

"What are you afraid of?"

"I'm not afraid. You should be afraid. I could kill you if I felt like it."

Olle smiles with unabashed delight and lurches forward as if his spine is collapsing. No flower bud appears this time. Instead there's a greedy expression in his grey eyes, the greed of a man who's sure he's struck gold.

"Could it be, Sven, that you call yourself a murderer to get attention? Could it be that your insistence on calling yourself a killer is nothing but a cry for help?"

"A cry for help?" Oh, Christ! Would you listen to that?

"That's what this is all about, isn't it, Sven? It's a natural development of your neurosis. Which means we can help you get better."

"You're an idiot," mutters Sven, shaking his head in disbelief.

"Now, why do you say that? Why does the truth bother you?"

"Truth or not, it's irrelevant."

"How so?" Olle raises his left eyebrow and licks his leeches.

"You're saying that if you go out and kill a person as a cry for help, then it's okay. Which means if I go out and kill ten more people and say I'm just crying for help really loudly, is that okay? You can kill if you have a good psychological reason?" Sven surprises himself by his reasoning, but firmly believes in his logic.

"No, I didn't say that." Olle smiles. "What I said was...."

"Oh, shut up."

But Olle isn't going to let Sven upset his diagnosis. It's a good one. Not quite finalized; it needs more dimension. Olle considers himself a thorough and methodical craftsman. A firm realist, he does not deal with abstracts, so he rummages through his box of labels and theories, diving to the very bottom for bits and pieces that will put the finishing touches on his work. He's inspired now, weaving back and forth in his chair, adding wrinkle after wrinkle to his sculpture of The Man Who Cried For Help. Sven continues to chain-smoke and sulk.

The sulking, of course, is significant in itself.

Olle writes a lengthy report on this most challenging case, stating that the patient still suffers severe shock which for the moment renders impossible an in-depth probe into the incredibly deep-rooted neurosis behind his bizarre behaviour. Sven Andersson suffers from severe psychological disorders. The recent incident is likely only the tip of the iceberg. He is definitely not the murderer he claims to be, and his insistence merely confirms that he is severely delusional. In all likelihood Andersson suffers feelings of guilt from having wished the young man dead. Constant psychiatric evaluation, together with pharmaceutical therapy, is recommended. More knowledge about the patient's childhood is essential for delving to the bottom of the neurosis, but the patient refuses to divulge any information in that regard. This is highly significant in itself. Consultations with a host of professionals are recommended. There is no doubt that the patient must be entrusted to a psychiatric hospital for long-term evaluation.

It comes as no surprise to anybody but Sven that he is declared unfit to stand trial. Arrangements are made for him to be moved to Östra Sjukhuset Psychiatric Hospital for long-term treatment. What that means, they tell him, wanting to mollify him — is a different kind of incarceration. Another kind of jail, more suitable for somebody with no previous record, they say, making it clear that he is by no means going unpunished.

"I suppose, with my background, I need to be investigated for inherited criminal tendencies," muses Sven to the Chief Inspector.

"That's about it, Sven," says the Chief. He has asked Sven a few questions, checked some confidential old files, and come to the conclusion that Sven is undoubtedly the son of Rune Andersson, a Nazi bootlicker who was killed in internment camp back in 1944. Cases like that were dealt with quietly at the time, and were still not common knowledge. According to the file, the man did have a young son named Sven, and there are facts in the report that Sven could not otherwise have known. But the Chief Inspector has decided to keep his conclusion to himself. It's nobody's business, certainly not the tabloids'. It has no bearing on the present and it certainly won't help poor Andersson.

When preparations are being made for his transfer, Sven insists on arranging to sell his apartment and get rid of his few belongings. He wants to keep only his two paintings, his old chair, and his red Christmas candleholder.

"There's some Armagnac in a cupboard in the kitchen," he tells the Chief. "I want *you* to have that."

For some reason he refuses to wear his old clothes. As he still has money in the bank, he requests that somebody take him shopping for a new wardrobe, preferably at the NK department store. He wants quality clothing, something suitable to the new man he is. His taste hasn't changed; he just wants brand-new things. Although it is highly unusual, the request is granted. It is a simple enough matter, and besides, Andersson has become the pet screwball of the division.

Sven buys two pairs of pants, four shirts, a blazer, and a wool sweater. One shirt, a dusty shade of rose, is a daring hint of flamboyance. *Rose du bois*, the colour is called. Pettersson, the police escort, chooses it. He also suggests a Saint-Laurent silk tie with a discreet matching pattern on a background of midnight blue. The price of the tie leaves Sven almost comatose. The price reflects the fact that Saint-Laurent is a very famous French designer, explains Pettersson, and the tie is high quality silk. You get what you pay for, he adds, and he says he thinks Sven ought to splurge for once in his life, go the whole hog. Sven admires this insight and, once he recovers from the trauma of the price tag, decides to buy the tie. The saleslady puts it in a box, wraps the box with expensive paper, and ties it up with a ribbon in a shade of pink that almost matches his shirt.

"You're gonna be one classy guy, Sven," says Pettersson, who can't afford designer clothes but likes to go shopping. Sven heartily agrees.

As they exit the store, Sven stops to have a last look at the world he'll be leaving after lunch. It's a sunny summer day. People are strolling, shopping, eating ice-cream, sitting at sidewalk cafés. Nobody's in a hurry. Doesn't anybody work any more? A tribe of drooling dagos block the sidewalk on the corner by Kalendegatan, busy ogling all the half-naked girls parading by.

It was down the street there, outside The Hippodrome, that he saw Ma stumble that time, way back when. In 1944. After Pa left. She was with the man in the blue suit and the stupid hat. She was laughing her head off. The Hippodrome was still there. Maybe Ma was still there too, still doing the jitterbug.

It won't be difficult to leave freedom behind. He never liked it much, never quite knew what to do with it. But as they walk to the car, the headlines outside a tobacconist's shop catch his eye. He sees a picture of that little slut from the apartment on it, and beside the picture are big black letters crying, "I WANT MY BABY BACK!"

"What's happened to the baby?" Sven asks Pettersson. "He's being looked after, isn't he?"

"Sure. He's in foster care. But I don't know...."

"What?"

"Oh, nothing."

"Is the baby all right?"

"The baby's just fine, Sven."

"That's good. That's all that matters."

Pettersson, who feels sorry for young Lillan Werner, doesn't say anything.

A block farther up, outside the Hotel St. Jörgen, a well-dressed man stands reading a similar bulletin. He turns pale as he recognizes his daughter Kerstin, nicknamed Lillan, whom he hasn't seen for more than ten years. He'd know his Lillan anywhere. He turns abruptly and runs back into the hotel, knocking a well-known actor out of the way. Just the day before, he called his ex-wife and demanded to know Lillan's whereabouts. Lillan is of legal age and can make her own decisions but, now that he is moving back to Sweden, he's decided to find her. And here she is, all over the newspapers.


Everybody at the division compliments Sven on his shirt and tie, the classy cut of his new pants. They shake his hand and wish him all the best. Sven sheds a few tears and the Chief Inspector pats his shoulder. Then it's time to leave. It isn't easy; it's much harder than leaving his apartment.

Pettersson and Arvidsson take Sven to the hospital. Sven, who's never been out in those parts, is pleasantly surprised by the idyllic setting. A bunch of two-storey buildings are spread across a vast parklike area. There are trees and lawns and rosebushes, and flowers in the flowerbeds. It will be like staying at a holiday resort. Not that he's ever been to one, but he's seen pictures.

"Why, it's really nice here!"

"You're so easy to please, Sven."

"I am?" He never knew that. "Why, thank you!"

"You're quite welcome."

He gets his own room. It isn't very big, but his chair is already there, and somebody has put his two paintings and his candleholder on a table by the window. His new home. Arvidsson and Pettersson say goodbye and hand him over to the staff. As they leave, Sven sheds another tear. They're his friends. He asks if they will come and visit, but they explain that they can't, it's against police regulations.

Later he has a chat with the head nurse, Mrs. Molin, a tall grey-haired woman in her sixties with a friendly, horsy face. She says yes, she will be happy to get somebody to help him hang his pictures, and yes, he can certainly help with the gardening. Not right away, but once he's settled in. She has a kind word and a smile for everybody. Before long Sven adores her, but she's used to that.

In Occupational Therapy, patients are allowed to weave rugs. Sven asks if he can weave one for his room. With blue stripes — he's quite adamant about the colour. They say that he can, a little later, when he is settled in and has started treatment. Sven wants to know how many shades of blue he can use for his rug. They tell him to please wait and see, not to worry about it for now. There will be plenty of time to weave.

Sven settles in from day one. He is a model patient, for he likes the hospital a lot. The food is good and there is plenty of it. He is a content man. After a month his new pants are straining at the waist.

He gets on well with his fellow inmates, and isn't at all afraid of them. It is good to have them around. They don't talk a lot, but they're there; he isn't alone. Some of them are pretty strange, which is comforting. It's good to have somebody to look down on.

For example, there is a bizarre young woman who always sits by the same window in the day room, still as a statue, her hands folded in her lap. Her hair is long and red, with some early strands of white despite her obvious youth. It hangs in a tangled mass and doesn't look as if she combs or washes it very often. She is skinny and her face is freckled. A scar runs from the left corner of her mouth down her chin, disfiguring what must once have been an attractive face. She never talks, never acknowledges other patients. They say she has long welts and scars all over her back. Her left eye is out of kilter, it sort of hangs down a bit, and somebody tells Sven that that eye is blind. She only eats if a nurse feeds her. Her name is Ann-Marie Eriksson, she is twenty-nine years old.

After Sven's arrival a subtle change can be seen in Ann-Marie's behaviour. Sven goes to the day room every evening after supper to watch TV, and lately she has started to smile, but only at Sven. Not an ear-to-ear grin, but a smile nevertheless. There is a spark of life in her good eye, and the corners of her mouth turn upwards. The attention embarrasses Sven at first, and he isn't sure why she reacts to him this way. At first he suspects that she may have designs on him. But that doesn't seem to be the case, because the rest of the time she just sits gazing out the window, ignoring him as she ignores everybody else.

Besides, she has a husband and a child. A tall blond man with a beard and a skinny little boy come to visit her regularly. The boy is about five years old, with a lot of unspent energy. He tears around the place and checks everything out, gets treats from the old people, but ignores his mother, who he thinks is just a statue with cracks in it.

Ann-Marie doesn't smile at her family, yet they visit every Sunday all the same. Her husband pulls up a chair, sits down beside her, and puts a bag of fruit and chocolate in her lap. He strokes her thin, freckled hand with its bitten nails and asks, "How are you today, Amy?" And all the while she continues to gaze out the window. Once in a while she will turn her head and look seriously into his face with her healthy eye, as if she's trying to figure out if he is real. Sometimes she will pat his hand. But she never smiles at him,

276

or at the rambunctious little boy. When it's time to leave, her husband kisses her cheeks, strokes her uncombed hair, and whispers, "See you next Sunday, Amy." Sometimes she nods a weak little nod. Other times she ignores him.

One evening, when Sven returns to his room, he's shocked to find the freckled apparition of Ann-Marie standing in his private space. There she is, right in front of his paintings. She doesn't hear him come in, she's so deeply absorbed in the two desolate scenes. Sven remains in the doorway for a second or two before he dares to say, "What are you doing here?" She turns to him, unfazed, and smiles. This is a bigger smile than before, and he notices for the first time that her front teeth are missing.

"I like these paintings," she tells him. Her voice is surprisingly clear and strong, but she has a slight lisp. He didn't realize she could talk.

"Thank you," he replies, not knowing what else to say.

"They're such empty landscapes," she goes on, as if they discuss art on a daily basis. "Desolate but not lonely. I feel at home in them." She smiles at him again, this time remembering to keep her mouth closed.

"I do too," says Sven, and puts his hands in his pockets. Looking at his shoes, he attempts to smile back, while wondering how she knew about his paintings.

"Can I come and look at them again some time? When you're busy with other things, so I won't disturb you?" Her good eye looks friendly; her dead eye stares right through him.

"You're not really allowed on this floor. This is the men's floor." He looks past her and notices that it has started to snow. Not heavily, but a few small flakes sail erratically towards the lawn. He focuses on his visitor. "Come if you want," he says.

"Good." She nods, businesslike, and walks out.

He's left wondering what just happened. It's still trying to snow. Feeble flakes fall randomly as he sits down by the window to do his crossword puzzle. This is a new interest he's developed. He isn't very good at it yet, but as Kurt, the orderly, said the other day, he's getting there fast.

Unable to concentrate tonight, he turns to study his paintings. Have they changed now that he's shared them, now that another eye has absorbed them? Does he want them to change? He isn't sure. There are no strange footprints in the mud by the river, nobody has splashed by in rubber boots. There is no sign that anyone has walked down the road by the old wall and disappeared. At least, not yet.

Don't be pathetic, Sven, he tells himself. Do your crossword puzzle.


On his first birthday at the hospital Sven turns forty-seven and, shockingly, there is a birthday cake with his name on it at mid-morning coffee. "Happy Birthday, Sven!" with red sticky stuff in the middle. There is a red marzipan rose with green leaves on it, too. Never having had a birthday cake in his life, he is stunned. His chin drops to his chest, and he cries in front of everybody, which is embarrassing but nobody makes fun of him. They sing instead. The nurse cuts him the biggest piece of cake and makes sure he gets the marzipan rose. Somebody has put a slender vase with a carnation by his place at the table. The carnation is as red as the marzipan rose, and surrounded by that gossamer green stuff they always put in bouquets. Just as they did when old Jöns had his birthday a month ago, or when Staffan down the hall turned fifty-four back in August. It is like being part of a big family. No doubt Mrs. Molin is behind it, it's the kind of person she is.

Afterwards he goes to lie down and unbuttons his tight pants so he can breathe more easily, and he thinks about what a wonderful birthday he's having. It's cloudy outside and a cold wind is tearing leaves off the trees in the yard, but he loves it. Inside it's cosy and warm, and the building is full of people he knows. Later he will go outside and rake leaves and get some fresh air. Work up some appetite for supper.

Thirty-seven years ago he'd been absolutely sure that they would celebrate his tenth birthday. Pa had turned forty the previous year so he knew that a birthday ending with a zero was something big. Something really special. Pa had had a party with lots of people — women in high-heeled shoes who stepped on Sven's toes, men who smoked cigars — and lots of food, lots of booze. Pa's cousin with the harelip had brought some home-made stuff. They'd partied all night, until the police came and broke up a fight in the yard.

But it turned out that ten didn't count. The number was probably too low. Asta and Kjell came over in the late afternoon of his birthday, mind you, but they had only come to play cards and get drunk. Ma and Pa hadn't seen them for a while, so when Pa poured the first glass he raised it in a celebratory manner.

"So, you bow-legged tin soldier, what shall we celebrate?"

"Hitler's imminent fall?" grinned Kjell.

"Watch it, you sick fuck!"

"It's my birthday," said a small voice.

They all stared at Sven and he blushed.

"I'm ten today. It's got a zero in it," he explained, already wishing he'd kept his stupid mouth shut.

"Jesus Christ! So it is!" Ma had forgotten completely. "How about that!"

"Is that right?" said Pa. "You're ten? I had no idea. Well, cheers, kid."

Down the hatch went the *akvavit*. Kjell, sentimental fool that he was, deemed such a day worthy of a gift, and hauled out a one-krona piece and gave it to Sven with hearty congratulations and a handshake, man to man. Not wishing to seem cheap, Pa repeated the performance, but gave the boy two kronor.

"What do you say?"

"Thank you."

They told him to go and spend it. He was dismissed.

What happened after that might have been a dream; he was never quite sure. On the way to Möllevångstorget, deep in thought about his sudden fortune, he kept his eyes on the ground. That was the way he usually walked. At the square he looked up and found that everything was deadly still, and the silence was so absolute that it pressed against his ears. The square was like a picture. The leaves left on the trees across the street were as immobile as the men in the statue, the stone workers eternally holding up the huge boulder. It was like entering a painting, but not the paintings at home. There was no comfort to be found in this barren cityscape.

Sven stood on the corner, his hands in his pockets, a tight grip on his money. The money was real. It was less certain that he himself was. Everything was closed. There were no people. Even the drunks who usually hung around the statue were gone. Like empty mirrors, hundreds of windows reflected nothing, revealed nothing.

Only death could be this still and silent, and Sven didn't want to be dead. To make sure he wasn't, he opened his mouth to make a noise. I'll sing and celebrate my birthday, he thought, but he couldn't make a sound. So he must have died. But he could still see, and dead people couldn't see, he was fairly sure of that. Here are my arms, here are my legs, my feet are right there on the sidewalk. He could move, too, and dead people definitely didn't move. He took his money out of his pocket and looked at the three coins in the palm of his hand. They were real.

He had an idea. Quickly he turned around to check his reflection in the store window behind him, trying to take himself by surprise. But there was no reflection. The windowpane reflected nothing at all. That was proof that he no longer existed. He must have died without realizing it. Frightened, he dropped the money and ran all the way home as fast as he could, his feet making no sound on the pavement. Galloped up the stairs, wooden clogs hitting the stone, and still he made no sound. As he flung open the door to the apartment, a wave of noise rolled over him, almost knocking him down. The familiar shouts and laughter, the drunken arguments and bluster. Faint with relief, he hurled himself into the room.

"Pa!" he yelled, and grabbed his father hard by the arm. A daring thing to do. "Pa! What happened?"

Pa stared at him for several long seconds, but then he grinned and showed him his five cards.

"What happened, kid? I'll tell you what happened. What happened is that tonight yours truly gets the fucking jackpot!"

Pa was a happy man. Sven sighed with gratitude. He was alive. He did exist after all. It was a horrible, horrible thing not to and he never ever wanted it to happen again.

# LILLAN

While Sven is out shopping for designer ties and permanent press pants, Lillan's moral character is on trial. Everybody has an expert opinion about this young woman they've never met. While the trial is under way in the tabloids, Lillan sits in Majken's cluttered living-room and cries. It's all she ever does these days, if she does anything at all. Her arms have become useless, and she's constantly cold without her child's yielding body to hug. They've taken Micke away from her, and Janne is dead and gone. He's been identified, cremated, and buried. You can't be more gone than that.

It was a quiet funeral. Some of Majken's relatives were there, her brother Uno and his family, a few cousins, two of her neighbours but not the nosy old bat next door. On Lillan's side there was no family, but Katarina was there, as were Eva and Hasse. Lisbeth, Isabella, and Åsa came with their boyfriends. Even Pelle and his Arab came to pay their respects, as did a couple of guys she didn't know. Afterwards the guests walked from St. Gertrud's Chapel through the cemetery, past the bench where Sven had sat less than two weeks earlier, over to the restaurant for coffee and sandwiches. It wasn't exactly a laugh-fest, but it was tradition, it was what you did after the service. Majken had insisted. She wanted to do things right.

Now the two women mourn, and it's exhausting. They miss Janne, and they're both still paralysed with shock. But they're both used to losing loved ones. Lillan lost both her father and her grandmother when she was a girl. Her mother and sister have always been lost to her, although they are both very much alive.

When Majken was ten she lost her only sister. It was a long time ago, but she will always remember Kristina coughing up blood, her blonde pigtails on the white pillow at right angles to her head. Majken would sit by her bed and read to her. Kristina would close her eyes and Majken would stop reading, thinking she was asleep.

Then she'd open her eyes and say, "Read some more, Majken." Selma Lagerlöf was her favourite. One day she didn't say, "Read some more, Majken," and she never opened her eyes again. Funny how you remember every little detail when it comes to things like that. They said she had soot in her lungs and Majken wondered how it got there and why it didn't come out when she coughed. Later she understood that it was tuberculosis.

When she was twenty-four, Majken lost her husband in the train accident, when Janne was only four. Now she's lost her good-for-nothing boy too. Well, he was a good-for-nothing, she admits it, she's not blind. And at the moment she's angry with him, she can't help it. But he's dead, and the emptiness left her breathless. She misses him sorely.

But it's his fault that Micke was taken away. His fault and nobody else's that the baby was handed over to Children's Aid. As if he were a rag-doll thrown in a box and given to a rummage sale. Sold for a couple of kronor. The state helped itself to their baby, and won't say where he is. It won't give him back. It makes out that she and Lillan have no right to him.

She was outraged to discover that Janne and Lillan went out and left Micke all by himself. Seven nights in row, until Janne was killed. If she'd only known, she keeps thinking. But it's too late for such useless thoughts. And she knows it isn't Lillan's fault, Lillan was just as upset. Janne nagged and nagged her until he wore her down. Majken is only too aware of how stubborn and persuasive the boy can be. Or could be, rather. She keeps forgetting he's gone. He's dead because he went out and left Micke alone.

Sometimes she's convinced it's all her fault for not being a stricter disciplinarian, for not spending more time with him. For falling asleep instead of playing boardgames with him at the kitchen table. For not being a perfect mother. Lillan says the fortune teller claimed to know what had happened before Lillan did. The cards told her. Figure that one out. Majken would like to meet that emissary of the occult and sit on her face until she could produce a logical explanation. Majken firmly believes that everything has an explanation. The problem is finding it.

She doesn't believe for a minute that it was an accident. That man Andersson confessed that he pushed Janne on purpose, and Majken's intuition has nodded and said, "Yes, that's what happened." She understands why the man lost control and shoved Janne to his death. Janne. Her son, Gösta's son. He was so like his father, just as stubborn, always right. What he didn't have was Gösta's easygoing personality and sense of humour, his way with people. So he wasn't the world's most affectionate son, so he wasn't the most responsible, thoughtful human being ever to saunter around this earth. He was her son. And he was slowly changing for the better, she knows he was. How could he not, with Lillan to guide him down the right path? He would have straightened out. But it's too late now. So, while she understands Andersson up to a point, she'll never forgive him. She wants him to be haunted by remorse for the rest of his life. She wants him never to sleep without nightmares. She wants him to wake up sweaty and anxious, wishing for the night to be over but for the morning never to arrive.

Majken sighs. She's spent the morning chain-smoking and drinking coffee, and she leaves late for her afternoon shift, red-eyed and puffy-faced. She might miss the ferry, and if she does she'll miss her shift. She doesn't care, though. Not now. She steps out into the street and finds the world awash in sunshine. The streetcar she just missed is clanging down the road. Old Ivarsson is out walking his dog, and he waves to her. Mrs. Rydberg from next door comes out of the café with a bag of pastries, and smiles at Majken, if you can call it a smile; it's one of those "understanding" smiles, more embarrassing than compassionate. It says she wishes Majken would go away and take her grief with her. Majken ignores the bitch and crosses the street to wait for the next streetcar.

Janne is dead. They've taken Micke. She can't stop thinking these useless thoughts.

The streetcar arrives five minutes behind schedule, so she will probably be late for work, but it doesn't matter. When she closes her eyes she can still see Lillan sitting in the rocking chair as she left her, pale and unwashed, staring out the window with broken eyes. She was always so sunny, their Lillan, and now look at her. She isn't

Lillan any more, she's just the shell of what once was Lillan. She doesn't eat, doesn't sleep. Majken made a pot of coffee and a plate of cheese sandwiches before she left, and pointed out for the fiftieth time that Lillan has to keep her strength up, poor girl, how else can she fight for her baby? Because they have to fight, don't they? This is what she tells Lillan. Life can't be so unfair, she says. It can't punish a baby for his father's perceived sins. They'll get him back somehow. They have to.

She checks her watch. Katarina will be over in another hour to stay with Lillan. She goes straight from work to Majken's apartment every day, and Majken has given her a key. If Katarina wasn't willing to do that, Majken wouldn't dare leave Lillan on her own. Lillan has lost her will to live, and Majken is frightened. If she loses Lillan, she'll have nothing at all left to live for.

Lillan sits where Majken left her, rocking dully in Majken's wooden rocking chair. She isn't thinking, because she can't think; it hurts her head, it breaks her heart and makes her nauseous. She sits straight and rigid, leaning back, her hands gripping the armrests of the chair, as if she was about to fall off a mountain. She holds on like that to counteract the emptiness of her lap, where her baby ought to be.

Nor does she want to acknowledge that her snug little world has imploded and gone kaput. She did her best. Lillan is mad at Janne. No, not mad. She's furious and disappointed. It's his fault they took her baby away, his fault and nobody else's. Never mind that he's dead, that doesn't exonerate him. That was his own fault too. He lied to her face, smiling sweetly; he betrayed her. And what she hates most is the ease with which he did it. He must have laughed himself silly thinking what a dope she was. A stupid naive nitwit brainless cow. The goddamn useless bastard. He'd been on his way out, he'd planned to leave Micke by himself all along. After looking into her eyes and saying, "I promise." Well, he broke his promise and it cost him his life. That's quite a price to pay, but she still can't forgive him. Strange people have taken her Micke. He is frightened to death, wondering where his mummy is. He's wondering why she's gone away and left him. He's afraid she doesn't love him any more. She can sense all this, and it's killing her. If she doesn't get Micke back, she's going to take her life. She's made up her mind. But it's her secret.

She was hysterical by the time Katarina screeched the car to a halt that night. She charged up the stairs, ignoring the cluster of men on the landing. The apartment door was open and she rushed straight into the arms of Arvidsson, who stood there tall, serious, and solid as a rock.

"What happened?" she yelled as she bounced off him.

He told her, and she wished he hadn't.

Lillan was frightened then, and she's still frightened. She feels as if some evil force is after her. Most of the time she can barely sense it, but there are odd moments when she's sure she can see it, like a slippery shadow that is laughing at her. How could the cards have told the truth unless there were strange forces involved? How could that fat sibyl have known? Dark forces are on the loose. Lillan isn't her mother's daughter for nothing. She learned all about evil at an early age.

Her second question that night was "Where's my baby?" He was in good hands, she was told. It was all for the best, for the time being — her best as well as the child's. They talked to her firmly, though not unkindly, but when she realized that Micke had been taken away she started to scream and didn't stop, thinking that if she screamed long enough and loud enough they'd have to bring him back to her. The moment she found out that they had taken Micke away, Janne's death became secondary.

They asked her to calm down, please, and answer some questions, but Lillan had other priorities.

"In good hands?" she screamed over and over. *"In good hands?"*

Somebody fetched Katarina, who was chain-smoking out on

the landing, and she came and held Lillan until she ran out of steam and had to stop shrieking. She sat on the edge of the bed in front of his cot, her hands inert in her lap, Katarina's arm around her shoulder, trying to imagine what had happened to her baby. Trying to imagine the "good hands" he was in. Were they as large as a cradle? Could they rock him like a hammock?

He was probably sleeping when the strangers rushed in and woke him up. It must have scared him half to death. They would have grabbed him, carried him out into the night, driving him away in a strange car. And poor Micke, not knowing what had happened, hearing only unfamiliar voices, seeing only strange faces in the glow from the streetlights as they drove through streets he wouldn't recognize. In good hands! He might have died from fright and she'd never know, they'd be too afraid to tell her.

"A child belongs with his mother," she said when she caught her breath.

"You should have thought of that before," they pointed out. The same thing would be pointed out by the bureaucrats, by the uniforms, by those who made the decisions, by those who ruled from behind desks and never had to raise their voices. They had the law on their side, they knew what was right. Lillan only knew what felt right, and she didn't count any more.

She's been bad. *Kvällsposten,* the evening paper ever ready to dig up dirt, quickly traced her mother back in Småland, and that good woman lets it be known that her daughter Lillan had never had a trace of moral fibre in her sinful body. She announced that the sad mess the girl now found herself in didn't surprise her one bit. Lillan has made her bed, now let her lie in it. However, being a good Christian, the long-suffering mother offers to say a prayer for her wicked daughter's soul. It is a mother's duty to pray for her child.

"What a miserable cunt," says Katarina. Then she has an idea. "Hey, I know what we'll do!"

"Huh?"

"I've got an idea! We're going to call *Kvällsposten* and give them your version of the story."

290

"Why?"

"Just wait and see!"

Lillan doesn't understand. Her brain doesn't work very well these days. Katarina explains what she has in mind and Lillan actually nods and lights up.

Majken comes home later that night to see a spark in Lillan's eyes, and she feels a ray of hope stab her in the chest. Katarina tells her that a journalist and photographer are coming over from *Kvällsposten* the next morning, and they spend the next hour feverishly chain-smoking, tense with the possibility that maybe something good is going to happen. When they can hardly see each other through the smoke, Majken sends Katarina home, after hugging her and saying, sweet, sweet Katarina, I love you, how can we ever thank you? Katarina won't be there the next day, when the journalist comes; that's something Lillan and Majken must do on their own. But she'll lie awake all night and keep her fingers crossed.

Majken runs a bath for Lillan, and then she starts to clean. She dusts and vacuums and polishes and tidies. Everything has to be perfect. The souvenirs from Rimini, Mallorca, and Torremolinos stand in a military row on the bookshelf. She straightens the black lace on the red silk of the flamenco dancer's dress, remembers something that brings a blush to her face. Sighing, she says to herself, I better go and have a bath too.

At nine o'clock the next morning, Lillan is sitting in the rocking chair, clean and sweet-smelling, her hair shining around her pale face. She's dressed in a clean white blouse and a demure blue skirt that belongs to Majken. It's too long but it looks rather sweet that way. She's even had a glass of milk and a sandwich, which has given her a stomach-ache. Now she's waiting nervously. Majken is wearing her best dress. The row of pearls she inherited from her Aunt Lina adorns her neck. Her hair is stiff with spray. She's even put on some lipstick she found in the bathroom cupboard. She looks as if she's going dancing.

At nine-thirty the guys from the paper arrive. There's a fat one, the journalist, with a tape-recorder under his arm. Behind him stands a skinny weasel with a beard. That's the photographer, laden with cameras. How many pictures is he going to take? The two men enter, their eyes shining in anticipation of juicy headlines, and they gush sympathy. The young widow tells them whatever they wish to hear, in a shy, breathless voice, so humble is she before these benefactors of the gutter press. The bereaved mother of the victim insists they have coffee and pastries, no more than they deserve for all the trouble they're taking. Such humanitarians. Such heroes. Such men of the people.

That evening, Lillan's pleading eyes stare out from *Kvällsposten's* first page, and from news posters all over the country. The headlines give voice to her desperate face: GIVE ME MY BABY BACK! Who, with their heart in the right place, can resist that? Her predicament sells a lot of papers. Tens of thousands of people read what she has to say, and feel for her. For God's sake, demands public opinion, give the child back to the poor girl. It's not her fault her boyfriend was such a jerk.

But the bureaucrats aren't influenced by gutter-press headlines, let alone broken hearts. They are on the side of the law — hell, they are the law — and the law has to be upheld at all times or Swedish society as they know it will crumble. Anarchy will reign. Sloppy quotes like "Without my baby I have no reason to live" doesn't cut red tape. Nor do feeble excuses like "I am quite capable of looking after my baby. It was Janne who let us down."

But Sven Andersson has given ample evidence about her irresponsible conduct. As has Lillan's mother. The proof is there. The decision has been made. Lillan Werner is an unfit mother.

That's why she now sits where she sits, pale and exhausted and very still. Thoughts and recent memories blink on and off on the surface of her consciousness, but they're starting to sink. Soon she won't be thinking at all. Which is just as well, as every thought upsets her. Mostly she thinks about Micke. She sees him, she hears him crying for her. She remembers Janne as he stood by the window between the freshly laundered curtains, holding Micke in his arms and waving her goodbye. Such a false picture. If only she hadn't trusted him.

Those curtains are packed in a case with the other curtains, towels, and sheets. Micke's clothes and toys. Janne's stereo and records and tapes. All down in Majken's storage space in the basement.

Sometimes Lillan wonders if Anja can be held responsible. If Janne would still be alive if Anja hadn't read her fortune. If Micke would still be with her if she'd declined to have her star interpreted. Has all this happened because Anja saw it? Or is it the other way around? How can you ever be sure? Anja mentioned Daddy too, Lillan does vaguely recall that, but at the moment her thought process is too dull and she's too petrified by misery to even consider reaching for that fragile straw.

Late one night, as she lies dry-eyed and rigid in the sofa-bed in Majken's living-room, Lillan starts to pray. That's how desperate she is. Whispered sentences addressed to God. She clasps her hands as she did when she was a little girl saying her nightly "God who holds all children dear." Dear God, she starts, a little awkwardly because she isn't too clear about who God is, or *if* God is. If there is a God, is it the same one her mother has such colossal respect for, the strict, unforgiving, hateful God who spends his time gloating about how everyone will burn in hell? No, not that God, she wants nothing to do with that one, he's a nasty human invention. She feels deep in her heart that no real God would behave in such a petty, small-minded way. There must be another God, a good one, the one who holds all children dear. Would a kind God just sit there in heaven and twiddle his thumbs while that kind of thing went on down below? Look down and say, well darn it all, Lillan, you can't expect me to interfere with the bureaucratic machine, can you?

"Listen to me, God," she whispers, afraid to wake Majken. "I need to talk to you." In the hush of the dark room she begins whispering her problems to the shadows. But suddenly she feels stupid, and stops. She turns around and looks out on the yellow glow of a streetlight. Out there in the dark where time's standing still is her Micke. She listens as the late night bus heads for downtown. Then there's silence. The nights never end. Nor do the days.

God, if there is such an omnipotent force, is not listening. If

293

there is such an entity he won't be able to hear her. He'll be busy getting several earfuls from Majken who is also lying awake in her bed, reaming out every damn deity she can get her mind on. Majken imagines God with a long white beard and she's pulling that beard so hard it hurts, hissing "Who the hell do you think you are anyway, playing around with people's lives like that? Why are you doing this to my family?" Majken has no respect for the concept called "God."

Whether it's God, dark forces, or a fluke — whether the fortune teller is responsible or not — something is happening while Lillan sits in her rocking chair. Something unexpected is going on while the thermos of coffee is sitting untouched and the edges of the cheese in the sandwiches are drying and curling up. Wheels are in motion.

The man at the Hotel St. Jörgen gets into a taxi and barks an address, and the taxi speeds away, passing close by the psychiatric hospital where Sven will arrive in a short while. The taxi stops at the tall *Kvällsposten* building, and the man gets out and strides into the building to see the editor-in-chief. No, he doesn't have an appointment, he snaps, but that doesn't matter. Trust me, he says, the editor-in-chief will want to see me. The man is Mikael Werner, Lillan's father. Head of a large corporation in France, he is a business genius who has tripled his corporation's profit, mainly through business in the Far East. But in addition to his wealth he has accumulated bleeding ulcers and has recently been diagnosed with rheumatoid arthritis, and he has decided to semi-retire, to move back to Malmö, his home town, which is conveniently close to the continent. He's a man with some influence.

He reads the paper on his way to *Kvällsposten,* and is appalled to find out what's happened to his daughter. Most disgusting are the things Lillan's mother has said about her. Mikael Werner is outraged. He is resolved to get his daughter back, then his grandchild. Then he will sue his ex-wife for slander.

The editor-in-chief is delighted to see yet another headline come rushing into his arms. How lucky can you get? But after Werner has obtained Lillan's address, he has a little heart-to-heart with the editor — quite a long heart-to-heart, actually — after that the editor is no longer interested in catchy headlines pertaining to Lillan Werner and her child.

By way of a thank-you, however, Werner puts a few other fleas in the editor's ear. They have to do with the paranoid delusions of a certain religious fanatic. He invites the editor to come up with whatever headlines he can in that regard. Mikael Werner knows when and how to play dirty.

The pair shake hands, and Mikael Werner hops in another taxi to go and see an old lawyer friend of his. Then he's going back to the hotel. He has a phone call to make.

Katarina is just putting the key in the lock when the phone rings. Lillan runs to answer it, positive that this time the authorities are calling to say that they've changed their minds, that she can come and get Micke right away. They'll apologize, they'll admit they were wrong, and the nightmare will be over.

"Lillan," says a man's voice. It's a deep, confident voice, but it sounds a bit breathless. "Is that you, Lillan?"

"Who is this?"

"It's Daddy, Lillan." The voice sounds unsteady.

"Daddy?" Lillan faints.

Katarina slams the door as Lillan crumples to the floor. She grabs the phone, and when Mikael Werner introduces himself she gives him the third degree, making sure this is no hoax. In the end she's convinced, and soon he is on his way, sitting in yet another taxi and thinking about everything that was. How he should have fought for his child, but didn't have the heart to take her from her mother as he should have. He really did believe that children are best off with their mothers — or was that a convenient excuse? He doesn't know and he doesn't want to find out. You can't change what happened more than ten years ago. All the things he should have done, and didn't. All the things he shouldn't have done, and did.

He walks slowly up the stairs, nervous and full of wonder. Here it is. M. Persson. The door of the neighbour — S. Rydberg, according to the mail slot — opens a few inches and an old woman peeks out. Mikael knows a snooping snout when he sees it, he was married to one, so he gives the old woman a cold stare. It's something he's extremely good at. It needs to be done because this is a moment he does not wish to share. The old woman quickly withdraws and he knocks on the door. A young woman with long dark hair opens the door and his heart sinks. It isn't Lillan.

"Mr. Werner? I'm Katarina. Come on in." She stands aside to let him by.

"Thank you," he says. As he steps inside, he looks over Katarina's shoulder and sees a small figure he could never mistake for anybody else. His heart goes all peculiar. She's pale and very thin, and in his eyes she hasn't changed, she's still a child. Lillan stares speechlessly at her father, who's appeared out of nowhere just as the fortune-teller said he might. He hasn't changed much either. There are lines on his face and grey in his hair, but he too is unmistakeable. They stand staring at each other for several seconds, until Lillan faints again.

"It's because she's stopped eating," explains Katarina. "She just sits there all day long, day after day, and doesn't eat."

Lillan's father picks her up and carries her into the living-room. He sits down on the sofa with her limp body still in his arms. He is weeping — very quietly, very discreetly — so Katarina makes herself scarce. She busies herself in the kitchen making coffee. After a short while Lillan revives, and Katarina can hear them both having a good cry. She's rather choked up herself. She doesn't particularly like the looks of Lillan's father; he seems too glib for her liking, too in control, and his suit is a very expensive Italian job. She doesn't trust men in expensive suits. Peter's father always wore expensive suits but Peter never did. But never mind. She gets the coffee tray ready, including Majken's expensive liqueur. When the sound of sniffles subsides, she enters the living-room with a convincingly cheerful smile and serves coffee.

Mikael tells them about his return to Sweden, and his French wife, Nicole, and their two young sons, Philippe and Jean-Pierre, Lillan's brand-new half-brothers. He'll be calling them later to tell them that he's found his daughter. And to surprise them with the fact that he's a grandfather. The boys will get a kick out of that, he says.

"Are you sure?" Lillan looks insecure. Her daddy is back but he has another family now. She doesn't know what to think of that, isn't sure if she's part of it or not. Or if she even wants to be. These people are strangers. They don't even speak Swedish.

"Of course I'm sure!" says her father, who is determined not to lose his daughter again. "I always talk about you. You've always been part of our family, I want you to know that. Okay?"

"Okay."

"Good. Now, tell me about Micke."

"I named him after you."

"I wondered about that. Thank you for not forgetting me."

"Will I get him back?" She asks as if it was ultimately his decision.

"We'll see what we can do." He smiles the way he had smiled when she was little and worried about something. It was a smile that said everything would be all right, he would see to it.

He doesn't bother to tell her that he plays golf with three of Malmö's top lawyers. He doesn't mention all the influential people who owe him favours. He's doesn't trouble her with the fact that he's already making plans and has started the ball rolling. He just promises her that everything will be all right.

While they are talking, Majken comes home and stares at the

suave man beside Lillan. When she finds out who he is, she just about drops too. She had no idea who Lillan's father was. So impressive! So well dressed! She somehow had the notion that he was just an ordinary guy. All her life she's known only working-class people. That's her world. Intimidated, she smiles at him. She almost curtsies. He asks her to please call him Mikael, and begs her to sit down. She gratefully does as she's told, and they pour her a glass of Grand Marnier, and fill her in. Things are going to happen, they tell her. Everything is going to work out. Everything is going to be okay.

The next afternoon, Majken is working and Mikael is meeting with some lawyers. Katarina comes over to stay with Lillan, who has changed overnight. She's even made coffee for Katarina and herself. She's talking again, almost as bubbly as in the old days. When they're on their second cup, Lillan says she wishes Katarina could be as happy as she is right then, waiting for her baby to come home where he belongs. Katarina says she's afraid that isn't possible for her. But, she adds, it's quite a relief that Lillan is no longer her little seagull, because it's been so painful to watch her and not be able to help her. Lillan demands an explanation. She never liked seagulls much; they're noisy and they leave shit everywhere. What do they have to do with her?

"I wasn't going to tell you, but I will. You see, I will *never* be happy," she informs Lillan. "But remember, it's confidential."

"Why not?" It comes as a big surprise to Lillan. Katarina is always so cheerful. "Because of Peter, you mean?"

"No, it's got nothing to do with him."

Katarina explains that she will never be happy because it's too selfish. That's what she says: too selfish. In her opinion you'd have to be deaf and blind to be happy. Mind you, she wants other people to find happiness as best they can, and it pleases her a great deal when they do. As for her, if she feels mental bliss coming on she always remembers a seagull she saw once in France, in the harbour in some town south of Bordeaux.

"It was so awful," she says. "This bird came tottering in at low tide, dragging this torn, useless wing over the slippery rocks along the quay. The wing was attached by a single piece of cartilage. You could step on it and it would come off. The bird didn't know it would never fly again, didn't know it would soon be dead. I mean, it was such an obvious target for human nastiness. Maybe that was the worst part, knowing that. On and on it tottered, dragging this useless appendage. And every so often it looked up at all the seagulls swooping around like crazy, and it just couldn't understand."

The memory still makes Katarina cry. She doesn't know why; there are so many worse things happening in the world. But it fills her with unbearable sadness. She's such a fucking wet blanket sometimes. The last time she broke up with Peter, she didn't manage to cry until she remembered the seagull. And then she wasn't able to stop.

The seagull also reminds Katarina of her father. An unskilled labourer, a factory worker with a bad back, the tenth child of a drunken shoemaker, he was not remarkable in any way. He was a man without influence. He didn't own a single Italian suit. When Katarina thinks about him, she always sees a framed picture of him. Not a photo but a memory. It was at a birthday party at Aunt Ines and Uncle Hugo's, when Katarina was sixteen. She couldn't wait to get the hell out of there so she could hang out with her friends. She was standing in the hall, ready to sneak away, looking into the living-room, where the menfolk sat, jackets off, white starched shirt-sleeves exposed, smoking, talking loudly, and having a grog. Cheap cognac and soda pop in tall grog glasses with golden edges. The fancy ones Aunt Ines got out only for parties. She had a dozen of them: three with the ace of spades, three with the ace of clubs, three with the ace of hearts, three with the ace of diamonds. Katarina's dad sat on the couch, between Uncle Hugo and Uncle Sten, holding a glass with the ace of hearts on it, still full. From where she stood, he was perfectly framed by the door-way. He was part of the group, yet very much alone. He sat silent, his head slightly bent, while she stood observing him, noticing the strands of white in his hair. After a while he looked up and saw her. Their eyes met and he smiled, and something broke in her young, self-centred heart. It was such an apologetic smile. "I've given up," it said, "I'm finished. My back pain is so bad I'll never get another job." And the worst thing was that, the smile revealed rather than hid his shame. It still hurts Katarina to think about it. Pain like that never goes away.

"He was ashamed, Lillan," she says, "because nobody needed him any more. A man who can't do an honest day's work is not a man — that was the philosophy of his generation of working-class people. He would have liked me to be proud of him. That's why he didn't touch his grog, you see. A man who doesn't earn his living doesn't deserve a drink, he has no right to sit and discuss union matters or even soccer. He no longer belongs."

The terrible thing was that Katarina was ashamed. She was ashamed because she'd let him see her, and he knew what she'd seen. She could only hope that he didn't see the pity in her embarrassed smile.

"My heart just broke," says Katarina. She isn't trying to sound dramatic. "I realized that he'd already gone somewhere I couldn't follow. It was like saying goodbye. And he died less than a year later. I think he died because there was nothing else left for him to do."

And that, she says, is why she can never be happy. "Do you see the connection, Lillan? Do you see the random injustice?"

"No," says Lillan. "I do not. Your father wasn't a seagull, for God's sake. Seagulls are stupid. The one you saw had no idea what had happened to it. It just went on. Your father knew what had happened to him, but how do you think he would've felt had he known that you could never be happy because of him?"

"Not because of him. Because of the seagull. What it symbolizes. That's different."

"I don't care. It makes no difference, the way I see it. It's your

300

duty to be as happy as you can. Life is so short."

"That's not what you said when they took Micke away."

"I know. To lose a child like that is different. Your own child will think you don't love him, and that's unbearable. But it's your duty to try to be happy."

"Duty, Lillan? Don't make me puke!"

"That's what the old king said. Gustaf VI Adolf."

"What? 'Don't make me puke'?"

"No! 'Duty comes first.' That was his motto. Grandma told me that. Every king has to have a motto."

"Christ, Lillan, he wasn't talking about happiness, was he? He was talking about what my father lost. The ability to do his duty. As in, duty is honour. It's a bit different, isn't it?"

"I don't care. Micke will be back with me soon."

"You *don't* care for the same reason I *do* care. I just choose to face facts, while you ignore them."

Lillan doesn't argue with her, she let's her eyes linger fondly on her friend's face. "Are you ever going to have children?" she wants to know.

"I don't need to. I've got you."

Meanwhile, Mikael Werner's bandwagon is rolling along. The bureaucrats who have been so unhelpful are rediscovering their humanity, under the light of his money and influence. An investigation by a journalist from *Kvällsposten* produces concrete proof of Lillan's mother's addiction to tranquillizers, and interviews with neighbours and a string of cleaning ladies reveal that a few years earlier, for example, she accused her neighbours of performing satanic rites in their backyard at full moon. Telling the police about the goings-on during the latest full moon led to an investigation where it was found that the neighbours in question were on an

African Safari at the time. However, somebody did break into their house while they were away and made off with their sound system and colour TV. But while the culprits were never caught the police found not a shred of proof that they'd performed any satanic blood-sacrifices in the backyard before, during, or after the break-in. Mrs. Kristiansson, a former cleaning lady lets it be known that Mrs. Werner fired her after listening at the bathroom door to confirm her suspicion that the cleaning woman used too much toilet paper. "More than half a metre!" she shouted when the woman came out.

An interview with Sven Andersson at the psychiatric hospital brings forth a few new facts. Janne and Lillan did *not* go out and leave their child every night for months on end; they'd only lived there for a month. And during that month Andersson was so beside himself that most of the time he didn't know what day it was. He's feeling much better these days, he says. He's a new man, he's doing crossword puzzles. He still fervently maintains that "the slut" isn't a fit mother. But did he actually know Lillan? No, he admits, he didn't. Did he ever talk to her? No, she wasn't the kind of person he wanted to get to know. She was the kind of person who has sex in sandboxes.

She what?

A police report confirms that there was a disturbance at that address and that time, and that a couple was found having sexual intercourse in said sandbox in said yard. The officers on duty didn't bother getting the names of the culprits; they just told them to put their pants on. Lillan hysterically denies that it was she and Janne who were thus entertaining their guests, and tells Mikael about Lena and Vicke. But Vicke can't be found and Lena claims she doesn't remember.

This new accusation derails Mikael's program to restore Lillan's parental rights. After a month of frustration he takes a different tack, and puts in a request to adopt Micke himself. That way, the grandfather would become the official father, and Micke would reside with him as his and Nicole's son in the sprawling villa he has recently purchased in Limhamn. Lillan would live with them as well, as Micke's official sister and unofficial mother.

This isn't what Lillan wants to hear. She's met her father's new wife, and she likes her. Nicole is quite plain, and kind in a cool, polite manner; Mikael says she's an intellectual, and fiercely intelligent. But Lillan doesn't want to live with them. Nicole doesn't speak much Swedish, and Lillan's two half-brothers don't speak Swedish either. They speak excellent English, but Lillan doesn't. They all smile at each other a lot.

Besides, she doesn't want brothers. She wants her baby. Daddy talks to her, tells her it's only on paper that he'll be Micke's father, only in the eyes of the law. At home the roles will be different. Lillan will be the mother, he will be the grandfather and Nicole will be the grandmother. Philippe and Jean-Pierre will be little uncles, they're really looking forward to it. They're in school learning Swedish and soon everybody will be able to communicate. Everything will be just fine.

Late on a Wednesday afternoon, Lillan is visiting her father and his family. Nicole has cooked an early dinner and they're just sitting down to eat when the phone rings. Mikael goes to answer it and is informed that Micke is dead. No, it isn't a morbid joke thought up by some twisted tabloid-reading citizen. It's a fact. Apparently Micke spent a lot of his waking hours crying, and refused to eat. Whoever tried to forcefeed him got a bit overzealous. A piece of cheese sandwich was shoved in his mouth while he was screaming, and he choked.

Lillan's father relays the message in a grim voice, his face white and determined. Flags labelled "lawsuit" are already flapping in his head. Lillan screams and faints, cracking her head on the sharp edge of the glass dining table. She's unconscious and bleeding when her father scoops her up and rushes her to the car. He drives her to the same emergency ward where Amy once took Lillan.

It turns out there's no permanent damage done. Lying on a gurney, Lillan soon regains consciousness, remembers what has happened, and starts to cry. Tests show that she's severely anaemic, bordering on malnourished, suffers from calcium deficiency, and is approximately nine weeks pregnant.

Hearing this news she cries even harder. She had hoped to die

303

and follow her little boy where he shouldn't have to go alone. She wanted to kill herself. But now she doesn't know what to do. Now another baby needs her. It must be Emma, her girl, who is on her way. She wants to meet her. The thought of a new baby holds a promise of life continued. But no sooner has she dared think about living than she remembers Micke and breaks down again. He died thinking that his mummy went away and left him. That she didn't care. How on earth is she supposed to live with that, for even a minute? She can't. She has too. No, she doesn't, she can't.

Her father scoops her up again and drives her back to his home. Katarina comes to see her there as soon as she gets off work. They hold each other and cry.

"I was wrong," sobs Lillan.

"About what?"

"It's not our duty to try to be happy. I tried, but it doesn't work. I was so wrong."

"It doesn't matter, Lillan. I was stupid to bring it up. I suffer from terminal reality fixation. It was selfish. I'm so very, very sorry."

"Don't be. I understand now what you meant. Now Micke will be my little seagull for ever. But I don't think I can live with that, I really don't."

She cries again and Katarina joins her. Later Majken arrives, destroyed, and joins the wailing chorus. Nicole cooks dinner — she needs to keep busy — and forces them to eat. They try but can't manage. All but Lillan drink a lot of wine. Mikael is busy on the phone with a lawyer friend, preparing a lawsuit against those responsible for his grandson's death. Sometimes he has to curb the urge to go and visit that man, Sven Andersson, who started all this, and tear him limb from limb very slowly with his bare hands. Never has he felt so helpless, so *not* in control.

The next day Mikael Werner goes to the funeral home, needing to see the grandson he never met. He needs to know the physical being who was his flesh and blood, the grandchild who was named after him. In the quiet room he has to force his eyes onto the face of the dead child. The moment he does, he becomes powerless. It's such a small face. He stands there, stunned, and doesn't dare think or feel. If he opens his mouth, his heart will fall out. He leaves quickly, takes a taxi to the Kramer Hotel, and does something he hasn't done for many years: he gets absolutely pissing drunk. Two hours later, he asks the bartender to call a taxi.

He sits in the back of the taxi as it drives along the road by Ribersborg Beach, and looks out over the water, almost seeing double. He feels so useless and insignificant that he isn't sure who or what he is. Back at the villa, he asks Nicole, "Tell me what my name is."

She tells him. Half reassured, he lies down on the bed and passes out. Nicole covers him with a blanket.

Having to face reality again the next day, he copes by keeping busy. There are funeral arrangements to be made. He and Majken help each other, both needing to occupy themselves. Lillan gets involved too, but at first her father refuses to let her attend the funeral. He knows she won't be able to cope with the sight of the small white coffin. He's not all that sure he can cope with it himself. Lillan's response is to get hysterical. That is when Nicole, who usually doesn't interfere, puts a cool hand on her husband's arm and has a little talk with him in private, in French, out on the patio. She points out that you do *not* prevent a mother from attending her only child's funeral; it's that simple. You might have to sedate her, but you do not deprive her of her last goodbye.

Werner is used to giving orders, but he's wise enough to realize that there are times when he has no say. Nicole is right, and in the end Lillan does attend her Micke's funeral, sedated to the point of catatonia. She doesn't notice who is present, apart from the little white coffin decorated with red and yellow roses. It's so small. So very, very small. Once she sets her eyes on it, she can't move unless somebody takes her arm and leads her in the right direction.

In the funeral chapel, when they lower the coffin below floor level she is supposed to be the first to step forward and throw her bouquet of forget-me-nots and say her farewell, but she doesn't move. Her body, like her mind, is paralysed. Her father and Nicole gently take hold of an elbow each, and very slowly lead her up. None of the people present can bear to look at her. Eva says afterwards to Hasse, "If I had looked at her, my heart would have ripped in half." Lillan's father dislodges the flowers from her hand and throws them for her. Nicole throws in twelve white roses, and says in a low voice, "Au revoir, petit." Then it's Majken's turn. Clutching a bouquet of red and white carnations, she collapses and has to be carried to her chair. Katarina is crying hard and trying to be quiet at the same time. She's too dizzy to stand up. She isn't even aware that she's still clutching her bunch of small white roses when she leaves after the service.

The priest doesn't say "from dust to dust," not when the deceased is so young. He says, "The Lord giveth and the Lord taketh away. Blessed be the Name of the Lord." When Majken hears that, she lets loose a querulous "Why?" The priest doesn't respond, but bows his head in the face of the higher power he humbly serves.

There are no hymns sung, not even at the end. There wasn't a suitable one, according to Lillan, who refused every suggestion. The only hymns she likes are the ones that celebrate the beauty of the world, and at her son's funeral such a hymn would be highly inappropriate.

"What about Psalm 21?" the priest had enquired. "Glorious is the Earth, Glorious is God's Heaven"?

"No! It's not glorious."

"Well, it is customary to at least end with a hymn. Perhaps...."

"No!"

Instead there is organ music. Some requiem that Mikael Werner chose.

The priest also suggested that he read "At a Child's Grave", from the Swedish Book of Psalms. It describes, he said, the child being carried to the Lord's garden, where the cold hard winter can no longer touch him. That to Majken sounded like a frigging abduction, which, she pointed out, is the reason they lost their baby in the first place. She flatly refused it. The priest then suggested "At a Child's Bed" instead, in which not only God guards the sleeping child, but also a host of angels in white. That, they all said, was much better. Micke is just asleep and angels are watching over him; they all found that comforting. Majken and Lillan both see angels as female entities, perhaps because of their long flowing gowns, and trust them to do a better job than God, who hasn't impressed them so far. Everybody prefers the image of a sleeping child to that of a dead one.

They told the priest to read the psalm at the end, when Micke has gone to bed, so to speak. This he does, and his voice is gentle, but Majken doesn't like the way he reads it. He's too mechanical, he lacks emotion. Well, to him Micke is just a dead kid in a box, so why should he care? Also, she remembers afterwards, as they gathered outside before the service, that she saw the priest give Katarina the eye, sliding an indulgent gaze up her long legs.

They don't gather at the restaurant after the service. Not this time. It wouldn't be appropriate, says Majken, when Mikael consults her. And anyway she can't face it. When an adult dies you can control your sorrow and anger, but when it's a small child you don't stand a chance. You can only go home and hide. Walking down the path from St. Gertrud's Chapel to the car, Nicole and Mikael lead the diminished black figure that is Lillan. Katarina and Majken follow them, holding each other up, Katarina still carrying the white roses. They're a pitiful sight.

Micke will be cremated and his ashes placed in the memorial grove with Janne's, Janne's father and Majken's parents and sister. That way, says Majken, they'll have each other for company, and we can come and visit them all together.

Time stands still as the months go by. Lillan notices the progress of time only because her stomach is growing bigger. She's still living at Majken's, sleeping on the sofa-bed in the living-room. She prefers that to living with her father and his French family. She likes them very much, but she doesn't fit in. Majken is her family now. Majken is only forty-six, but losing Janne and Micke in such a short space of time has aged her. Her brown hair has turned grey and she's shrunk. She needs Lillan as desperately as Lillan needs her. They both need Katarina and her strength.

In the fall Mikael Werner buys them a three-bedroom house. He insists that his future grandchild live in a house with both a garden and a grandma. Buying the house is partly an effort to coax Lillan to try to go on living, and partly a way to say he's sorry. He takes Majken house-hunting and in Södra Sofielund they find a renovated house where a second floor had been added. They're both convinced that it's the one, it has the right feel to it, and they take Lillan to see it the next day. When she lays eyes on the pear tree, so large it covers the small garden like a roof, she knows they are meant to live there. She also knows that she's not meant to die yet, even though not dying will be very difficult.

Majken agrees to the purchase of the house, but only if she's allowed to pay for half of it. She doesn't want any hand-outs, she'd rather go into debt. She feels right at home in the neighbourhood. Södra Sofielund is the old part of the city where her grandparents had lived, right around the corner on Idunsgatan in a three-room house with no indoor plumbing and an outhouse in the back yard. Their house is gone now, replaced by a brand-new one in yellow brick. The cobblestones are gone too, as are all the old people who had lived there. But the area still has a village atmosphere, and Majken can sense her past nestled like shadows amid everything new. She needs her past now more than ever.

Katarina is invited to live with them as well. They feel their increased number will increase their strength. But she refuses. She needs her own space, she says. They'd get on her nerves within a day, and that wouldn't be good because she loves them dearly, they're her family. She visits often. There are fewer tears now, but there still isn't much laughter. When Majken is working, Katarina takes Lillan for long walks in Pildammsparken. They walk slowly and don't talk much, Lillan holds onto Katarina's hand.

The first Sunday of Advent, the three of them go for a visit to Memorial Grove at the cemetery. They bring bouquets of small roses, yellow, red, pink, and white ones, tied with matching ribbons. They bring candles as well, and light them by the edge of the fountain. Majken lights candles for her sister, her parents, her husband, her son, and her grandson. So many candles. Katarina lights a candle for her father. The yellow roses she brought are for him, except for one, still in bud, which is for the child she never met. Lillan lights two candles and puts her roses beside them.

It's a cold afternoon but the arbour has a lot of visitors. A ring of lit candles surrounds the fountain, which is still dry in this season. Inside the burning circle is a circle of flowers attached to the rim of the fountain by a cast-iron strip. It looks very beautiful, almost unearthly.

They are all standing silent with their thoughts, a dozen or so mourners bundled up in winter coats, when it starts to snow. The flakes are large and thick and perfect in their symmetry. Soon one candle is extinguished, then two, three. They watch as white flakes float into the grove and coat the grass and flowers. It takes a while for the flames to be overpowered, they're quite persistent. Lillan stares in a trance at the candle she lit for Micke, waiting for a sign that he is somehow with her, that he can see her standing there, and realize that she did not turn her back on him. She wants him to see her face and know how much she loves him. If that is possible, she says to herself, then the flame of her candle will continue to spread its light through the dark afternoon, and the snow, which is falling heavier and thicker, will have no power to put it out.

"Let's go," says Majken. "I'm freezing." She's been crying and her face is icing up.

"Micke's candle is the only one still burning," says Lillan. "He's sending me a message. He understands, you see? He knows I love him." She is glowing with an urgent need to believe. "His spirit is here, isn't it?"

Katarina and Majken look at each other over her head. Thank God she's so short. Their eyes have an intense conversation and they come to a wordless agreement.

"I think you're right," says Majken. "I can feel him."

"Did you see the seagull fly over the grove as we stood there?" asks Katarina, on a spur-of-the-moment inspiration.

"A seagull?" Lillan stops and stares at her. "Was it a small white one?"

"Yeah, that's right! You saw it too?"

"I thought I saw something. I wasn't sure if it was a bird or just snow."

"It was a seagull," confirms Majken, who has no idea what all this is about. "I saw it too. Rather unusual, I thought."

Lillan looks at the sky, hoping for the white bird to come back, but fluttering crystal stars land in her face and she is forced to close her eyes. Still, she's pretty sure she saw something, way up there.

"We'd better go," says Majken. "We'll miss the bus." She takes Lillan's arm and turns her around. Lillan is still gazing skyward, trying to distinguish the bird in the falling white, and doesn't notice that Micke's candle has gone out.

"Isn't it amazing," says Katarina when they're sitting on the bus. "That candle was still burning when we left the arbour. I turned around and checked. Did you see it?"

"I sure did," Majken agrees. "Quite incredible."

"It was Micke," says Lillan. "I didn't have to check. I knew that candle wouldn't go out." She thinks that maybe she might be able to go on living, to wait for Emma.

SVEN

On the first Sunday of Advent, Sven is sitting in his room, at the table by the window, doing a crossword puzzle. Lately he's been spending more time in his own room than in the day room. Ever since the news that the hooligan's baby died, he's felt strange. The baby wasn't supposed to die, he wants to protest. He was only trying to help the little guy. He doesn't sleep well any more, he has trouble even closing his eyes. If he falls asleep he dreams that a seagull is sitting on his chest, staring at his sleeping face. It is very disconcerting.

On top of that, Ann-Marie has stopped smiling at him. She glares at him now, her good eye hurling icicles in his direction. He has no idea why she's doing it and he doesn't know how to handle it. He asked her one day if she'd been to look at his paintings recently, trying to reach out, to give her a chance.

"Fuck your paintings," she snarled. With her disfigured face she had no difficulty looking nasty.

That was the last thing she said to him. The next Sunday she smiled at her husband and her son; she kept her mouth closed, but there were signs of life in her good eye. Halfway through the visit the boy crawled up into her lap and she held him awkwardly for a while, until he got bored. As they left, she leaned forward in her chair and waved out the window to them. The staff are beside themselves with excitement over these signs of improvement. Yesterday Mrs. Molin herself washed and combed Ann-Marie's hair, and trimmed it. Now it looks all glossy and smooth.

"Hey, Sven!" The door opens and Kurt, the orderly, is standing there. "Guess what?"

"What?"

"You got a visitor!"

"What?" Sven's just put down *lilac* for *shade of purple*, five letters.

"I said, you've got a visitor." Kurt is an unhurried sort of guy who likes to spread a bit of joy whenever possible. Mind you, with the people in this building it's easier said than done.

"A *visitor?*" repeats Sven, as if he's trying to fit it into his cross-word. *Visitor.* Sven never has company. He doesn't know anybody.

"That's right." Kurt smiles and waits for more signs of life. "I bet you're surprised, eh?"

"Well, yes, I suppose. Who is it?" He hopes it isn't a lawyer or a psychiatrist. It would be nice if it was the Chief Inspector or Arvidsson. But more than likely it's a mistake. The hospital must be full of lunatics named Andersson.

"It's your mother," says Kurt, and looks so proud you'd think he's conjured her up out of a hat.

"My *mother?*" Sven looks stunned. "I don't think so."

"Oh, it's your mother all right. She's here and she wants to see you. Aren't you one lucky guy?"

"She can't be here."

"Well, she is."

Sven feels sick to his stomach. "What does she look like?" he asks.

"Well, you know. An old lady. Grey hair and wrinkles. Tall, mind you. And she uses make-up. Lots of red lipstick."

That sounds like Ma. But no, it can't be. He doesn't want it to be. His past is locked up in a room at the back of his head. Lately he's sorted through it and thrown most of it out. There's no way she could get out.

"It's a mistake," he decides. "I don't have a mother."

"You don't?" Kurt looks puzzled. "But she's got papers to prove it. Her name is Edith Boman. She's remarried, she says. But she must be your mother."

"No! She's lying!"

"Why would she lie, for God's sake?" Kurt is losing patience. "She's an old lady, for crying out loud. Why would she come all the way out here on a cold Sunday afternoon, and then lie, just to meet you? Nothing personal, buddy, but hey...."

"Society is full of sick and twisted people," Sven points out.

314

He's full of opinions these days. "They come in any age, sex, and size. Why she came here, who she is, I don't know," Sven declares. "I don't care, either. But she's not my mother." He's breathing deeply and carefully because his heart is slamming against his ribcage, trying to break free. "Besides, how would she know where to find me after all these years?" He stares furiously at poor Kurt, who only wants to spread a little light in the dark of December.

"Her husband's daughter just started working on the ward with the stroke victims in the building behind ours," he informs Sven. "So I guess the information travelled along the old grapevine."

"She's lying."

"Does that mean you don't want to see her?"

"I'm just saying that I don't have a mother," Sven insists. "The woman is an impostor. Talk to the police. They're my friends. Tell the Chief Inspector to call. Tell the Chief Inspector I told you to call. They'll believe me. And go away. I have to do my crossword puzzle."

"Have it your way." Kurt shrugs. "I can't force you. But I have to tell you, I feel sorry for the old thing, I really do."

Sven doesn't deign to reply. A sentence like "I feel sorry for the old thing" can hardly apply to Ma, can it? He concentrates on his crossword puzzle. He has to finish it before evening coffee, that's one of his rules. *Like some Christians*, six letters down. First letter an R, third letter a B. *Robber?* He giggles. He needs another letter to help out; what about *heroic poetry*, four letters across? *Epos*. That one he knows. It was in a crossword last week. That gives him an O to help solve the mystery about the Christians. The word, it turns out, is *reborn*. He likes *robber* better.

It starts to snow. The leaden sky softens suddenly, as if it's letting out air, and big white flakes, perfect and lazy, fall to a harsh and colourless earth.

*Aphorisms*, four letters across. Now, what the hell could that be? What about *untrustworthy types*, six letters down? *Humans?* No, the third letter is an E. *Cretins?* No, that's seven letters. Never mind.

If he leans very close to the window he can see the gravel path leading to the main building, where the exit is. He gets up and presses his nose to the window. He can't open it, it's permanently locked. He sees the back of an old woman carefully making her way towards the main building. She has a slight limp. She's wearing a black coat and a green hat, but no feathers. He can see white curls poking out from under her hat. Her shoulders are drooping so much that she looks like a black bottle of wine with a green cork. Is that Ma out there bobbing in a sea of white?

She disappears from view. Was that her? After all these years?

He trembles, his heart hammering again. He doesn't want to see her. It would be like a bad dream come true. He made his life despite her, she has no right to turn up now and destroy it, he doesn't want anything to do with her. She's supposed to stay in the past. He doesn't want her.

Was it Ma?

He sits down. What does it matter? What the hell does it matter if she wants to come and intrude? She's not going to see me, she's not going to get me, I'm going to be all right. I don't need her, I never did. This is what he tells himself.

How old would she be now? In her seventies? He can't imagine her as a pensioner. Not Ma with the blonde hair and the big tits. Old and withered and used up. Ma in a stupid hat playing bingo? Is that what she's reduced to? Serves her right if it is. Serves her right.

To hell with her, I'm not a kid any more. Sven is quite firm with himself. *Ombrometers measure them*, five letters down. He has no idea. *Anatomical prefix*, five letters across. He hasn't got a clue. He's stumped.

It could not have been Ma. She was a tall lady, was Ma. The old woman who tottered by out on the path was short. Mind you, people shrink as they grow older. It's as if at the end, when you walk towards death you turn into a child again, you become innocent again and you forget the sins of long ago. Maybe Ma is turning into a child again. Wouldn't that be something. Does she want him to come home and look after her now? Feed her with a spoon and change her diapers?

*They give you fits*, seven letters across. *Mothers*? No, doesn't work. The third letter is a Y.

Suddenly Kurt is at the door again.

"Hey, Sven!" he says. "That's some weird lady, that mother of yours, or whatever you want to call her."

Sven looks blank. "How do you mean?"

"Well, when I told her you didn't want to see her, she got really pissed off. She stared at me, real mad like, and said, "Well, if the little prick doesn't want to see me, he ain't getting no chocolate!" You see, she brought this box of chocolate, I saw it, she was carrying it in one of those netbags, a big frigging box of Aladdin. You know, the kind in the red box? I'm so sorry, I said to her, there's nothing I can do. So she turned around and stalked out, nose in the air and all, mumbling to herself. Didn't even say good-bye. Some old babe, eh?"

"I can imagine." Sven nods mechanically. "Doesn't surprise me a bit."

Kurt shrugs and rolls his eyes.

"What colour coat was she wearing?" Sven wants to make sure.

"What colour coat? A bright red one. Had one of them fake leopard-skin collars."

"Was she wearing a hat?"

"Uh...yeah, she was. Why?"

"Did it have a feather in it?"

"A feather? I don't know. I wasn't admiring her hat, was I? Why do you ask?"

"Just wondering. She sounds crazy. Crazy old ladies usually wear feathers in their hats."

"They do, eh?"

"Yes, they do. I've seen them."

"Well, there's no telling about some people, that's for sure." With that ambiguous insight Kurt leaves Sven to his crossword.

Sven's relieved that it wasn't Ma he saw walk by. That means he hasn't laid eyes on her after all. He never will. He'll survive if he has to sit in this room for the rest of his life.

It's still snowing. Huge white Christmas-card flakes fall with an almost studied elegant nonchalance towards earth. They fell like that on a Christmas long, long ago, when he lived in his big bright room at Mrs. Hultén's. The year before she died. Late on Christmas Eve, close to midnight, it started to snow, just as it's doing now. Looking up from his new mystery, he noticed the large soft flakes passing slowly in the glow of the streetlamp outside. He put the book aside and got up to open the window. He felt something calling him. The air outside was mild and smelled of snow. There was no traffic. The world was holding its breath. Soundlessly the white stars fell before him, blanketing the parks and the street, melting in his outstretched hand. He stood gazing at the trees, the grass, the paths, gazing onto a world that was white, untouched and new, a world only he had the privilege to see.

As he looked out, his very soul ached with the beauty of this world. And with the sadness of his life. He had cried then, very quietly, so as not to disturb the silence. Not sure if he cried tears of joy or of sorrow, he realized in that instant that if you reach in deep enough, down to the core of your being, to your very soul, you find that joy and sorrow becomes the same emotion, the same intense pain that leaves you breathless. At least, that's how it felt in that brief moment. Despite being so light and so subtle, it drained him with its intensity. Every neuron in his head became charged with electricity, every nerve end sparked like a fire-cracker. His consciousness reached a level of clarity and insight that he could never hope to attain again. It was a gift, he realized that. Looking out at the snow now, he wonders if he will ever be handed another gift like that, if he will ever feel like that again. He doesn't think so, but he is grateful that he remembers that Christmas Eve long ago, when he was blessed.

He puts down his pen and checks his watch. The crossword will have to wait, it's almost time for evening coffee. They're supposed to get gingerbread tonight, Mrs. Molin said, because it's the first of Advent, and they will light the first candle in the Advent candleholders. Soon it will be Christmas. There will be a tall tree in the day room, and everybody will help decorate it. This year, instead of books, he will be giving himself a rug he's busy weaving. It's almost finished and he's very pleased with it. Woven with thin strips of cotton fabric, it's in bright shades of blue that bring to mind summer skies, cornflowers, and bluebells.